CLASH
OF
EMPIRES

THE RED SEA

William Napier

First published in Great Britain in 2012 by Orion Books,
an imprint of The Orion Publishing Group Ltd
Orion House, 5 Upper Saint Martin's Lane
London WC2H 9EA

An Hachette UK Company

1 3 5 7 9 10 8 6 4 2

A CIP catalogue record for this book
is available from the British Library.

ISBN (Hardback) 978 1 4091 0534 3
ISBN (Trade Paperback) 978 1 4091 0535 0
ISBN (Ebook) 978 1 4091 0536 7

Typeset by Deltatype Ltd, Birkenhead, Merseyside

Printed in Great Britain by Clays Ltd, St Ives plc

The Orion Publishing Group's policy is to use papers
that are natural, renewable and recyclable products and
made from wood grown in sustainable forests. The logging
and manufacturing processes are expected to conform to
the environmental regulations of the country of origin.

www.orionbooks.co.uk

To Ann
and Iona

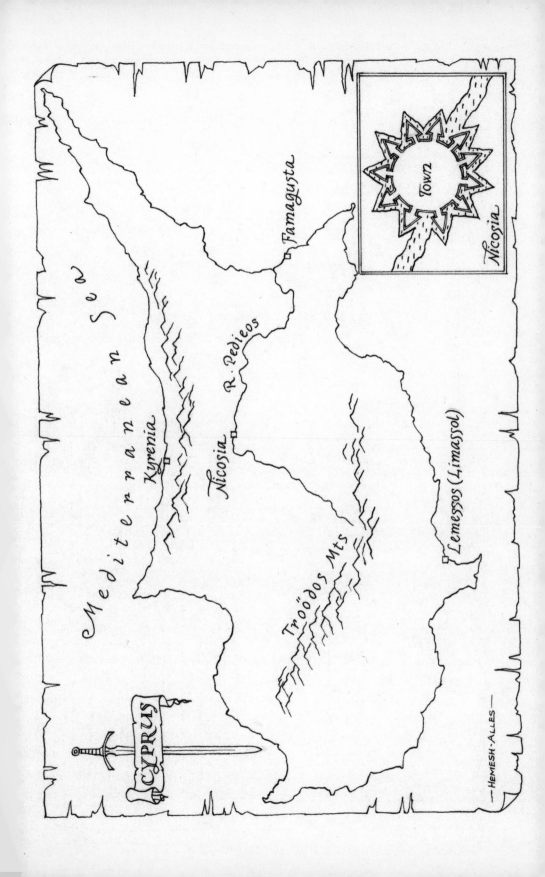

Mediterranean Sea

Kyrenia

Nicosia

R. Pedieos

Famagusta

Troödos Mts

Lemessos (Limassol)

CYPRUS

Town

Nicosia

— HEMESH·ALLES —

Bristol
London

HOLY ROMAN EMPIRE
Warsaw

Vienna
1529

Bay
of Biscay

Paris

Geneva
Venice
Marseilles
Toulon
Nice
Genoa

Adriatic Sea

1543

Rome
Corsica
Naples

Madrid

Messina
Sardinia

to the
Americas
Cadiz

Sicily
1565

Tangier

Algiers

Tunis
Malta

Barbary Coast
Djerba

Sultanate
of
Morocco

Tripoli

— HEMESH·ALLES —

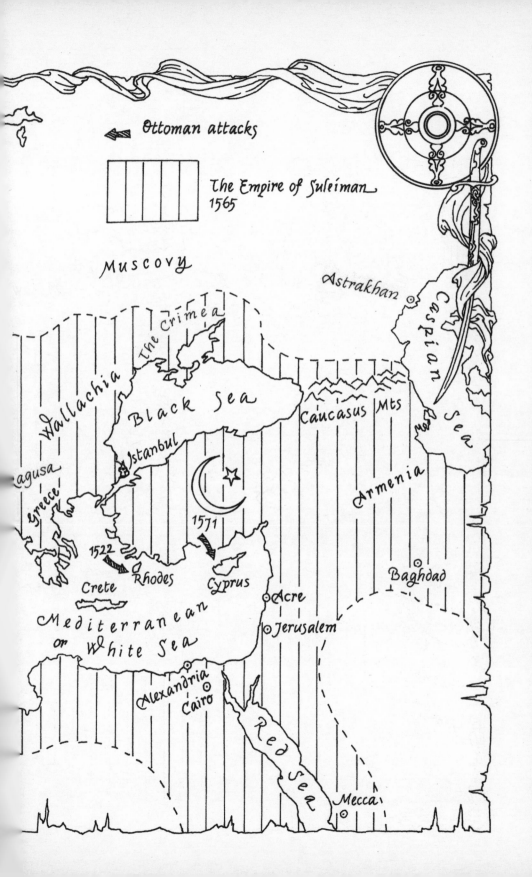

Ottoman attacks

The Empire of Suleiman 1565

Muscovy

Astrakhan

Wallachia

The Crimea

Black Sea

Caucasus Mts

Caspian Sea

Istanbul

Armenia

Ragusa

Greece

1522

Rhodes

Crete

1571

Cyprus

Baghdad

Acre

Jerusalem

Mediterranean or White Sea

Alexandria

Cairo

Red Sea

Mecca

Since the Dark Ages it had been called the Mediterranean: the sea at the centre of the earth. The Romans had called it Mare Nostrum, Our Sea, and such arrogance was no more than the truth, for it was Rome alone that ruled her.

Now, in the sixteenth century of the Christian era, the Papacy still called her the Roman Sea, but it was wishful thinking. There was only one great power in the Mediterranean, and it was no Christian power. In its relentless conquests it carried the rayat al-sawda, the black war-banner of Islam. It was the Empire of the Ottoman Turks ...

PROLOGUE
Spring, 1571

A hush fell upon the gilded audience chamber of the Topkapi Palace in the heart of Constantinople. Every head bowed. There came a swish of silken robes over the polished floor, and then a herald declared, 'Bow knee and head for the Sultan of the Ottomans, Padishah of the Black Sea, the Red Sea and the White, Guardian of the Holy Cities of Islam, Lord of the Lords of this World, son of Suleiman the Lawgiver: Selim.'

But first appeared a tall, lean man in a plain dark robe, striding swiftly, his broad forehead and keen eyes betokening the highest powers of observation and intellect. Behind him waddled a much shorter man in gorgeous golden robes and a huge silk turban, beneath which showed puffy eyes, a round nose and plump, sagging jowls. His feet slapped the marble-tiled floor with a sound like a duck on wet flagstones, then he shuffled over the priceless carpets of Tabriz like a slippered octogenarian.

All eyes followed the commanding figure in the dark robe. His footfall made no more sound than a cat's. He halted before the Imperial Throne. His plump follower hitched up his skirts, and made his way laboriously up the seven steps to the throne as if ascending Mount Ararat. Thus symbolising his perpetual elevation seven planes higher than the world of mortal men.

A monkey in a tree sat higher, thought Sokollu Mehmet.

At the top, Sultan Selim turned and sank back into the throne in an unregal slump. His doughy complexion shone with sweat and he breathed hard. You could smell the wine on his breath at five paces.

3

Sheitan, ruler of the seven hells, thought the Grand Vizier, bowing before the panting sultan. Was this truly the sole surviving son of Suleiman *Kanuni*, The Law Giver, whom even the Christians called *The Magnificent*? What in the name of Azrael had gone wrong?

He stood upright again and regarded his Sultan directly, as Ottoman court etiquette expressly forbade. Never in his life had Sokollu dared to look into the eyes of Suleiman the Law Giver. But Selim's he held steadily, until the Sultan's own bloodshot, bulging orbs dropped away. Sokollu nodded and stepped back, and Selim took a roll of paper from his inner robe. He unfurled it with pudgy, shaking hands, resting it on the tight little mound of his belly. Sokollu bowed his head to listen to the address along with the rest of the assembled dignitaries. The delivery was hopelessly weak and hesitant, but the meaning strong and clear, as Sokollu knew it would be. He had written every word.

'It has long been Our Duty to carry the religion of the Prophet to the farthest corners of the earth,' declared Selim in his reedy, diffident voice. 'Beneath the benign shelter of a single world empire, an Islamic Caliphate, we are called upon by the Just, the Merciful Himself, to save all primitive peoples and idolaters from the error of their ways. To bring mercy, peace and the heavenly law of Sharia to reign from the mountains and deserts of Asia to the Straits of Gibraltar, and from the heart of Europe to the sands of Africa.'

The court murmured polite assent to this noble plan.

'Muslim merchants, eager to spread their wealth over the globe, have already carried the word of the Koran with them on their voyages to the farthest east, to the ports of Goa and Jakarta and the Spice Islands. We have even heard that there are records of Chinese voyages a hundred years ago, which discovered a vast new continent in the southern ocean, the antipodes.'

The Lord of the Lords of this World had a sudden attack of coughing, and reached out for a cup. He always drank from a beaker of dark red glass, so that the more orthodox among his courtiers should not see that it was wine rather than water. But everyone knew. The wine-loving Sultan. Selim the Sot.

'The antipodes,' he resumed waveringly, eyes scanning the page to find his place again. 'Er. Ah.' He coughed once more. 'The

4

greatness of the world, and of our task in bringing light to its dark-est corners, is a heavy burden of responsibility upon Our Shoulders.

'And in addition to that, the Truth has many enemies.'

There were angrier murmurs.

'The Empire of the Persians claims to follow true Islam, although Shia is mere mockery and heresy. The many kingdoms of Mughal India, although its Emperor Akbar claims to be a true Muslim, allow the worst idolatries of Hinduism to flourish, in the name of tolerance. And in the west, most implacably of all, are the Christians. They have conducted brutal Crusades against Islam and its holy places for centuries, they continue to lord it over lands once and forever rightfully Muslim, from Cyprus to Sicily to Spain, and at the forefront of their aggression have ever been the Crusading Order of the Knights of St John, may their name be accursed.

'The Sultan will not divulge His plans further, for as you know there are spies and deceivers everywhere.' Selim swallowed at these words, and for one painful moment Sokollu thought he was going to stare around with those bulging hare eyes of his, as if expecting to see a couple of Knights of St John, maybe, standing at the back of the hall in their red surcoats, listening to his every word. But he controlled himself and resumed.

'Yet the Sultan knows that, in his Grand Vizier and closest advis-ers, he has the wisest counsellors any ruler could wish for. And so it is with them, his admirals and commanders, that he will discuss further plans. Know that the holy war continues. And that the shame of Malta will soon be avenged.

'In the name of Allah, the Just, the Merciful, I give you good day.'

Then Selim was helped down from his throne by a bodyguard and shuffled from the chamber.

Sokollu followed close on his heels.

As darkness fell that day, two of the three most powerful men in the Ottoman Empire met to discuss strategy. Selim was not among them.

The absent third was Lala Mustafa Pasha, Commander of Land Forces, currently away planning for the coming Cyprus campaign, much to Sokollu's satisfaction. Both men were ambitious, ruthless, immensely talented, and inevitably the bitterest enemies.

Grand Vizier Sokollu Mehmet, supreme intelligence and manipulator behind all the doings of the Sublime Porte, was born into a Bosnian Christian family. Taken as a young child into Ottoman service, he had risen to the top by supreme ability. Though never a military commander in the field, yet he could master any discipline he set his mind to.

With him sat Muezzinzade Ali – Ali, 'son of the muezzin singer', born into a humble family in the ancient Ottoman capital of Edirne. Like Sokollu, he too had risen by sheer ability alone. Turkish and Muslim from birth, Muezzinzade was devoted and loyal, with the simplicity of true greatness, and recently appointed *Kapudan Pasha*: Supreme Commander of the Ottoman Fleet. He was of slight, wiry build, yet powerful enough still to draw the compound bow. Many times Muezzinzade had fought in the forefront of battle – and would once more.

Sokollu pushed a fruit bowl aside and ordered various maps of that Turkish cartographer of genius, Piri Reis, spread across the table before them.

'As you know,' said Sokollu, 'I have long argued for a continued land assault on Christendom, through Hungary, Austria, the Danube valley. Our Janizaries are the finest infantry in the world. Even the Christians acknowledge it. But it seems fate has offered us another chance of victory in the Mediterranean.

'Yet we must wait. Three dangers remain on our flanks, as we look west.' He moved a long, lean forefinger over the maps. 'To the east, the Persians are and always will be our enemies, until the blessed day when Allah gives us victory over them. But this victory will not come soon. The Shia rebels in the mountains of Yemen also remain in revolt against us – stirred up by Persia, I have no doubt. And to the north, the Grand Duchy of Muscovy grows ever greater in power. Her ruler, Ivan, with ludicrous presumption, even calls himself Caesar, or Czar in his barbarous tongue. There is no Caesar but Selim.

'We must strangle this new Christian power at birth, or she will grow ever stronger, a constant threat to our northern border. Her potential empire is all of Scythia. We landed forces at Astrakhan, but ... the campaign was a difficult one, and we were obliged to change course. Instead our trusted ally, the Khan of the Crimea, is even now riding north with his Tatars, carrying the finest Ottoman muskets, arquebuses and guns. He will raze this upstart city of Muscovy to the ground.

'Then, having secured our borders to our satisfaction, all our strength may be turned upon the Inland Sea, and the push west. A *Jihad fil-bahr*: a Jihad of the Sea. We will take back Cyprus, then the Adriatic coast. Already our galleys rule that sea, and Venice does not stir. We also possess the vital port of Avlona, ruled over by our dear friend, the Black Priest, Kara Hodja.'

Muezzinzade smiled grimly. The renegade Dominican friar, Kara Hodja: corsair, cut-throat, and now Bey of Avlona. His reputation was so terrible it caused almost as much anxiety to his Ottoman overlords as did the Christians.

'We will take the squabbling city states of Italy piece by piece. Even Venice, and the Papal States.'

'And Malta,' said Muezzinzade. The very name was like a dark stone dropped into water.

Sokollu's expression was unreadable. 'Yes. This time we will finish it.'

Muezzinzade shifted in his seat. 'Grand Vizier, I have heard it said – and I do not wish to believe it – that as we sow discord among our enemies, so they sow discord among us. The work is done especially by agents of the Knights of St John. They seek to harass and weaken us by working in Russia, they have fomented rebellion in the Yemen, they even send secret embassies to the Sultanate of Morocco, encouraging the Moors to view us as enemies.'

'Rumours fly faster than facts,' said Sokollu tersely. 'Because they are light and insubstantial. The Christians do not have that kind of intelligence.'

'And the Grand Master in Malta,' persisted Muezzinzade, 'Jean de la Valette, sold his Order's lands in Cyprus just before his death. As if he knew of our coming invasion.'

'Mere chance. His beloved Malta will fall soon. And Morocco is our Muslim brother and ally now. Remember that in ports such as Larache and Rabat, Sultan Abdallah possesses harbours which face not east, but west: out across the Atlantic, where a whole new world lies. From the Moroccan shore, they hear the cries of their oppressed brethren, the Moriscos, in the lost Berber kingdom of Andalus. And to sharpen the insult, they see an endless stream of Spanish treasure ships returning from the New World. The trade winds carry them from Havana to Cadiz in little more than twenty days, laden with all the silver of the inexhaustible mines of Potosi.

'Which brings us to the greatest prize of all.' Sokollu spread his fingers wide over another map. 'Spain. And her vast new territories in the Americas.'

Here Piri Reis had truly excelled himself, showing the coast of Europe, Africa and the Americas enclosing the mighty Atlantic Ocean. Upon the coast of Brazil there were images in pen and ink of elegant beasts and fowl, and also men with their faces in their chests. Piri Reis himself did not credit such far-fetched travellers' tales, but they made for amusing illustrations.

'With this unimaginable wealth,' said Muezzinzade, his eyes roaming over the Americas as if he could devour them, 'we will reign over earth and sea.'

Sokollu said, 'Do you not feel the force of destiny?'

Muezzinzade nodded, slow and solemn. 'Yet if all the kingdoms of Christendom were to stand together against us – the powers of Spain and Portugal, the superb soldiery of the German princes, French chivalry, the armies of the Papacy, the vast resources of Genoa and Venice—'

'Perhaps aided by some small contribution,' Sokollu interrupted sarcastically, 'by that rain-lashed little island, England, ruled over by a *woman* ...'

Muezzinzade smiled.

Sokollu waved his hand. 'Perhaps then the Sublime Porte might have something to fear. But it will not happen. The Christian princes fight amongst each other like scorpions in a sack.

'The French hate the Habsburgs. The Genoese and Venetians hate and mistrust each other. And that is only the Catholics. Germany and the Netherlands are riven by Protestant rebellion, France massacres its own Protestants, England begins to persecute its Catholics. Christendom is now in a permanent state of low-level war with itself. It would take some man of genius to unite her. Yet' – he reached out for the fruit bowl – 'the hour is come, but not the man. Christendom is a fruit close to rottenness, and overripe for picking.'

He pulled a grape from the stalk and crushed it between his teeth.

Part I
COMRADES

1

The sun burned white in a cloudless sky, and spangles of sunlight danced on the placid sea. Occasionally dolphins broke the surface, their oilskin flanks darkly gleaming, before curving back into the green silence below. Away to the south, on the distant horizon, the sky was a dusty ochre over the burning deserts of Africa.

Tiny fluttering shapes of flying fish skimmed over the small waves, disturbed by a long dark shadow cutting through the water behind them. And the clean sea air suddenly soured with the stench of a Barbary slaver.

It was a low-slung black galley with a single mast, little more than a brigantine. The wind was so light the sail was furled. Fast, light and nimble, made for lightning raids on sleepy villages and lumbering merchantmen. A hawk of the sea.

They said you could smell the stench of a slave galley a mile away, and a downwind gust from this one would surely make any man tighten stomach and craw as he fought the urge to vomit. It was the stench of fifty men chained and rowing under the lash, the bilge water around their rotting feet a stew of salt water, urine and faeces. For slaves like these lived on the rowing bench until they died. But it was also the stench of permanent exhaustion, and despair so deep that death was all they longed for.

The Barbary slaver was some sixty feet in length and carried a single centre-line gun at the bow. Her primary armaments were the crew of twenty or so corsairs who lounged at the stern under the sun-blanched canopy, naked to the waist, flashing teeth and eyes, hooped gold earrings and elaborate henna tattoos. And armed with every variety of knife and dagger, mace and club, scimitar and half-pike imaginable.

One or two scanned the horizon from east to west, keen eyed and hungry for carrion. The rest diced or dozed, chewed qat or smoked kif. Other than men, the slaver – her name was the *Sweet Rose of Algiers*, without apparent irony – carried nothing more but the ballast of pebbles below, and the captain's chest, an iron-bound treasury of gold and silver coins of every nation: Spanish escudos, Venetian ducats, Ottoman akçés, as well as a pair of bejewelled crucifixes they had looted from a little chapel on the coast of Sardinia. There was also, in a small velvet pouch, the dainty curio of a sun-dried nose, sliced from the face of a Sicilian nun they had captured onshore a few weeks ago and taken with them for a while. Eventually they had tired of raping her and tumbled her over the side.

The dip of the oars was slow but steady. If any rower faltered, the bull-hide lash of the boatswain would cut his back open. A rower on a slave galley was unlikely to last a year, and was usually grateful if he died before.

Among the Sardinians and Neapolitans, the Sicilians and Spaniards, there were two blue-eyed Northerners. A thickset young fellow with an impassive expression, and another with burning gaze and a pale beard that showed he was fair haired. Thin but strong, his torso showed many scars. Each wore nothing but filthy loincloths and rags on their heads to protect them from the Mediterranean sun. Still the sun blistered ears and cheeks, shoulders and hands. Slave owners commonly tried to keep their slaves in good condition, as they would any other of their possessions, and shielded their rowers with crude canopies. But not these corsairs. They were the dregs even of their low profession.

They were also careless in other ways.

On a Barbary slaver it was usual to work your slaves to death, ditch their corpses and then capture more on a further raid. The supply was endless and free, and that was what the slave galleys did: they consumed men. They existed to enslave their rowers, who rowed that they might exist.

And the life itself – the lawless raiding and ravaging – was itself so dark and seductive a pleasure. Erupting out of the night upon some huddled fishing town, cutting a swathe of bloody terror through its wailing streets, destroying and looting as the fancy took you. A corsair was nothing but a penniless back-street cut-throat in the shadowy alleyways of Tunis or Algiers or Tripoli, a poor fisherman's son from some desolate dust-blown village of the Barbary Coast. But on a corsair slaver he was free to follow every desire, to heap up other men's treasure as his own, to do what he wished with their wives and daughters. None ruled the sea but the gun and the sword alone. And a captain was the king of his ship. Even of so wretched a vessel as the *Sweet Rose of Algiers*.

Each rower pulled a single oar, but one had collapsed and moved no more. Immediately the rhythm was lost, other oars fore and aft clonking into his trailing blade.

The boatswain was upon him in an instant, beating him and howling curses, but he was too far gone. A fisherman's son, taken from Sardinia only a few weeks ago. The light was gone from his eyes and his heart had already shrivelled and died within him.

The blue-eyed English youth with the fair beard was called Nicholas Ingoldsby. He glanced at his countryman, Hodge, across the narrow gangway. His eyes blazed. More than the single manacle that fixed a galley slave to the rowing bench in front, it was the manacles of the mind which held him enslaved. Few there dreamed of freedom, most dreamed of death. But in Nicholas Ingoldsby's burning blue eyes there was no despair.

And the manacle round his ankle was loose.

Five days ago the galley had pulled into a narrow bay on a deserted island and the carpenter had gone ashore to find decent timber. The repair took some hours and the rowers rested, aching with longing to see land so close. But the corsairs' scimitar points were always at their throats.

'Slaves you are and slaves you will remain!' bawled the boatswain. 'Rebel and you will lose your ears, your noses, your eyes – a blind man can row as well as a sighted! I have seen rebellious slaves skinned alive. And then your throats will be cut and you will go down to feed the fish. No flowers on a sailor's grave. None on a galley slave's either. Your seed will die out and you will be forgotten for ever. Now do not stir while we work.'

They did not stir. Anger still burned like a red fire in Nicholas's belly. As long as he still felt that, he might live. Others here would die. Most of them. But not I, he thought. Not I. Nor Hodge either. Soon our time will come.

They had been through worse than this before.

The corsair who doubled as ship's carpenter replaced a spar, but in a moment of carelessness let a short iron bolt drop beneath the rowing benches, to subside in the foul water. In a trice Nicholas had clenched it between his toes and kept a hold on it, knowing a man's life might depend on such a trivial thing. He clung to that iron bolt like a sinner to the Cross.

The boatswain raised his whip. The Sardinian fisher boy was about to be beaten to death before their eyes.

Nicholas bowed his head. He could never bear to watch this final scene, this epilogue to so wretched a life, though he had seen and endured many horrors himself in his twenty-two years. There were many scars on his arms, his lean torso, and a lumpy white cicatrice over his left elbow where a musket ball had once smashed into him as he swam desperately across a harbour. Long ago now. Upon the island of Malta ...

The boy groaned at his trailing oar but could not move himself. The whip cut and cut in pointless cruelty.

For five days now that iron bolt had been passed around, mostly at night, going from one rower to another. It was terrible work, and their punishment had they been caught would have been beyond imagining. Skinning alive would have been the least they suffered.

After five days of agonised filing and wrenching at their manacles, in the snatched seconds when the boatswain was not overseeing them, when they were on rest watch, in moments of darkness when clouds covered the face of the moon and dulled the brilliant Mediterranean stars, they had prayed to God to help them break their single cursed manacles.

And now for three of them, just three, their manacles were broken. Nicholas, Hodge, and the great bear-like Easterner whose language no one else spoke, but who said he came from '*Rus, Rus*'. It was scarcely believable. He meant the Grand Duchy of Muscovy, they thought, an almost unknown realm in the heart of snowbound

Scythia. None knew how he had come here. But his expression was one that even the corsairs did not like to consider too long. As if the moment he had the chance, he would rise up and tear each of them limb from limb with his bare hands.

The slaves could have waited longer. The precious iron bolt might have been passed on night after night, freeing more and more. But then they might have been discovered. And they could have better chosen their moment to rise in revolt too. A natural time would be when the corsair galley came in sight of its next prey, when they were attacking a Christian merchant ship, and battle was engaged. Then they might just be saved. But to rise up now, only three of them, was suicidal. Patience was as important as courage.

The Sardinian boy groaned, blood coursed from his head and face, and he began to shake and tremble violently all over, his eyes closed. He could no more pull an oar than he could fly. He would die soon, before their eyes. Then his emaciated body would be unlocked from the bench, hauled up and rolled over the low gunwales. He would make barely a splash, his soul already flown to other spheres.

The bearlike Rus turned his great head on his rounded shoulders and glowered at Nicholas from beneath dense black brows. Whether it was a smile was impossible to say. But he showed his teeth. And then he made a noise that Nicholas did not understand. Blowing softly through his lips, he made a sound like a great, distant explosion.

The boatswain gave up his beating and leaned over, unlocking the boy's manacle. He angrily ordered two of his men to haul in and stow the oar, and drag the half-dead boy aft.

The corsair captain in the stern grinned, his teeth stained with qat. 'Row on, my Christian gentlemen, row on! Do not be troubled by your dying comrade there. For there is gold still to be discovered, emeralds, amethysts, bars of silver – and of course your white-skinned maidens …'

The dying boy was dragged to the gunwales.

Nicholas flexed his hands.

The oars were far too long and unwieldy to be drawn in and used for weapons. What else was there?

'For St Nicholas and Mother Russia!' cried a voice as deep and cavernous as a great bronze cannon. The huge Rus had hauled himself up on to the narrow gangway over the rowers' heads, and was standing there facing the open-mouthed corsairs at the stern, huge and adamantine, his arms flung wide, his broken manacle still trailing from his ankle. He was virtually naked, though back and shoulders were matted with dark hair, and quite weaponless. Yet still it was a few shocked moments before the boatswain ran at him with drawn sword.

The Rus somehow evaded the sword-thrust altogether and took the boatswain in an embrace. He lifted him from the gangway and squeezed. The boatswain's eyes bulged in their sockets and his scimitar clattered on the planks. The Rus grinned.

In a scrambling panic, a couple more corsairs fitted arrows to their curved bows and one of them shot. Just as the bowstring thrummed, the Rus turned a little, and the arrow thocked hard into the boatswain's back. His breath sighed from his mouth and his head rolled free. The Rus thrust his arm between the dead man's legs, twirled him above his head, and flung him like a straw doll at the onrushing corsairs.

Other corsairs ranged their broad blades over the rest of the rowers below, ready to strike their heads from their necks if any more should stir. Nicholas cursed as he felt a cold blade touch the back of his neck. They were trapped. But what the devil was the Rus thinking of?

The Rus had run to the prow and turned again, still grinning like a deranged bear just loosed from its chains. He leaned down to a wooden hatchway. An arrow thudded into his belly and he paused for a moment, and then continued.

It was the powder store.

The corsairs were screaming and running at him, but everything happened in no more than a few breaths. With his mighty strength, the muscles of his arms and shoulders bunched like knots of towing rope, the Rus wrenched the locked door of the hatchway free, flinging it upright to give himself momentary cover just as two more arrows thudded into its planks.

The narrow gangway between the rowing benches allowed only one corsair to attack him at a time, and the first came sweeping wide with a side-bladed glaive or half-pike. Again the Rus's agility belied his size, not to mention the two arrows that now stuck in him, belly and thigh, narrow rivulets of blood trickling from each. He ducked the half-pike and then swiped his assailant backhanded as if he were no more than a troublesome fly. The corsair reeled, blood erupting from flattened nose and split lips, and dropped to the deck.

The Rus leaned down and dragged him to his feet and held him tight to his flank in another crushing one-armed bear-hug. He shuffled near to the open hatchway again, his constricted captive trying to suck in air, his mouth a horrified gaping O.

Another corsair darted forward with a wheel-lock pistol hurriedly primed, and the Rus grinned widely, savagely, as if this was all that he had hoped for. Not even looking, he put the heel of his hand under his captive's chin and shoved his head back with terrifying force. Nicholas heard the neck vertebrae snap. Again he threw a corpse into the arms of his onrushing assailants, then in a blur of speed he seized the arm of the fellow with the squat wheel-lock, snapped his arm at the elbow, and caught the pistol in his own paw.

He turned and leapt into the hatchway.

The air was filled with screaming, from the corsair with the shattered arm, and behind, from the captain himself. A scream of genuine panic and terror.

Nicholas's eyes too flared wide with terror. Now he understood that sound the Rus had made. The soft explosion. He would kill them all in his madness. They would all go down together, Mohammedan and Christian alike, equals at last in the drowning sea.

Corsairs came struggling over the bodies of their fallen comrades, but it was too late. The Rus had moved with astonishing swiftness, his movements planned weeks and months before in bitter dreams of vengeance.

He reappeared from out of the hatchway like a demon in a stage dumbshow rearing up out of hell, deranged, filthy, triumphant – and holding upon his left shoulder a barrel of gunpowder that it would take two normal men to lift. In his final triumph now he was actually singing, some old Russian hymn, in deep baritone. *Blagoslovi, Dushe Moya ...* He smashed the barrel down upon the rest of the store below, waved the wheel-lock tauntingly one last time at the captain as his desperate screams fell silent, his mouth still open, disbelieving. Finally the Rus crossed himself, dropped to his knees, gritting his teeth at the arrow's agony in his belly, held the sparking mechanism of the pistol to the spill of serpentine black powder – a scrabbling corsair leapt on to his back with a knife raised high in his fist – and fired.

2

The massive explosion blew the bow clean off the galley. After that, events unfolded in a strange, dreamlike silence but for a faint distant ringing. For the explosion had deafened every man aboard.

The single centre-line gun pitched head first through the flaming timbers and sank directly down to the ocean floor, a few last air bubbles trailing from its black mouth. The rest of the slaver seemed to rear back for a few moments, as if in horror at its own mutilation. Spars and scraps of burning sailcloth turned and wheeled high in the blue sky, and among them, heads and limbs and limbless torsos of corsairs and slaves alike.

The decapitated galley crashed down again and immediately her hold was swamped by the inrushing sea. Rowers on the benches scrabbled desperately at their manacles, but it was useless. There were only seconds left. Groaning forward, the galley began to slide down below the surface. Bubbles and eddies came up from the drowned hold, a casket of oranges floated free, a severed arm revolved in a small whirlpool. The captain held his chest of treasures clutched under his arm, looking wildly around. The *Sweet Rose of Algiers* carried no longboat or dinghy, and few of the corsairs could swim. The galley had been their home, their mother, their country.

The water swirled in around the rowers, and the salt made them reel in agony as it coursed past blistered thighs and backsides, chafed by months on the accursed bench. But swallowing their pain and shock, Nicholas and Hodge managed to move. They levered their broken manacles from their legs, and Nicholas thought to snatch the loosely draped headcloth from his bare skull and tie it around his neck, shouting at Hodge to do the same. Another of the rowers held on to him in desperation, pulling him down beneath the swirling water, nearly drowning him, screaming to be set free. The galley gave another lurch and, gripped by a maddened, dying man, chained to a sinking ship, Nicholas was momentarily dragged beneath the water. He strained every sinew and came up above the surface sucking in air. Then all he could do, loathing himself, was ram his elbow into the fellow's face, driving his nose-bone back into the brain so that his grip loosened and he fell silent. That was the only way he could set him free.

He saw Hodge take another cloth and wrap it round his waist, and Nicholas grabbed a floating corsair by his belt – what remained of him – and took his dagger. There were so many other things they might do, so many things they might try to salvage, in faint hope of rescue before the *Sweet Rose of Algiers* took everything with her to the unknown deep. But his head was screaming, the water was swirling ever more powerfully and carrying him away. He clambered and waded back to the stern, stuck his dagger in the captain's chest as he stood there wild eyed, wiped it clean and wedged it between his teeth. The captain dropped his treasure chest and sat down in the water, holding on to the whipstaff of the rudder, his face ashen and dying. A whirlpool of water coursed around him and Nicholas. Even the chest, heavy with silver and gold and precious stones, lifted and turned. Somewhere in the distance, his ringing ears heard Hodge shouting. 'Save yourself! Get away from the ship!'

Nicholas staggered in the powerful surge, then set his foot on the captain's throat, grabbed the rawhide thong around his neck and pulled. It came free, with the key attached. The captain's head fell back and he went under water, his last words a curse in slurred Berber.

'May it carry you down.'

The ship itself then gave a colossal gulp, like the last gasp of some dying leviathan, as its stern was finally sucked beneath the surface of the sea and it tilted and began its slow dive to the ocean floor, many dark fathoms down. Nicholas abandoned himself to the turbulence, eyes closed, mouth clamped shut, the dagger still between his teeth, his lungs filled with one final breath. You could not fight the sea. You had to wait until it let you go.

Seeing nothing, tumbled about, all sense of direction lost, he was aware only of an iron key in his right hand, and a heavy locked chest under his left arm, dragging him downward fast. So fast that even through tight-closed eyelids he was aware of the sunlight fading, the water around him darkening, deeper and deeper green, as he fell away from the sunlit upper world. In his blindness he groped with the key, tumbling over and over, and at last drove it into the lock of the chest.

The captain had kept it well oiled. He counted his loot nightly. With his last strength, his lungs feeling as if he'd inhaled a line of pure gunpowder, Nicholas turned the key and wrenched the lid open with main force. The weight of the sea at this depth was trying to keep it shut, as if Old Father Ocean had already stretched out long green fingers of weed, decreeing these treasures *Mine, mine, for all eternity ...*

Let it be something decent, he thought. Even at that extremity the wry thought crossed his failing mind that, knowing his luck, he would probably come up with a fistful of English pennies. His fingers closed around something like a chain, and then he let the chest go and it dropped away into the depths. He kicked the opposite way from its descent, towards the light. He could barely kick more. But he must, or he would not rise fast enough to save his life. He must swim.

He began to see visions, colours. But he held himself in his right wits, eyes bunched tight, though longing to open them and look down, for one last glimpse of those corsair treasures sinking away into the midnight deep. But he denied himself. That second or two of delay alone might kill him. He kicked for the sunlight, eyes screwed so tight he saw stars, mouth leaking bubbles now, eardrums throbbing and hissing.

He imagined himself kicking upwards through glinting silver reales, cascades of pearls and glittering clouds of gold dust. Turning and falling, winking and revolving like some strange sea creature, at last losing even its light, an emerald necklace that once graced the alabaster neck of a queen.

He never remembered the last of his ascent but came to the surface and lay there with a roaring in his ears, a thunderous sound. After a while he realized it was his own breathing, as his burning lungs sucked in air. He lay spreadeagled on his back in the water like a starfish, just floating, blinded by the sun. Still alive. A dagger blade still between his teeth.

Then a familiar voice called his name.

If the ship had sunk entire, they too would have been lost. But the Rus's act of mayhem had blown timbers and spars widely over the sea, which offered the remote chance of reprieve, at least for a few hours. Straws to drowning men.

Hodge was draped over such a spar. Nicholas stuck the dagger in the knotted waist of his loincloth and swam slowly over to him.

After the months of enslaved horror, then the sudden violence and the gigantic explosion, there was an eerie calm. They bobbed in a flotsam of shattered timber and drowned men. Now the *Sweet Rose of Algiers* was gone, they looked out on nothing but boundless sea. They almost felt a longing for the filthy brigantine. Here, so far from land, so far from other living men, was the loneliness that drove men mad.

After a while they found the energy to exchange their single spar for a broader, more promising timber. A plain piece of pine from the mountains of Lycia, all that saved them from death. They draped their arms over it. Their blistered backsides and legs under water, their rotted feet, had gone strangely numb. Perhaps it was better that way.

'What's that you've got? Round your fist?'

He hadn't even looked at it. A rope of colourless stones that flashed every colour of the rainbow as he twisted his fist about.

'Looks like it was diamonds you very nearly perished for,' said Hodge.

Nicholas almost smiled. 'So far,' he said, 'I've had a very lucky day.'

Hodge closed his eyes. When he opened them again, Nicholas had checked the links and then awkwardly managed to drape the necklace over his head.

'As drowned men go,' said Hodge, 'you'll make a very pretty one shortly.'

24

'We're not drowning,' said Nicholas. 'I'm not done with this world yet.'

It was very quiet but for odd splashes and groans. Nicholas looked around for the Sardinian boy, the only other slave unmanacled at the end who might have survived.

'Save your breath,' said Hodge. 'You'll need it.'

'He might still live,' said Nicholas.

'He died,' said Hodge. 'Look around you.'

It was true. Among the gently rocking detritus, one or two terrified corsairs still clung to bits of wood. But no boy.

'How long can wood float before it's waterlogged?' asked Hodge.

'Weeks,' said Nicholas.

'How long can *we* float before we're waterlogged?'

'We shouldn't speak. Breathe through your nose.'

Hodge fell silent. Then he fumbled underwater at the cloth tied round his waist, and produced ... four oranges, salvaged from those that had floated up from the hold. He laid them carefully in a deep rut on the timber. But still seawater sluiced over them.

'Eat them now. They may save us.'

Such paltry things a man's life could depend on. Man whose mind ranged the whole universe – yet his life could depend on a single iron bolt, the thread of his life be cut for want of an orange.

They ate slowly and deliberately, knowing this could be the last thing they tasted before they died.

'They were good,' said Nicholas.

'They were sweet.'

After a time Nicholas said, 'We've got a day and a night. After that we will die of thirst. I remember Smith and Stanley telling me.'

'Smith and Stanley,' repeated Hodge. 'We could do with their company now.'

Nicholas smiled faintly. What would they do now, if they were us?

It was a question they had asked themselves many times over the last few years. What would the mighty Smith and Stanley – old acquaintances from their past lives, adventurers, knights, warrior monks – what would they do? Nicholas and Hodge had whispered it to each other in filthy Tripoli dungeons, yelled it to each other as they fled through almond orchards pursued by hunting dogs and a hundred maddened villagers, murmured it to each other drunkenly in many a dubious quayside tavern, surrounded by half a dozen cut-throats they had just insulted. *What would Smith and Stanley do now?*

'Smith,' said Hodge, 'would swim about with a knife in his hand, finishing off any corsairs he could find.'

'Stanley would be making terrible puns. He'd say he'd be surprised if the *Sweet Rose of Algiers* ever *rose* again.'

'Both of 'em,' said Hodge sharply, 'would have the wit to remember to cover their heads.'

Hurriedly they unknotted the cloths around their necks and tied them over their heads. At least they might delay the hour when the Mediterranean sun stewed their brains in their skulls. They also took off their loincloths and draped them round their reddened shoulders.

'We've survived worse,' said Nicholas, still ignoring his own rule about not speaking. The desolate silence sapped the spirit. 'Remember when we stood at arms at Elmo. Our comrades, Lanfreducci, Luigi Broglia, the Chevalier Bridier de Gordcamp – those gallant souls. Remember the nights at Birgu, when the Turkish cannon roared. The basilisks spat flames that lit up the sky.'

'Remember?' said Hodge. 'I will never forget.'

It was a comfort to talk, despite the thirst. Every little trick helped in survival. Nicholas looked around at the barren plain of the sea. There were no men coming to help, no comrades. It was a saltwater wilderness that cared nothing, for no one. Where was God?

Yet they prayed. Dying men always prayed.

'What current are we in?' said Hodge. 'The Atlantic rushes in past Gibraltar and heads north, does it not?'

'Aye. And we know we're near the African shore. The yellow sky to the south tells us so. The current here heads back west. A great wheel. We live long enough, we may paddle into harbour at Cadiz or Tangier. Should only take some three months or so.'

'I wonder about all the blood,' said Hodge. 'From the corpses. What fish and monsters it will bring.'

'We have hardship enough already, friend Hodge. Don't add sea monsters to it.'

For the rest of that day, they watched men flounder and die. Some simply fell silent on their timbers, their faces dropping into the water. The sea gradually pulled the other survivors farther apart and cast them wide over the ocean. Towards dusk one still living came kicking past them very slowly. He wore a white turban.

'Salaam,' he croaked. He tried to smile but his cracked lips made it impossible.

'Die, you maggot,' said Nicholas, his voice a hoarse rasp. His throat was so parched, his lips so burned, he hallucinated wildly that his words were being spoken by a ghost. He had a mouthful of cobwebs. The sun made a malevolent humming noise in the sky as it went down in the west. 'Die, or I will kill you.'

The corsair rested, exhausted, his head on his arm. His voice too was like the wind through dry grass, only just audible. 'We are equal now. No longer slave and master ... equal before the gates of death.'

'Die,' whispered Nicholas.

Then night came on, and the corsair died. The loneliness began to unhinge their minds. There was nothing but silence under the star-light, an empty world, the lapping of small waves at their timber of pine. Exhaustion and fragmentary dreams. Nicholas saw a Maltese girl called Maddalena. Hodge saw the woods and green fields of Shropshire. The constellations wheeled overhead, the moon came up and blinded them. Each of them had a horror he would close his eyes, and open them again to find the other one dead. They talked in slurred words with swollen tongues, hallucinating, lips splitting and bleeding, dreading the rising sun. For tomorrow would kill them.

Nicholas tilted his head back to the sky because it was raining. But no, it was not raining. He was dreaming. He wondered whether there was dewfall at night on the sea. He opened his red mouth wider, wider. The moon burned his black tongue.

Then he looked round and Hodge had gone. Slipped below without a word. His childhood friend, his manservant, his

27

comrade-in-arms through the atrocity of Malta. Hodge was gone below and he was alone. Now he would surely die.

'Hodge!' he tried to cry out across the starlit sea. 'Hodge!'

But no sound came from his throat. Not even a whisper.

Some time later Hodge reappeared, but Nicholas knew he was just seeing visions. It was the Devil's torment of a dying Christian. Hodge, he thought, came back very slowly through the sea, dragging a set of three timbers tied together. He pulled them up against their own, and tied them loosely to it with his waistcloth. It made a very crude, narrow, unstable kind of raft.

'And look,' said Hodge, producing something else. 'Two more oranges were still afloat. Breakfast.'

He hauled himself on to the four lashed timbers, which sank a little but held. Nicholas stared up at him.

'By day we stay under water or we'll cook,' said Hodge. 'But by night we can crawl out like turtles and lie on deck. Aboard the *Fair Maid of Shrewsbury*, as she's called.'

Nicholas smiled. It was a comical vision. There was the Devil for you. Gentleman, liar, joker.

He was cold in the night and towards dawn he stirred. Water lapped shallowly round his chest and legs where he lay. But he lay flat across four timbers. A light wind blew.

'Master?' came a strained whisper. 'I thought you'd never come round.'

Nicholas raised his head. His neck ached abominably, his head throbbed with merciless pain, and the thirst was agony. But then Hodge waved an orange before his nose and he could smell it.

'Hodge?' he whispered. 'I thought you were dead.'

'Not yet. Eat.'

Hodge helped him roll on to his side. Everything was hurting – his joints, his legs, his feet, his hammering skull, his pulsing, bloodshot eyeballs. Every bare inch of his flesh felt as if it had been rubbed raw with sharkskin.

He sucked on the orange, and after a few minutes he felt a small trickle of strength in him. Enough to say, 'This is our last day isn't it?'

Hodge lay beside him, his eyes closed. Both of them were half in the water. 'I think it will prove so, master. Aye. And soon the sun will be up and we must drop back in the sea.'

'I cannot, Hodge. I cannot.'

Hodge turned his face towards him. 'Master. To get this paltry raft, knotted with old clouts, I had to drown two Moors.'

Nicholas heaved himself round. 'I have a dagger.'

Hodge look at him. 'Not yet,' he said. 'Hold out a little longer.'

'For what?'

'For a last hope.'

The sunrise was beautiful and terrible, a few trails of cloud in the east scattering the burnished light. God's blessed daylight come to kill them. Every minute that the sun climbed to the zenith brought their death closer. They rolled back off the raft into the water with barely the strength in their arms to hold on to the spars. Their feet were bloated and white, legs blistered and weeping. Little fish came and nibbled at their sores but they could do nothing. They rested their throbbing heads on their forearms and made their last confused peace with God.

Nicholas thought he heard a splash near by and raised his head again. Twenty yards off there was a corsair corpse lashed to a spar, half submerged. His face was turned upwards, and the sun had burned his eyes dry in their sockets. But he seemed to move strangely, to twitch and bob. Like a dead dancer.

Then he understood. Something was tugging on the corpse from below, making it jerk spasmodically. Teeth were taking chunks out of his stomach.

To the dumb animals, flesh was flesh, alive or dead. Sailors' tales told of rats biting into sleeping men's faces. Meat was meat. He did not even know whether he would feel it when they in turn began to be eaten. His head drummed in hot agony, but the rest of his body below felt bloated and numb.

He could not speak but touched Hodge on the shoulder.

They watched a dark triangular fin passing back and forth through the water near the corpse. No, two fins. Three. Another splash. It was the fish fighting over the meat.

Hodge spread his hand wide, very calm. The old signal from their boyhood deer hunts. Keep still. Make no noise.

One of the dark fins, driven from the corpse by the others, was coming towards them.

3

'On to the raft,' whispered Hodge. He tried to pull himself up, but had no strength left.

Nicholas reached out across the raft to the next spar and strained with all his might. His skinny forearms nothing but bone and sinew. Feebly his legs kicked in the water. The dark fin veered a little and made towards the movement. He pulled and pulled, desperate to drag his emaciated body from the sea to safety. But he might as well have tried to lift a hundredweight sack of grain.

Hodge said, 'There's a ship's mast. I saw one.'

He was hallucinating.

Then the dark fin cut through the water right beside them, and Nicholas saw the horrible grey shape of a huge fish, longer than he was, with small eyes in a massive head, and a wide mouth that seemed to be smiling. He fought with every inch of his will not to move, not to kick out, and the fin turned suddenly, whipping away through the water. It moved off some thirty yards, and then he saw it turn. It was coming back again.

'Both of us,' said Hodge. He felt like his throat was bleeding from the effort of speech. 'Same side of raft. Weight down.'

Nicholas did as he said, and the raft dipped down into the water at an angle. Nicholas rolled on to the submerged edge. Hodge swam slowly round to the other side and hung on. The raft flattened out and Nicholas was just out of the water. Hodge was not.

'Keep still,' whispered Nicholas. 'Do nothing.'

The fin came closer.

Nicholas pulled the small dagger from his waist. As well fight a lion with a twig.

The fin passed by again and he swiped clumsily at it with the blade, nowhere near, almost rolling from the raft into the sea.

Hodge shook his head.

Nicholas knelt up precariously on the four lashed timbers. One of them was coming loose.

Hodge shook his head again more strongly.

Nicholas's swollen fingers struggled with the knot where it was tied with a piece of cloth, but it was impossible. Tight with salt water. He crouched over the knot, swaying like a drunken man, and began to saw at it with his dagger. It came free. He clamped the dagger back between his teeth and, with his very last strength, hauled the spar from the sea. It was the broken shaft of an oar, splintered in two by the explosion, and the far end was jagged.

The shark was gaining speed, making straight for where Hodge hung now, its fin cutting a tiny trickling bow wave. That was how they attacked.

Nicholas tried to roar out, to steel himself, but only a croak came. He lifted the splintered oar in both hands and squinted, and there was a great grey flickering form in the water. He lunged down. The jagged end struck something very hard and dense, like a side of beef, and Hodge was suddenly barged aside, losing his hold on the raft. Nicholas dropped the oar crosswise and seized hold of him.

Out of the corner of his eye he saw the dark fin curve away and round – and then come again.

Hodge's eyes were closed, his head lolled. How could Nicholas drag him on to the raft? Yet he must. He hauled the semi-conscious body to his side. Looking up, he saw three fins around the raft now, circling wide. Four fins. Five. And he saw a dolphin leap.

A dolphin. Several of them.

And as if by magic – or a miracle – those dark circling fins vanished.

Another of the dolphins gave a great curving leap, and then they too were gone, and all was silent.

Nicholas looked down, but there was no blood in the sea. He could have wept. But he didn't have the tears.

There was only the stony silence of the sea, and the burning sun.

32

After a while he dropped back into the water, and looped Hodge's arms around the spar beside him. They were sunk very low now, their mouths only just out of the water. The raft was failing them.

'Dolphins,' whispered Nicholas. 'Dolphins came.'

It was like a miracle. But he had heard of such things. Dolphins and sharks were ancient enemies, and dolphins had been known to save a drowning man, aslike in the myth of Arion.

Hodge's eyes were closed, his expression one of dull agony. But he said, 'Sharks fear dolphins. Christian and Turk.'

Still, they both knew the sharks might yet come back.

A little while later, Nicholas said, 'I am happy to die beside you, Hodge.'

Hodge stirred and spoke one last time, as if remembering something, his voice barely audible now. 'I saw a mast. You ... on the raft.'

He was dreaming. But in a last act of faith and trust, after many minutes of effort, Nicholas rolled once more on to the raft, having first knotted Hodge's upper arms to a timber. Trembling under the burning sun as if he were dying of cold, he pulled himself first on to his hands and knees, and then, shaking violently, arms outstretched for balance, feet astride, he managed to stand upright.

He looked out, as best he could.

Hodge's dream was infectious. There was a mast.

He drew off the wet cloth around his neck and very slowly, almost sobbing with the effort, raised it above his head. But it was far too wet to flutter. A sodden rag made no signal.

He prayed she was a Christian galley. The odds were even, the toss of a coin: Christian or Mohammedan.

Yet this was only a hopeful lie. They were but forty miles off the Barbary coast. There was every chance it would be a Tripoli merchantman – or another corsair galley.

She had no sail up, but she was coming towards them under oar. It must be a dream.

But no. It was a nightmare. She was black hulled and lean. She was a corsair.

Hodge murmured something from the water below him.

Nicholas took out his dagger from his waistband.

'Is she Christian?' murmured Hodge.

'Aye,' lied Nicholas. 'We are saved.'

Now he had but to kneel down again, trembling with the effort, and cut his friend's throat.

For it had all been for nothing after all. If they still breathed by the time the corsair came by, they would be quickly dispatched as too weak to row, and this preposterous lady's trinket that still sparkled round his blistered neck would be lifted from his corpse. It was time to die now, with what shred of dignity they had left, at their own hands.

'It was a banner of St John,' slurred Hodge. Seawater lapped at his chin. 'I saw it from the sternpost.'

Dying men had dreams. How could he have seen the ship when they lay in the water?

Yet Nicholas, still clutching his dagger in readiness, shaking from head to toe, half blinded by salt and sun, eyelids red and inflamed, lashes encrusted, stared out westwards still. He could see nothing but a white dazzle, his brain throbbing in its bone cave. Nothing but the glaring pain of the world.

Yet he heard the boom of a single cannon, and no cannonball's whistle to follow.

It was a signal. A sign.

He bowed his head, and the dagger dropped from his hand.

4

For three days they nursed the two near-dead men they had dragged from the sea.

They washed the crusted salt from their skin, and dressed their terrible sunburn with bandages soaked in vinegar, two strong men holding them down as they applied the dressings. For pain could sometimes be so great that a man might arch his back from the pallet and crack his own spine. They poured water mixed with a small pinch of salt and some honey down the castaways' throats, a few drops at a time, but constantly, hour after hour, holding their heads up. Their hands were the powerful, knotted, scarred hands of swordsmen and warriors, but now they were as gentle in their ministrations as Carmelite nuns. They continued to make the two men drink water until, long after nightfall, they urinated. That effort alone exhausted them, and they both lay back again, barely conscious.

'I thought you medics drank a patient's urine,' said one of the warriors. 'For diagnosis.'

The medic looked down at the dark bronze liquid in the bowl. A mere spoonful, but the odour was ... penetrating. 'In this case,' he said, 'that will not be necessary. My diagnosis is that they are still thirsty.'

They made them drink and drink, sometimes mixing the water with a squeeze of lemon juice. They dabbed their many sores and wounds with alcohol, rubbed fat on their atrociously blistered lips, placed and regularly re-placed cool cloths on their hot and feverish heads, and finally poured tincture of opium, blessed opium, down their parched throats. Both castaways soon became delirious and talked effusively.

'Your Majesty, Your Majesty,' slurred the fair-haired, emaciated one, 'I am your most loyal subject ...'

'Market day in Shrewsbury,' muttered the other, 'a bad business ...'

'Malta,' said the first. 'Elmo is lost ...'

'Elmo?' repeated the knight, and stared at the medical chaplain.

The chaplain stared likewise. 'And Englishmen? So we have been ministering to a couple of Protestants.'

Suddenly the fair-head gripped the medic's wrist hard, eyes wide but unseeing. 'Does the banner of St John still fly?' he whispered.

'Yes ... yes, it still flies.'

Again the chaplain and the knight exchanged bewildered glances. There was something very strange here. Something of destiny.

The fair-head collapsed back upon his sweat-stained pallet. 'Christ be thanked. More opium.'

The knight nodded, and the chaplain poured a few more drops of the precious tincture on to a silver spoon.

'May your visions be sweet ones,' he said.

Nicholas swallowed down the few bittersweet drops. 'I doubt it,' he said, and slipped from the waking world.

Three days later, after the two castaways had slept many hours, and drunk numberless pints of sugared and salted water, and then taken softened bread, and finally a little meat broth, they were just strong enough to sit upright on their pallets and swing their legs round to meet the floor, and not topple over sideways.

'If there were more opium ...' said Nicholas.

The medical chaplain shook his head. 'No more is needed. It creates an appetite in a man and makes him a slave.'

'*I have been a King, I have been a slave ...*' said Nicholas in a strange sing-song voice.

He was not driven mad, this one – not yet. But he had seen many atrocities, and borne much in his short life. The medical chaplain could see it in his eyes. He had seen it many times before. Such a one could easily turn into the very worst, most aimless cut-throat, a man with no heart or soul left in him – or a helpless slave of opium, lying reeking and glassy eyed in some backstreet den in Tangier.

The other seemed an altogether stouter, quieter, more imperturbable fellow. If they were old friends and comrades, then the fair-head was lucky to have him.

'Where are we?' demanded the fair-head now. He spoke good Spanish. 'Who are you men? Whose ship? And what year is it?'

'With respect,' said the medical chaplain, 'you are our guests now. And it is we who ask the first questions.'

They were joined at that moment by a couple of knights, and a tall, noble-looking Knight Commander. He had a splendid, iron-grey forked beard, close-cropped hair of the same colour, and large, thoughtful eyes that might have been those of a scholar.

The medical chaplain stood immediately and gave a small bow.

'Brothers,' said the Commander. 'Fra Bernardo. And ... newcomers. I am glad that you have lived through your ordeal. You are strong.'

'We were on the galleys.'

The Commander nodded. 'We guessed as much. What happened?'

Nicholas shook his head and told the tale of the Rus and the gunpowder. The Commander gave a low whistle. 'You have survived by a miracle. The Rus must have been maddened – but that is not unusual on a galley. You would have died, but by a strange irony, it was the explosion of gunpowder that we heard, and the plume of black smoke that set us rowing towards you. A murderous act became a distress beacon. We thought it might be an engagement between corsairs and Christians.'

'The Rus knew we two were unmanacled. He might have thought we could survive, at least.' The fair-head looked down. 'His was an act of sacrifice, maybe. Another small sacrifice in this unending war.'

The Commander asked, 'Your names?'

'Nicholas Ingoldsby.'

'Matthew Hodgkin,' said the other. 'Hodge.'

'You are Englishmen, and Protestants?'

'Englishmen, and Catholics.'

'Ah,' said the Commander. 'I like this better.'

'You will like this better yet, if you believe it,' said Nicholas Ingoldsby. 'My father's name was Sir John Ingoldsby. Long before

I was born, when our King Henry attacked the monasteries and destroyed them, he also abolished the Order of the Knights of St John in England.'

'I know this.'

'But before that,' said Nicholas, 'my father was a Knight of St John. Of the English Langue.'

The Knight Commander stared at the emaciated youth on his pallet. His blue eyes were exhausted but unflinching.

'My father even fought at Rhodes, in 1521. He knew Grand Master Jean de la Valette, and he—'

'Hold,' said the Knight Commander. 'You mean you are ... you are the two English volunteers who fought with our brothers at Malta? Even in the inferno of Elmo?'

'That was us.'

There was a long silence. The chaplain, Fra Bernardo, could have sunk down on his knees before the two of them. He had heard of them both, and of their exploits. Who had not?

'I was fighting at sea that summer,' said the Commander softly, surveying them. 'But truly Christ is with us today. Look what a fine couple of fish we just plucked from the water.'

He reached out and clasped first Nicholas's and then Hodge's hands in his own, and his face shone with heartfelt emotion 'My name is Gil de Andrada. Truly you are welcome aboard this ship. Truly.'

Nicholas felt shaken within. Let me not weep, he thought, and bit his blistered lip.

'But this is a corsair galley?' he said.

'We captured it. We have been patrolling the east coast of Spain against the Turk, along with the Chevalier Romegas – you remember the great Romegas?'

Nicholas smiled very faintly. 'We met him. He still sails?'

'Of course. Still the greatest sailor among all the knights, and an unceasing terror to the Ottoman ships. We captured this mean little galley off Tripoli and are now sailing back to Malta. You will be greeted royally there.'

'I cannot go back to Malta,' said Nicholas. 'I beg you, this one favour. Do not take us back to Malta.'

The chaplain moved swiftly to the side of his captain and had low words with him. 'It is said, Captain, if you recall, that the English boy was in love with a Maltese girl during the Great Siege. And she was killed by a cannonball, near the very last day of the battle.'

The Commander bowed his head briefly. Now he remembered. So sad and heroic a tale.

'Then it is settled,' he said briskly. 'It is the least we can do. We are equal sailing now from Malta or Cadiz. You will go to Cadiz. But what then?'

'Then home,' said Nicholas. 'We want to go home to England. We are ...' He searched for the word. 'We are very tired.'

'But you are Catholics.'

'Aye.' Nicholas looked puzzled. 'But Englishmen still.'

Fra Bernardo and Gil de Andrada exchanged agonized glances. It was such a curse to bear bad tidings.

'England,' said De Andrada – he clenched his fist. Damn it, so sad a tale for these broken heroes, these boy volunteers at Malta, the greatest siege in Christendom's history. Afterwards they should have been welcomed home with hymns of praise and palms before their feet. But it would not happen. And damn the fate that it should be he, De Andrada, who must tell them.

'Alas,' he said, 'it is now the year of salvation 1571. April, with Easter just past. You do not know? Malta was six years ago.'

'Six years?' whispered Hodge.

'Where did it go?' said Nicholas.

'In Algiers prison,' said Hodge. 'On the galleys. In the desert hills. But mostly in Algiers prison.'

'What befell you after Malta?' asked Gil de Andrada.

'There was a family,' said Nicholas softly, 'that we had grown close to. The Maltese family of a man called Franco Briffa, a fisherman. After the Siege, my friend Hodge and I stayed on with that family, for four happy years. And we helped to build the fine new city of Valletta, over the water.'

'Where else had we to go?' said Hodge. 'And as the city took shape we were proud of it. Maybe it will stand as our finest work.'

De Andrada nodded. 'Valletta is a wonder.'

'But at last our hearts sickened for home,' said Nicholas, 'as men's do. And though we were still penniless vagabonds, and had come to love our new island home of Malta very much – yet it was not truly our home. Not our native land. So finally we said sad farewells to our friends there, and sailed for England. But luck was a little against us, and our voyage home was interrupted – by corsairs.'

'And they had other plans for us,' said Hodge.

'Yet for two years we survived, by God's grace alone. On their stinking galleys, in their jails, or trying to flee. Hiding, afraid—'

Gil de Andrada said, 'No need to hide more. You are with the knights again now.'

A thought struck him. 'Smith and Stanley. Our comrades-in-arms at Elmo, and at—'

At last some happier news. Gil de Andrada smiled broadly. 'Fra Eduardo Stanley and Fra Gianni Smith live and breathe and quarrel and fight still like true brothers. They may have a few grey hairs now, and move a little slower – but they remain among the most ferocious of the Knights. And the keenest for this last great sea battle to begin.'

Nicholas looked questioning.

'Later. But as for England – my friends, my heart is heavy beyond telling.' De Andrada took a deep breath. 'Only last year, the Holy Father in Rome, Pope Pius V, issued a bull declaring your Queen Elizabeth excommunicate.'

The words sank slowly in. Excommunicate. Denied membership of the true Church, and eternal salvation. Pronounced a heretic, and so a false claimant to the throne of England. Now it was the duty of every Catholic prince in Europe to bring her down.

And Nicholas and Hodge were Catholics – and therefore traitors. They could never go home.

The silence was bitterly painful to all there. Fra Bernardo and Gil de Andrada could have wept for sorrow. These two were like Odysseus the wanderer, forever kept from his home in Ithaca by the malice of the gods.

At last Nicholas reached out his hand and laid it on the shoulder of his friend and comrade Hodge. Exiles and eternal wanderers together.

Hodge's shoulders began to shake.

'Bring them wine,' rapped Gil de Andrada.

They drank only a little before they felt they could sleep again, heavy with weariness and sorrow.

'There is more to discuss, but enough for now,' said Gil de Andrada. 'What is past is past. What is yet to come is in the hands of God. All things rest in God.'

Hodge and Nicholas lay down in the gently rocking cabin. Perhaps each time they slept would be less nightmare-ridden than the last. Perhaps their minds would heal eventually, along with their bodies.

'When your skin can bear them,' said De Andrada in the doorway, 'there are clothes in that chest. And there is also this trinket that came off your neck.'

He was holding up the diamond necklace. Nicholas had quite forgotten it, a worthless thing compared to life itself.

'I am no great judge of stones,' said De Andrada. 'You'll need an Antwerp Jew for that. But I would hazard a guess this necklace is worth more than a peso or two.' He tossed it over with a smile, and then a leather belt. 'The belt has a hidden pouch within it, like a snakeskin. Hide the thing well in there. Perhaps you might even live long enough to change it into gold one day.'

5

They had fine sailing westwards to Cadiz, with the shores of Africa a few leagues off to port all the way. At any time another corsair galley might have been spotted, slipping out of some narrow sandy lagoon past the date palms where it had its lair. But they felt little apprehension. No corsair galley would dare to attack a ship flying the standard of the Knights of Malta. Even an entire squadron of them would hesitate. Corsairs were cowards, preying upon the weak and defenceless. And the knights were most certainly not defenceless.

Nicholas took only one look down below, where the captured corsairs were now chained to the benches in their turn, straining under the lash to speed the sails. His eye roved blankly over them as he squatted at the top of the steps, staring down, hearing them groan, his stomach turning at the familiar stench. Other than that, he felt nothing at all. Christ, he wondered, has my heart turned to stone? Suffering turned few men into saints. Most men it simply made hard and unfeeling.

He and Hodge sat out on deck in the shade of the sails and breathed in the fresh salt wind and felt a little stronger each day. They passed the time telling their rapt shipmates tales of Malta. The younger knights had missed out on the Great Siege, to their bitter chagrin, and wanted to hear every moment of the story. Nicholas told them as much as he could bear, and Hodge too was a fine raconteur, plain and clear sighted and with the exact memory for telling detail of the true countryman, having passed his Shropshire boyhood

42

noting the changing colour of the haws each passing month, or telling the print of a dog otter from a bitch in the riverside mud ...

He also had his forthright opinions on foreigners, not a whit abashed that, apart from himself and Master Nicholas, everyone on this ship was a foreigner.

'The Grand Master, this Valette,' he declared, 'knew how to give orders, and wasn't a bad fellow for a Frenchman.'

'What do you mean by that, friend?' asked the young Chevalier de Rochefort.

Nicholas smiled and looked away.

Hodge said, 'Only that your Frenchman, with only a few exceptions, is a deceitful simpering cotquean with not enough blood in him to fill a chicken, and a great friend of the Turk to boot.'

De Rochefort, of impeccably noble ancestry, French to his fingertips and still only a hot-headed nineteen, looked as if he might go below for his sword. But Gil de Andrada near by, enjoying Hodge's account enormously, called out in stentorian tones, 'Respect to our heroes of Malta and guests aboard, De Rochefort, sir! Let him speak! If you dislike his harsh opinions about the conduct of France in this great war – and his opinions are by no means unusual – then get below and wad your ears with gun cotton! Speak on, Master Hodge. Fine entertainment.'

'He has opinions on other foreigners too,' said Nicholas.

'I'm heartily grateful you plucked us from the water back there,' said Hodge. 'We'd have been dead in a day. But this is what I learned at Malta, among other things. Your Spaniard is full of hot wind and boasting, but he can fight hardily enough if he's in a corner. They gave a good enough account of themselves at Elmo, those Spanish pikemen, I allow that: almost as good as Englishmen at times. Portuguesers, well, they're just like Spaniards, only shorter. Your Italian, he'll fight best if there's a pretty woman watching to admire, it, or some such reward at the end of it. Otherwise he's another one full of hot wind, and treacherous and incestuous to boot. We met some Greeks, and they're a snivelling wretched race. I don't see how they could ever have been heroes like in the tales of Homer. Frenchmen you know about. Germans are fat, greasy barbarians, as are the Dutch. Others – well, they're worse. But I don't care if I am aboard a ship full of foreigners, I won't fear to say it – there's not a dozen foreigners of any nation who would be worth a single Englishman.'

At that, Hodge folded his arms and glared around to meet any challenge.

De Andrada led the applause. 'You, Master Hodge, are truly one of these dauntless Englishmen we've heard about, with hearts made of oak.'

Hodge nodded acceptance.

'Just promise me – you will never work for your country's diplomatic service.'

Nicholas asked, 'Why are you patrolling off Spain?'

The Italian knight, Luigi Mazzinghi, answered him. An elegant young Florentine nobleman with a gentle voice, dark and lustrous hair down to the shoulder, flashing-eyed and with a ready smile, he was one of those knights for whom it must have been hard to keep strictly to the vow of chastity. The ladies would besiege him like the Armies of the Turk.

He explained, 'The rebellion of the Moriscos in Spain. You know of the Moriscos?'

'I have heard of them. The last Moorish subjects still living in Andalusia, but converts to Christianity.'

'Converts in name only,' interrupted Giustiniani, a grizzled veteran of a knight with a broken nose and a beard peppered black and grey. 'They are Mohammedans still, and their loyalty to King Philip and to Rome is worth less than nothing. A Mohammedan population among a Christian will always cause trouble. Now with the power of the Ottomans in the East growing once more, the Moriscos have risen in revolt from their mountain fastnesses in the Alpujarras, dreaming of Spain being Muslim again. Perhaps all Europe, under the rule of the Caliphate in Istanbul.'

'And you are patrolling – because the Turks are trying to supply them by sea?'

'Correct. In fact the Turks have already supplied them. A previous coastal patrol under the Marquis de Mondejar was wrecked in a storm, and the Turks, or their corsair allies, took the opportunity to slip in under nightfall. They must have made contact, and supplied generously. When the Moriscos rose in revolt, they

44

were armed with the finest blades, muskets and arquebuses from the Ottoman armouries, and full of confidence under their leader, Aben Humeya. It has taken nearly a year to suppress the revolt, and it is still not done. And now King Philip has made his base-born half-brother, Don John of Austria, commander of his home forces.'

Nicholas could tell from his voice that Giustiniani had no high opinion of Don John of Austria. He said, 'I met him once.' He gave an abrupt laugh at the strange memory. 'In a quayside tavern in Messina. He was making for Malta too.'

'But he did not quite make it?'

'King Philip ordered him home.'

Giustiniani harrumphed.

Nicholas said, 'He was wearing white kidskin gloves, a suit of pure white velvet, and soft white leather top boots to above the knee.'

'And this is the man charged with extirpating the Morisco rebellion!' cried Giustiniani.

'I remember thinking,' admitted Nicholas, 'that if he hadn't mentioned his mistresses at least twice in as many minutes, I would have taken him for a ... well, the kind of gentleman who prefers the company of other gentlemen.'

Giustiniani's expression suggested he'd just eaten a bad oyster. 'Though the truth is, he devours ladies like a fox in a hen coop.'

Mazzinghi smiled.

When he had possession of his feelings again, the older knight said, 'There have been many atrocities. At times it looked like outright civil war. The Moriscos spread terror across Andalusia. Men, women and children have been burned alive in locked churches, priests tortured to death, their own crucifixes used against them as instruments of torture. Nuns raped and their mouths filled with gunpowder to prevent them uttering the names of the Virgin or of Christ at their moment of death. Then burning linstocks touched to their lips ...'

Nicholas closed his eyes, but the picture did not improve. War always produced rumours of imaginative savagery. But he had seen enough of war to know that some of these rumours were true.

'So far,' said Giustiniani, 'three hundred Christian villages have been destroyed, and perhaps four thousand people killed. Their leader, this Aben Humeya, calls himself "King of Andalusia", and his right-hand man, Aben Farax, is even worse.'

'The revenge of the Spanish militias will be terrible,' said Nicholas quietly.

'That it will,' said Mazzinghi. 'Nothing breeds so readily as cruelty.'

'But it's a well-timed revolt, however cruel.'

'Ah,' said Giustiniani. 'So you see the wider picture?'

'I think so. Spain is the only Christian power that could conceivably face up to the might of the Ottoman Empire – though still no match for it, in truth. But if the Turks can ruin Spain from within—'

'And Spain's vast possessions in the New World?'

'You think the Turks dream of taking the New World?'

'If Spain lay in smoking ruins … what would stop them?'

Nicholas felt as if he were looking into an abyss. And he remembered something Stanley had once said. This was not just a war of the Mediterranean. It was a war for the world.

'Spain is financed by the silver of Peru,' said Giustiniani. 'Portuguese ships exchange cannon fire with Turkish off Goa, in the Indian Ocean. The whole world is implicated. And then closer to home, there is still a little island called Malta.'

Nicholas looked at him sharply. 'The Turks would sail against Malta again?'

'The Armies of Islam will always come again.'

He felt sickened at the thought. 'It cannot have all been for nothing.'

'It wasn't for nothing,' said Mazzinghi gently. 'That summer, six years ago. It was one of the noblest stands against Islam in a thousand years. All Europe was saved by it. Would to God I had been there.'

'You were still suckling at the teat,' said Giustiniani. 'But as you must understand, English comrade – even Malta was but a battle in a far greater war.' Giustiniani looked out to sea, and even this warrior monk of St John, his austere life dedicated to never-ending crusade for the faith, showed an expression like regret. 'Cyprus is under siege again. And there is a great sea battle coming soon. I think it is a war that will never be done.'

46

They sailed into Cadiz harbour as dusk was falling, the whitewashed houses glowing warm in the last rays of the sun. There were fine churches, warehouses, mules and muleteers, a babel of seamen's voices, wheeling seabirds, huge catches of fish being offloaded on the quayside.

'It is against the words of the Scripture,' said Gil de Andrada, smiling broadly and holding a purse out. 'But here, my sons of Belial, flown with insolence and wine. This is for your services, to go and get drunk in a tavern. But try to stay out of trouble.'

'Our services?' said Nicholas.

'Your tales of Malta. They were worth a few ducats.'

Still he hesitated. He hated taking money like this, but then again, stepping ashore on Spanish soil with not a penny to their name might have caused problems, until they found a Jewish dealer in diamonds.

The pragmatic Hodge took the purse anyway. 'Much obliged, sir. I'm looking forward to a good hot meal myself.'

Gil de Andrada raised a hand, and behind him, Mazzinghi and Giustiniani and Fra Bernardo and the rest. 'We bid you farewell. Perhaps you will make it back to England, and somehow keep your heads there. Play the scurvy politician and turn Protestant, for comfort's sake.'

'Never,' said Nicholas. 'My parents were Catholics. Their parents, and theirs. I am a Catholic.'

'Well, said De Andrada. 'Just supposing. Then write a letter to the Grand Master in Malta. Though I don't suppose it will ever get past your English spymaster Cecil, the most cunning in Christendom, they say.'

'Our thanks again,' said Nicholas. 'And fair sailing to Malta.'

They climbed down the ladder.

It was only when their feet touched dry land that they felt truly free again. Back on Christian soil, free men, and with a dozen ducats in their purse. The surge of joy and animal spirits, the warm Spanish night, were almost overwhelming.

'By God, Hodge, we've made it. We've actually made it!'

They embraced and danced like madmen on the quayside. Fishermen stared.

'Food,' said Hodge.

'Wine,' said Nicholas.

They went to a quayside tavern and sat down on a bench in the gathering dusk and wiped their sweating brows.

'Wine. And fresh water.'

'Lemons,' said Hodge, 'or oranges. Bread. Shrimps, mussels, anchovies, sardines, olives. Those little sausages, how d'ye call 'em, *churiscos*—'

'There's bread and stew,' said the girl. 'So bread and stew you'll get.'

She brought them a loaf and two platefuls of steaming stew, and two jugs and cups. They drank. Nicholas raised his cup to her.

'Freedom. Sweet freedom.'

'You are drunk already,' she said.

'Only drunk on the sweet wine of freedom, lady, and your unearthly beauty.'

She said, 'You should know, if you vomit in my tavern I will beat you so hard you will crawl out of here on all fours.'

Nicholas laughed, and then stopped and regarded her. 'Did you ... did you used to serve wine in an open-sided shack on the quayside down that way?'

'What of it? I work hard, I am thrifty, I save the money that is thrown my way by drunken fools like you.'

The tone of voice, the stance, hands on hips, the wonderful haughtiness, the arched brows – and her flashing dark eyes, along with her haughtiness, and her fine figure ... 'Hodge,' murmured Nicholas, when he had drained another cup and the girl turned away. 'Think back, six years ago – when we first came to Cadiz, whenever it was. You remember that quayside bodega that Smith and Stanley took us to?'

'And started a fight, and then ran and left us to it. They said it was for our ... martial education, or some such horse shite. And we got badly beaten about too. I remember.'

Nicholas nodded at the girl. 'That's her, isn't it? Our ministering angel.'

Hodge remembered back to the fight, and the bruised aftermath, when a pretty bar-girl of sixteen or so, fierce of speech but gentle of hand, had tended their wounds. When Smith and Stanley had returned she gave them such a tongue-lashing for their conduct that the two knights had cowered visibly. Now Hodge stared at her where she stood in the shadows, filling another jug from a barrel. Her dress was modest, she was no whore. Yet still it showed the outline of her neat bosom, her hips. He swallowed. It had been a while. 'I think you're right. And better preserved than we are too, I'd say.'

'Eh! Señorita!' called Nicholas.

She came swiftly. 'Señora.'

'But you wear no wedding band?'

'What business is that of yours?' She was more cold than haughty now, verging on real anger.

'I ... I am sorry. It is none. Forgive me.'

Well, he had manners after all. And the carriage of a gentleman too, she had to admit, though he wore a patched old linen shirt and scuffed boots and had behaved like any other drunken churl in her tavern. And on his bare arms, she now saw, he had cuts, and scars, a great white cicatrice on his left elbow, and gunpowder burns as well. They may have been no more than tavern brawls, of course. Yet something told her – something in their eyes, these two with the strange accents, and blue eyes in sun-darkened faces – something told her that they were no ordinary tavern braggarts.

'My husband was killed,' she said. 'Soldiering in the Alpujarras. The Moors killed him.' She spat and twisted her foot in the dust. 'And you? Where did you come by those burns? What is your accent?'

'We.' Nicholas hesitated. 'We—'

'We may need more wine before we divulge all that,' said Hodge, tapping the side of his nose.

She softened a little more. They were no ruffians. 'And more food too,' she said. 'Both of you together have hardly enough meat on you for one man.'

'That's life on the corsair galleys for you,' said Nicholas.

'The galleys!' She tossed her head scornfully. Her hair was

49

midnight black and glossy. 'Now you are a bag of wind.' And she went for more bread and wine.

The wine worked quickly, and they ate ravenously in between swilling.

Hodge sat back and belched. 'I'm going to be sick.'

'Then get outside and hurry up about it,' said Nicholas, tearing off more bread and dunking it in his wine. 'Or there'll be nothing left when you come back.'

He reached out and tried to take the girl's arm. She slapped him.

'Six years ago,' he said, 'we were in a fight in your quayside tavern. There was a blubbergut boastful Frenchman—'

'What other – *hic* – kind is there?' said Hodge.

'And we beat him. We were with two Knights of St John of Malta.'

The girl frowned. A hazy memory did come back to her. 'They were ...' She scrutinised Nicholas. 'You are English?'

'And you are,' he said, delighted with himself for having dredged up the name from so wine-hazy a memory, 'you are Maria de l'Adoracion!'

For the first time she smiled, showing perfect white teeth. Then it went again as she took a hold of herself.

'Perhaps I am,' she said.

Darkness was falling, and a small scruffy boy appeared in the doorway. 'Where are the strangers?' he said in a piping voice.

'Out, out!' she cried, waving her apron.

'They came off the knights' ship. They fought at Malta, someone said.'

Maria stared back at the two drunken Englishmen, and then waved the urchin away.

She came back and stood at their table. 'You really fought at the Siege of Malta? That is where you got your scars?'

Nicholas looked at her dreamily. Women loved a hero. Maybe he was on to something now.

'We did, señora. And after ... Algiers, Tripoli, the Greek islands ... the galleys.'

With her dark hair and dark flashing eyes, he knew he was confusing her with a girl he had known and loved on Malta. This

Maria was a bar-girl and a widow, though yet only twenty or so, and more radiantly beautiful with every cup of heady wine. Well, let him be confused. Let confusion reign, he thought.

He pulled her to him. 'Sit on my lap.'

She slapped him again, a considerable blow. He laughed.

'You think to come swaggering back into my tavern after ten years—'

'Five years,' he said. 'Six at most. How my heart has yearned for you.'

'—and expect me to fall into your arms? What kind of arrogant swine are you?'

'Women always insult those they are drawn to.' He beamed at her.

'Doh, you are impossible. *Impossible.* Touch me once more and you will see my stiletto.'

She went to serve another customer, her cheeks flushed red.

'As lovely as a rose in the gardens of the Alhambra,' murmured Nicholas, leaning after her and nearly tumbling off the end of the bench.

Hodge poured them both large tumblers of plain water. 'King Solomon didn't sweet-talk his one thousand concubines in the Bible any more sweet than you do. 'Tis a *Song of Songs* to hear you woo her. Here, drink this.'

'Water?'

'Water. We need it.'

They drank, and almost immediately Nicholas felt his head become a little cooler and clearer. He sighed. God save us all from beautiful but virtuous widows, he thought.

They drank three more tumblers of water each.

'Well, Hodge,' Nicholas said, with a small watery belch. 'I am not proud to say it, but there's another appetite must be quelled before I sleep. And this tavern is too virtuous a place for it. But the whorehouses of Cadiz are highly reputed.'

'Aye, Master Nicholas,' said Hodge, an address used only sarcastically now. 'I am equally filled with disgust at myself for saying but. But – my britches cannot lie. Lead on. To the whorehouses of the Street of the Christmas Flowers.'

They staggered out of the door arm in arm, singing 'Farewell, O You Sweet Spanish Ladies'.

Maria de l'Adoracion watched them go.

Men.

6

They awoke the next morning with burning heads, the daylight making them wince, their eyeballs aching. They lay on straw pallets in an upper room, in an insalubrious house at the end of the Street of the Christmas Flowers. Nicholas tried to speak but his throat was too dry. *Water.*

He lay naked on top of his own britches, and could feel the necklace still concealed within the belt. His fist clutched his purseful of ducats. He opened it and peered inside, and found the correct number remained. The girls last night – four of them, wasn't it? Five? – from what he could remember, were hardly the finest Venetian courtesans in looks or in conduct. But they did what whores are paid to do cheerfully enough, and they were honest.

He and Hodge dragged on their clothes groggily and stared at each other. No man can feel proud of himself after a night in a whorehouse.

'Water,' they both croaked simultaneously.

'And opium,' said Nicholas.

Hodge looked at him.

'For my head,' he snapped.

There was no bright sun today, and they were grateful. Grey clouds rolled overhead, and a cold wind came down from the north, off the Sierras, where the high passes were still thick with winter snow. As they stepped outside, a chill drizzle began, and they pulled the hoods of their cloaks over their heads.

They found a drinking fountain at the end of the street and

washed and doused their heads and drank like camels and felt a little more alive. Girlish voices called down the street from an upper storey, 'Come back to us soon, English stallions!'

'*Stallions*,' muttered Hodge. 'More like mules with the mad staggers, we were.'

An old woman behind them, veiled and clad in black from head to toe, clucked her tongue against her few remaining teeth and pushed in beside the fountain.

'This water is for purity,' she said. 'Not for cleaning off the filth of the whorehouse.'

'You speak right, señora,' said Nicholas gently. 'How I would love purity.'

She stared at him, unsure whether he was mocking her, and then shoved them both out of the way.

After some enquiries they found a jeweller's shop in another side street, the air filled with the clink of little hammers from the coppersmiths' workshops. Nicholas presented the aged jeweller with the diamond necklace he had saved from the corsair treasure chest. The jeweller stared at it, breathed on it and held it to the daylight.

'Fake,' he said. 'But skilled work. You may have two ducats for it.'

'Two ducats!'

'Very well,' said the jeweller. 'Three.'

Nicholas shook his head and stowed the necklace away in his belt again. 'I'll keep it. Treasured memories.'

'A fake,' muttered Hodge as they walked away. 'Emblem of our whole poxy lives.'

There was a hubbub in the square. A crowd of people was surging along as if being harried from behind. They carried their possessions in rolls of blankets, improvised sacks or wooden barrows, as if they had packed hurriedly. And their baggage had the strange and ungainly look of fugitives' baggage: expensive silks were bound up with cheap twine, cooking pots blackened with smoke clanked alongside silver candlesticks and fine glass ornaments, a mule carried two cages full of songbirds, cheeping and bright eyed and bewildered.

Men, women and children, crying infants, old ones, huddled and frightened, looking around, keeping close to one another for comfort. The children shivered, ill dressed for such a cold day. One boy wore nothing but sandals, a pair of baggy britches and an embroidered satin cloth around his skinny shoulders: a fine piece of work, but no warmth in it. What he needed was wool. Without thinking Nicholas stepped forward to throw his cloak around the poor lad. He too had been a fugitive and a vagabond once, shivering in the woods and ditches of his native Shropshire. *And you shall not oppress a stranger, for you too were strangers in a strange land ...*

But even as he stepped towards the fugitives, a woman, perhaps the boy's mother, looked up at him with an expression dark with fear and hatred. He began to speak, to draw his hood down, but she spat on the ground and then she and her shivering boy moved on. It was too late. Enmity ran too deep and was as old as the generations of men, and the time for peace and for gifts was long since gone.

The drizzle became weightier and fell as rain. Hodge and Nicholas stepped back and watched from the entrance to a side alley, their hoods shadowing their faces. The atmosphere was bitter and ugly. Instinctively Nicholas's hand dropped to his left side to check his sword. He had none.

The crowd numbered some two or three hundred people, being driven down to the harbourside. The men were all bearded and wore skullcaps, and women wore headscarves, some of them half-face veils. The wind caught at their veils and they held them in place with slim brown hands decorated with henna tracery.

Behind them came a gang of thirty or forty well-armed ruffians and irregulars, the cruellest and most unpredictable kind. Not disciplined Spanish *tercios* but a motley militia, untrained, underpaid and vengeful. Ready looters and thieves from any weaker than themselves, and made bolder by the additional presence of a couple of squadrons of pikemen and musketeers.

A low murmur came from the shuffling, dispirited crowd. Some of them were reciting prayers in singsong voices, praising Allah for having liberated them from this land of tyranny and unbelief. Others muttered '*Allahu akbar, Allahu akbar, have mercy on us, Allah the Just, the Merciful ...*'

'So these are the Moriscos who have committed such atrocities,' said Nicholas softly. 'There seems an irony here to me.'

'Civil war.' Hodge shrugged. 'The innocent get it in the neck along with the guilty.'

'Get that filthy burqa off!' screamed a fat woman, suddenly enraged. 'You're on Christian soil still, you dirty Mohammedan slut!' And she clawed at a younger girl and snatched off her face veil. The girl cried out, but her father touched her on the arm and cautioned her. In deep shame, exposed in public before all men's eyes, and infidel eyes too, the young Moorish girl followed after her father, her face suffused with scarlet. Rain and tears ran down. They were nearly at the harbourside now, and there were ships come to take them from unkind Spain to a new life in the Islamic Kingdom of Morocco. It was as Allah willed it.

'Still,' said Hodge, 'hard to think they are of the same religion as the Turks, or those corsair savages.'

'They are not of the same religion,' said Nicholas.

'They are all Mohammedans.'

'Every man has his own religion. You think those thugs who drive these people out of Spain are the finest Christians?'

Hodge said nothing.

Down the alley behind them came more Moriscos, driven loosely along like cattle.

'*Allah ma'ak*,' muttered Nicholas as they passed by. God go with you.

The father of the family stared at him, this Christian who spoke the forbidden language of Arabic. In his eyes was nothing but suspicion, as if the blessing itself were a trap. He looked him up and down, as if trying to identify who he was, where he came from. Then he raised his arm and pointed at him very deliberately, looking hard towards an upper window above. Nicholas glanced up too, puzzled, and thought he glimpsed a figure move behind the wooden grille. When he looked back the father had moved on.

They ventured out into the square.

A wealthy Morisco merchant carried a fine bundle of silks on his shoulder, moving forward plump bellied but dignified, refusing to be hurried. A militiaman with a pike shouted out, 'Hold!'

The Morisco merchant stopped.

'Hand me those,' the militiaman demanded.

'They are not mine to give you,' said the merchant. 'They are promised in payment for our passage to Morocco.'

'Hand 'em over, you snake-tongued devil worshipper, or I'll open your belly!' He lowered the wicked-looking pike. The merchant's daughter, a girl of fourteen or so, cried out, 'Abu! Abu!' and clutched him.

The militiaman sneered at her and then viciously jabbed the butt of his pike down on her foot, encased in a fine silver-filigree slipper. Nicholas stared in horror as the girl fell to the ground howling, clutching her foot. Her father instantly dropped his bundle of silks and knelt at her side. The militiaman triumphantly seized the bundle and threw it over to his comrade.

'Your purse too!' he shouted through the rain and the girl's agonized screams. 'A rich man like you, it must weigh heavy!'

Hodge was already gripping Nicholas's arm, holding him back, knowing his master of old. 'We're not even armed,' he muttered, 'don't be a damn fool.'

But Nicholas twisted and was gone. He seized the militiaman's pikestaff in both hands and shoved it back hard into the fellow's startled face, knocking his helmet back off his forehead. He shoved it back a second time, a short swift jab. The heavy wooden staff clonked audibly against his skull, and blood spurted from his nose. He reeled. Nicholas whipped the pike clean from his grasp and spun around.

Immediately he was surrounded by a semicircle of half a dozen unwavering pikes, lowered to belly height. Heroes of Malta they might be, but this was suicidal. Hodge raised his face to the rain in despair. Barely a week free men, and they were going to go to jail again. At the very least.

There were a few moments of angry shouting, the pikemen looking ready to run this miscreant through on the spot. A Mussulman sympathizer, friend of the Moors, perhaps he'd like to take ship for Morocco too?

'Have your cock chopped like a filthy Jew!' bellowed the sergeant. 'Maybe we should circumcize you in advance!' He jabbed towards his groin, then looked around. Some hubbub was spreading through the square.

A rumour had run through the nervous crowd that a general massacre had begun. The Spaniards were intent on slaughtering them all before they even got to the harbourside, taking their last possessions, their daughters for prostitutes and bedroom slaves. Finally, to add to the pandemonium, someone had untethered some horses in a nearby street and tied lighted torches to their tails. Now the poor, terrified beasts came careering into the square with hindquarters smouldering and smoking in the downpour, lips back and teeth bared, rearing and trampling, the air filled with their screams and the evil stench of burnt horsehair. The crowd began to stampede and the pikemen turned away from Nicholas, starting to panic themselves.

Then urgent hands grasped Nicholas and Hodge and pulled them away down a narrow alleyway. Too startled to resist, Nicholas dropped the pike and allowed himself to be led. Moments later they found themselves crossing a tiny, rain-soaked inner courtyard, and bundled through a wooden doorway. They passed down a pitch-dark passageway, those that drew them on knowing the way, then through an archway so low they had to duck, and into a dimly candlelit chamber. They were pushed through heavy curtains at the back, into another still-smaller chamber, also candlelit. It was bare but for a single divan, and the air was full of the sweet smell of sandalwood.

'Wait here,' hissed a voice.

And then they were alone.

'What the bloody hell *now*?' said Hodge. 'Once again you have landed us in the middle of a cowpat the size of Shropshire.'

'That I have,' said Nicholas, shaking the beads of rain from his cloak, drawing his hood off and sitting down on the edge of the divan with infuriating equanimity. 'That I have.'

In the candlelight, Hodge actually saw the damn fool *smile*. The smile vanished again. 'But I could not watch what they were doing.'

'They were all Moors. The atrocities they have done, the terror they have spread—'

'Hodge,' said Nicholas quietly. 'You know that is not true. Not those merchants and their families. Not that girl, her foot now broken by a Spanish pike.'

'I bet they supported the uprising anyhow.'

'Are you surprised?'

Hodge held his gaze and then his eyes dropped. 'Damn it all,' he said, 'but the world's a mess and a half.'

7

It must have been half an hour later that the heavy curtain was drawn back and a man stepped lightly into the chamber. He wore a long robe in the Moorish style, and there was a dagger on a thin gold belt round his waist. They stood.

'Please,' he said, and indicated the divan again. 'You are my guests.'

They sat, warily. A boy brought in a beaten copper tray bearing two more candles, and three tiny cups of steaming coffee. They took theirs and held them until the man took the first sip from his own. He smiled. 'Please,' he said. 'Drink without fear in your hearts that you will be poisoned.'

The coffee was very hot and sweet. *Hot as hell, sweet as love, and black as the devil*, as the saying had it.

'So,' said the man. 'How is your homeland?'

It was important to show nothing, give nothing away. They were in a very peculiar situation, irony piled upon irony. Threatened by Catholic pikemen, they had now been rescued, it seemed, by Spanish Moors.

'She flourishes,' said Nicholas.

'*Alhamdulillah*, God be praised.' The Moor smiled. 'You would like to know of our progress? Assuming the ... gifts are to be shipped soon?'

Nicholas thought rapidly. They were mistaken for someone else. He said, 'Tell me of the fugitives first. Out there. Why are you not among them?'

He sighed. 'Cadiz has not yet been ... cleansed. These that you

60

see, the family that you so gallantly and foolishly fought for – and risked all our plans for, I might add – these are fugitives driven down from the Alpujarras.'

'Where the atrocities have taken place?'

'What have you heard?'

'Of churches burned, whole families massacred. Christian priests murdered.'

'And you too are a Christian. I understand that.' The man was thoughtful. 'It is a civil war, and nothing that the worst criminals among my people do has my support. Aben Farax in particular is driven more by hatred of the enemy than by any love of the Prophet. There are men like this in your world too. Yes? Driven more by hatred of the Moor, the Turk and the Saracen than by any love of your Christ?'

Nicholas nodded. 'We worship different gods. But the devil is always the same, and men commit the same atrocities the world over.'

'Then let me tell you how it has been for my people in Cadiz. And this has been by no means the worst. In Granada it is worse.

'Three years ago we were told that we must become true subjects of King Philip, no longer stand apart. We must abandon speaking Arabic, and learn to speak only Castilian Spanish. The language of the Prophet, the language of the Book, was to be *proscribed*. As if a filthy thing.'

'What did you do?'

'We did what any oppressed people does. We smiled, and bowed our heads humbly, and agreed. And in secret we did differently, speaking Arabic with ever more love and relish. So that we soon increased our reputation for dishonesty and treachery.'

'But this is hardly an atrocity.'

'Listen longer, English friend. We were then ordered to hand over all books in Arabic to Pedro Deza in thirty days, including the Koran. You know of Pedro Deza?'

They shook their heads.

'Doubtless you will. *Why do you still harbour copies of the Koran?* they said. *You are Christian now.* Of course, of course, we said. We believed the books were to be burned. We were then forbidden to wear any Moorish garments. Women must go in public with their faces uncovered, in case they posed a danger, or they were really Moorish men in disguise, intent on assassinating Catholic princes and cardinals. Our private family ceremonies, such as betrothals and marriages, must take place with the doors of our houses open on to the street, so that nothing nefarious could take place. What did the Christians take us for? So they could watch us – and the lesser ones, the peasants, jeer at us and even spit at us over our threshold as we gave our daughters away in marriage.

'Moorish names and surnames were banned. A father could no longer name his son Mohammed, he must call him Jacobo, or Rodolfo. Our bathhouses were closed down, because they said they were nothing but places where we practised our filthy lusts. We were forbidden to own Negro slaves – although as you know, Negroes are made by Allah to be slaves, for they are the accursed sons of Ham.'

Nicholas sipped his coffee.

'Our madrasas were closed, all our children were to be placed in Christian schools. To save their souls. And so you see, humiliation piled upon humiliation. Eventually a million little humiliations – do they not add up to their own kind of atrocity?'

'So you rose in revolt?'

The Moor nodded. 'Though we had no arms, no training, no fortresses and little money. Yet the Turks and the Moroccans promised us much. So we rose in revolt. At first Aben Humeya and Aben Farax led a band of no more then eighty followers. Young men full of blood and fire, and all the recklessness of the young. They had nothing else to look forward to but a life scratching a living herding goats in the Alpujarras, or running a stall in the market square. Why should they not take the golden road to martyrdom and paradise? More and more flocked to join the revolt.

'We fought from the natural fortresses of the Sierras – though we must not call Spain's highest mountain Mulhacen now, must we? It is an Arab name. Like the Alhambra. Like algebra and alchemy, and the Christians' favourite, alcohol, which is forbidden to us. Surely Allah plays jokes upon mankind, to instruct him!'

The Moor smiled, and the smile faded. The boy came back and whispered to him, 'The four are here for you.'

'Tell them to wait,' he said.

Four, thought Nicholas and Hodge. And they had not so much as a dagger between them.

The Moor resumed. 'One law said that any Muslim, of any age or sex, could receive a hundred lashes if he came near a town. For speaking Arabic you now spent thirty days in chains. Then bitterness and fear erupted in atrocity, and fed more atrocity. Christian villages were attacked by armed bands and put to the sword, though our leader Aben Humeya tried to restrain it. And then the whole Moorish quarter of Albacin, of Granada. Our men sold captive Christian women and children into slavery, under cover of night off the coast, to the Barbary corsairs. In return they received arms and munitions. A few Turkish supplies also came through the coastal blockades.

'And so for the Spanish, any Moor was now suspect by race, regardless of conduct. In some villages, Moors were hunted down with hunting dogs, for sport. Whole families were slain and buried in mass graves.

'There were still six hundred thousand Moors within Spain. A great number. But we could not oppose the Spanish army, and it destroyed us. Of course it did. We were only villagers, townsmen, merchants, and with families to protect. We were utterly defeated. Many of our people were herded down from their villages, broken up and divided, some sent on the long march to new settlements in Castile, or concentrated in camps in alien valleys, on the poorest land.

'A few fanatics still fight on now, in the Sierras and in lonely valleys. But what for? The Morisco people have already begun their long walk into exile. And this is really what Spain wanted all along, I think. What men such as Pedro Deza had long since dreamed of: a pure Spain, white and clean and Christian. That day has nearly come now. Pedro Deza has triumphed.

'And after all we have suffered, perhaps we are glad, or at least resigned, to be going. Those fugitives you witnessed, out there in the rain. They are not really weeping to go. They are weeping to be driven out in such ignominy, so unjustly robbed of their possessions. Many have lost relatives and loved ones in the wars. But they are not sorry to go. Here is another fine irony, my friends. I am in agreement with Pedro Deza after all. I do not think that we

63

Muslims and Christians can live in peace side by side. Not for very long. And so, after nearly a thousand years in al-Andalus, we go.

'Into exile, and betrayed too by the Turk. Constantinople promised us soldiers – none came. Just guns. And already we hear that in Morocco we are further preyed upon and robbed even by our brother Muslims. In Spain we are despised as traitororous *Mohammedans,* but in Morocco, we are thought not true believers, tainted by centuries of living under the infidel. They jeer at us as we step off the ships at Tangier or Ceuta, saying we sold our pigs just before embarking. It gives the Moroccans the excuse they need to practise their most ardent belief of all: cheating and stealing from those who trust them. It is a disgrace to the Faith.

'It is the flight of King Boabdil. You know of him?'

'The last Moorish king of Andalus.'

The Moor nodded. 'Who reined in his horse on the last high pass over the mountains of Spain, and looked back one last time over his beloved, lost kingdom of golden Granada – and sighed. That pass that has ever since been called *El Suspiro del Moro.* The Moor's Last Sigh.'

He said very softly, 'The history of men is but sadness and sorrow, always and for ever. Trust not in men and their history. Trust in Allah only.'

After a while Nicholas said, 'Yet – though your people are going and passing away from Spain for ever, you still wish to receive these ... gifts, from England?'

'Very much,' said the Moor, still with his head bowed, dwelling on the past and his people's sadness – and unguarded. 'We still wish to distract Spain, to prevent this Holy League from forming a while longer. Then when it forms, let it be drawn far eastwards, to Cyprus, so that the Ottoman fleet can sail west and take—' He bit his lip. This was too much to divulge, even to this gallant English ally – who was yet a Christian.

At that moment the boy returned with another whispered message. The Moor turned his head sharply, then said, 'Forgive me. There is a ... I will return.'

And as he vanished behind the curtain, he glanced back at his two guests, a look of puzzlement on his face.

*

The only possible weapon in the chamber was a tasselled silk cushion, which might stop a dagger-thrust for a second or two. They were well and truly trapped. Before, their situation has seemed so absurd, Nicholas had smiled. His smile had gone. The Moor had talked far too much for them to walk out alive now.

'I'm not sure,' said Hodge quietly, 'we've not hopped proverbially out of the frying pan straight into the fire, like a couple of stupid sausages.'

Nicholas nodded. 'Hiding from the Spaniards, sheltered by a Moor. Truly Lady Fortune is a whore.'

'You'll be a poet yet.'

They sat in silence for a while. At last Hodge said, 'Nick, this is agony.'

Nicholas said nothing. *Surely Allah plays jokes upon mankind, to instruct him!*

'The minute we came into this house,' said Hodge, 'dark and candlelit as it was, there was the coffee and tobacco smell, and mint tea, and the shoes left at the door. And I said to myself even then, Hodge, dearest friend, you are in a bugger's pickle now.'

'We cannot betray,' said Nicholas. 'They saved our lives here, though mistaking us for someone else, I think. But is England really to supply the Moors with armaments, to weaken Spain from within? Is our own country so treacherous?'

'Is she really our own country still?' said Hodge. Nicholas looked pained. 'Politics,' said Hodge, waving his hand. 'Like you said of the devil, it's the same the world over. No one comes out of it smelling like my dad's sweet williams.'

There was whispered conferring and then the Moor reappeared.

'Quickly, there are soldiers. In here.'

They hurried after him. In the outer chamber was a large cedarwood chest, which the boy and a woman had cleared of its contents. They stacked the various blankets and coverlets beside it on the floor.

'Inside,' said the Moor.

Nicholas hesitated. Such a hiding place wouldn't fool anyone. And once in the chest the lid might be locked or weighted down, and they would be left to starve. Who could they trust?

A thunderous drumming was heard far off. Pike butts being thumped against the bolted wooden door on to the alleyway.

'House search! Open up in the name of King Philip!'

Hodge was already getting into the chest. 'Mind you leave it open a crack.'

The pikes drummed again, and then they began a steady, rhythmic battering at the door. There soon followed a crash as the bolts gave and the door was flung back against the wall.

'Give me your dagger,' said Nicholas. The Moor looked puzzled. 'Give it to me!'

There was the sound of running feet and ruffianly shouts. 'On the floor! Don't move! You, kneel!' A muffled sound that might have been a cry of pain.

The Moor drew the thin gold-handled dagger from his belt and handed it to Nicholas without a word.

Nicholas stepped into the chest and crouched. As they lowered the lid over them, Nicholas laid the dagger blade on the rim, jamming it open a crack.

The chamber emptied and they crouched in silence.

'I hate small spaces,' said Nicholas.

'I didn't enjoy the dungeons of Algiers jail that much myself,' said Hodge. 'Can you see out?'

Nicholas craned painfully and tried to put his eyes to the crack. 'No. Only darkness.'

From the rest of the house, and the warren of chambers and passageways and courtyards that was the old Morisco quarter, came a range of thumps and bangs and cries, all the more unnerving for being unseen.

After some time there came a long silence, and then they heard the door of the chamber open. A voice whispered, 'Friends!'

It was the voice of the Moor.

They didn't move. Nicholas's grip tightened on the handle of the dagger.

'Friends! It is safe. Come out.'

Still they hesitated. 'Are you sure?'

'Quite sure.'

Another pause, and then Hodge slowly pushed the lid up, Nicholas ready with the paltry dagger.

There were two burly Spanish pikemen at the door, and another had his arm gripped around the Moor's throat, half-throttling him. In his left hand he held an evil half-pike, the tip under the captive's jaw. A fourth soldier had a knife to the throat of the boy, whose eyes rolled white with terror. In the brown eyes of the Moor there was no hint of treachery, only pleading and sorrow.

He whispered, 'I am sorry, I am so sorry—'

'Shut it,' growled the soldier, screwing the point of his half-pike into his cheek and drawing a trickle of blood. 'Or you'll lose the boy.' He looked back at the two wretches rising from the chest and smiled. 'Chain 'em up.'

8

The day was still dark and rain-sodden when they were dragged out of the maze of dark passageways into the street. They were driven into the main square, now empty of fugitives. But as they passed by a wide puddle, Nicholas saw that the rain was mixed with blood. They crossed to the imposing courthouse, and were dragged down some narrow steps into a lower passageway, though a narrow iron gate, down more stone steps in air clammy with damp and decay, and finally thrown into a fetid dungeon. The iron bars clanged shut behind them and were triple-locked.

It was pitch dark and silent as the grave. Some other sense, perhaps hearing, perhaps smell, told them that dungeon was not large.

They lay still, twisted, chained and blind. After a while they rolled over on to their sides and tried to pull themselves against the damp walls. They lay and breathed. This was going to be bad. They could see absolutely nothing.

'Dark as Egypt in the eighth plague,' muttered Hodge.

All they could hear was each other breathing. And then another sound. A skitter of little paws.

'Rats,' said Hodge.

The skittering grew. More and more of them.

'Shite,' said Hodge, and tried not to think of the tales he had heard. Of men chained in dungeons, unable to move, while rats feasted on their hands, their feet, their faces ... He kicked out with his hobbled boots and the rats shrieked and trotted away. Then he could hear them coming back, chattering. Could picture them in the darkness, raising their narrow muzzles, noses twitching, scenting fresh meat.

Suddenly, from the other corner of the dungeon, not two body lengths away, there came a violent thump and the rats squealed and were gone. For now.

'Who's there?' demanded Nicholas.

Silence.

'Damn you, speak. How many of you?'

Water dripped from an overhang, a drop every few seconds. Nothing else.

'If you don't sing, I'm going to,' said Hodge. 'And you won't like that at all.'

After a pause, a soft voice said, 'I am Abdul of Tripoli.'

'A goddam Mohammedan?'

'As you say. You have any light?'

'Of course we don't have any light,' said Hodge. 'You think they gave us a tinderbox and a sirloin steak when they shoved us in here?'

After a while something rasped in the darkness, and to their astonishment a small flame appeared. A stubby candle was set on the floor, blinding them for a moment, and then as their eyes grew used to the light in this dark place, they saw a slim brown face beyond. He grinned.

'Some of us come prepared.'

'But you're not chained!' said Hodge indignantly.

'And you are, I see. Pedro Deza must have caught two very big fish indeed.'

'He's got a surprise coming,' said Nicholas. 'What are you in for?'

'For following my own business,' said Abdul. His smile was very wide. 'But I shall soon be free again. I am of too much service to Pedro Deza.'

'You work for him?'

'I work for whoever is the chieftain. Always keep an eye on the leader of the monkey pack.' He ran his middle finger along an eyebrow in an enigmatic but expressive gesture. 'When I am in the dungeons of Grand Inquisitor Pedro Deza, I work solely and loyally for Pedro Deza. Once I am free again – Pedro Deza can go and kneel beneath an aroused camel.'

'You're an Algerine, then?'

'Abdul of Tripoli is also Abdul of the world!' He rocked back and forth where he sat cross-legged, smiling delightedly. Maybe he'd been in here a long time. He certainly seemed keen to talk to someone. 'You know that *Abd'ullah* means *slave of Allah*. But then when I am Greek I am become Petros Christodoulos, which is, in Greek, Peter, the slave of Christ. It is all one, you see, and means everything and nothing.'

'So you're a liar and a Judas.'

'I'm a philosopher,' said Abdul. 'And a survivor. I have been whipped in Spain, whipped in Sicily, scourged in Jerusalem and stoned in the streets of Cairo. But I survive. And like an old dog, I have learned from my whippings. I laugh at other dogs who are too stupid to learn.'

He regarded the candle. There was plenty more to burn.

'In Rome I'm a Christian, in Mecca a Muslim, in India I lie down in the dust and let the sacred cows walk over my prostrate body. I am all things to all men. And then Abdul climbs a hill in his imagination, as the sun sets, and looks down on the churches of Rome, the minarets of Mecca, the temples of India, and he sits back and laughs in the sun! He laughs at them down there, trapped in their gloomy churches and temples, while he sits high and free on the windy mountainside, a song in his heart like an uncaged bird. You wish me to sacrifice or swear devotion to any god? Willingly. Then let me go in peace, showing my bare arse to your gods as I go.'

'You're a blasphemer,' said Hodge.

'If it is blasphemy then God will punish me for it.'

'He is right,' said Nicholas wearily. 'Perhaps he is a man with no soul.'

'No, I have my soul.' Abdul lowered his eyes and stared into the candlelight. He said again softly, 'I have my soul.'

They heard the sound of footsteps in the passageway and Abdul cupped his hands around the candle flame. Then they heard a stertorous breathing and he took his hands away again.

'My tubercular and tabefied friend Diego the Jailer!'

'Tabefied?' said Hodge.

'Phthisic,' said Abdul. 'Marasmous. No hope for him, poor fellow.'

A gaunt, grubby figure with slumped shoulders and keys at his belt, Diego laboriously unlocked the door. Then he handed in a bundle of fresh candles, a large flask of water and, to Nicholas and Hodge's astonishment, a wooden trencher steaming with some roast fowl. Abdul took them from him and sat down cross-legged again before the candle and began to eat. Diego locked up. Nicholas watched his movements closely.

'Don't even think of it,' growled Diego through the bars, then hawked and spat. 'Not a chance. There's two soldiers at the end of this passage who'll skewer you like hogs the moment you stick your head out of the cell.'

'These two,' said Abdul with his mouth full, pointing at them, 'they escaped from Algiers prison *three times*.'

Now their jaws dropped open. 'How in the devil's name did you ...'

Abdul smiled infuriatingly and tore another strip of glistening meat from a slender bone. 'I must say, this is an excellent bit of guineafowl. Well done, Diego. How is the girl?'

Diego ran his tongue over his black teeth. 'Goes like a drunk mare,' he said.

'She is a generous-hearted soul. I owe her. And when do we expect ... His Excellency in town?'

'Tomorrow, I heard.'

Abdul looked back at his two cellmates. 'Don Pedro Deza will be in town tomorrow, and will then want to question you. Pedro Deza is a genius of his kind. He knows how to set one man against another. He could make a man betray his own mother. You should start praying to your god. Did he not once send an angel to rescue St Peter and St Paul in a similar predicament?'

'If I had a fist free,' said Hodge, 'I'd lam you.'

'But you have not. Which is why I shall continue to taunt you. But you should understand,' he ran his finger round the trencher and sucked up the juices, 'that there is teaching in my taunting. I may not love you as my brothers. But it would please me, nevertheless, if you were to avoid having every bone in your hands and feet broken by Pedro Deza and his ingenious machines. Before you die.'

*

Abdul slept for a while. Nicholas and Hodge bowed their heads but did not sleep. Their cellmate revived very suddenly and yawned and said, 'I must be out of here in another day or two. It dampens my spirits.' He looked at them sharply. 'You are sure you have nothing to sell?'

Nicholas shook his head.

'Even information?'

'No.'

'And there are things Pedro Deza, peace be upon him, would want to know of you?'

'I suppose.'

'But you are of heroic temper, and will resist telling him?' He shook his head. 'Pedro Deza knows how to make a man spill the innermost secrets of his heart. It does not take long either.' He belched. 'Mm, that was a lovely bit of guineafowl. Would you care to gnaw the bones?'

'Up your arse,' said Hodge.

'I do not know,' said Abdul, 'how men so foolish and ox-like and undiplomatic as yourselves ever survive long enough to breed.'

They were in front of Pedro Deza in less than two hours. They sat on wooden chairs in a lofty stone chamber – still chained at wrist and ankle. Two soldiers stood behind them. In front of them sat a man at a wide desk. He had a narrow, ascetic face, so white that it might have been powdered, and watery fish-eyes that blinked too rarely. He kept himself very still.

'So,' he recapitulated. 'You come ashore under cover of darkness in Cadiz, blue-eyed English Protestants, and from Moorish Africa. English thieves. Your Queen Elizabeth has dealings with the Sultanate of Morocco, does she not? Because both she and Morocco are enemies of Catholic Spain.'

'I do not know,' said Nicholas. 'But I repeat, we are Catholics, we did not come from Moorish Africa but from a sunken galley, and we are not thieves. You have seen our manacle sores and scars. Look.'

Pedro Deza remained quite expressionless. 'What do you know of Cyprus?'

72

'Cyprus?'

'And of the great sea battle that is to come? The Turk is building new war galleys on the Bosphorus at the rate of three a week. Where will they sail?'

'I do not know.'

'Because you are mere humble vagabonds and thieves?'

'We are no thieves.'

'You have never stolen? What do you eat – air? Wandering vagabonds like yourselves, mercenaries, spies?'

'Gentleman adventurers.'

Deza smiled. It was not a reassuring smile. 'You tell me you have never stolen?'

Nicholas shrugged. 'In the back streets of Algiers, when we fled through the alleyways with the manacles still on our wrists. Just like now. Yes, we stole.'

'You escaped from the jail in Algiers? This is impossible.'

'Not if you know how. We escaped three times.'

Deza laughed. A thin sound, more like a cough.

Nicholas said, 'The first time we filed through the bars. The second time we started a fire. The third time we faked that we had a noisome fever. We rubbed our faces with plaster dust, played the delirious madmen.'

'Then you were recaptured and put on the galleys? How long did you slave?'

'Time is not counted there. But in all, it seems – two years.'

'Two years a prisoner or a galley slave. And you are still alive, and not maddened?'

'I wouldn't say not maddened,' said Nicholas drily. 'But we still have a shred of reason in us. We had many adventures. Yet all we wanted to do after Malta was get home to England. I have an estate there, but it is in the hands of—'

'You were at Malta?'

'Six years ago. We were.'

Deza drummed his elegant fingers. He was getting impatient. 'Now that caps your tall tale, *Inglés*. Only heroes were at Malta six years ago. The Knights of St John. It was the greatest, most heroic siege in history. And you tell me you were there. You fought there?'

'We did.'

'I have been to Malta. You lie.'

'I do not lie.'

Deza leaned forward. 'Be very careful what you claim, my friend. If you lie to Pedro Deza, he will find you out, as he has found out ten thousand before you. In the dungeons below there are machines that can break every bone in your hands and your feet. Crack them into shards like a nutshell under a hammer, and ensure you are still in your senses, though voiceless from screaming with pain.'

'I don't doubt that your machines are very efficient.'

Pedro Deza sat back. 'So. Tell me about Malta.'

Nicholas looked sidelong at Hodge, then cleared his throat. Then he told Pedro Deza about Malta.

At first Deza took notes. After a while he laid down his pen and just listened. A long time later, he sat and stared in silence.

'Truly,' was all he said, shaking his head very slowly. 'Truly.'

At last he stood. '*Inglés*, your tale is persuasive. But tell me this. Why did you ask your cellmate, Abdul, if he could get you back to Algiers?'

'I did not!'

'He tells me you did.'

'That double-crossing bastard,' cried Hodge, rising from his chair until cuffed heavily from behind.

'Below with them,' said Pedro Deza.

9

They began with a beating, the soldiers wearing heavy leather gauntlets, Nicholas and Hodge roped to the wall, naked but for loincloths.

'There is no plan,' said Nicholas yet again, hearing his words bubble malformed through the blood in his mouth. He spat. He had learned long ago that nothing makes you sicker than swallowing your own blood.

'We had no plan,' he said more clearly. 'We are no spies, no allies of the Moors. You know as well as I that the word of that Abdul of Tripoli is worth less than a beggar's purse. In the square here I saw a girl being beaten by two soldiers in armour, with pikes.'

'Chivalry indeed,' said Deza. 'But it is only when such a treacherous people as those Moriscos are driven from Spain that our kingdom will be safe. Not until.'

'Kingdoms and policy,' said Nicholas. 'These are not my interests. I saw a girl being beaten.'

'A Morisco girl. An unbeliever, a Christ-denier and devil worshipper. These Moors are the enemy within. Their souls are dark, their very blood is dirty. And you went to her aid. A dirty Moorish whore.'

'No whore. But your mother was.'

Not a wise thing to say. Hodge bowed his head and closed his eyes. Nicholas had often been unwise. Deza raised an eyebrow and the soldier hit him hard with a bunched fist. He managed to pull back a fraction as the fist connected, softening the blow. But only a little. It hurt very much. He drew himself back from the pain, as

75

Stanley and Smith had taught him. The pain was very great, but it was there, look, there, in his left eye, his nose, his jaw, throbbing in his ribs and his belly. But he was not there. He, Nicholas, was here, safe and deep inside the bone cave of his skull, looking out. Aware of that pain there, but not part of it. Unaffected by it. He was somewhere else, something other.

When he came to his full senses again, Pedro Deza was standing in front of him holding something bright and gleaming.

'And this?' he said. 'Concealed in the ingenious belt that held your britches up?'

It was the diamond necklace.

Nicholas could not help but smile as he told the truth. 'I took it from the treasure chest of a corsair captain as his galley was sinking.'

'You have a romantic imagination,' said Deza. 'But I think you were carrying it to pay for a large shipment of arms and munitions from Africa to the Spanish coast, to help England's Moriscos allies.'

'You have a fine imagination too, kind sir,' said Nicholas. 'It's a fake.'

The jester was quite unbroken.

One of the soldiers asked about the machines. Deza considered briefly and then shook his head. 'It is enough for today. Throw them back in the cells.'

The machines tomorrow, perhaps. But there was much here he did not understand. Though all they had told him so far was mere fairy tale, and the diamond necklace looked real and was damning evidence, yet Pedro Deza had been interrogating men long enough to know the liar from the truth-teller. And in this one's quiet and steady voice, to his puzzlement, he heard nothing but truthfulness.

They were unmanacled and shoved through the barred door. They lay on the floor of the cell, trying not to move. Everything throbbed. There was no Abdul.

'I will meet him again, I swear,' said Hodge. 'And when I do—'

'I wonder,' said Nicholas. His mouth was so swollen his voice sounded strange and slurred to him.

'Wonder what?'

'If he really told Deza such lies. Or if Deza himself was inventing. He is more cunning than a fox.'

Hodge breathed out. 'I hate lies.'

Nicholas started to feel about, and to his surprise found the stub of candle still set in its own melted wax on the stone flags.

'Strange,' he muttered.

In the blackness he could feel a trail of candlewax leading away from the source into a far corner. Yet the floor did not slope.

He followed the little ridge of hardened wax until his fingers encountered a hole in the far corner, and within, his fingers closed on ... a fire-steel.

With the candle lit, he explored again, and in the same shadowy hole, barely large enough for a mouse, he found something else.

'What?' said Hodge, voice tight.

Nicholas turned back and smiled as well as his face would allow. 'If this was a romance, it would be a key, or a bag of food at least. But this is no romance, it's the life of mortal men. So instead what we have here is' – he held up a tiny bottle, barely longer than his forefinger, popped out the cork and sniffed – 'what smells like truly filthy Spanish grape spirit.'

They took turns pouring it down their throats. It tasted even worse than it smelt.

'Filthy,' said Hodge. 'Filthier than Wagg's cider brandy back home.' He tipped it back again. 'Stings like hell too.'

'I think,' said Nicholas, when they had finished and sat gasping, eyes watering, throats burning, 'that Abdul of Tripoli, like all men, is maybe a mix of good and bad.'

Hodge belched and then gasped again. 'Hell itself doesn't belch out vapours like that from the lake of fire and brimstone.'

'Keep away from the candle,' said Nicholas.

He slept badly, had restless dreams. Once again he was in prison. Only twenty-two and doomed to die, the days and the years running by, time like a smooth evil river. His whole life would waste away in manacles, in jail or on a stinking galley. The sun came up and went down in the beautiful sky, white birds flying, wings translucent in the sun. Girls singing, combing their hair, the warm wine of life ... And here they lay, he and Hodge, rotting in another filthy dungeon. He dreamed there was a black monk in the cell with them, and the black monk was really Death. He raised his skeletal hands to bless them. *Vivite,* he said. *Venio.*

Live. I am coming.

He stirred. The cell was still dark but somehow he knew it was day, and there was someone with them. Not in the cell, but just outside the door. Someone rattling the bars.

'Wake up, idlers and fools. Move yourselves!' A girl's voice, whispering harshly.

His eyes were clotted. He rubbed them and stared. It was Maria, from the wine shop. Maria de l'Adoracion.

'You!'

'Over here, fool. Unless you want me to throw you food like a dog.'

'You brought us food?'

'The more fool I for doing so.'

'How did you get in?'

'Persuaded the jailer.'

'How?'

'How do women usually ... oh, do not ask. Here. Bread. Watered wine in here. Some almonds and some oranges. It stinks in there.'

'The lack of privies is a disgrace, in a tavern of this quality. We will complain to the landlord.'

'You are such fools. Look at your faces.'

'We cannot. No looking glasses either. A disgrace.'

He and Hodge slurped from the flask of watered wine.

'You look terrible,' said Maria. 'So they are beating you?'

'With enthusiasm. Can you help us?'

'I? Don't be ridiculous. You are in the dungeons of Pedro Deza. Pedro Deza is the Chancellor of Granada. He has personal audiences with King Philip himself. You have made an enemy of a very powerful man.'

She could have wept but she held herself. Soon they would be put to the torture, these two. Then they would either die, or emerge trembling into the daylight in another day or two, speechless, tongueless, and crippled for life. She had seen it before. Yet they still joked. Englishmen and fools. But she did not weep. Let them be ignorant of it a few more hours.

78

Nicholas chewed on the bread as best he could.

'Your lip is bleeding.'

'One kiss from you, and—'

She pulled a face of genuine disgust. 'Kiss a dying man through the bars of a dungeon door!'

'You are cruel.'

'Cruel but fair,' she said.

Nicholas couldn't help but laugh.

'And all for the sake of a Morisco girl, so I hear,' she said. 'What possessed you?'

He shrugged. 'It seemed right at the time.'

'You are a fool.'

'Surely you mean a great and chivalrous hero, and conqueror of your beating heart?'

Then she seized his arm through the bars and held him urgently. 'Do anything that they ask. Co-operate with Pedro Deza.'

'Turn traitor?'

'Just survive,' she whispered. 'Just survive.'

Then she was gone.

The hours of waiting were a torment, though they tried to remain calm. Both had a terrible sense of foreboding about today.

Then keys were rattling in the locks, and they were dragged out of the cell and along the passageway to a heavy wooden door studded with black nails. They heard the voice of Pedro Deza behind them.

'Today, my English friends, we will hear the truth.'

'You have heard the truth,' said Nicholas. He could hear the pleading in his own voice, and despised himself for it. Yet he was very afraid now. Afraid of the excruciating pain of torture, but more of the way it sent a man mad, never to be sane again.

The door swung open and they gasped. Within was a large, high-arched chamber, brightly lit with twenty or thirty flaming torches all around the walls. There was a table set with a jug and some beakers of coloured glass, and arranged in a rough circle, a number of machines comprised of strong wooden beams, ropes, manacles, weights and metal bars with their ends hammered into hooks and claws. High up on the wall at the far end of the chamber was a large wooden crucifix. Christ's eyes were raised to heaven.

Both of them were pleading now, saying Please, please. Trying to keep their voices calm, as befits men, but desperate and afraid. Please, we have told you everything. Please, this is not needed. Please.

They were strapped into seats with rapid efficiency, and Nicholas found his right arm laid on to a thick oak board, manacled tight down. His fingers were splayed around some nails.

Above his hand hovered a long wooden arm with a lead weight at the end of it.

'Please,' he said again. 'Let us talk.'

'Let me show you this first,' said Pedro Deza. He ordered the torturer to unlock his arm again.

'Move your hand out of the way. Quickly now.'

'I swear that my friend and I have told you—'

'You see the wooden board there, where your hand was just lying? You see the holes and the gashes in the wood. And there in the gashes, the dark stains? That is blood, of course.' He pointed up to the weight above. 'No larger than an apple, but you see it is like an inverted pyramid.' Deza spoke with soft admiration for his machines. 'When we release this lever it will come down very fast and hard, and it will smash into the back of your hand, like this.'

He signalled to the torturer, and they pulled the lever. The heavy lead weight punched down into the wooden board and made a hole half an inch deep.

'It both punctures and smashes at the same time, you see?'

'I see.'

The weight was raised up again. 'Now. Lay your hand down there once more.'

Naturally Nicholas struggled against it, but two of the torturers forced his arm back down and splayed his hand and manacled him tight.

Across the room, Hodge had closed his eyes.

'Open your eyes,' said another of the torturers, 'and watch your friend.' He touched a cold blade to Hodge's cheek. 'Or I will slice off your eyelids.'

Hodge knew he meant it. He opened his eyes. The tears ran down.

'Aw,' said the torturer. 'There, there. Don't cry. It'll soon be over for him. Then it'll be your turn.'

'Eat shit,' said Hodge.

The torturer grinned.

'Look at your right hand,' said Pedro Deza to Nicholas. 'Thin but strong, with a nice scar or two, as befits a dashing Protestant agent and spy, in league with the Moors against Spain. I see some powder burns too. But alas, your hand is not strong enough. In perhaps – half a minute, shall we say? – this weight will slam down again, and this time it will not be bare board to meet it, but the back of your hand here. Look at the bones, delicate as chicken bones when you consider, when you compare the bones of a mortal man to a hard lead weight. And the soft flesh between. Most of all, the nerves and the sinews that make a hand strong. These will all be cut away and pulped by this machine. The first time will hurt very much. Then we will give you a sip of this special drink,' he gestured over to the table with the coloured glass beakers, 'to ensure that you remain conscious, though in great pain. In very great pain. Then the machine will smash down again, and again. Each time will hurt more than the last. By about the seventh or eighth time, you will have screamed yourself hoarse and no more sound will come from your throat. This will be a relief to us, as men's screams can be very trying.

'Finally the right hand that you knew so well and loved so much will be completely smashed. Nothing but a bloody mess of meat and bone. Little bits of it falling away over the side of the board there. Little chunks. Then we will gently take your left hand, and lay it down there and do the same. Then over here, there is a similar machine which will also pulp your right foot to nothing. Then your left foot. And you must understand: this is only the start. Yet it will be the longest hour of your life.

'And so, one last time. Answer me these questions truthfully. What do you know of the Turkish war fleet? Where are they sailing? What did you ask of Abdul of Tripoli? What is your connection to the Moor in whose house you were found hiding? What was your code word, your name? What is the Moor planning? What are the names and residences of all his accomplices? And where is the current hiding place of Aben Humeya and Aben Farax?'

Nicholas shook his head, preparing himself. 'I do not know.'

Pedro Deza waited a long time. Then he said, 'I am not a cruel man. But I have a task to do. You understand this. We must get at the truth.'

He signalled to the torturer behind to release the lever.

10

There came a loud thump from the passageway outside, and angry shouting. Then the unmistakable sound of tempered steel clashing with steel.

Pedro Deza glared around and touched his sword hilt. 'Take up your pikes. You, flank the door. You – open it.'

The door was cautiously opened on to the darkened passageway, and there stood a figure dressed in an immaculate white velvet suit trimmed with ermine, pulling off his kidskin gloves and examining his fingernails for damage. He looked up, arched his eyebrows and then strolled into the chamber. He was followed by two more burly fellows. Hulking figures in dusty travelling cloaks, shaggy haired, bearded, long heavyweight swords slung at their sides. One of the torturers ill-advisedly made a movement with his pike, as if to block their entrance, and one of the two ruffians swiped him backhanded with a kind of absent-mindedness that was almost comical. Yet there was nothing comical about the effect. Such was the power behind that casual blow that the torturer reeled backwards and slammed against the wall behind him, upsetting the table of glass beakers, bringing them crashing down around him as he slithered senseless to the floor. The black-bearded ruffian strode on into the chamber, not turning a hair at the din, and stationed himself near the door.

Nicholas stared, his thoughts in a whirl. There was only one man he had ever known who could deliver a backhand blow like that. But it could not ...

The fellow in white velvet looked around. 'Damn it, Deza, but this is a curious show you run here. One of your pikemen dared to stand in my path, so I had to run him through. Just in the arm. I expect he'll live, in a vulgar sort of way. Oh, and the smell is quite *execrable*. Have you rosewater?'

'I, I ...'

'No rosewater? My man, do you want me to stink like a civet? And kneel when I address you! I may be the bastard son of a bosomy German whore, bless her venereal soul, but I am also half-brother of King Philip. Down on your knees to Don John of Austria!'

Deza knelt, chewing his lip furiously.

The young prince, perhaps twenty-four years of age or so, tall and willowy of build, strolled languidly around the chamber, examining the various machines. At last he said, 'What a *nasty* set-up. Is it really all necessary?'

'It is, Your Excellency.'

The prince pulled a face. Then he raised an eyebrow in the direction of his two ruffians, and pointed at Nicholas and Hodge.

'Are these your comrades?'

The two strode over. Their physical power was palpable. Their commanding presence had the other torturers skittering back to stand against the walls like naughty schoolboys before an angry master. One of the ruffians stood before Hodge and the other in front of Nicholas. Nicholas stared back at him. He was dreaming. The torture had started, and he had gone into a madman's dream, his only escape.

The big flaxen-haired, ruddy-cheeked fellow in front of him grinned and nodded. 'Aye, Your Highness. I'd know this reprobate anywhere.'

''Pon my word, Deza, you unconscionable *booby*,' said Don John. 'But you choose your victims carelessly. You are only torturing here two of the most gallant heroes of the entire Siege of Malta.'

Nicholas wept openly as the manacles were sprung and he and Edward Stanley embraced.

'Aye,' said Stanley, 'relief can do that to a man. You came damn close to being broken for life. What a place.' He looked over at Deza with disgust.

'You are in my Chancellery still, Sir Knight,' said Deza. 'Have a care.'

Stanley turned from Nicholas, still shaking, and bore down on Pedro Deza, his broad sunburned brow furrowed with a ferocious glare. Six foot four of muscle and anger. His voice rose in volume, and the chamber echoed as with the bellowing of an enraged bull.

'A Knight Commander of St John answers to none but his Grand Master, the Pope in Rome, and Almighty God! These two youths here that you have reduced to shivering wrecks with your vile contraptions fought at Malta as heroically as Jean de la Valette himself. While you were shuffling your papers and presiding over your interrogations, *Don Pedro Deza*. So vex me no more. Or I may lose my sweet temper altogether.'

Deza quailed visibly, but said, 'It was important to discover more about the Morisco rebellion. We have heard rumours that the Mohammedan rebels are being armed from England. And here were two Englishmen, hiding in the house of a Moor—'

'Then you are credulous fools!' replied Stanley. 'The knights have information – not rumour, *information* – that the Moriscos are being armed from Constantinople, not England.'

Pedro Deza said not another word.

Don John of Austria was pulling on his kidskin gloves again and smiling thinly.

Smith gave Hodge a drink from his flask. Stanley laid his hands on Nicholas's shaking shoulders.

'Easy, old friend, easy. None will hurt you now.'

Then he too gave him his flask to drink. Nicholas glugged and gasped and managed a tremulous smile.

Stanley cuffed him on the back. 'Let's get some air.'

They marched out of the chamber led by Don John of Austria himself. Rescued by a prince of the blood! Well, half of the blood.

Life was a dream.

Two of the torturers hovered a little too near as they departed. In the blink of an eye, and in utter silence, Smith embraced them in his mighty hands and clonked their heads together. They dropped like meal sacks.

*

'I know a tavern on the quay,' said Nicholas.

'We don't doubt it,' drawled Don John of Austria, barely looking at him. 'And a delightful stew it may be. But we have our ship out there in the harbour. Which one do you think it might be?'

Beyond the bobbing boats, fishing smacks and coastal barges, there towered a gilded and magnificent galley flying the flag of the two-headed Habsburg eagle of Spain.

'That one, possibly,' said Nicholas.

'Your judgement is uncanny,' said Don John. Then he looked him up and down. 'We met at Messina, I recall. Then you and your manservant went on to fight at Malta with Sir John and Sir Edward here.'

'We did.'

The young prince's eyes flashed with jealousy. 'And then you served on a corsair galley as your reward?'

'We love rowing. Both day and night.'

Again Don John gave his thin smile. He liked this one, he recalled. Sharp tongue, fighting spirit, and he followed all his sarcasms point for point.

He looked out over the harbour, to the royal galley and beyond. 'We are sailing first for Messina, there to await further orders from Spain and learn more news of the movements of the Turk. Will he fall upon Cyprus, upon Crete? The coast of Italy?' The foppish young prince looked grave for once, his gaze upon the far horizon. 'His fleet is vast, the threat to Christendom is as real as ever. There is a great sea battle coming, I am sure of it. You might as well join us again, since your native England is now under the rule of Elizabeth the flame-haired frigid heretic, who will burn you at the stake the moment you set foot on home soil.'

'She is my Queen still,' said Nicholas.

'Your Holy Father in Rome has declared her no queen but a usurper.'

The English youth looked a picture of torment, his eyes pained and hunted. Don John relented a fraction. 'Well, I do not envy you your position. But I do not think you can ever dream of England again. Come and die with us fighting the Turk, and have your troubled head blown off by an Ottoman cannon. You will sleep easier thereafter.'

'For my part, I have missed every single encounter yet with the Mohammedans, being too occupied panting in the arms of my mistress – whichever trollop it was at the time – or prevented by my caring brother Philip. But for the coming sea battle, this watery Armageddon ...' He touched a kidskinned finger to his own chest. '... for once, this perfumed, velveted fop and whoremonger bastard will show his royal blood.'

Such a mix of pride and self-mockery, thought Nicholas. Such quicksilver intelligence and cutting humour. He gave a small bow.

'You acknowledge me a fop and whoremonger?' snapped Don John.

'I, I ...' stammered Nicholas.

Stanley and Smith were both grinning.

'Mercy, Your Excellency, you test him worse than Pedro Deza.'

'Tch. Then off to your sordid peasant tavern with you.' Don John turned on his heel and made for the quayside. A long rowing boat with a crimson awning and elaborately curved and gilded prow and stern, something like a Venetian gondola, was bumping against the harbour wall. He turned back.

'But come to sea with us afterwards, English vagabonds! Perhaps you'll prove too skeleton thin for a cannonball to hit you!'

Nicholas led them back to a certain tavern on the quay.

'We heard you were to be racked and strappadoed,' said Stanley as they walked. 'Word came back from Gil de Andrada that you had been picked up. We heard more from ... other sources useful to us. And when we heard that you were to be *questioned* by the great Pedro Deza, well, we had at least to *visit* you in prison. Before you got too lean and stringy. A few sessions on the rack and you would have looked like a two-yard earthworm.

'Then Brother Smith here was going to sing soothing lullabies to you as you were stretched, in his unusual baritone, which would surely have taken your mind off your agonies. You should hear him singing "Greensleeves". Ladies swoon at the very sound. Some actually burst into tears and run away, unable to bear such unearthly beauty.'

Smith growled, his voice more bear-like than ever with the passing years. 'You see that Ned Stanley has lost none of his lacerating

87

wit. Many's the time I've burst my doublet laughing at his brilliant jests and sallies.'

Stanley roared with laughter. Smith glared from under his thick black brows. They had not changed.

Nicholas had almost forgotten why he loved their company so much. Not just their strength, their prowess at arms, their badinage, Smith's grim sallies and Stanley's smile. It was their nobility he loved. Their lives were a testament to lives nobly lived, strictly disciplined. Beneath those shabby cloaks, there were hearts and souls that served something higher than most men ever dreamed of. You have to serve some high ideal. Serve only yourself, and you soon shrink down to the small, petty size of yourself. Most men lived that way. But serve something high and noble, and in time you grow towards it, as an oak tree grows towards the sun. That was Smith and Stanley.

They came to the tavern, and there was no Maria. Instead, no sooner had they pulled up the benches and sat down than a tiny boy came running in, wide eyed, open mouthed and breathless, and stood by their table. He was barefoot, wore ragged breeches and shirt, and could not have been more than four or five.

'You are the landlord here?'

The boy stared.

'Well then,' said Stanley. 'A jug of wine, bread, water, whatever there is.'

The boy nodded and sped off.

'I'm sure they're getting younger,' said Smith.

The food and wine came, and Hodge raised his cup. 'Wish it was good English ale to toast you with, but still. Here's to you, Brothers Smith and Stanley. What a turnout. Who would have believed it?'

Nicholas said little and drank hard. Both knights noticed. After Malta, the galleys, and Algiers jail ... the boy from Shropshire, son of a knight himself, was deeply wounded and scarred within. Their hearts ached for him. He would take more than a good meal to mend. And he hardly touched his plate of food as it was.

'Eat,' said Stanley. 'You need it.'

'I'd eat some opium if you had any,' said Nicholas. 'For my head.'

Not your head, your heart, thought Stanley. He could well foresee the thin English boy passing the last few months of his young life in a smoke dream, on a filthy divan in a den in Tangier, living for nothing but the pipe and an easy death.

It was not only from Pedro Deza they had saved him.

11

'So now,' said Stanley, settling back and turning his cup of wine in his hand. 'Let us understand this clearly, old comrade-in-arms. After the Siege you and Hodge spent four long happy years in the house of Franco Briffa. Then we bid sad farewells to you, and you sailed from Malta, bound for England. But you were taken by corsairs on the passage to Spain.'

They nodded.

'You were galley slaves, you spent time in jail, you escaped, were recaptured ... Finally you survived the destruction of the very galley you slaved on, and were picked up from the sea by Fra Gil de Andrada, our brother Knight. 'Tis not improbable. The western Mediterranean is still our sea as much as anyone's. Then, for reasons unclear, you arrived upon the soil of Holy Catholic Spain – after two years of bitter tribulation at the hands of Moors and Barbary pirates – and promptly hurl yourself into a fight *on behalf of the Moors*? Against Catholic Spain?'

'He always did have a noble heart,' said Hodge, with what sounded much like sarcasm.

'Nobility, bravery,' said Stanley, 'often look so like idiocy on a moonless night.'

Nicholas grinned. This from two warrior monks who, though they would hate to hear it said, had shown more crazed bravery at Malta in four months than were told in a library of *Iliad*s.

Smith said, 'What *were* you doing in the house of a Moor? I can see why Deza might have had his suspicions.'

90

Nicholas explained as best he could. Smith grunted. 'Fool. *Hiding in a chest* indeed.'

'A fool to his fingertips,' said a woman's voice behind. 'A fool and addlepate beyond measuring.'

It was Maria, hands on her hips. The small boy came in and stood half hidden in her skirts. She tried to sound angry, but there was a light in her eyes.

'So you were freed from the dungeons of Pedro Deza?'

Nicholas nodded, swallowed, wiped his lips. 'Close-run thing.'

'And now what will you do? Ride off to Madrid and insult King Philip to his face, perhaps? Go and seek the north-west passage to the Indies, a hundred years too late? Or sail off in a sieve to find the Golden Fleece?'

'I think we might go to Cyprus.'

Hodge looked resigned. Maria cried, '*Cyprus!* It is full of Greeks.'

'One or two, I believe.'

'But then all Greeks are liars and fools. At least you will not be noticed there.'

Maria turned her attention to her little boy. He had a new graze on his knee.

'She likes you,' said Stanley.

'Pour me more wine,' said Nicholas.

'In fact I'm sure I remember her. Wasn't she the one who salved your bruised sconce all those years ago ... ?'

'A young widow, I surmise,' said Smith. 'And as pretty as ever.'

Nicholas grabbed the wine jug.

'We have free passage to Messina if we want it,' said Stanley. 'With plain sailing we will be in Sicily in five days. You are sure you want to join us?'

Nicholas looked at Hodge. They had been together so long, through so many trials, they could read each other's thoughts without speaking. England was closed to them for now. After all their sufferings, it was a terrible thing to learn.

Nicholas sighed. 'Let us sail east after all. Into the cannon's mouth, as ever. Let us go and fight the Turk all over again.'

'Might as well,' said Hodge.

*

On the quayside, porters were piling up cedarwood chests, five, six in number. An elderly Spanish gentleman was overseeing them.

'What the devil are those?' asked Smith. 'They don't look like armaments.'

'His Excellency Don John has ordered more vestments for his wardrobe,' said the elderly gentleman. 'He felt he had insufficient for the voyage. Six more suits, two cloaks, linen and undergarments, hats in the latest styles, and six pairs of boots of finest Spanish calf leather.'

'For a voyage of five days?'

'Just so.'

The sun was going down as they moved off from the quay. It had been quite a day, beginning in terror in a torturer's dungeon, ending now in magical reunion with old friends. Nicholas could have wept with exhaustion and elation.

When he looked back towards the quay, a young woman was standing there, a small boy close beside her. Nicholas raised his hand in farewell. She raised her hand likewise, and then turned swiftly away and was gone into the crowds.

'This arrant new Florentine order,' observed Stanley mockingly, 'the Knights of St Stephen, our callow imitators. They are laymen, not monks, and allowed to marry.'

'Really?' said Nicholas, settling back and yawning and closing his eyes. 'Fascinating.'

As they drew near to *La Real,* Don John's flagship, Nicholas marvelled at her beauty. He and Hodge had been on fat-bellied Genoa merchantmen, stinking corsair galleys, lean warships of the knights, that funny little bucket of a vessel that sailed them out of Bristol six long years gone – but never anything quite like this. A palace afloat on water.

She blazed in the setting sun. Her hull below the water was black but above, her waist was crimson, her gunwales deep yellow and her railings crimson and gold. Her poop-deck awning was of finest crimson satin, and above it hung the two-headed Habsburg eagle of the Holy Roman Empire, the quartered standard of Spain, and even the eight-pointed cross of the Knights of St John.

'He is not, strictly speaking, permitted to fly that one,' said Stanley quietly, 'even though he's a Knight Commander in the Order, and we are his acting aides-de-camp. But he may yet prove the Knights' best ally. So we say nothing.'

At the prow of *La Real* shone the dimly gleaming barrels of her main guns, thrusting out from beneath her fighting deck. Sakers and culverins flanking, but the centre-line gun most definitely a full-size cannon, perhaps as much as an eighty-pounder. The whole ship would shudder when a linstock was put to her breech.

They climbed the ladder on her larboard – even that was elaborately carved and gilded – and were beckoned to sit on luxurious velvet-padded benches on the covered admiral's deck. The small windows were of colourful stained glass, depicting the lives of the apostles and the saints.

'Clear glass would be better,' grunted Smith. 'Get a view of the approaching Turk.'

The elderly gentleman from the quayside appeared again and ordered wine to be brought for them. He introduced himself with a little bow.

'Don Luis de Requesens, tutor to His Excellency. Who is now at his evening toilet. He will join you presently.'

'Has to pluck his eyebrows,' said Smith when Don Luis was out of earshot.

Nicholas grinned and cradled his silver goblet of wine, cool to the touch and beaded with water droplets. The goblets had been chilled on beds of ice. In early summer. How on earth … ?

'Brought down by muleteers from the Sierra Nevada,' said Stanley. 'Snow lies up there till June.' He grinned 'The things you can have if you're a prince.'

'Or sail with a prince,' said Nicholas.

He took a gulp of wine, sweet and white and deliciously cool on a sultry Cadiz evening. Then he said, 'So. Tell us about Cyprus.'

Stanley drew breath.

'You remember I said to you once that Malta was but a minor skirmish in a much greater war?'

'Minor skirmish!' said Hodge bitterly.

Stanley nodded. 'Not in heroism and endurance, of course. But

93

the greatest battle is yet to come. Perhaps the final battle. And a sea battle, we believe. It will make or break us. If we win, it will mean the end of Ottoman dreams of conquering Europe. If we lose ... well, there are already Ottoman forward bases in the Adriatic, Ottoman war galleys harrying Venetian shipping right to the mouth of the lagoon.'

'Raids led by that devil-born traitor, Kara Hodja,' growled Smith, his eyes burning like coals, 'who was once a Dominican friar.'

'We will meet with Kara Hodja one of these days,' said Stanley, his voice soft but chilling. 'The Black Priest will have his last rites soon.'

'But,' said Smith, 'the raids of Kara Hodja will seem as nothing if the fleet now being assembled on the Bosphorus succeeds in destroying the Christian navies piecemeal, and comes to dominate the Mediterranean end to end. Then Europe will be theirs for the taking. St Peter's Rome will be a mosque, as Constantinople's St Sophia became a mosque a hundred years ago.'

'A far more beautiful church than St Peter's, incidentally,' said Stanley.

'You have seen it?' asked Hodge, wide eyed.

The knight gave an enigmatic smile. Then he was serious again. 'So you see, bit by bit, Christendom falls to the Armies of the Prophet, and still we are divided against each other. The Turk gobbles us up singly, like a fox among chickens. Long ago Jerusalem fell to Islam a second time. All the ancient heartlands of Christendom. Then in 1453, Constantinople herself. And since then, Trebizond, Rhodes, Belgrade have also fallen, with further attacks on Corfu, Venice, Vienna ... The dark shadow of Islam creeps ever westwards.'

Smith thumped his boot on the deck. 'And the Turk *must not win*! This battle that is coming will decide the fate of the world. Nothing less. If the Turk destroys us in the Mediterranean, sails free past Malta and Sicily into the west, then that fanatical empire can command the Atlantic seaports of the Sultanate of Morocco. Asilah and Agadir, Larache, Mogador, Azzemour ... '

'And once established there,' said Stanley, 'the Turks can attack the Spanish treasure ships coming from the Indies. That treasure, I sometimes think, is all that keeps Christendom afloat and able

94

to fight at all. Lose that treasure and we are doomed. We can no longer build warships, can barely hammer out a few swords in a smithy. We are finished.'

Smith said, 'The Turk will go on to Madeira, the Cape Verde Islands, the Gold Coast. This mightiest of Islamic empires has always had a land army second to none. Now they are learning to become sailors, there is no knowing what may befall. We must stop her armada. And soon.'

Stanley said, 'But what with? The knights have the Chevalier Romegas, the greatest naval commander of the age. Even the Turks would admit that. And he commands ... six galleys. The Turk is building three galleys *a week*. The Ottoman fleet that is soon to sail out of the Bosphorus will number three or four hundred galleys. We Knights of St John give a good fight, and are reputed gallant. But not that gallant.'

'And now you believe that the Turks will first sail on Cyprus?' said Nicholas.

'Aye. And Cyprus *must be held*,' said Smith, thumping his boot again for emphasis. 'It is Christendom's forward bastion, from which we will—'

Stanley looked sharply at him, and Smith bit his lip.

'How much do you know?' asked Stanley.

'How much do you think?' said Nicholas. 'Our corsair overlords were shockingly remiss at keeping us up with the affairs of the world.'

'Well then. Cyprus, as Brother John here says, must be held. It is indeed Christendom's eastern bastion. Look.' Stanley began to move objects around on the gently rocking table, to represent a rough map of Europe. His wallet was Spain. His dagger served for Italy. His sword laid crosswise was the north coast of Africa. Smith snapped a frayed lace from his shirt and formed a thin crescent where Constantinople stood.

'Such artistry,' said Stanley. 'So then. Cyprus, here,' he laid down a gold coin, 'is a mere sixty miles from the coast of the Holy Land and the lost kingdoms of Outremer. If we are ever again to march through the streets of Jerusalem, to pray in the Church of the Holy Sepulchre on Calvary hill, it is from Cyprus that we'll sail. Cyprus is now a Venetian possession, but it is surrounded by Ottoman.

Turkey itself to the north, Palestine east, Egypt to the south, and even west of her, the new Ottoman possession of Rhodes. The Venetians have always maintained a friendly neutrality with the Turks. You know how they value their trade.'

'Gold hoarders,' growled Smith. 'Soulless bankers, Mammon-struck mercenaries of the Adriatic. Yours for a ducat.'

'Thank you, Brother,' said Stanley. 'But now, inevitably, as we had long warned, the Turk is about to invade Cyprus anyway.'

'And we will have to get Venice to awaken at last,' said Smith, 'and join with the Papal States, and with Spain, with Genoa and with Savoy, at the very least. If we are to have a fleet anything like big enough to face the Turks.'

'And the thought of Venice, Genoa and Spain all agreeing to fight on the same side,' said Stanley, 'instead of against each other, is about as likely as Brother John here taking up embroidery.'

Hodge shook his head. 'This all sounds to me like what my old dad would call a pig's arse of a muddle.'

'Worse,' said Stanley with a grin. 'It's a worldwide pig's arse of a muddle. But if we fail, make no mistake. We will all be slaves of the Turk.'

'So,' said Nicholas, 'if the Ottoman Empire attacks Cyprus – a Venetian possession – Venice will *have* to join the war against them.'

Stanley looked the picture of innocence. 'Wicked tongues say that the warmongering knights have worked behind the scenes, spreading certain rumours, to *encourage* the Turks to attack Cyprus. But of course this is nothing but malicious slander.'

Nicholas grinned. 'What you really want,' he said, 'is for the Turks to attack Cyprus, but not to succeed in capturing it.'

'That,' said Stanley, 'would be ideal. We want Cyprus to be another Malta.'

'But there are problems,' said Smith. 'The locals, for one.'

'The Greeks hate the Turks, don't they?'

'Yes. Unfortunately they also hate their current Venetian over-lords, who have taxed them ruthlessly. As Eastern Orthodox, they also have little love for Rome.'

'Utter pig's arse,' muttered Hodge.

'I know that Suleiman is dead, at least,' said Nicholas.

'So he is. Died campaigning in Hungary back in 1566. His son succeeded him, a fool they call Selim the Sot. But an empire as mighty as the Ottoman Empire goes on, even when ruled by a fool. The true brains are the ministers and viziers. One Mehmet Sokollu, Grand Vizier, is every bit as cunning as any ruler in Christendom – probably more so. He is loyal to the memory of Suleiman the Magnificent, however much he may scorn the son Selim. And with their North African and Arabian allies, the Ottoman dream remains the same. The conquest of all Europe for Islam.'

'After Malta,' said Nicholas, 'I thought they would never come again. They lost so many.'

'They can afford to lose so many,' said Smith. 'Their empire stretches from the gates of Vienna to Aden, from the Maghreb to the Persian Gulf. Beyond that, there are more Islamic empires. The Persian itself, and the Mughal Empire of India. Christendom is a little nest of squabbling princedoms in comparison. Once again we must unite to fight them, if we are to have any hope. But once again, we are failing.'

'The Florentines, Genoese and Venetians are bound to each other only by mutual hatred,' said Stanley. 'No one trusts France, and all envy and fear Spain her silver and gold. King Philip's Spain is rich beyond dreams with the wealth of the Indies, which keeps her great galleons well armed and ready, and yet at the same time – behold, I give you a mystery – Spain is utterly bankrupt. Thirty pieces of silver ruined Judas. Thirty million pieces of silver, and Philip is ruined as badly, so they say. It would take a better financial brain than mine to explain this to you.'

'A wise professor of Salamanca,' said Smith, 'has tried to argue that the more silver and gold there is in a kingdom, the less it is worth. So the price of a loaf of bread increases accordingly, and the people are poorer. Hence Spain's troubles.' A very faint smile showed through Smith's thick black beard. 'God is telling us something here, perhaps. About true worth.'

'A loaf of bread's worth a loaf of bread,' said Hodge stubbornly.

'Friend Hodge,' said Stanley, 'you are an English empiricist to the marrow, and could teach those professors of Salamanca a thing or two, I do not doubt.'

'I could an' all.'

Stanley waved his hand over the table. 'But back to our map here. In the north, Protestant England watches and waits. Perhaps her days of glory will yet come. In Germany, Catholic and Lutheran princes slaughter each other's peasantry at will, and in Hungary the wind-blown marches are stripped bare and left vulnerable, where those splendid Hussar horsemen used to ride out defending the Danube valley and the whole eastern flank of Europe against the Turk. The flower of Hungarian chivalry was destroyed at Mohacs forty years ago, where Christian skulls now lie whitening on the plain. The regiments of Janizaries – the world's finest foot soldiers still, do not doubt it – could be back at the gates of Vienna in weeks.'

'Then the situation is desperate,' said Nicholas.

'Of course!' said Stanley, slapping him on the back. 'It is always desperate! That is why we sail for Cyprus, and prepare for siege by the Turk. Spain promises help, but none will come.'

Smith touched the hilt of his sword. 'Yet the knights will go, as always.'

A servant brought them dishes of almonds, dates and salted biscuits.

'There is still another twist in what Hodge here calls our current pig's arse of a muddle,' said Stanley. He devoured a salt biscuit whole. 'Not only do the Cypriot Greeks detest Venice, but the Venetian commander there is no Jean de la Valette.'

Smith said, 'In the heart of Cyprus stands the well-fortified capital, Nicosia. But its commander is one Niccolo Dandolo, and what we have heard of him does not inspire confidence. And then down on the east coast, facing across the sea to the Holy Land itself, is the ancient port of Famagusta, also well fortified by the Venetians.'

'Famagusta's governor is Marc'antonio Bragadino,' said Smith, 'of an old Venetian family. We hear he is a strong commander, at least. But as for Dandolo ...' He shook his head.

Nicholas said softly, 'If only we still had Jean de la Valette.'

That superb old warrior, who led the knights through the Siege of Malta, to final, unbelievable victory. Now laid to rest in the new capital city of Malta which he founded: Valletta, named in his honour. That noble old man. Nicholas often grieved that he would never see him again. But of course he would be near eighty now if he still lived, an implausible age for one who followed a life of such striving and danger. And all men must die. The thing was to live rightly, nobly, and with honour. And by God, La Valette did that.

'His successor, Piero del Monte,' said Nicholas. 'Is he a good Master?'

'He is a Grand Master,' said Stanley.

Nicholas rolled his eyes.

Stanley laughed. 'He is a fine new leader, as bold and honourable as we could wish. But his place is at Malta, not leading an army to Cyprus. And then of course there is the new Holy Father in Rome.'

Yes, Nicholas knew of him. Pius IV died in the Borgia Tower, back in 1565. The cardinals wintered on it, and when the smoke signals went up in January 1566, their choice was one Michele Ghisleri, aged sixty-one, born a mere shepherd boy. He took the name Pius V. Known to be simple and devout, he wore a hairshirt instead of silk, mistrusted worldly power and despised wealth. It was said he didn't even keep a mistress.

'A story goes,' said Smith, 'that immediately he was raised to the See of Rome, his family came to him expecting all kinds of favours and preferments. He graciously received them, and told them he was sure that being related to the Pope would be honour enough. They left in some pique.'

'And he has excommunicated Elizabeth,' said Nicholas.

'In no uncertain terms. He denounced her as a "slave of wickedness".' Stanley nodded. 'Yes, he is fierce, but he is incorruptible, and he is the Holy Father we need in this desperate hour. A mild-mannered Elijah would hardly have dealt aright with the priests of Baal.'

'And he preaches a new crusade,' said Smith. 'He dreams of a Holy League of all Christendom, and works and prays tirelessly to inspire it. Not enough for him that Christendom should be defended, Cyprus be saved from the Turk. He already refers to the Mediterranean by its old name, the Roman Sea, and dreams that Hagia Sophia might again resound to Christian choirs, and the Cross return to the Holy Land.'

'But it has been a while now since the Pope himself led his armies into battle personally,' said Stanley. 'What is needed is a Christian military leader who can unite and inspire all the squabbling forces of Europe.'

Smith stirred. 'And that man may just be, as some say – the bastard Don John. Implausible as it may seem.'

Nicholas looked up and coughed.

'Though he may be, in his own words, a velveted fop and whoremonger—'

Nicholas coughed more loudly and bulged his eyeballs at Smith.

'—looked on with contempt by all the crowned heads of Europe. Even his own half-brother Philip does not want him attaining glory. But I think that if that vain and coxcombed head could raise itself for one moment from the plump bosoms of his whores, he might just yet—'

Smith became aware of something. A figure stepped out of the deepening shadows.

12

Don John had been listening for the last minute or more, silent in his gold-braided lambskin cabin slippers. Behind him was the venerable Don Luis de Requesens, looking anxious.

Smith stood, and Don John stood eyeball to eyeball with him though only half his width.

'Pray continue,' he said softly. He was quite expressionless but for a certain blaze in his eyes, six inches from Smith's. 'Don't mind me.'

Smith did not flinch. He had faced worse in his time than an offended prince. 'He might just yet ... pull us all together.'

It was impossible to tell Don John's mood. His gaze flicked between Smith and Stanley. 'Which is the better swordsman of you two?'

'Smith, by a whisker,' allowed Stanley. 'Though he's a clumsy great oaf in every other respect. The gallant Hodge here delivers a hefty blow, and the thin lad Ingoldsby knows a trick or two.'

'I may tup my social inferiors,' said Don John, 'I do not duel with them.'

'My father was a Knight of St John, as you are,' said Nicholas angrily.

'I am a Knight Commander Grand Cross,' snapped Don John, 'and of the royal blood.'

'My father always said there are noble births and noble hearts, and the two do not always coincide.'

Don John smiled thinly. The lad had fine spirit, and now his blood was up.

'Stand!' Don John moved out on to the deck.

Nicholas's anger abated. 'It has been a long day, Your Excellency, and I am very weary.'

'Not as weary as you were at times upon the walls of Malta.'

Nicholas looked rueful. 'That is true. But I still don't see why I should be punished for my comrade Smith's ... intemperate speech.'

Don John had already drawn his Toledo blade and was swishing it through the night air. Then he vaulted lightly on to the gangway and thrust once or twice at the standard post.

'To duel with a prince of the Habsburgs is hardly a punishment,' he said. 'More of an honour. Then come, let us exchange a few *passados*.'

'Sire,' said Stanley, 'the moon is thin, and the stern lanterns give barely the light of a glow-worm. It is dangerous to duel in such darkness.'

'He is right, Your Excellency,' put in Don Luis de Requesens. 'Do you think this is entirely—'

'Danger,' said Don John – *cut, cut, guard, thrust* – 'is the salt and pepper upon the tedious meat of life.' He raised his blade and kissed the cold steel to his lips. 'And absolute fearlessness is the surest sign of a true nobleman ... along with eighteen different varieties of pox. *In guardia!*'

'Give me your sword,' hissed Nicholas.

'Don't be a fool,' said Stanley quietly, standing between him and the table where the sword still lay. 'Though he's still wearing his cabin slippers, and I've never seen him wield a sword before, he'll have had the finest fencing masters in Europe since the day he first walked.'

'He'll not kill me.'

'What if he divests you of an eye?'

'I've got another.'

The boy moved with his usual lightning speed, ducking under Stanley's outstretched arm, snatching the sword from the table and spinning away before Stanley had time to stop him.

It was the first time he had held a good blade in years. He swished and whipped it, felt the weight and the counterweight, the fine balance, and the sinewy strength in his lean arm. How quickly it came back. And the thrill too, the fierce delight. He began to feel alive again. As if the darkness were clearing and a hot sun burning instead.

He drew up before Don John.

'Good fellow,' said the Prince. 'Ingoldsby, eh? There's gold in that name.'

'That there is,' said Nicholas.

In the shadows behind them, around the mainmast and along the side walkways above the sleeping rowers' heads, the *Real*'s mariners had gathered to watch the fight. Sicilians, Sardinians, Marseillans, Andalusians. It was forbidden for them to look the royal prince in the eye, but they might be quiet spectators at this lunatic dancing duel. *Noblemen*, they muttered among themselves. All loons and inbred crackbrains.

The two swordsmen made a quick bow, and then all was a flurry of flashing blades and metallic rings. Their skill was astonishing. Neither Nicholas nor Don John dealt much force, but such was their speed that their blades were a blur. It was evident immediately from their different styles that Stanley had spoken the truth. The prince fenced with a kind of schooled and fluid perfection, show-ing mastery of every style, every move and stroke. The unexpected *riverso*, the dancing *schivar di vita*, the flamboyant and frankly pointless *guardia alta*, sword held high above his head like a mata-dor about to slay the bull.

But more important than this flamboyant display, there was a steady blaze in his eyes which showed he meant to win. Yet Nicholas, schooled only in the bloody hand-to-hand fighting on the walls of Malta, and whatever backstreet skirmishes he had survived since then, matched him cut and thrust. It was his speed which saved him. He could see each blow coming in and block it without any apparent difficulty. But that speed of movement could not be long maintained on so still and sultry a night. They broke off after a mere minute or so, both panting and heated.

'More wine!' called Don John. 'Well watered!'

They threw back their goblets and tossed them empty to Smith and Stanley.

'In the name of Mohammed and his thirteen fat wives,' said

Don John, slashing and flexing his blade again, eyeing its edge, 'but you make quite a satisfying opponent.'

They resumed. Thrust, parry, thrust, parry, lock blades, apart. And then Nicholas, roughly schooled as he was, made a half-turn and executed an entirely unorthodox blow that succeeded only by virtue of surprise. His blade cut Don John across the upper right arm, a long though shallow cut. Don John stopped and took a backward step. He did not glance down for a second at the wound, nor clutch it with his hand, look pale and aghast, or even remotely surprised. He stood and bled gently upon his white satin shirt, and raised his eyebrows.

'Good tap, begad. I did not see that coming. What blow do you call that?'

'My best,' said Nicholas. He risked a smile. 'The *passado alla braggadocio.*'

'New to me.'

'I just made it up.' He raised his blade *in guardia.*

Don John smiled too. This English commoner Ingoldsby was quite a fellow.

'Sire,' called Don Luis de Requesens. 'You must desist! This is madness!'

Don John gave no sign of hearing him. 'I had best finish you quickly before you cut through my sword arm altogether, Don Niccolo. For Christendom is lost without me, you know.'

And with that the prince pressed forward hard, unrelenting now, all his years of experience showing. He wrong-footed the boy with a move called a *ballestra,* one of his favourites, a bewildering mix of feint and hopping lunge. He used the layout of the deck against him, had him stumbling back against the rail, and then with an extraordinary looping movement of the wrist, seemed to wrap his sword in a spiral round Nicholas's and flicked it free. The blade arced away over the opposite rail towards the sea.

'Catch that,' drawled Don John, not looking back.

Stanley was already hurling himself across the deck, trying to catch the sword at the last instant before it went overboard, even if the tempered steel did cut into his palm. He failed, and the sword vanished. He gave a groan. That was no mean weapon.

Don John meanwhile had the point of his sword at the boy's throat.

'Don Luis!' he called. 'A gold ducat for the first mariner to dive down and fetch that blade for Fra Eduardo here.'

'But sire, 'tis three or four fathoms down, and inhospitably dark.'

'A gold ducat!' Don John turned to the mariners in the shadows. 'From my own princely purse.'

It was a month's wages. The mariners eyed each other. The moon was no more than a splinter. They'd have to grope around on the sandy seabed like blindworms. But the sea was warm, and a ducat was a ducat.

There was a splash as half a dozen of them promptly went over the side.

Don John returned his sword to its sheath. Nicholas rubbed the dent in his throat.

'Not ineffectual,' murmured the prince. 'Though clearly schooled in the Duelling Academy of the Backstreet Gutter. Yet that very lack of schooling can sometimes spring the winning surprise. As in chess.' He fixed his eyes on the boy. 'You honour your father. Who is dead. Am I right?'

Nicholas frowned. 'How did you know?'

'You referred to him in the past tense.' He added with a certain gentleness, 'Besides, it is obvious. I honoured mine also. I sometimes think that sons honour their fathers more in death than in life.'

Then he turned away and said with his usual drawl, 'We dine at eight.'

'You need that cut stitched, sire,' said Smith.

'Indeed I do. Wouldn't want me dying of poisoned blood, now, would we, Brother? For then who would lead Europe to victory over the Terrible Turk, if not this whoremonger bastard in white velvet. Hm?'

Smith bowed low, perhaps to hide his smile.

The prince retired to his cabin.

Stanley smacked his mighty fist into his palm, eyes shining.

A dripping mariner had just come up the ladder with a very fine sword in his hand.

*

The prince reappeared precisely as the bell towers of Cadiz tolled eight.

His four fellow diners tried manfully to keep their expressions neutral as they stood and surveyed him. Don Luis de Requesens, appearing beside his lord and master, wore a look of ancient resignation.

'A man who has just been cut in a duel,' declared Don John, flicking his cuffs of finest Bruges lace, 'should always dress his very finest. Just as a man should step up to the gallows wearing every pearl and ruby in his jewel box.'

He took his seat at the head of the table. All sat.

'The Almighty has so ordained the lives of men to be a series of preposterous jokes and humiliations, for our sins. So we may as well laugh along with him, dressed in our finest, always maintaining our wit, our poise and our ... *sprezzatura*. "Nonchalance", I think, is the best translation of that dancing Italian word.'

'Intriguing theology,' murmured Stanley.

Don John inclined his head gracefully. 'And do we not look the part? Do we not look *the very thing?*'

The prince was now freshly shaved, his neat beard immaculate, his cheeks high coloured and smooth as an infant's behind. He wore a pinked shirt of white satin, narrow-sleeved to the wrist and fastened with silver hooks, and then those flamboyant lace cuffs. Over this he wore a crimson doublet of a colour ordered precisely to match the crimson of his ship. The doublet was embroidered with cream-coloured flowers and gleaming pearls. He wore a hat rakishly on one side with a large feather, and a fresh posy of flowers with another pearl and a ruby at the sprig. His breeches, stockings and fringed garters were all white, and his shoes were so highly polished they could have served as a lady's looking glass, had they not been so encrusted in gold buckles, sequins and precious stones.

'Very fine, Your Excellency,' said Smith gravely.

'A picture of majesty,' said Stanley with equal gravity, 'and surely the terror of the Turk.'

'We thank you,' said Don John. He glanced cursorily over the dress of his aides-de-camp: much-darned linen shirts, worn breeches and scuffed leather boots. 'Though I have my doubts, brother knights, whether you yourselves are the most perspicacious judges of fashion.'

As he raised his sardonic eyebrows, Nicholas realised that the prince really did have them plucked, arched high and thin over his pale forehead. Even for a simple dinner with this quartet of vagabonds and travel-stained knights, he had clearly powdered his face and touched a dab of rouge to his fine high cheekbones. Piss o' the nettle, what a mincing cotquean! Yet he knew how to handle a sword, that was sure, and seemed to disdain all pain and fear. You could never judge a man by first impressions. And if you looked beyond the exaggerated courtliness, the absurd wardrobe, the pea-cockery, you saw that his dark eyes flashed and burned when he talked of crusade and war.

'Don Luis de Requesens here, my devoted tutor,' drawled the prince, 'whose life's work has been to raise me to virtue and right-eousness' – he smiled at the solemn old man – 'what an abject *failure* you have been, incidentally, Don Luis. I mean, *look* at me. When I usurp the throne of Spain, I shall have Don Luis beheaded immediately, along with my beloved brother Philip. Secondly, I shall establish a large harem of dusky maidens in the Escorial, for my sole delight.'

'You should not make such jests, sire,' said Don Luis.

'Very well,' said Don John. 'Let us forgo the harem. Aha. Here comes the soup.'

They dined in a soft breeze, the great galley barely rocking, candles in lanterns, moths fluttering around them, nightjars hawking over the coast. They made the most of the fresh fare from the markets of Cadiz while they could. There were sardines, Serrano ham, wheaten bread, spiced rice with raisins, the last oranges of the season, apricots, cherries. Soon enough they would be living on simpler fare.

'Sea voyages,' said Don John, 'are bad for the complexion but excellent for the waistline. I tend to survive on wine alone.' He sipped delicately. Nicholas couldn't imagine him drunk. It would go against his perfect poise.

Then the prince raised his goblet. 'To Cyprus!'

'To Cyprus!'

Stanley set down his goblet again and said carefully, 'You are ... coming with us to Cyprus, sire? In person?'

'My brother will not stop me again,' said Don John, his voice sharp edged.

'But your mission is also a diplomatic one. To unite the Holy League.'

'A mere bagatelle. My brilliant Machiavellian mind has already planned it. I will warn the Genoese that they risk being outshone by Venice if they do not join with us. I will tell Venice the same thing regarding the Genoese, and further intimate that they stand to lose Cyprus to Genoa, not to Constantinople, if it falls.'

Stanley and Smith looked nonplussed.

'Diplomacy and a poetic imagination are closely allied,' said Don John. 'How to persuade my brother to commit the Spanish navy to the fight? I am still dwelling on this. I will conceive some noble lie. He thinks only of defence, like all cautious spirits. But he who stays within his own fortifications is lost.

'The knights, of course, we can count on, and the Papal States are fully committed. But France is more and more divided within, and that foul old witch – beg pardon, I mean Her Majesty Catherine de' Medici – is not entirely sympathetic to our cause either, I fear. The Turks are still outplaying us in diplomacy, as on every other front. Brilliantly setting us against each other.' He broke bread. 'Tearing us apart.'

'The revolt of the Moriscos was – is – a cunning move,' said Smith. 'And we know Constantinople was behind it.'

'And what a foul war that was,' said Don John. His mocking lilt vanished. He took a sip of wine.

'His Excellency was hit on the helmet by an arquebus bullet,' put in Don Luis. He shook his head and clacked his teeth. 'He simply took off the helmet and glared at it, and said, "Damn me, that dent has simply ruined the symmetry of the thing."'

They smiled.

Don John said, unsmiling, 'It was no true war. A campaign, against maids and children, against fugitive rebels. Moorish women fighting with nothing but daggers and dust. A civil war in all its ugliness. It made me sick to the stomach. You see why I long to face the Turk openly? Give me a clean war, a true enemy, a fight for good against evil. Any other war soon sickens the soul.'

'We saw a Moorish family dying in the snow,' said Stanley, his voice soft and low. 'In the snowy passes of the Alpujarras. Their house had been burned out, the man killed, I think the woman and her daughter ravished. King Philip had lately given the troops the right to take booty. They had nothing.'

'And so?'

'And so – we found a wagon and took them down to Malaga. By the time we got there, all three children were dead of a fever. The mother went on alone to Morocco.'

Don John's gaze was far away. 'Hernando de Talavera, saintly archbishop of Granada, said that the Mohammedans ought to adopt our religion, and we ought to adopt their morals.' He dipped some bread in his wine but did not eat it. 'Christians drunk in the streets, women arguing with their men, orphans and widows uncared for ... and then enriching themselves at the expense of the expelled Moors. But this is the way of the world. Edward of England took the property of the Jews, did he not? Philip the Fair of France fell upon the treasures of the Templars. That fat villain Henry – begging your pardons, Englishmen – destroyed the monasteries for their gold. And in Muslim lands, of course, Jew and Christian have always been taxed and oppressed.'

He sighed and then became spirited again. 'All a melancholy business. Trust not in the princes of this world. Except myself, of course. Let us talk no more of it. To Cyprus, and a clean war.'

He clicked his fingers to one of the servants and murmured something.

He turned back. 'Now I shall play you a piece of my own composition upon the lute. A gallant love ditty, serenade, or amorous dirge addressed to my beloved Diana de Falangola. Or Ana de Toledo, or Maria-Theresa, or whichever really. They're all much the same when they're lying underneath you.'

Smith almost choked.

The servant handed over a beautiful instrument of finest Neapolitan make, inlaid – excessively inlaid, perhaps – with mother-of-pearl.

Don John stroked it with long, elegant fingers. 'My own design,' he said.

And then he began.

'*O mistress mine, now hearken to my sad plaint ...* '

They listened with perfect politeness, and afterwards they applauded at length. Don John stood and bowed, and then, bidding them all a good night and good sleep, retired to his cabin.

Smith said, 'I wonder if he knows any songs that cannot be heard?'

They went and stood at the rails, the four of them, and looked out across the harbour. The night was warm and sweet and there was night jasmine on the air.

'Penny for your thoughts, Brother,' said Stanley. 'Well, a groat anyway. Let us not overvalue them. The devil knows, you're no St Thomas Aquinas.'

Smith showed his teeth. 'I was thinking that this prince – for all his outlandishness, his courtly absurdity – he appeals to me more and more. Recall what he said about our lad Ingoldsby's unschooled blows, and the element of surprise, the unexpected.'

'And?'

'I begin to think, though he is a very different man to Jean de la Valette, he may be our best hope to lead the Holy League against the Turk.'

'With an extensive wardrobe, but little real military experience, except against the wretched Moriscos, and none whatsoever of naval command?'

'Aye. Because it is, like an unschooled blow, so unexpected – it might just make sense.'

'*Credo quia absurdum,*' murmured Stanley. 'As Tertullian said of our Christian faith itself. *I believe it, because it is absurd.*'

Then they saw a small boat coming towards them in the darkness.

Nicholas peered.

It was the Moor. Abdul of Tripoli.

'You again,' called Nicholas.

'You know him?' said Smith.

'We shared a prison cell.'

'Permission to come aboard?' asked Abdul.

'Denied,' said Smith.

'What do you want?' asked Nicholas.

'To sail east with you.'

Smith didn't even reply, just laughed.

'Why?' asked Nicholas.

'I want to get to Aleppo.'

'Chained to the bench?' said Smith. 'As a volunteer oar slave?'

'Certainly not,' said Abdul. 'I am a man of fine sensibility, of delicate soul, I do not—'

'Then find your own ship. We don't take Moors.'

'I know much that can be of use. I have travelled widely.'

Smith pondered. He knew the type.

'He did leave us a flask of spirit in the prison cell,' said Nicholas. 'He did not betray us.'

Eventually Smith said, 'You can tie up and sleep in your boat. You will know tomorrow.'

'Do you have a blanket for me?'

'No.'

Surprisingly, Abdul agreed, and curled up to sleep in the bobbing boat.

Smith said sotto voce, 'He must really want to sail with us. I wonder why?'

Later there were just the two of them on deck, Nicholas and Hodge, and they were both a little drunk. The moonlight and the light of the swaying stern lanterns rippled on the gentle sea, and they looked out at the scattered lights of the great city, and then the darkness of the waterlands and the delta of the Guadalquivir. Beyond, the mighty ramparts of the towering Sierras, and the gaunt and austere tableland of Castile. It was very beautiful. Nicholas's head swam with sweet Spanish wine and disbelieving joy. He could not only scent night jasmine on the air. He could scent adventure.

Here they were, aboard a princely galley, reunited with the two men he loved as he had loved his father. They were still young, and free again, and sound in wind and limb. His blood burned within him. Perhaps it was all a dream. Perhaps they would wake tomorrow morning and find themselves back in Pedro Deza's dungeons, or on a corsair galley. But for now they were young, and the wine was sweet, and life was very beautiful.

'Well, friend Hodge,' he said, his eyes shining with a strange, mixed excitement. 'Shall we sail into battle once more, for Christendom and the Holy Catholic Church? Shall we go east with Don John of Austria in one last glorious crusade, we two exiles and comrades-in-arms, to meet with the numberless Ottoman fleet sailing under the crescent banner of Islam?'

'How much wine have you had?'

'Shall we drown in far Orient seas, or shall we live to find glory and honour and the love of fair maidens, there beneath the burning Levantine sun, upon the fabled coast of Palestine? Shall we walk once more the streets of Holy Jerusalem?'

Hodge burped deeply. 'Buggered if I know what else to do with myself. But for now I'm going to bed.'

Nicholas stood alone a while longer, his vision swimming with dreams of medieval chivalry in which he couldn't quite believe. Surely the age of Crusades was past, the age of paladins, and lionhearts, and golden castles standing proud upon the shores of Outremer? But oh, that the ancient heartlands of Christianity – Alexandria and Antioch, Damascus, and Jerusalem itself, long since overrun by the savage Saracens – that they might yet be Christian again! And that he, Sir Nicholas Ingoldsby, Knight Grand Cross (but with a special clause remitting him from chastity), might yet ride into the Holy City, *urbs Zion aurea*, resplendent as Bohemond upon a white charger, gleaming with gold and crimson trappings, crowded around by dark-eyed, adoring maidens . . .

He smiled to himself, drained the last of his wine and weaved his way down below, and slept for eleven hours.

13

They were awoken eventually by Smith hammering on the door and bawling, 'The day is half gone, you slovenly slug-a-bed toss-pots! Up on deck and show me your swordplay, girls!'

They came up to find that Abdul of Tripoli had indeed been allowed on board, if he agreed to sit down below with the galley slaves during the day, sleep on deck at night, and keep silence throughout.

Again, he agreed.

'Interesting,' said Stanley.

Hodge exchanged a few minutes' thrust and parry with Smith, and then gave Nicholas the blade. Nicholas danced round Smith and nearly tripped over a coiled rope. Smith grinned through his black beard. Nicholas parried, another parry, locked his blade with Smith's and then flicked it aside and, so fast that it surprised even him, had the point of his sword pressing just under Smith's chin. Smith froze.

Stanley clapped and hooted. 'He moves like a snake still, this English galley slave! Fra John, you are fairly skewered!'

Smith batted Nicholas's blade away with his bare hand and shot his own back home in its scabbard. He stumped away to the taffrail.

'Well,' said Stanley pityingly, looking after him, 'he is nearly eighty now.'

Nicholas gave the blade back to Stanley and said quietly, 'One of the saddest things about being taken by the damned corsairs was that they also took my sword. The sword of Bridier de la Gordcamp, remember?'

'I remember. Never a knight more gallant. He died as any man would wish to die.'

And then there were shouts from the mariners, the creak of oars back-rowing over the anchor, and the great quadruple hook lifting off the seabed and rising up to the cat-head, where two barefoot urchins tied it up. Then each bank of oars rowed against the other, the galley slowly turned, and they headed out to open sea.

As they rounded the cape and felt the first Atlantic gusts come up behind them and buffet them on the right, another cry sounded from the master. The great square sail came down from the main-mast. The oar slaves below were slackened off so as not to tire them, yet still they surged forward with that fine wind off to starboard and stern. The blue sea swelled and their hearts swelled with it.

'To Sicily! And the last crusade!'

Yet once they had passed Gibraltar and were into the quieter waters of the Inland Sea, the mainsail sagged again and it was oar power once more that drove them.

'It seems an antique way of moving a ship, after all,' murmured Nicholas.

'It is,' said Stanley. 'Antique galleys upon an antique sea, barely changed since Homer's day. The future is sailing ships, and the Atlantic winds, westwards, ever westwards.'

'But we are aboard this handsome but lumbering vessel, as haughty as Cleopatra,' said Smith. 'Lumbering and slow. We'd move much faster in something small and light, well sailed, sleeping on deck with nothing unnecessary. But for Don John of Austria to voyage in such a humble craft, without his wardrobe of six chests of suits ...'

Nicholas grinned, but Smith looked grim. 'Meanwhile the Turk still builds his three galleys a week, his land army swells with re-cruitment across his vast empire, his Janizary regiments train with-out ceasing, his cavalry champ at the bit. And soon the Ottoman cannon will roar once more, and Cyprus fall to ruin.'

Just at that moment the drumbeat changed, and the sweating oar slaves were slowed still further. Energy must be conserved, if they were to reach Alicante at all without running out of fresh water.

'Another advantage of sails,' said Stanley. 'You don't have to keep feeding and watering them.'

Smith had goaded himself into impatience. 'Devil take it!' His great hands gripped the rail as if he'd squeeze it into splinters. 'Too slow, too late, always too damned late. Cyprus will be done for by the time we hove into view. Like the Valley of Siddim, nothing left but smoke and ruin.'

Stanley said nothing. He glanced over his shoulder and there was Don John himself at the admiral's position, standing resplendent in a new suit of burnt orange with trimmings of Tyrian purple. His hat was like something Hermes would wear in a fancy Italian painting, made of orange felt with a white egret feather. Was he really to lead them to victory against those massed armies of Ottoman veterans? Stanley's heart felt heavy with foreboding. Throughout the pages of history, it was commanders like Don John – vain and inexperienced, little trusted by their men and desperate for personal glory – who had led their own armies to destruction.

And time was desperately short, every day counted. Yet Don John seemed to regard it all as a leisurely exercise in style and ... *sprezzatura*. Entertaining though he might be to dine with, was he really a Caesar, a Hannibal, an Alexander?

Cyprus stood in urgent need of relief, the sun burned, summer was moving on, and *La Real* cruised eastwards with as stately a grace as if they were going to a Christmas wedding in Alexandria.

After watering at Almeria, and again at Alicante, they began the crossing to Sardinia and thence to Sicily.

There was a thin mist one morning and then from the lookout above there came a cry of 'Galley to the south!'

Don John was up at the admiral's position in a trice, demanding more detail.

It was a lean Barbary corsair by the look of her, a low black shape upon the twinkling, blinding, sun-spangled sea. No more than a galliot really, with perhaps – the mariners strained their salt-wrinkled eyes – twenty oars a side? At the most.

A mile off? Less.

The instant she became aware of this huge flagship moving in stately fashion over the sea, appearing with horrible suddenness out of the thin morning mist to the north of them, flying both Hapsburg and Spanish standards and bristling like a fortress with cannon and saker, the Barbary captain of the galliot was screaming at his slaves to head her round and make south.

'Back-row and turn about!' called Don John.

'We can't possibly catch 'em, sire,' said the master, 'we'd need—'

Don John's languid voice changed abruptly to a note of harsh command. 'Follow orders, you impertinent rascal, or I'll clap you in your own irons!'

The master followed orders.

La Real's own one hundred and eighty slaves groaned and strained at their oars, three men to each huge oar, and slowly, slowly the great galley moved round, her stern swinging out and her prow coming to face south. Meanwhile Don John had also sent orders for the bow guns to be primed and ready.

Smith squinted over the blinding water and muttered, 'This is going to be interesting.'

The moment *La Real* was in line, Don John shouted, 'Fire the culverin!'

'That'll be a fine-judged shot if we hit, sire,' said Stanley.

'Then we had best judge it finely,' snapped Don John.

There was a tense silence while the two twenty-pound culverin were swiftly loaded and rammed, back-loaded *sabots* or seals made of no more than papier mâché were wadded in behind the balls to trap the explosive gases, powder was precisely measured in and the slim, elegant fourteen-foot-long barrels raised at an angle of some thirty degrees and given a final sighting squint by the master gunner.

Then the smoking linstock was put to the touch-hole, and they roared.

The range was truly impressive, both covering some fifteen hundred yards.

One ball ploughed into the sea not far short of the fleeing galliot, but some way wide. The second hit ball hit the water only just off her stern, sending up a plume of water that arched high over the boat and soaked the captain and crew. They could hear the babble of voices across the sea.

The master gunner ordered reload.

'Show me one of those bouncing shots over the water,' said Don John. 'The *tiro de fico,* don't you call it? A Portuguese speciality.'

The master nodded. The first culverin was depressed again as low as it could go, cleaned and reloaded in lightning-fast time, under a minute, and then the gunpowder exploded once more. The ball shot low, almost hitting *La Real*'s own spur. It bounced twice over the water and then sank, not more than three hundred yards off.

They heard the master gunner ordering reload again.

'Cease fire!' called Don John. 'Master gunner, report!'

The master gunner came back, a grizzled old hand far too proud to look discomforted by this inevitable failure.

But Don John had no interest in scolding him for failing at the impossible. Instead he looked thoughtful.

'Rest the guns,' he said. 'Leave those pox-ridden pirates there to scurry back to their flea-infested hovel in Algiers. Tell me, master gunner, that *tiro de fico* there – it did almost shear off the spur, did it not? Or did my handsome eyes deceive me?'

'It nearly did, sire. It's not unusual. If you try to lower a gun, for a bouncing shot or a close one low into an enemy hull, it can happen.'

'What does a spur *do,* exactly?'

'Do? Well, it's part of the ram.'

'And do we ram much these days?'

'Not much these days, no, sire. The Turk still does. Ram and engage. Like fighting a land battle at sea, you might say. Then they'll swarm aboard ye with scimitars flashing. And unless you've got some bloody good soldiers or marines of your own aboard—'

'Or Knights of St John,' said Smith.

'Or knights, for instance, aye – then you're pretty much dogmeat to 'em.'

'But if we don't ram, we ... what?'

'Well, your Spanish galley or your Genoese will hope to return fire and hole 'em before they come close. But in the end it's going to come to a musket and sword. The Turk still likes his bow and arrow too. Fast shooting.'

'So ramming is ... what, old fashioned?'

'You could say, sire.'

'Then why do we have rams and spurs if they only get in the way of the guns?'

'I couldn't say, sire. I don't build the galleys, I just fire the guns.'

'Quite right. Good man. Now back to your station.'

Stanley observed the master gunner closely as he stumped back fore bandy legged. He looked as if he thought this ludicrous peacock of a prince might not actually be such a stupid bugger after all.

'Guns will come to rule the world,' said Don John crisply. He turned to Smith and Stanley, sweeping off his hat and running his hand back over his smooth-combed hair. For the first time, they saw in his expression something of the steely decisiveness and leadership of the true military commander. It was there, after all, under that peacockery and orange velvet. Even the men could see it.

Don John said, 'We need more guns. It's all going to be about guns.'

Only five days later they came into the great harbour of Messina in Sicily and the slaves at last lay back from the hated oars.

Nicholas squatted down and looked under the awning where they sat slumped below in the shadows, the stench indescribable. The boatswain went around loosening their manacles. Several of them were too sick or exhausted to stand, but the rest would be marched off the galley under close guard, and fed and watered on the quayside like cattle. *La Real* herself would be carefully sunk by two or three feet, the sea allowed to flow through her and wash away the accumulated bilge, and then stopped and refloated. After that she might smell just bearable, when the slaves were driven back on board again and manacled once more to the benches.

Nicholas's heart went out to them a little. He had been there too.

Hodge near by him muttered, 'I hate it. That men should be treated so, Christian or Mohammedan or worshippers of Baal himself.'

But it was the way of the world. And war galleys must be manned.

'They may have their reward yet,' said Don John behind them.

Nicholas turned. 'By Christmas, perhaps they will have heard their manacles sprung back from their limbs for the last time.'

Nicholas looked puzzled.

Don John just smiled.

14

There was a counsel in the Governor of Messina's palace, attended by various dignitaries and ambassadors in fine robes, carrying an alarming weight of scrolls, ledgers and sealed documents. Don John was given a royal welcome by two heralds blasting down long brass horns.

Then their deliberations began, slow and ponderous. What should be the next step? What did the Papal Legate from the Holy Father in Rome have to say? King Philip of Spain urged caution, as did Venice. Certainly nothing should be too hasty. It was important to keep negotiations going with the Sublime Porte in Constantinople. Diplomacy might yet achieve peace in the Mediterranean.

To Nicholas and Hodge it was a bore, to Smith it was infuriating. After a while he could stand to listen no more, and stomped up and down in the hall outside, chewing his lip to tatters.

Stanley grinned to see him, but with sympathy. 'Peace, Brother. You'll have a seizure.'

'I'll be at peace when we start fighting!' said Smith in a strange, strangulated whisper that wanted to be a roar.

Later, both of the knights were summoned before the counsel to give their opinion.

'The Turks will be sailing upon Cyprus soon,' said Smith bluntly. 'The knights are sending one galley to aid the defence – all we can risk. But it is not enough. Cyprus will fall.'

The Venetian ambassador raised his eyebrows. 'Really, Fra ...'

'Fra John. John Smith.'

'An Englishman?'

'A Knight of St John. Who fought at Malta. Where were you?'

Don John raised a gloved hand. 'Please, Brother John. Some courtesy.'

Smith scowled. Stanley nudged him with his foot to be silent, and said, 'The counsel may not like what we say, and regard the knights as warmongers. Crusaders from another age, out of their time. But reverend sires, you know full well that we have an intelligence network second to none. You also know that in September last year a considerable Ottoman fleet, some sixty-eight galleys strong, appeared off the coast of Cyprus, under Admiral Ali Pasha.'

'Of course we know,' said the Venetian ambassador smoothly. 'A state visit, quite unthreatening. We gave them a silver bowl of a thousand piastres as a courtesy.'

'With which to buy more arms,' said Smith.

Stanley kicked him harder.

'The Turks came ashore at Famagusta and were welcomed amicably,' said the ambassador, speaking to the rest of the counsel now. 'They were given a tour of that celebrated city, and because they courteously asked to take four classical columns with them back to the Sultan for his palace, they were permitted to travel throughout the island of Cyprus in search of columns to their taste.'

'So they took a leisurely tour of Nicosia and Kyrenia, Cyprus's other principal fortified cities,' snapped Stanley. 'Even though the finest classical columns in Cyprus, as everyone knows, are to be found at Salamis.'

The ambassador inclined his head. The knights were always so belligerent, so disagreeable.

'Just *six miles north of Famagusta*,' said Stanley.

The Papal Legate shifted in his chair. 'Is this so?'

The Venetian ambassador waved his hand. 'I ... that is to say, we—'

'There's more,' said Stanley. 'Among their party was travelling one Josefi Attanto, a traitorous Italian who works for the Ottomans now. By profession, *a military engineer.*'

The Venetian ambassador at last looked discomposed, to the delight of his Genoese counterpart. 'How do you know this?'

'The knights know everything it is their business to know.

121

Unlike the Republic of Venice, it seems. We also know that the Grand Mufti in Istanbul, Mufti Ebu's-su'ud, lately reminded the Sultan Selim of a cardinal principle of Islam: that any treaty or promise with the infidel may be broken if it brings advantage to Islam. The principle of *taqiyya*.'

'You are versed in Islamic theology too,' said the ambassador with heavy sarcasm. 'Is there no end to your wisdom, dear knight?'

The Genoese ambassador muttered something about low wit, and he and the Venetian exchanged time-honoured scowls.

'It pays to know your enemy,' said Stanley.

'And you have spies in the very courts and chambers of the Sultan Selim himself?'

Stanley glanced at Smith and gave an enigmatic smile that he knew would infuriate this reptile of an ambassador. 'Some of us know Constantinople better than you think.'

The Papal Legate said, 'All this interests me very much, sir Knight, as it will the Holy Father in Rome. You know that no one has worked harder to bring the Christian powers into a league against the Turk.' He paused meaningfully. 'Despite many obstacles. Tell us what more you know.'

'You should be aware,' said Stanley, 'if you are not already, that the Ottomans are planning a canal between the Don and the Volga, in southern Russia, so as to dominate that region. They have allied with the Mohammedan Tatars in the Crimea, to destroy this burgeoning new power of the Grand Duchy, and will soon attack Moscow itself, we believe. That would secure their northern border and increase their power enormously. They are also planning a canal to link the Mediterranean to the Red Sea at Suez, thereby circumventing the Persian Empire, as well as the whole of Africa, on the trade route to India.'

'Preposterous,' said the Venetian ambassador.

'Extraordinary,' said the Papal Legate.

'Can it be done?' asked Don John, hitherto silent and watchful of his fellow counsellors, assessing the character of each in turn. So far his only liking was for the Papal Legate, a Dominican monk of small stature but sharp wits.

'Anything can be done,' said Smith, 'with enough will and manpower. Even defeating the Turk.'

Don John smiled.

'The Turks have quelled the rebellion in the Yemen,' said Stanley. 'They are at peace with Hungary, and with Charles IX of France. And so now they are all ready to turn again to the Mediterranean.'

'And Cyprus?' said the Papal Legate.

'And Cyprus,' said Stanley. 'Regiments of Janizaries and Sipahis are already mustering at the new fortress of Finike on the shores of Turkey opposite. The fertility of Cyprus will serve them well when they arrive there – unlike Malta – and the Greek populace, alas, may well greet them as liberators. It is for the Venetian ambassador, not me, to explain why this might be.'

The Genoese ambassador chuckled.

The Venetian said, 'Now you insult us, sir.'

Stanley ignored him. 'Indeed, the Turks may well have sailed already. Even as we sit here talking.'

'Preposterous,' said the ambassador again. But his voice carried less conviction now. The rest of the counsel sat in thoughtful silence.

'Gentlemen,' said Don John, 'the knights' intelligence is grave. And I for one have never known it to be wrong. Let us reconvene in one hour, no more. Decisions must be made, and with dispatch.'

The two English knights were standing in a courtyard with Nicholas and Hodge, Smith grinding his fist into his palm for want of anything better to grind. Two slim, slightly built noblemen approached them, their demeanour courtly but reserved. They might have been brothers. They had green eyes and secretive smiles, and it seemed to Nicholas that there was something indefinably dangerous about them. Each carried a pair of ivory-handled knives on his belt. One knife usually served for most men.

They bowed.

'Ambrosio Bragadino, of Venice,' said the first.

'Antonio Bragadino,' said the second.

All bowed.

'Our father, Marc'antonio Bragadino, is the Venetian Governor of Famagusta.'

Stanley nodded. 'We have good report of him. I do not think that Famagusta will fall easily to the Turk.'

'We thank you,' said Antonio. 'But you should know that Governor Dandolo, of Nicosia is less well reputed.'

Stanley grimaced. 'We have heard as much.'

'We cannot go with you ourselves,' said Ambrosio. 'It pains us, but we cannot. Our duties lie in Italy. But we will work ceaselessly to bring our beloved but reluctant republic into the war. And understand this. If our father should come to harm at the hands of the Turk – then we will sail east. And our revenge will be terrible.'

He spoke so softly, his green eyes unblinking, that Nicholas's heart felt chilled.

These two would indeed make evil enemies.

'We go to fight with your father if we can,' said Stanley. 'Rest assured, the Turks treat their nobly born captives with respect. If only to get a ransom.'

The brothers Bragadino bowed one last time and departed with silent, padding footsteps. Like leopards.

'Interesting,' said Smith quietly.

'Worth remembering,' said Stanley.

Tempers were on edge that evening, discussions fraught, mistrust and fear of betrayal everywhere.

'*Politics*,' snarled Smith.

Over a candlelit supper, Don Luis de Requesens said courteously to his master, a silent Don John, 'His Majesty King Philip has forbidden you to go to Cyprus, sire.'

Don John sipped his wine.

'It is a Christian territory!' said Smith. 'How can Spain not go to her aid?'

'Greek Orthodox,' said Don Luis, 'not true Catholic.'

'And how can a single galley of volunteers and knights,' said Don John, 'even Knights of St John, defend an island the size of Cyprus?'

'We cannot,' said Stanley, 'and we will not. We will go there to advise, and fight and likely die there, vastly outnumbered as we shall be. But we will die content that we have done our oath-sworn duty. That is what the Knights do. What they have always done.'

'But we are owed better than this!' cried Smith, beating so hard on the tabletop with his bear-like paws that several glasses jumped and one smashed to the floor.

124

'Calm, Brother,' said Stanley. 'You should cultivate more of His Excellency's *sprezzatura*.'

'*Buggery and damnation to His Excellency's sprezzatura!*'

Nicholas glanced anxiously at the prince, but Don John only smiled. Don Luis de Requesens pursed his lips.

Smith stood and strode out into the courtyard.

'My apologies,' said Stanley. 'It is not in my brother's nature to be cool and urbane.'

Don John inclined his head. 'No apologies necessary. It is the passion of such as Fra John that will save us all from the Turk.' He considered. 'If I went with you to Cyprus—'

'Your Excellency!' said Don Luis, scandalized.

'If I went with you to Cyprus,' repeated Don John, 'what is the worst that could happen?'

'The worst?' said Stanley. 'We arrive offshore, in secret, ensign down.'

'Certainly not. Don John goes nowhere in mean disguise.'

'Ah well, in that case, we arrive offshore, and word quickly spreads among the Greeks that none other than Don John of Austria is come to the war, still flying the double-headed eagle of the Habsburgs like a damn fool – the Greeks' words, Your Excellency, not mine. Word is passed on to the Turks, for a price. And the Pasha promptly sends out a squadron of his fastest galleys to take you hostage.'

'I am *not* going to spend my time in a Turkish dungeon,' said Don John, examining his fingernails. 'Imagine how the ruffians there would *admire* me. My elegant shape and figure.'

'Worse, we would have stupidly given ourselves away, and gifted the Turks a powerful bargaining coin. Their preparations are far advanced, and we need to exercise caution.'

'*Semper non paratus*,' snapped the prince, and stood abruptly. 'Caution is the daughter of punctuality and the mother of gastric disquietude.'

The rest of the table stared.

Don John forgot his dandyish poise for a moment and laughed out loud. A harsh little *hah*! Then he turned on his high heels and departed, Don Luis hurrying after him.

Nicholas laughed too. He was really beginning to like this preposterous prince.

'Mad bastard,' muttered Smith, standing in the opposite doorway. 'Words merely descriptive, not disparaging.'

'And he is to lead us against the Turk?' said Hodge. 'Christendom must be desperate.'

The comrades met again soon after the early summer dawn. A breeze was blowing and the eastern sky was red.

'You should go,' said Don John, regret in his voice.

'Excellency?'

'Get aboard your own galley. There she rides at anchor, look, under her Maltese Cross so red. I stay here. Thence to Rome, and perhaps to Venice after. Not out of milk-livered obedience to my brother. But my task is here. The delicate, unheroic work of diplomacy, forging the Christian princes into a unity. Like herding cats.'

Stanley and Smith both bowed.

'Get you to Cyprus, and my bitter envy go with you. I mean, my heartfelt blessings.' He smiled a wan smile. 'To Famagusta, right under the glare of the Grand Turk. In his very courtyard. If Cyprus falls, then it will all come down to the great sea battle at last. But I need you back for that. I need you by my side for it.'

They shook hands, and then the prince lowered himself to shake the hands of Nicholas and Hodge as well.

'English gentlemen volunteers. Believe me when I say, I hope we may meet again on a happier day.'

They bowed.

The ladder was being lowered with a clunk, a longboat pulling alongside.

'Get your bags,' said Smith. 'The fate of Cyprus will decide much.'

When they came aboard the galley of the knights – she was called the *St John of Jerusalem* – there was Gil de Andrada to greet them with a broad smile.

'We meet again.'

'Don John has other business,' said Smith. 'A deal more tedious. But we are for Cyprus.'

'And happy to have you as captain,' said Stanley.

'Vice-captain,' corrected De Andrada. But he looked quite content about it.

'Then who . . . ?'

Up from below appeared an older man with a long, fine nose, a thin beard, and extraordinary, burning eyes, deep set and circled with dark rings.

All bowed.

The Chevalier Mathurin Romegas. The most brilliant naval commander among all the Knights of St John, the most feared sea-wolf in the Mediterranean.

Nicholas knew all about Romegas. It would be an experience to sail with him.

'Gentlemen,' said Romegas. 'We sail at sundown.'

'There is a Moor travelling with us. Might he sit below?'

'A Moor?' said Romegas. 'Why?'

'It will become clear in time, I think.'

On the second day out of Messina, far to the south upon the burning sea, there was a small sun-brown island.

Malta. Malta of the knights.

Nicholas's heart ached to see her. But they would not step ashore there. Most of those he had loved there were dead. Jean de la Valette in his grand stone catafalque in Valetta's new cathedral. Bridier and Lanfreducci and Medrano and all the brave knights who were slain. And a young girl called Maddalena, too, lay sleeping in her narrow grave until the Judgement Day.

The handsome young Florentine knight, Luigi Mazzinghi, was standing by him.

'She is so small a place, our island home. The island that you fought for, you and your comrade Odge.'

'Hodge,' said Nicholas. 'H. H.'

'*Hodge,*' said Mazzinghi carefully. He smiled. 'And while you and he fought, I was bent over my desk in a room in a Florence palazzo, learning my mathematics and my Latin grammar. How old are you now?'

'Twenty-two.'

Mazzinghi tapped his chest. 'Nineteen. Thirteen when the guns of Malta roared all summer long. Yet there were boys of thirteen fighting at the siege?'

Nicholas nodded. 'Boys of ten, boys of eight. Boy soldiers, slingers, women, entire families fighting near the end.'

'Everyone thinks Cyprus will be different.'

'I think both better, and worse.'

'I pray God,' said Luigi Mazzinghi softly, crossing himself, 'I only pray that I am worthy in the battles to come of the heroes of Malta.'

In the squalor and poverty of the last two years, Nicholas had half forgotten about the knights. Not only Europe's most elite warriors, but monks too. Most devout swordsmen. Now Mazzinghi prayed he would be worthy of the heroes of Malta – such as himself! A whoring, drunken, roving, brawling English vagabond, lost in the world, with neither family nor home, nor country.

He smiled a bitter smile. In whatever firestorm was to come, he prayed he would be worthy of such simple, noble souls as the Chevalier Luigi Mazzinghi.

And the firestorm would surely be upon them soon.

Time was hurrying on. The sun sailed across the sky.

The Turk was coming.

15

The rugged outline of Crete lay ahead, with Cape Matapan to larboard, backed by the mountains of the Peloponnese. A fresh wind out of the north-east, the *St John* under oar only. The lookout called down. Something approaching.

'More detail,' said Romegas.

There was a tense silence while the lookout, a boy of fifteen, strained his eyes. The best lookouts were boys of eleven or twelve.

'Squadron!' he called.

Smith moved to the hatchway.

'Black sails!'

Smith grinned. 'Time to arm up, ladies.' And he was gone below for his treasured Persian jezail, an elegant, long-barrelled weapon that those at the Great Siege said was the most accurate musket they had ever seen in battle.

Smith invariably retorted, 'Depends who fires it.'

Stanley waited a while longer. A *squadron*. Knights disdained to turn and run, and Romegas would attack an entire armada single handed. The Turks feared him as they would a mad dog – but a mad dog with exceptional tactical intelligence. An entire squadron of enemy galleys was quite a challenge, nevertheless. They would need a plan.

'Gunners to your stations!' roared Romegas. 'All guns primed and loaded. Crew at the munitions hatches, ready to serve the guns!'

'Six!' called down the lookout boy. 'Six galleys under slow oar and sail. In a loose file.'

Romegas was squinting down his brass eyeglass, set on a tripod clamped to the rail. His hands shook badly. It wasn't fear. Once his galley was capsized by a monstrous sea, and he was trapped underwater for twelve hours with his head in an air pocket. There was nervous damage. Men were supposed to grow more fearful as they grew older, and Romegas was past sixty now. But he still hadn't learnt the meaning of fear.

His eyes strained. He prayed to God to give him better sight. God never answered that prayer. But the eyeglass would do. It confirmed that there were six galleys under oar, they were rounding Cape Matapan westwards and so heading for the Adriatic ports, and they weren't Venetian. And something – a sailor's deep, inborn sixth sense – could discern relaxation and relief in their very oar stroke. They were sailing into home waters.

There was more to be deduced. The squadron could see the *St John of Jerusalem* and vice versa. But they were not turning to attack, although so superior in numbers. Was that because they were heavily laden with booty, and only wanted to make landfall back in their pirate lair, Ragusa or Avlona?

'The standard they fly!' called Romegas. 'Tell me it is a black standard with a white crescent!'

'I cannot see, Captain.'

Romegas stroked his beard. 'Then we will have to row closer.' And he gave the order. The boatswain blew his whistle and the mariners got stirring, the helmsman leaning hard on the whipstaff to move the great stern rudder round a few perfectly judged degrees.

Smith came back up through the hatchway carrying his jezail in a roll of finest oilcloth and singing a psalm.

'*I shall give the heathen for thine inheritance, Thou shalt break them with a rod of iron, thou shalt break them in pieces like a potter's vessel.*'

'I've heard crows sing sweeter,' said Stanley. 'Recite it rather than sing it, Brother, I pray you. You'll bring Leviathan up from the deep with that caterwauling, and in a foul humour too.'

Smith sang on.

Nicholas and Hodge stood upon the larboard walkway near to where a pair of gunners were rapidly readying the *verso*, a small cannon that swivelled broadly left and right on its pivot and could deliver a hefty fistful of grapeshot at close quarters.

'Remember our first corsair skirmish, Matthew Hodge?' murmured Nicholas.

'Well enough,' said Hodge. 'Considerin' I got a blow to me poll that I never quite came right from again.'

The *St John of Jerusalem* was now rowing fast due north, towards the lead galley of the six, as if to hit it broadside. Which would also leave the *St John*'s own broadside exposed to the following five galleys. Lunacy.

'Standard flies!' cried the lookout boy. 'Black standard with a white crescent.'

'And on the forward ship,' Romegas shouted up to him, 'tell me there is a shaven-headed villain with a topknot, who still wears the tattered robe of a Dominican friar!'

The boy strained his eyes, swaying back and forth in the tiny netted crow's nest as if that would help, then called back, 'There's a fellow in a long black robe, I think, looking our way. Cannot tell the style of his hair.'

Smith gave a strange guttural growl, and Romegas drummed his fists on the rail. 'That dung-munching, idol-serving Gibraltar baboon!' Then he plucked the eyeglass from the tripod, stowed it inside his doublet and leapt back to the captain's lookout position with the eagerness of a man half his age.

Stanley saw Nicholas's and Hodge's enquiring expressions.

'Kara Hodja,' he said. 'The Black Priest, and the evillest corsair in all the eastern sea. Shame on him that he was once a Christian. He still wears his Dominican robe in mockery, even as he is beheading Christian captives on the deck of his ship.' He looked out across the narrowing gap. 'But Judgement Day is coming.'

'Six galleys against one,' said Hodge.

Gil de Andrada joined them. 'Watch and learn.'

The six galleys had slowed and were hoving to uncertainly.

'Fire the centre-line!' called Romegas.

A few moments later the great centre-line gun roared and they heard the rush of the forty-pound iron ball through the air, then saw the geyser of white water where it struck, many yards short of the enemy.

'Well out of range,' said Hodge. 'Waste of good powder and shot.'

Gil de Andrada shook his head. 'Shows we mean business. Romegas wants them to think we are bent on attacking with all guns blazing, and he reckons on a certain response.'

And he got it. Moments later all six corsair galleys were seen turning sharply to the north. They were fleeing. Now the sharpest eyes on the *St John*, Nicholas and Hodge included, could see their black sails straining and filling as they turned into the nor-easter. Their mariners scurried about the decks and up the rigging. And they could hear the drumbeat sound.

'Romegas bewitches men's minds,' said De Andrada. 'Makes them see things which are not, makes them do his bidding like whipped slaves.'

Meanwhile Romegas stood leaning hungrily forward from his post, dark-circled eyes burning, muttering like an incantation, 'Give us a shot, God rot your bones! Just one shot.'

Then it came. A vague, half-hearted warning shot from one of the fleeing galleys' stern guns. The ball fell nearer its source than its target.

But it was enough.

'Helm about! Battle speed due east, and don't spare the lash down below there!'

'Now I am *truly* confused,' said Nicholas. 'We are going into battle against, what, thin air? And hurrying due east, with our enemy now rowing away north? Chevalier Gil de Andrada, we need a commentary.'

The *St John* came sharp about, sails tight reefed, and surged into the oncoming waves. They could hear the groaning slaves, the creak of the thole pins down below.

'Even I cannot always read Romegas's mind,' said De Andrada. 'And he rarely shares his thoughts. But here is my interpretation. We encounter an enemy, far more numerous than us. We feign an attack. They flee. This tells Romegas the enemy has valuable booty, and wants to keep it. They will row fast north, almost into the wind. What else does it tell us? That they judge they can row faster than us. What, laden with booty? Then they must be carrying very few heavy guns. Unlike us. So we outgun them.'

'Romegas indeed reads men's minds,' murmured Stanley.

'And of course he reads the wind,' said De Andrada, 'and knows every rock, every current, every vagary of the sea. So then he waits until the enemy return fire – as they did, just that one feeble shot – and then feigns to flee east. At battle speed. Not to attack anything, young Ingoldsby, simply because that is the fastest sustainable oar speed there is. Only ramming is faster, but that can be kept up by the slaves below for only a few hundred yards. Meanwhile our guns are all readied and waiting. The enemy are heading north in file. Then there comes a moment ...'

The *St John* was already a mile east of the vanishing corsair squadron, apparently heading away fast. The squadron finally rounded Cape Matapan and the mad dog Romegas was out of their sight.

'Head her about ... NOW!' Romegas roared. 'Hard on the starboard oars, face her about to nor'ward! Then give me full sail, master mariner!'

'We'll swamp her sides, *Capitán*! And salt all the starboard guns to boot!'

'Full sail and quick about it!'

'Galleys must be low sided, low in the water,' said De Andrada, 'so the oars can reach the sea, obviously. But that limits how far they can roll. Unlike a high-sided Atlantic galleon, there's a limit to how much sail they can carry. But Romegas knows every wind around Cape Matapan.'

'Ship oars!' called Romegas.

'To rest the oarsmen,' said De Andrada. 'Because battle speed cannot be sustained more than a few minutes either.'

Out of sight of the enemy, the *St John* came hard about to face westwards now, and her two fine sails, foresail and mainsail, billowed forth under the fresh nor'easter.

'Ah,' said De Andrada, shaking his head. 'Masterly. You see? The enemy have gone north, they cannot use a nor'easter so are condemned to oars alone. But we are now coming back westwards, with the wind on our side. They have also gone into the lee of Cape Matapan so there is little wind for them anyway. We are still in full wind so can gain on them with little effort. And they cannot see us coming.'

Now the *St John* surged exultantly forward again with the wind, the waves running with her. They crowded fore, hair blowing about their faces, breathless with excitement.

A minute … two minutes … Nicholas squatted and looked over the muscular, filthy backs of the rowing slaves, still sweating and panting from that punishing battle speed. How ironic, how potent – he had thought it many times, when he was chained to the bench himself – that a galley slave faced always backwards. Could not even see where he was going.

The master mariner's doubts about full sail in such a wind very nearly proved justified. As the *St John* leaned perilously under a stronger gust, the larboard rowers had to raise their oars still higher if they weren't to get the blades caught in the passing sea, slamming them backwards, badly injured, off their own benches. Men had even been killed that way. Meanwhile, to starboard, the oars would have been unable to reach the water even if they'd tried.

But it was only a gust, and then the wind dropped off markedly.

Cape Matapan.

Romegas knew every wave, every eddy.

'Hence his risking full sail,' said De Andrada.

The lessening wind still filled the sails, but the *St John* now moved forward on an almost even keel. From his position Romegas gazed keenly forward.

'See to your guns! Report from larboard!'

A moment later a gunner ran up to say, 'Front *verso* got a faceful of salt, *Capitán*. No other.'

'Then clean her down. I want every gun ready to fire in two minutes.'

They were cutting perilously close to Cape Matapan now, far nearer than the corsair squadron had dared to sail, even though these were Kara Hodja's home waters. But Nicholas felt a growing trust in every single thing the extraordinary Romegas did. He could sail between Scylla and Charybdis blindfold, this wolf of the sea.

There was a spike of rock not ten yards off the starboard bow, and heaven knew what ragged monsters lurking immediately below the hull, down in the sunless gloom. The *St John* surged merrily over them all. The rocks of the cape itself were barely fifty yards off. They were sheering round, and any moment would emerge, perhaps with an extra gust of wind as they moved offshore again, the rowers rested and ready for ...

'Battle speed!' called Romegas.

And then they were surging out from the cape, the file of six corsair galleys spread away towards the Dalmatian coast and their lair. The rearmost of the six was merely ambling. Not a soul aboard had yet seen the *St John*'s red hull appear round Cape Matapan, coming to destroy them.

Nicholas had rarely seen such ferocious aggression, with never a moment of hesitancy or doubt.

Romegas signalled now, rather than shouted. The helmsman brought the prow around to just ahead of the hapless, unwitting rear galley, and the oarsmen left off battle speed for a slow stroke, just enough to keep her steady and moving forward.

Romegas raised his hand. The master gunner beside the centre-line gun held a smoking linstock. Nicholas felt what it was then to have absolute power. A wild, dark pleasure.

Later the lookout boy swore he saw one of the corsairs glance back at that moment, and his eyes flare wide with terror.

Then Romegas dropped his arm, and all five prow guns fizzed and roared in a rolling volley of less than a second.

'All guns reload! Hold fire!'

From the crow's nest the lookout boy saw men turn and stare aghast from several of the corsair galleys, and clapped his hands in delight.

Then two of the five cannonballs struck home.

The galley rolled helplessly under the iron hammer-blows, and both balls passed clean through her hull, erupting from her far side in a mighty explosion of splintered timbers and spars. A howling went up from her depths as the oar slaves panicked and ceased rowing, crying out for mercy, their drivers flailing their lashes but to no avail.

The five other galleys seemed to give a moment's pause at the shocking fate of their companion – and then the order ran through the squadron to row ahead with all speed. They fled.

The crippled rear galley floundered and turned in a quarter-circle. Already her stern was beginning to sag in the water.

'Fast ahead!' roared Romegas.

There was many a Christian captive aboard her. And in but a minute or two they would be dragged down in their chains to the deep.

The corsair crew were standing fore with hands clasped on their shaven heads. Smith kept his jezail on them from the *St John*. They jabbered and rolled their eyes. The deck tilted.

A handful went aboard. Stanley whipped the key from the captain's belt and tossed it to Nicholas.

'Here, you can swim. Move fast.'

Nicholas clamped the dismayingly small, fiddly key between his teeth and waded down among the benches. In the stern the wretched slaves were already up to their waists in seawater. And the bilge that had lain around their feet, rotting the nails from their toes, was now afloat.

Nicholas crossed himself. A cholera sea, this was. Welcome, the bloody flux.

Back at the stern, the captain smiled a lazy smile. 'That is not the key,' he said.

Stanley thundered at him.

The captain shrugged, wasting time. 'That is not the right key. That is the key to my treasure chest, such as it is.'

Stanley gripped him round his jaw. 'Then give me the right key.'

He still smiled. 'There is none. It is lost. The Christian slaves will drown. Because you have destroyed our ship.'

Nicholas had not heard. The manacles were on their ankles. They cried out to him. He knelt in the foul water as the galley juddered. A huge current came gushing in from somewhere below where the *St John* had holed her. Nicholas groped beneath the water. There was the lock. He plucked the key from his teeth and turned it underwater. It was damnably stiff. In God's name let it not ...

Three things happened in a single instant. Smith's jezail sounded its whipcrack shot. The galley gave another terrible lurch and Nicholas was up to his neck. And the tiny key snapped off in the lock.

He dragged himself to his feet, yelling out, 'Another key!'

Stanley was shouting back to him. One of the corsairs was lying across the deck, shot through the head. He had tried to pull a dagger and stab Stanley in the back, but Smith had shot him instantly. The rest cowered and cursed him for a fool. You do not take on the knights, nor any galley that flies the white cross on red. Fools die.

Nicholas was wading back through the sluicing bilge. 'Another key, for God's sake!'

In the sinking stern the first and second benches were now under water. Men were drowning, crying out for help. Some voices were very young, those of beardless boys.

Stanley crossed himself, De Andrada muttered a prayer to Christ Jesus.

The captain smiled.

'For God's sake!' cried Nicholas again, dripping and filthy.

Stanley shook his head. 'There is no key. An evil day.'

'To the longboat!' cried Giustiniani.

Nicholas was seized then by … he knew not what. That blind fury that came upon him at times, ever since Malta. A red blind fury. A mariner near by was holding a boathook as a weapon, loosely pointed towards the crew of corsairs. He snatched it from his grasp and made to attack the murderers, to smash the iron hook into the sides of skulls. But a huge bear-hug seized him from behind and flung him away. Stanley. The galley was all but below the water now. Any moment she would be sucked down to the deep. All was chaos. The longboat was filling up, only Stanley and Giustiniani remained. Then Giustiniani leaped into the sea. He would find the longboat after.

Nicholas floundered, his head alternately above and below water. The current among the benches was like a huge snake coiling around his legs. There at the rear benches were two slaves, one of them screaming.

He jammed the boathook down again and again until he felt it hit metal and then twisted it violently. It was lodged. Another current, the ship rolled and seemed like to capsize, then settled again at a crazy angle. Somewhere beyond the screams and the ringing in his head, there was Stanley shouting. He gripped the far end of the boathook, half expecting it merely to snap, and fell on it with all his weight. Something sprung loose and he was thrown. He floundered in reeking salt water. A huge bubble came up from the hold, perhaps all that had been floating her, and the ship was going now. Two men, still chained to each other, were clinging to him, drowning him. He struggled against them in the water, kicking furiously, windmilling his arms, the foul sea lashed white. All coherence gone. Then there was a powerful, unmistakable sucking force upon everything and he was being pulled down. Down in a dark silent vortex of rushing emerald sea.

16

There was sun on his face, and his nose was clotted. He was completely deaf. He choked on air. He was vomiting.

Someone slapped his back so hard he juddered. He vomited again. Was he being beaten?

The sun reeled overhead and he opened his eyes. He was alive.

He was hauled up the side of the *St John* like a kitten rescued from a tub. Flopped on to the deck.

When he came to his better senses again there was blinding sunlight, and a dark shadow standing over him. More shadows beyond. A gull in the sky. Someone playing a musical instrument, for the love of God.

Romegas's shadow loomed across him.

'You, lad, are almost as much a brainsick fool as I am. You drowned yourself to save two oar slaves, one of whom died anyway. It was I who killed the rest. Damn the day.'

He struggled upright. Someone helped him on to a bench. The sky and the sun still reeled around him.

'Stanley,' said Romegas. 'Watch him. If he escapes the bloody flux from that vile dunking, he must have the luck of the devil.'

His clothes were dumped overboard. Smith said they'd poison all the fish between Cape Matapan and Crete. He was sluiced naked until he felt his skin half salted off, and given the freshest, purest water to drink, straight from a spring ashore. They made him drink until his belly was swollen like that of a mother with child. And for a day and a night they watched him like hawks, felt his brow, demanded to know of his stools. By the end of the next day, as he wearily reported on the state of his bowels, they shook their heads. Aye. He had escaped it. The Lord alone knew how.

'Swallowed several firkins of galley slaves' bilge,' grumbled Smith, 'and never a whit the worse for it.' Smith grumbled with a kind of paternal pride, like a father grumbling about how much his son ate, how tall he was growing. 'Lad, if every man had your stomach, then camp fever and bloody flux would be things of the past.'

Nicholas grimaced. He still didn't much like to be reminded of it.

The two slaves whose manacles he had sprung had nearly drowned anyway, but one was finally hauled, choking but alive, aboard the *St John*'s longboat by Smith, clutching the wretch round his bare throat. The knight nearly gave him a hanging.

'This is your saved man, the Christian you almost drowned for,' said Smith, his voice sardonic. 'He cut his wife's throat.'

Stanley grinned broadly. 'This day is full of little ironies, is it not?'

Nicholas refused to look shaken. 'Who am I to judge his sins?'

He was an Italian, a fellow with a narrow face and dark, lank hair, called Aurelio Scetti, and a lute player, of all things.

'You are now his rightful owner,' said Stanley. 'Not in bad shape, he might be worth thirty ducats in the market at Venice, if you get him there alive. Not bad work, Master Ingoldsby.'

Thirty ducats! Nicholas had hardly considered it. But he now had more wealth than he'd had since leaving England.

'Perhaps it will be the beginning of a great Ingoldsby trading empire,' continued Stanley mockingly. 'You know your way around certain Mediterranean cities, you speak fair French, Spanish and Italian as well as your native tongue, and now you have your first assets. Become a slave trader, Ingoldsby! There's no end of demand. You could take to gunrunning and arms dealing between Turk and Christian as well, and end up with a palazzo of your own overlooking the Grand Canal of Venice, with the prettiest wife *and* a couple of mistresses too.'

Nicholas looked at him sourly. 'Don't tempt me,' he said. 'The

140

older I get, the more likely I'll think in such ways. But it's not why I came here.'

Why did he come here? Stanley watched him at the rail. He knew why.

Ingoldsby – still an orphan boy at heart, at twenty-two – Ingoldsby came here hoping that in the nobility of some last crusade he might redeem his life and his soul. A foolish hope? Vain, naive, impossible? Stanley was glad it was not for him to say.

Romegas was silent and stared his horizon stare for long hours from the captain's post.

'It was an evil day,' said Stanley quietly. 'That any captain, even the most villainous corsair out of the Barbary Coast, should lock his slaves to their benches and then lose the key. Knowing that in storm or shipwreck he could not release them. It was a villainous thing. But—'

Romegas shook his head. 'I'll not be comforted. It was I gave the order, I who sunk her. It is I must bear responsibility. And I heard talk among the mariners that this is an omen for Cyprus.'

'Do you believe in omens?'

'I do. But I also believe men always read 'em wrongly.'

Nicholas negotiated with the boatswain, and his new possession was allowed to sit on the rowing benches unmanacled, down beside Abdul of Tripoli, fed and watered but not rowing, to restore his strength. Aurelio Scetti said nothing. He was a man far gone inside himself and his own misery.

Nicholas gave Abdul a piece of bread.

The Moor said, 'Your magnanimity drowns my very heart in tears of most humble gratitude. Surely your beneficence is like unto a beacon of golden light, shining out across the cruel darkness of—'

'Cease,' said Nicholas. 'Have you ever rowed on a corsair galley?'

'That I have. A misunderstanding between myself and a powerful imam concerning his daughter. I can say no more, decency forbids. But you think that corsairs only use Christians on their galleys?' He shook his head. 'They use any man with two arms and a heartbeat.'

*

At dawn they came in sight of an island and Smith and Stanley went ashore in the longboat. They came back to report a single spring, the water drinkable. Not a goat, not a rock dove, not a human soul. A few skittering lizards. The whole island but a thousand paces across.

They took barrels over and filled them with fresh water. Then they went back with the corsair captain and his crew and marooned them there without a blade or a gun between them, only the clothes they stood up in.

Curses followed them across the water as they rowed back to the *St John of Jerusalem*.

'May Allah bring you and all your children to hell!'

And, 'We will kill you! We will kill you all!'

Three days later the lookout boy said he thought he could see mountains on the horizon. Romegas examined a chart and ordered the rowers to slacken off. They drifted until dusk and then moved on under darkness.

It was the Troödos Range. They were nearing Cyprus.

The dark bulk of the mountains loomed up beneath the moon, beyond a broad coastal plain. Between them and the coast, laced white with small waves in the moonlight, there was the lantern of a single small fishing boat at sea. The *St John* herself moved forward in complete darkness, her stern lanterns unlit, orders passed for'ard in whispers, the rowers commanded to move their oars as silently as possible.

Romegas eyed the little swinging lantern of the fishing boat a mile off. 'Now begins the business of distinguishing friend from foe. This will be the story of your Cyprus campaign.'

Romegas said his farewells to them and embraced his brother knights heartily, the tears in his eyes betraying his fear that he would ever see them alive again. Gil de Andrada too would stay aboard, far more value as a naval captain than a land soldier. They would return to Malta.

'God give you the victory,' said Romegas, clasping Stanley about his broad chest. 'I wish to God that I was with you, but I am a seaman, and it is at sea I do my best work.'

'We know it,' said Stanley, 'and the Turk knows it too.'

'Sail away fast with our blessing,' said Smith. 'Cyprus is a lone Christian outpost in a Turkish sea, surrounded by the enemy. Flying the cross of St John of Malta, this galley is like a straw man on an archery green.'

'The *St John* is no straw man,' said Romegas.

'And you'll prove it yet, I have no doubt.'

'Fortune go with you, Brother,' said Giustiniani gravely. The two old veterans had fought side by side for forty years or more. 'And may you hear good news of Don John and the Holy League. We need it.'

'There *is* no Holy League,' said Romegas with sudden bitterness. 'It is a figment of the Pope's.'

'A noble lie,' said Giustiniani. 'A noble dream. Wait and pray.'

Smith, Stanley and Luigi Mazzinghi went out in the longboat with barely a sound, and moved towards the fishing boat, their swords under their cloaks so as not to catch the moonlight. But the sharp-eyed fisherman had already seen them and the lantern went out. Yet his boat did not move. They rowed towards him.

Finally they pulled back on the oars only a few yards short. They could see the shadowy outline of a man, sturdy looking, holding his boathook like a pike.

'Ho there,' whispered Stanley. 'Your name.'

'What do you want with me?'

'Nothing of you, friend, but your name.'

After a long pause, the fisherman said, 'My name is Nikos. The Turks are on the coast all around. And your galley there is nicely lit up by the moon.'

'We thought to have sailed round to Famagusta. But we cannot.'

Nikos shook his head. 'The Turks already have Lemessos and Larnaca. The seas all around Cyprus belong to them now. You would not get round in your galley unseen, they would destroy you in the water, and it is too far in that longboat.'

'Then will you guide us ashore here?'

'How much?'

'We come to fight for your island, man.'

'How much?' said Nikos stubbornly.

Stanley sighed. 'A ducat.'

'Done.'

They moved as fast as they could in silence. Mazzinghi, Smith and Stanley remained in the longboat while swords and muskets were lowered down in wrapped blankets, and Giustiniani climbed down to join them. Then two Sicilian mariners, who would row the longboat back to the *St John*. Then Smith stood up again, setting the longboat rocking dangerously. Stanley told him to sit, for the love of God, but Smith ignored him and climbed back up the ladder. At the rail he spoke quickly to Romegas, who then lowered one of the small standards of the Maltese Cross from outside the stern cabin and handed it to the Englishman. Smith sat back in the longboat and rolled up the standard on his knee.

'An excellent idea, Fra John,' said Stanley. 'Ensuring that if we are captured by the Turks, as is more than likely, they will search your knapsack and discover that we are Knights of St John, going in disguise in Turkish territory. And what do you think they will do to us then? More than tickle us in the ribs, I imagine.'

Smith ignored him, carefully stowed the tightly rolled standard at the bottom of his sack, and then sat back looking almost pleased.

Stanley sighed. 'It's like trying to reason with a small child.'

Mazzinghi grinned in the darkness, as nervous and excited as any of them.

Finally Nicholas and Hodge came down the ladder, and one other with them.

'Why is he coming?' hissed Stanley.

'Just a hunch,' said Smith. 'Don't you have hunches?'

'Yes. And they're usually wrong. A Moor. Brilliant. Seven of us going to liberate Cyprus from the Mohammedans, and one of us is a Moor.'

'Seven against Thebes,' said Nicholas. 'The Seven Sages.'

Stanley laughed sardonically.

'What happened to the Scetti fellow?' asked Smith.

'I sold him back to Romegas,' said Nicholas. 'Twenty ducats.'

'A poor price,' said Abdul.

'You keep silent,' said Smith. 'You may be a free man, God help us, but no Moor speaks aboard *my* boat.'

'Enough talk,' said Giustiniani, and flung his arm out.

'Off we go,' said Stanley, slowly moving his oar. 'Why, I can feel that army of a hundred thousand Turks trembling at our very approach.'

Part II
THE SACRIFICE

1

Nikos guided them into a small, shallow cove, hidden by tall cliffs.

'We're trapped already,' said Smith, glancing round, as if half expecting Turkish musketeers to appear above, forewarned by some secret signal from Nikos, to slaughter them where they sat.

'You can hardly step ashore on a broad beach,' said Nikos, 'not in this moonlight. But look, there is a gully in the cliffs. That is your route.'

'You are coming with us.'

'I am not. It is enough for me.'

Mazzinghi was already wading through the shallows with the bundles of weapons.

Stanley squinted up at the cliffs. Even he was feeling daunted at the absurd task they had set themselves. 'And then we make inland, and across the Troödos mountains. I think it will take us ten days.'

Nikos stroked his moustache. 'You would be strong for that. More like twenty. The Troödos are no mere hills, and then the burning plain beyond – it is May now, and very hot.'

'We can come down to Kyrenia from inland, or else to Nicosia.'

Nikos eyed them. He was an old man, his eyelids drooping like his moustache, his eyes like those of an old dog that has seen all. He spoke without pity for them, and without enmity, but with sorrow for his native island. 'The Turks have already taken Kyrenia.'

All heads turned. 'Impossible! Not so quickly as that, not with those fortifications.'

'Not by conquest,' said Nikos. 'Kyrenia surrendered without a shot. They saw the size of the Turkish armada, and they held up their hands. It was a wise decision for men who want to live.'

'Without honour, despised by all,' said Smith.

Nikos inclined his head and made no comment. Instead he said, 'Now Nicosia is already under siege.'

The words sank in, a bitter double blow. They were come too late, always too few and too late. Smith hung his shaggy head. It was worse, far worse, than he had expected.

'Brace up,' said Stanley to all of them, but mostly to his old comrade. 'We will not sit here and watch Cyprus go up in flames.'

'Yet what good are we now,' said young Mazzinghi, wide eyed, 'so few as we are?'

'We know a thing or two about sieges,' said Giustiniani, 'and experience counts more than numbers. We make for Nicosia. We can do some good, if Governor Dandolo will listen to us.'

'If,' said Smith, 'is a very big word.'

Giustiniani also knew that there was nothing so demoralising for men dismayed as mere talk. Whereas labour worked wonders.

He dropped over the side of the longboat into the warm water with agility, for all his sixty years, took up a bundle, and rapped out orders to the rest of them to follow. Once men got going, their spirits rose accordingly.

They knelt on the narrow beach and divided the muskets and swords, gunpowder and balls between them, as well as their food rations of dried meat, hard cheese and ship's biscuit. The rest would have to come from forage. Stanley and Mazzinghi both carried crossbows for hunting. Most precious of all were the water flasks.

'Every time we find fresh water,' said Giustiniani, 'you drain your flask, you drink until you can drink no more, then you fill your flask again and walk on.' He turned to Nikos the fisherman.

'Very well,' said Nikos. 'You ascend that gully. It is steep and crumbling but not impossible. You will come out on to a flat clifftop, a hundred or so paces of bare rock, and then scrub will hide you. Far ahead, right of the Pole Star, you will see a hill with a church dome on top, the village of Agios Nikolaos. Do not go into the village, or only in secret at nightfall. Many there would sell you to the Turk.'

'Shame on them,' said Smith.

'They are hungry,' said Nikos. 'Their children starve. Some cousins of mine live there also. So do them no harm in the night, steal not even a loaf, or you will pay for it.'

There was an awkward silence. They had to admire the grim old Greek. Unarmed, surrounded by a group of heavily armed strangers, he was still threatening them.

'We will circumnavigate this fearsome village,' said Giustiniani.

Nikos nodded. 'Beyond the village is forest, and a deep gorge carved by an ancient river. Follow the gorge up, it is good cover, but remember that it is also sweet water from the mountains, and Turks may come there to fill their flasks. A day's hard climbing, over rocks, over boulders, the gorge still flowing with snowmelt, a night's sleep, and you will come out on to the dry plateau. Ahead of you then will be the Troödos, the mist of morning upon them.

'After that, I do not know. It is not my country. But that hard sunbaked plateau is a dry country, the people have fled, and may have poisoned what wells remain for the Turk.'

The gully was as steep and crumbling as Nikos had said, and dark too. They moved slowly and carefully, finely balanced, each foothold tested before they committed their weight, leaving plenty of space between them in case of rockfalls. Several fist-sized chunks of sandstone were torn loose and rolled down the gully to land with a crack on the rocks below. But none of them was struck, at least.

At the top they crouched low and took in their surroundings. All were in a muck sweat already, thinking of water. Out to sea, gilded with the rising sun now and magnificent with her white sails and fluttering banners, the *St John* was moving westwards. Returning to Malta and the sea battle to come.

They were alone.

'Into the thorn scrub,' said Giustiniani, 'and quick about it.'

As they ran, Nicholas's sharp eyes saw a movement away to his left. He stopped and shielded his eyes and made out a peasant in a loose turban, naked to the waist, gathering salt in a leather bucket from a dried-out rockpool. The peasant stopped too and looked over at this strange apparition of men come from the sea. More Turks, were they?

'Keep moving, boy,' said Stanley, trotting past. 'Ignore him.'

By the time Nicholas got to the cover of the thorn scrub and looked back again, the salt collector had gone.

They took swigs of water from their flasks, gasping. Mazzinghi began to chatter with elation.

'Silence,' said Giustiniani harshly. He raised his hand.

They kept still. There was nothing but the silent land, the sun rising in a burning blue sky, the skitter of little lizards. The distant murmur of the sea.

And then Smith too heard something. He cupped his ear with one hand, and laid the other flat on the ground.

Time passed, sweat trickled down. Their legs ached where they squatted. A fly found them and tormented them, then another. Another skitter came from beneath a nearby clump of low thorn. Too big for a lizard. A snake?

Smith looked at Stanley and then Giustiniani. 'A marching column. Men only, I think, no pack animals.'

'And pray, no hunting dogs or we are dead men already. Stanley, leave your bundle and go on. Report back soon.'

An agony of waiting. More flies. Nicholas began to feel dizzy and shook his head. The damned Nikos had sold them to the Turk already. The bare bleached rock between the scrub was blinding. He closed his eyes and rocked on his haunches.

Stanley came back some minutes later, silent as a deer. His eyes shone with that mad humour of his.

'Brothers and gentlemen volunteers,' he said. 'We have come ashore right next to a fair company of Turkish infantry, come here, I think' – he indicated around – 'to build a lookout station on the coast, against enemy invasion.'

'Darkness and devils,' muttered Giustiniani.

'And,' said Stanley, rapidly taking up his bundle and hitching it over his shoulder, 'they have hunting hounds.'

At that very moment, there came an excitable bark from not far off – the unmistakable bark of a hound that has found fresh traces.

'Run!' cried Giustiniani.

It was farcical, humiliating, but not one of them was unafraid. If the Turks caught them, their deaths would be prolonged. They went back down the gully they had just ascended in an undignified scramble, skidding and sliding, sending loose scree slithering and dust cascading. Abdul made sure he went down first, on his bottom. Smith and Stanley knelt at the top of the gully as a rearguard, though what they could do against a column of infantrymen was unclear.

The barking sounded nearer: two of them. Two lean hunting hounds straining at the leash, tongues out, tails wagging. Their handler becoming curious as to what this fresh scent might be. The entire Turkish army on the lookout for any invasion force.

Hodge and Nicholas were down, and Mazzinghi, and now Giustiniani was descending, rapidly and without fuss, face to the cliff.

Smith reached into his bundle for his jezail. Stanley laid his hand on his comrade's.

'No, Brother. It is madness.'

'I'll die fighting.'

'No doubt. But not yet.'

The barking was barely a hundred yards off, more and more excited, and they could see low thorn trees stirring as someone passed beneath them. Smith and Stanley dropped to their bellies, pressed themselves into the ground like snakes, their dark canvas bundles cradled on the far side of them, covered in white dust.

The handler called out in Turkish to his comrades. Telling them to come to him armed. Something was up. Now he was at the spot where they had crouched, the hounds snuffing up their very drops of sweat.

Stanley loved dogs as much as any nobleman, but at that instant he could have shot the stupid beasts. Did they not know they were hunting Christians?

At last he and Smith were scrambling over into the steep gully, almost on top of each other. Smith glanced back, wondering whether to cast a handful of gunpowder over their last traces. But it was pointless, the ground was scuffed and bore the traces of where they had just been. The spoor glared back at him in the sun.

Flee, flee.

By the sea, Abdul was wild eyed, and all were staring back at the clifftop, trying not to look stricken. Nikos and his boat, the longboat, the *St John* were all vanished.

Giustiniani said, 'Lace your boots round your neck. Take nothing more in your bundle than you can swim with. Take too much and you drown. You judge. Then follow me.'

He was up to his waist in the water already. As an example to them, he took the musket from his shoulder, held it by the barrel and flung it far out to sea. All he had left now was a blanket, a sword and his provisions.

Then he struck out.

The deep cove was flanked by two great dark headlands, dropping almost sheer into the sea. Giustiniani was leading them westwards. No one knew what lay beyond. Drowning would be easy.

Abdul jabbered. 'Sea does not agree with me. Nor mountain, nor forest, nor desert. I am a man of the cities, urbane, sophisticated, erudite—'

Nicholas told him to save his breath. He would need it.

Soon they were out of their depth, clawing forward through the clear water, kicking their bare feet, their clothes and the bundles on their backs making swimming hard. Smith glanced back. Still no one on the clifftop. They might just make it.

Giustiniani was already under the thin shadow of the headland, the swell washing him up and down the rock. Impossible to hang on to even the tiniest spur or crevice, the swell would only take you off again, and the skin off your hands with it. No rest.

Hodge looked hollowed out and afraid.

Smith glanced back once more and there was a silhouette on the skyline above the cove. A man with two hounds. Then another man stepped up beside him, a long musket cradled in his arms. Smith ducked down underwater and made the last few yards round the headland. No shot was fired.

'What comes next?' gasped Hodge, moving his arms wide in the swell, muscles already aching and beginning to tremble, desperate not to reach out and hold on to Nicholas.

'Keep going,' said Giustiniani. 'There may be a cave, a break in the cliff, anything. We're out of sight for now, so move as slowly as you can without drowning.'

'If I move at all it'll be a bloody miracle,' muttered Hodge.

They floundered on. Exhaustion was approaching. Their blankets were sodden; most of them had not unburdened enough and were weighed low in the water, making swimming still harder. There were no waves but the swell was powerful. At least no currents seemed against them. But they must find rest soon.

Nicholas took his mind elsewhere and ploughed on. Salt stung his eyes. They passed beneath a tiny crystal waterspout from the gaunt cliff face, a glistening fault green with algae. No handhold there, no rest, not even safe fresh water to open the mouth to.

'Nick,' said Hodge suddenly, 'I'm going.'

Nicholas grabbed the strap of Hodge's bundle as they were both pulled underwater and wrenched it off. The bundle fell away – all Hodge's water, his provisions, his last weapon – and Hodge surfaced again, gasping.

'Breathe,' said Nicholas. 'Breathe. Lie back spreadeagled. You cannot sink in salt water, and we cannot be seen from above. Breathe.'

After a minute or more, Hodge bucked upright, hawked and spat and scooped his hair back.

'Go on,' he said.

'You first,' said Nicholas. 'I'm behind you.'

At last they came to a sharp needle of rock just a few yards off the cliff face, and clung to it like shipwrecked men. Above them the cliff was huge and ominous, but eroded at the top so they could not see the edge. So they too could not be seen. The barking of the hounds was out of earshot. It was just them and the indifferent sea.

Stanley was already hitching his bundle over Smith's shoulder, and then his laced boots.

'I go to *reconnoître*, as the French would say.'

Giustiniani nodded.

The fair-skinned Englishman with sun-bleached hair and brown arms ploughed away through the sea as confident as Neptune himself. He was back a few minutes later.

'Another couple of hundred yards and there is a low sandy beach and scrub. Very easy.'

'And very visible.'

'Aye.'

Giustiniani shook his head violently; droplets flew from his beard.

'Moor, drop your bundle. You are almost drowned.'

Abdul did as ordered. 'Your worshipful magnanimity—'

'Mazzinghi, you are struggling too. Lose your sword.'

'My father and my grandfather fought with this sword, my father at Djerba.'

'It will drown you.'

'Then, Commander, I ask permission to drown with it.'

Giustiniani swiped his brow with the back of his hand. They were all sweating, even in the sea. 'Permission granted. Young fool.'

He looked in the direction of the beach.

'We make towards it and huddle out of sight there until night-fall.' He pushed off from the rock. 'And pray for cloud tonight.'

Nicholas glanced up. The sky mocked them with its benevolent azure from east to west. Tonight would be as bright and moonlit as ever.

2

They huddled, panting, half in and half out of the water, on the seaward side of one last broken outcrop of rock before the coast flattened out into a wide sandy bay. The sun was halfway down the western sky. They fumbled for flasks in their bundles with white wrinkled fingers, and each tasted. Two of them were turned salt.

'Damn it all,' said Smith savagely.

'Speak only necessities,' said Giustiniani.

The other flasks were handed round and they drank small draughts. They would take more every half-hour or so. The summer day was long, nightfall was far off. They covered their heads with cloths. Waiting like this, sun-baked yet waterlogged, their mission already half ruined, was more exhausting than swimming.

At last it was dusk, and then darkness, and their hearts were as heavy as their sodden possessions. They would have an hour before the moon came up on their left as they walked north. They would have to go.

They crawled on to the sandy beach, all eyes, all ears. Not a sound came to them. They left off their boots and Giustiniani began the long walk, just in the shallows to kill the scent. But moving painfully slowly so as not to make a splash. They walked out across the wide bay feeling like actors crossing a bright stage. The whipcrack of Turkish musket, the skull-splitting impact, their slow fall into the small waves, the billowing red stain ... They could picture it all.

*

Yet they made it across the bay without mishap. They knelt in the deeper shadows below a ridge of rock, and Mazzinghi began to unbundle so he could wring out his blanket.

'Not yet,' said Giustiniani.

The young knight looked puzzled. 'It weighs so heavy. Like carrying a mule on my back.'

Giustiniani gestured back towards the sea.

Mazzinghi rolled his eyes. 'Oh no, for the love of—'

'For the love of God and our duty,' said Giustiniani, 'it is back to sea with us. The country is swarming with Turks, the moon is nearly up, and we must put miles between them and us. So it is round the coast we go, weary as we are. And in darkness.'

Mazzinghi hung his handsome head, curly locks plastered to his cheek.

'But come, Brother, we are still young and vigorous, are we not?' said Giustiniani. Born in the Year of Grace 1509.

Mazzinghi managed a weary smile. If this old dog could do it, so could he.

They were allowed a hard biscuit or two, salty and damp, and more freshwater. 'But pray we find a decent spring soon,' said Smith.

The coast beyond was more broken and rocky, and there was less danger of drowning. But the water was now liquid black, spangled with starlight, the rocks eroded and rough, their hands and feet already pitted and scratched, stinging and humming with the salt sting. There was little wind and small waves, but strong currents and eddies hauled them to and fro, dragged at their leaden limbs, tormented them. Water slopped and boomed in caves beneath the cliffs so dark they could not even see into them. What monsters lurked there? Nicholas and Hodge could not help but picture huge dark-finned fish circling, jagged jaws agape. This was the landscape Andromeda was chained in. The thought of a beautiful naked girl chained to a rock might usually heat the loins. But no, thought Nicholas with bitter humour, squeezing his reddened eyes free of blinding salt water. Not a stirring. Nor would any Perseus come to save them. It was just them and the sea and the sky, and their strength and stubborn will to embrace their predestined fate.

They scrambled repeatedly up over rock, dripping wet, boots laced round their necks cascading water, descended the other side, dropped back into the water, swam a few yards, scrambled out over another rock; or swam along a sheer cliff face, trying to clutch to whatever tiny fragments of mica or embedded quartz they could find, fingers torn, fingernails now as soft as wet rag, bony flanks buffeted and bruised by the swell.

And then, their eyes now accustomed to the starlit darkness, they were suddenly blinded by the appearance of the moon over the western sea. No comfort at all. Like a white burning torch, a flare of pure magnesia, held in their faces, burning their eyeballs. A cold interrogator.

'Some trick of Pedro Deza's,' muttered Nicholas.

Part joke, part exhausted hallucination.

They were all in a dream when they heard a bell tower tolling midnight from far inland. Some priest would be kneeling defiantly in a lonely church, dedicated to some saint they knew nothing of – St Spiridon, St Mamas – before a single taper, an icon of the Virgin, praying for the destruction of the Turks.

Giustiniani lay on his belly on a flat white rock. Soon the others were sitting around him, heads bowed, puddles of water spreading round them.

'That priest should learn to worship in silence,' said Abdul. 'Or the Turks will teach him soon.'

Smith said at last, 'I suppose we walk now.'

Giustiniani raised his head, and then rolled over and hauled himself up from his undignified position.

'We walk until dawn,' he said, pulling on his boots. 'But let us get over there, under those trees.'

They drained their flasks and ate half their cheese and some biscuit. After half an hour's rest they felt slightly more alive again.

They stood and wrung out their woollen blankets – a two-man job, one at each end.

'I can't believe we brought blankets,' said Nicholas. 'In this heat.'

'They make fine sacks,' said Stanley, 'soft bedding on hard ground, and in the Troödos, you will be glad of their warmth, believe me. It snows in winter there as hard as in England, and in spring the snowmelt comes down the gorges in torrents.'

They wiped their swords dry as best they could, and the last firearm among them was broodingly inspected. Smith and his treasured Persian jezail. There was no way he would have abandoned that. But it needed a soak in fresh water soon, and then a good oil. As for their gunpowder – it would need a week of drying. Until then, they felt as vulnerable as lambs.

'Do you think Nikos sold us to the Turks?' asked Nicholas.

Smith shook his head. 'He didn't have time. There was a marching column there anyway. Just our ill luck. Turks everywhere. The island is swarming.'

Lala Pasha had brought an army of a hundred thousand men to Cyprus, it was said. An exaggeration, surely. Yet some forty thousand had come to Malta, six years before. The Ottoman Empire seemed inexhaustible.

'Don't look now,' said Stanley, and all froze at his tone. 'But there is a pair of yellow eyes watching us from behind that carob tree.'

Nicholas whipped round – he couldn't help himself. And there was a curious goat, staring at them out of the darkness.

He sighed. 'I'd call you a damned fool if you weren't a knight and I a mere penniless vagabond.'

'And don't you forget it,' said Stanley.

Smith was reaching slowly for his crossbow, salt-encrusted though it was, his eyes never leaving the munching goat. But just as he brought the quarrel towards the stock, the goat turned and ambled off unhurriedly, soon lost to view in the thorn scrub.

'Run after it,' suggested Stanley helpfully.

Smith dropped the crossbow, scowling. 'You run after it, blubberguts.'

'We can't risk a cooking fire anyway,' said Mazzinghi.

'You mean you have never eaten raw goat?' said Stanley. 'Bloody liver, still warm from the paunch? Brother John here wouldn't eat it any other way. Though admittedly he is rather *primitive*.'

'On your feet, you gossiping women,' said Giustiniani. 'The Turks are wasting no time at Nicosia, be sure of that. So neither may we.' He glanced up. 'Five hours till dawn. I want to be fifteen miles along the coast by then. You can sleep in the day. And after that, it's inland, and the mountains.'

Even getting to their feet was weary work. Their boots were sodden and chafing.

They went west.

3

After hours of walking, stumbling, eyes closing as they walked, they came to a desolate peninsula. The moon now hanging in the west, the faintest hint of grey dawn out over the sea. It was a barren spit of land, wind-scoured rock and scrub, soon baking under the burning sun. There were small caves cut in the rocks.

Nicholas came to the edge of a drop and there before him, entirely below ground level, hidden from view until now, was a substantial courtyard with fine stone columns, and further chambers opening off into darkness so thick it was like black dust.

'What is this place?' he murmured.

'Some kind of ancient burial ground,' said Stanley. 'But a good place to find shelter in the day.'

Hodge said, 'I'm not steppin' down there. This place is brimful of witchery or my name's not Hodge.'

'Then lie out on the rocks and cook like a side of beef,' said Stanley. 'There is no other shelter.'

Abdul squatted and stared down, more fascinated than afraid.

'I know such places,' he said. 'In my country we say they are the haunt of djinns, but really they are more like the tombs of the Egyptians, in the time of Jahiliyah.'

Smith said roughly, 'Speak a proper tongue.'

'That is to say, in the time of darkness. Before the coming of the Prophet, peace be upon him.'

'Plague and boils,' muttered Smith. 'Travelling to war with a Mussulman. We must be moonstruck.'

Abdul smiled. 'Where there is chaos there is opportunity.

Besides, you know we Moors are not always the closest friends with the Turk.'

'You are for yourself and yourself alone, is that it?'

'No one cares for me as well as I do. Now,' he nodded downwards, 'the tombs of the Egyptians are famous for their hidden treasures.'

'That is all you have come for, in this accursed war? To hunt for treasure?'

'You keep your God, I'll take the gold.'

He had less soul than a dog, this one.

Abdul read Smith's thoughts and grinned, and then began to climb down the rock face into the hidden courtyard.

They lay up in the shadowy recesses of the courtyard, ate and drank, talked softly.

'Do we believe the army of Lala Mustafa is really a hundred thousand strong?' said Mazzinghi.

Stanley grimaced. 'We do not know, and will never know. But it is certainly enough for the job.'

'And seven of us,' said Mazzinghi, 'one a Moor. We must be crazy. Why are we here?'

'A knight is worth his weight in gold to any Christian army,' said Smith. 'We are the elite. We are worth a dozen Janizaries apiece. Four of us, that's . . .'

There was a long pause.

'Forty-eight,' said Stanley kindly.

'Of course. Any fool knows that.' He half-drew his sword and then slammed it back home. 'Anyway, the devil invented arithmetic.'

They were so exhausted, Giustiniani did not move them on at dusk. Instead he sent Smith and Stanley out to find fresh water under cover of darkness. Smith was also desperate to clean off his jezail, in a horse trough if necessary. They might steal some bread too, God forgive them. The rest could have a few more hours' sleep, but must go before dawn.

'Neither Turk not Greek will come here,' said Giustiniani softly. 'They will all believe it is haunted by demons.'

Smith and Stanley returned with water and wine, bread and olive oil. Smith used the oil on his jezail. Not the best thing, but it would serve for now. His powder had been drying all day, although what the addition of salt might do to the mix was uncertain. Anyway, he could not fire. The sound would only bring worse danger.

Abdul returned from several forays into the dark chambers within, only to return with nothing but the stains of bat droppings on his knees and elbows. 'And even I do not care to go farther,' he said. 'It is an ill place.'

He slept seated cross-legged, as if ready to flee more quickly.

Nicholas slept uneasily on his damp blanket. There was a stale odour of something ancient and unholy in this place. Above them the square of starlit sky.

He woke some time in the dead of night to hear scuttling in the darkness. He propped himself up on one elbow. It came again. Not a scuttling. A slithering. His blood froze.

'Stanley,' he whispered. 'Stanley.'

The knight awoke and tousled his shaggy blond hair and stared at him.

'Listen.'

They listened.

'A bat,' said Stanley. 'Come, Ingoldsby, you are too old for such childish imaginings.'

'Don't condescend to me,' hissed Nicholas, fear making him angry. 'Your ears are so deafened with years of cannon fire, you hear as well as an old maid. I know a snake or a bat when I hear one, and that was no damned bat.'

There was another sound. Stanley looked puzzled. Beggars, orphan children seeking shelter ...?

Nevertheless he shook Smith awake. Smith was on his feet with drawn sword in an instant.

And then, with sheer terror, Nicholas saw the demon crouching in the mouth of the chamber, eerily lit by the moonlight, hollow black eyes staring at them. His face otherwise was horribly feature-less. Nicholas was shaking. He could not even stand.

The palpable dread in the air had made the others stir and begin to waken too.

But Smith was already driving his sword back home in its scabbard. 'Fine spies we make,' he growled. 'Gentlemen, we have been sleeping in the middle of a spital-house. A leper colony.'

Abdul was up the walls and out on to the plateau like a monkey, jabbering about leprosy.

The rest rose quickly and gathered their belongings.

'Our brother Reynaldo, medical chaplain back on Malta,' said Stanley, 'always said that a strong and healthy man will not be stricken with leprosy, even if he sleep with a leprous whore.'

'For my part,' said Giustiniani, 'though I esteem Fra Reynaldo as much as any, it is a thing I'd not put to the test. Gentlemen. It is time to march.'

They came out on to the plateau, rubbed their eyes and drank water.

Behind them came a strange, small figure. In the bright moonlight, Nicholas now saw that it was a boy of some thirteen or fourteen years of age. He wore a loincloth and his legs and feet were hale and bare. But his poor ravaged arms and hands were covered in filthy bandages, and his head and face completely hidden under more bandages but for his eyes. In his hand he clutched a small bell, fingers round the clapper for silence. He stared at them intently.

'Move on,' said Giustiniani.

Something made Nicholas hesitate. The boy wanted to communicate with them. Yet how could he talk with bandages over his mouth? What mouth he had left from the ravages of that terrible affliction. His heart went out to him.

The boy stood and watched as Nicholas went towards him. Those dark Greek eyes stared back at him. Then the boy touched his chest, gestured out to all of them, and then widely eastwards. Towards the Troödos mountains.

'He wants to come with us.'

'We have a dubious Moor with us already,' said Smith, 'and only one firearm between us, well salted. Time runs on, and Kyrenia is already fallen. All we need do now is add a leper to our party to cook up a truly filthy broth.'

'Wait,' said Nicholas. 'I remember you saying about all the monasteries in the Troödos. The holy men.'

'What of it?'

'The holy men and ... *healers*.'

Stanley looked at him very steadily. 'You think the leper boy wants to come with us to find a healer?'

Nicholas nodded. 'And perhaps be our guide?'

'Our guide?' Smith snorted. 'He cannot even speak, his tongue is rotted in his head.'

'But he can walk. Look.'

Smith and Stanley exchanged glances.

'And nothing happens without the hand of Providence. You have said this yourself many a time, Edward Stanley.'

Giustiniani looked undecided. The boy was inching closer to them, but not too close, like a dog many times whipped, but desperate.

A few minutes later they headed out across the plateau. Seven of them, barely armed, led by a leper, against an army of a hundred thousand.

The plateau was burning hot and exposed in the day, and the rock glaring white. Their eyeballs throbbed, their heads hurt.

'Speak if you see a fire-pit,' said Smith.

After a time Hodge pointed. Giustiniani called a halt and Smith went over and squatted beside a shallow blackened pit. He laid his hand flat in the ash.

'Not recent.' He picked among the cinders. 'Take up a handful of black ash, spit, and then blacken around your eyes.'

'All of you,' said Giustiniani. 'Help each other. It will lessen the glare off the ground, and keep us dark as blackamoors in the night.'

Stanley smeared Nicholas's face. He stood back. 'You look like a beaten husband.' He grinned. 'Such is marriage.'

Later a thorn went right through Hodge's boot and they had to stop to dig it out. Even then the tip remained, reddening and painful. Smith made him bandage it. 'It'll dissolve in your flesh in time.'

They walked on a while more, Hodge limping. At last they stopped as the sun rose high, lying up in the paltry shade of sparse thorn trees, pouring with sweat, dry with thirst. The mountains seemed far off.

'Prickles and thorns,' cursed Mazzinghi. 'Every leaf on this island is barbed.'

After a long while Smith said, 'What's the difference between a cypress leaf and a French rapier?'

They shook their heads wearily.

'A cypress leaf has a prick at one end, a French rapier has a prick at both ends.'

Stanley raised his head and stared, mouth agape. 'Brother John has made a jest!'

'It's the delivery,' said Nicholas.

'A crude and amateur sort of jest, admittedly,' said Stanley. 'Well laboured. But for him to summon enough wit in his battered head to make any jest at all is indeed a historic occasion. O for a bottle of hock to celebrate this remarkable event.'

'Ah, shut your trap,' said Smith. 'Save spit.'

At night they approached the village on the hill that Nikos had spoken of, setting dogs barking and straining on their chains. They skirted round and into a wood of pines, and ever deeper darkness. The leper boy led them. Once they lost him, he had gone so far ahead, scampering over rocks and up steep slopes as if he were in perfect health. And then they heard the silvery tinkle of his bell, and made towards it, and there he was, squatting beside a boulder, unable to smile. But his eyes shining.

'We must find water,' said Giustiniani. He mimicked the action of drinking from a flask.

The boy nodded and gestured ahead. They followed him. Always uphill.

And then abruptly downhill again, slithering on steep slopes of pine needles, and a strange coolness in the air, rising up from below. And the sound of water.

He had brought them down into a great gorge, thickly grown, full of boulders and fallen tree trunks. One great black pine was smashed in two by a boulder that lay alongside, hurled into it by the force of the torrent. But the gorge was well hidden and, best of all, held fresh flowing water, even at this time of year.

The gorge deepened and the walls rose either side of them, dank and ominous. The rock was clay and chalk, thick with ferns, slippery as eel-skin, impossible to escape from now. They felt horribly trapped.

'If the Turks find us here,' said Giustiniani, 'if they have dogs, or if some goatherd sees us and betrays us – we are dead men.'

The leper boy gestured onward.

At last the gorge rose up steeply and they had to climb hand and foot the last hundred feet out on to a plateau, their breathing shallow, afraid, clutching on to ferns and roots and dubious rock. Nicholas glanced back at one point. But for a jutting spur it was a sheer drop behind.

They made it out alive. The leper boy managed to climb too, even with his withered and bandaged hands. What it must cost him. Then Nicholas remembered that at least lepers feel no pain in their diseased limbs. A tingling then a numbness are the first signs of that affliction.

They came to a village more like the skeleton of a village. A mill creaked in the desolate wind. They moved cautiously between the huts, hands on their sword hilts. They called out. Deserted.

The well was poisoned and foul smelling. Some carcass was down there, sheep or goat, and fattened flies arose in clouds.

'Many villages will be like this,' said Giustiniani. 'Many Greeks have fled to Crete, or drowned on the crossing. We can expect no great welcome here.'

A bell tinkled. It was the leper boy, summoning them onward.

It was a day of the uncanny. Once there came a loud boom from the mountains ahead.

'The Turkish guns?' said Mazzinghi.

Stanley shook his head. 'Only thunder.'

Yet there was not a cloud in the sky.

In the dusk they came to a small rocky outcrop with a thin cross atop it and a cave below, and in the mouth of the cave sat a starveling figure in goatskins.

They paused. The figure did not move but only stared at them with hollow eyes. Not one of them there did not feel a chill. Then the figure stirred and said, with a voice like the wind among dead leaves, 'You have come.'

Giustiniani stepped forward. 'Who are you?'

The skeletal figure raised a stick-like arm, spotted with unhealed sores, and pointed up to the cross on the rocks above. 'As for my name,' he said, 'it was long since taken from me.'

'You are a healer?'

'For the healing of the nations and the sins of mankind,' he said, then took a deep breath, as if already exhausted. 'And for my soul, I pray.'

'Have Turks passed this way? Is there fighting?'

Eyes rolled white in his skull. Smith muttered that there was little point in speaking with this creature, more crackbrain than hermit or holy man.

'We are haunted by dogs, by Turks, by the moon itself. The mountains are against us, the pines groan all night in their sickness.'

Smith was already turning away in disgust.

'The Turkish cannons roar, they tear open the sky, heaven itself bleeds, red rain rains down.'

'Peace, old father,' said Giustiniani more gently, then, catching Stanley's eye, shook his head and indicated they should press on.

They began to move away, bowing uncertainly, disconsolate, half afraid. Everything they had seen on Cyprus so far had filled them with foreboding, made them feel accursed.

Then the hermit said, 'The leper boy has come far to see me. Kneel, boy.'

And they watched astonished as the leper boy went slowly back to him and kneeled down, and the hermit laid his hand on the boy's bandaged head.

'Whatever healing may come, Lord, send it soon,' said the hermit softly.

Finally the boy rose again. Then he held his bell up and tinkled it and marched onward.

They slept in a dry gully. The mountains rose ahead of them and a cooler wind came off them. Nicholas drew his blanket round him, against the cool night air, and some nameless fear.

In the morning the leper boy had gone.

'Look to your weapons,' said Smith, 'he may have betrayed us.'

'He has not!' said Nicholas hotly. 'Unlike most men he has no speech, he is wordless and so as innocent as a faithful hound that has no language and so cannot lie.'

Smith looked at him broodingly from under his black brows. 'I'll track him,' he said. 'Wait here.'

It was half an hour before he returned, and his expression was distant and strange. He sat down as if in no hurry, though they must press onward, ever onward.

'Brother?' said Stanley.

'He lies up yonder,' said Smith. 'Half covered in leaves, lying as if asleep. He led us so far, and then went away from us in the night in solitude, to commit himself into the hands of God.'

Nicholas bowed his head.

Smith stood again and briefly laid his huge hand on him.

Stanley said, 'So that was his healing. Death's ending, which is the great beginning.'

On the brow of the hill, Smith looked back one last time and said to Nicholas, 'God will make it right. This life is but a chapter, and there is more to come.'

Nicholas said bitterly, 'I trust so. Otherwise,' he held his arms wide, 'this whole majestic starry universe is not worth a dunghill.'

Then they could see the mist among the pine-clad slopes of the Troödos, as Nikos had said, and they were climbing steeply into mountains higher than any in all of Britain.

There were springs of water, and bramble and ivy, 'just like Shropshire,' said Hodge delightedly. And there were wild brown trout in the streams. Hodge took great pride in tickling them and providing good fish for their supper.

''S not tickling really,' he said. 'It's more sliding your hand gently under, and' – he gave a deft flick – 'scoopin' 'em out on the bank before they can escape. Like that.'

Giustiniani said they could risk a small cooking fire, and so they ate trout skewered on greenwood twigs over a spitting pinewood fire, and this journey of theirs, hitherto so sad and strange, did not seem so bad. Though ahead of them, as they well knew, lay only the Turkish guns and the agony of Nicosia.

Nicholas wished they could fight up here, in the coolness and the pine-scented air. But it would be down below, there on the burning plain, that they would fight, and some of them would die.

4

There were thunderstorms, precipitous mountain paths made of nothing but sloping scree above thousand-foot canyons, and a ransacked monastery inhabited by just one old priest. He had nothing to give them, and they nothing to give him, yet he laid his hand on his heart as if to say thank you to them. He never spoke a word, sitting among the smoking ruins.

Smith said, 'So the Turks have passed this way.'

Then they ascended a last slope on to a saddle of the mountains, with higher peaks rising to left and to right of them. And ahead, out on that burning plain below them, they could just make out a walled city, almost obscured by the great ochre cloud that hung over it.

'A sandstorm,' said Mazzinghi, trying to sound wiser than his years. 'It's early in the year for it.'

The air shuddered with a hollow distant boom.

'That's no sandstorm,' said Abdul softly.

'No,' said Smith. 'That's the Turkish bombardment. And that dust cloud there was once Nicosia's walls.'

Mazzinghi blanched visibly, and Nicholas shivered with a mixture of dread and excitement. But the dread was strong. Dread that he could not take it all again, after those four terrible months of siege on Malta. Dread that he would dishonour himself, crack and run in the hell and din of battle.

He caught Hodge's eye. What were they doing here, after all?

Hodge read him instantly. 'We don't have to be here,' he said quietly. 'If we can't return to England, we could still find some-where more peaceful than this.'

'But it'll be something to tell your grandchildren. How you fought in the Cyprus wars.'

'They'll never believe it. They'll just have me medicined and put in Bedlam.'

'We're already in Bedlam!' cried Nicholas, laughing that wild, sudden laugh when the fit was on him and a silver light shone in his eyes.

He knew why he was here. For the memory of his father. For dreams of a pure cause in an impure world. For days of hardship and grandeur, and pity for those who lived in lesser days.

The older knights were studying the plain before them gravely, as if it were a military map. Nicosia was in a terrible position, on flat low land surrounded by hills.

Giustiniani said, 'That great engineer Savoragno did his damnedest, pleading with the Venetian senate for more work to be done on the defences, but those wise elders did nothing. He had only enough time and money to reduce the old nine-mile circuit to three, add some ramparts, and eleven decent enough bastions. And that was all.'

'Now Venice will pay for its parsimony,' said Stanley.

'Not if we can help it,' said Giustiniani. Yet at that moment another great bombardment juddered through the air, mocking his words. Turkish cannon big enough for a man to crawl inside, belching flame and black powder smoke and iron balls of two hundred pounds or more.

Another plume of ochre dust rose slowly into the still-hot air.

Smith brandished his sword. 'Nicosia, endure! We are coming!'

They descended out of the mountains for a long night and more cautiously the next day, keeping to the edge of woods or ravines thick with undergrowth. Creeping like animals. But Turkish patrols could be anywhere. Indeed, a warier commander than Lala Mustafa would have stationed lookout troops on the heights of the Troödos, but there was no sign of any. An indication of confidence. He commanded an army of tens of thousands, and a fleet that already owned every port on the island except Famagusta. Why should he worry?

And he was right. No Venetian force had come against him, no Holy League. Just a reckless, ludicrous band of seven knights and adventurers. And they had got through so far as much because of Lala's negligence as their own skill.

Then they were down through the last foothills, past deserted farmsteads and villages, and on to the plain. Nicosia was a few miles off, and the rows upon rows of Turkish tents much nearer.

They dropped down behind some rocks. There was no wind, it was midday. The dusty ground at their feet was soon spotted with their sweat. They might as well have rested in a bread oven.

'So,' said Nicholas, 'how do we break into Nicosia?'

'Break in?' said Stanley, a mocking light in his eye. 'Ah yes. We crawl in through a secret tunnel, do we not, unknown to the Turks? Through an ancient water culvert, perhaps, or even a cavern piled high with Orient treasure?'

Nicholas looked sour.

'I have been thinking,' said Abdul.

'So have we,' said Smith sharply.

'Yes, but if you will permit me. As a shifty and unchristened Moor, my mind is doubtless more subtle and devious than yours.'

Giustiniani smiled. 'Let him speak.'

Abdul said, 'We need to act the part of those whom the Turks would not kill, but would actively want to enter the city – and whom the Venetians would receive in peace, not shoot dead from the walls as we approach. Now hear my plan.'

A few minutes later, Smith was arguing furiously with Giustiniani. 'They will take our weapons! Even this jezail, made of the very finest Indian wootz steel, the best rifled musket perhaps in all of—'

The older knight said, 'Brother John, we have argued enough. I am in command here, and I say we may trust this Moor, at least so far, and I like his plan as the best – or the least foolish – that I have heard. Now be silent and obey.'

Smith dropped his head, teeth grating.

174

'Oh, and one more thing. That banner of St John you are carrying. It will have to go.'

Smith looked up again, his eyes blazing. But Giustiniani's grizzled features were set hard, and he was indeed in command. Smith slowly reached into his knapsack and drew out the furled banner. For a man of his temper, obedience was always far harder than poverty or chastity. He walked slowly away and dug a hole in the shadow of a wall.

They walked in single file across the plain. Giustiniani went first. Smith carried a white sheet knotted to a stave. The noise of the Turkish bombardment falling on the wretched, beleaguered city ahead never stopped. It filled them with foreboding.

So intent were the Turks on their prize, so negligent of the most basic guard duties, that the seven were in among the conical tents before they were challenged.

A single Turkish infantryman turned and stared at them, stony faced, disbelieving. Then he raised his musket, which was unloaded, and called, 'Halt!'

His finger twitched on the trigger. Then two more infantrymen ran up, and some pikemen, pike-heads lowered at the crazed intruders.

'Where is your commander?' asked Giustiniani with such quiet authority that one of the infantrymen immediately ran off.

'Put your hands on your heads!' said the first infantryman.

They did so.

Another was loading his musket, ramming down the ball. He raised the muzzle again until it was just a few inches from Smith's head.

The sweat trickled down.

A burly Turk with a broad gold belt around his middle and a thick black beard appeared before them.

'Who the hell are you? Who is the Moor? Is he a Christian?'

Giustiniani still spoke quietly, in fluent Turkish.

'We are come from Venice to order Governor Dandolo to surrender.'

'How did you come here?'

'Across the mountains. The Greeks betrayed us, we were set upon in the night and robbed of even our mules. Yet we would not fail in our mission. The moment we awoke and drew our swords, they fled.'

The Ottoman commander approved of this portrait of the accursed and cowardly Greeks. They would rob their own grand-mothers. And the surrender of Nicosia would save them a heap of trouble. He eyed them from under bushy eyebrows. 'You go well armed for mere ambassadors.'

Giustiniani said, '*It is hard to borrow a sword on a battlefield.*'

There was a light in the commander's eyes. 'You know this Turkish proverb?'

Giustiniani gave a little bow.

The commander scowled again. 'Perhaps you are spies? I will send to the Pasha.'

He ordered his men to march them under close guard to the ground before his tent and sit them in the dust, hands still on their heads.

They sat, eyes blinded by the hot sun. Their swords still at their sides, Smith's jezail across his back.

'Now comes the difficult part,' whispered Stanley. 'Lala Mustafa is a savage in a silk robe.'

It was a long, long time before the commander returned. No one offered them water.

He stood before them, two Janizaries at either side. Towering men, fair skinned, extravagantly moustachioed. Slavs more than Turks.

'The Pasha is pleased to learn that Venice has come to its senses,' he said. 'You will pass on into Nicosia unmolested, and we expect a written surrender from Dandolo by nightfall. You will leave your arms behind.'

'That we cannot do,' said Giustiniani.

The commander's midnight brows contracted again. 'You are in no position to refuse.'

'A word, sire,' said Stanley.

The commander grunted.

Stanley took a couple of steps closer to him and spoke sotto voce. He stepped back.

The commander scrutinized this broad-shouldered, powerfully built Christian, with his ruddy and sunburned cheeks, tousled fair hair, and laughing blue eyes, taller even than his two Janizaries here. Yes, the women would go for this one. Was he truly only an ambassador?

He smiled. 'This is very funny.' Then he laughed abruptly. 'Very funny indeed! Let me send to the Pasha again.'

They sat for another hour. Even during a siege, Ottoman ritual and etiquette remained famously leisurely.

'The devil knows how they conquered half the world,' muttered Smith.

The commander returned once more, and this time he ordered them to stand and pass on into his spacious tent.

The sides were folded up to catch any breeze, and after the oven of the sun-baked plain outside, it felt refreshingly cool. To their astonishment, wordlessly, they were brought sherbet in silver goblets. Iced sherbet. In May. The ice was brought down in straw-packed panniers from the heights of Mount Olympos. By June it would all be melted. But for now ...

Nicholas could have laughed at the dreamlike unreality of it all. He reclined on a large satin cushion and raised his goblet to Hodge.

'Enjoy it while you can.'

'Aye, we'll be in Nicosia soon, and no iced sherbet there, I wager. We'll be glad to drink mule piss.'

When they had finished, they filed from the tent and were given ponies to ride. The commander had one last word with Stanley. He said, 'The Pasha was amused by your tale. He says he hopes it was good sport! You may keep your weapons.'

Under escort of a dozen Janizaries, they went on their way.

'What the devil did you tell him back there?' demanded Smith. 'You crafty devilish schemer and liar, more snake than that Moor there.'

'Please do not derogate me,' said Abdul. 'I am *far* more of a liar and schemer than this noble knight.'

Stanley rode on, his silence infuriating.

'Ned Stanley, you swine, tell or be damned.'

'Aye,' said Giustiniani, 'that's an order. I had no idea of any more tales.'

Stanley said, 'I simply told him that we had to stay armed, because we couldn't wholly trust Dandolo's conduct towards us. The reason?' He smoothed his handsome fair beard. 'I said that Governor Dandolo had once caught me in flagrante with his own wife.'

All looked admiring except Smith, who looked disgusted.

'This both amused our enemy,' Stanley went on, 'pleased them to think that Governor Dandolo was but a ridiculous cuckold, and made them still more friendly towards us, the Venetian party come to have Nicosia surrender, and save the Turks a deal more trouble and gunpowder. You see, Fra John, what a little quick wit can do? Instead of mere blockhead muscle and bluster?'

'You devil,' muttered Smith. 'You born devil. I swear all this time in the East is turning you into a damned lying, snake-tongued Oriental.'

'I do not think,' said Abdul politely, 'that Orientals have the monopoly on lying, sir knight. Was not Adam, the father of all mankind, less than honest in Eden?'

'Eden was in the Orient too,' said Smith, and thumped his heels so hard into the flanks of his mount that the poor beast sounded like a kettledrum.

5

The long ride through the vast Ottoman encampment showed them nothing they didn't know already. The organization of the Turks was impeccable, the ranks and files of tents arrayed in gigantic squares across the plain, with broad avenues in between. And the resources of Lala Mustafa were limitless. His cannons nestled behind strongly built earthen ramparts, the gunners hidden from enemy snipers behind wicker breastworks. Unlike on Malta, there was plenty of timber on Cyprus, and plenty of earth too, compared to that barren rock. They saw cannonballs stacked in pyramids as high as a man, powder barrels by the hundred under canvas awnings, and sensed a besieging army indeed in the tens of thousands. Every nation under the Ottoman sun was here, and more besides: Bokharans, Armenians, Syrians, Egyptian Mamelukes ... Stanley swore later that he heard one powder-blackened gunnery team speaking Dutch.

As they passed out in front of the Turkish line to cross the bare no man's land beneath the walls of Nicosia, approaching the southern gate, a strict order ran along the line and the guns fell silent. Their ears rang in the silence. They had bought the city a brief respite, perhaps a quarter of an hour.

'Probably the biggest contribution we'll make,' said Smith sourly.

Coming closer, they could see how damaged the walls were already.

'Sweet saviour,' said Stanley.

The huge angled bastion to the right of the facing wall was already half pounded into a slope of rubble. Another couple of days, and Lala Mustafa would be sending in his Janizaries to finish it off.

If they thought Ottoman etiquette was slow, etiquette in Nicosia was sorely wanting. The gatekeepers kept them and their Janizary guard waiting for ten minutes before any answer came. The main gateways themselves were so deeply bulked they could not be opened, so a sally port would be unbarred, a low door in the wall just wide enough for one man to enter at a time, bent almost double. Meanwhile, on the walls, Venetian musketeers appeared and had them closely covered.

As he passed into the darkened archway, Nicholas saw a cannon-ball actually buried in the stonework beside him. He reached out and touched it. Still hot.

The sally port was heavily barred again behind them.

'Who the hell are you?' demanded a sergeant with a bloody bandage round his ear. The second time they had been asked that today.

Giustiniani ignored him and pointed back at the sally port. 'It is not being used?'

The sergeant shrugged. 'Not that I know of.'

'Let me see the walls.'

'Your weapons first.'

'Damn it, you cur, we are Knights of St John. Out of the way.'

And the seven swept past the Venetian pikemen and their ser-geant as if they were kings.

No, six. Nicholas stared around.

Abdul was gone.

Smith realized too and ground his teeth. 'How could we lose him? Fools. He'll be fighting with the Turks now.'

'No.' Nicholas shook his head. 'He's no fighter. He just wants to survive.'

Smith muttered another obscenity about Moors, and they hurried up the shallow stone steps to the bastion right of the main gate. The soldiers followed nonplussed.

Below they could see the Janizaries returning to the Ottoman lines at a fast trot with seven riderless ponies.

Stanley said, 'We'd better get off the walls. The bombardment will start again soon.'

Sure enough, across the two hundred yards of no man's land, they could already see gunnery teams cleaning and reloading the guns.

They reached the street below just as a huge cannonball struck somewhere not far ahead and brought down a last tottering wall. The narrow street filled with billowing dust. They crouched and spat, their eyes closed, and then out of the dust cloud ahead wandered an old woman carrying a kitten. The kitten was dead, she carried it by its swollen head.

'That bad already?' whispered Nicholas.

It was. The kitten was the old woman's supper. And if she got home before someone robbed her of it at knifepoint, she would count herself lucky.

The sergeant said, 'Each day the worst yet. Tomorrow we'll be in hell.'

'To the Governor's palace. Urgently.'

Everything they saw as they hurried through the shattered streets of Nicosia made the sergeant's words more real. Barely a building was untouched; the dust hung in funereal wreaths. There was a stench of sickness, of decay, perhaps even of the dreaded fevers that came with siege and bad water. But still worse was the sense of listless defeat. This was a city nearly finished in spirit, regardless of the state of the walls. They passed by a child's body lying in the gutter, unburied, not even covered for decency, and at the end of the same street, four exhausted soldiers playing dice.

'Why not dice over there!' roared Smith at them with abrupt ferocity, indicating a crucified Christ in the wall of a church. 'At the foot of the cross!'

The soldiers stared back at him, begrimed, exhausted, half starved, not understanding.

By the time they came to the Governor's palace, Giustiniani had changed his plan. He would not be requesting an audience.

'Where is he?' he demanded.

181

They stormed into a wood-panelled chamber to find the Governor of Nicosia finishing a late lunch. He had just turned angrily on a fellow in a battered breastplate standing near, and hissed, 'Knights of St John! It was the knights who began this whole accursed war!'

He saw them, mopped his mouth and stood.

Niccolo Dandolo, scion of one of the noblest Venetian families and direct descendant of old Doge Dandolo, was a lean man of middle years. His stockings betrayed calves that would win him no admiration from court ladies or courtesans, he wore his dull grey hair brushed forward low over his forehead in an unbecoming style, and his eyes were small and mistrustful.

Giustiniani spoke before he did, explaining who they were and why they had come in just two rapped-out sentences, a miracle of concision.

'Knights of St John,' said Dandolo. 'You are welcome here.' His tone managed to convey quite the opposite meaning. 'And so Venice has sent no more aid, nor instructions to negotiate with the Turk?'

'Neither.'

Dandolo looked bitter. 'Well then. Every extra sword is welcome. My sergeant-at-arms here will show you to your positions.'

Giustiniani bowed.

And then, infuriated by this late lunch and this smooth false talk, the dicing soldiers and the dead child left uncovered in the street, and Nicosia slowly falling to the ground around them, Smith butted in, voice raised.

'We come to give you our counsel, man! We who stood through the Siege of Malta for four long months, and made it one of the famous victories of Christendom. But this siege is a bloody shambles! Will you not listen to us?'

Giustiniani turned on him with a savage expression. 'Brother!'

Dandolo mopped his mouth again, unnecessarily. His voice was cold. 'Your passion is admirable, Brother ...'

'Smith. John Smith, Knight Grand Cross.'

Somewhere not far off, another cannonball hurtled home. The coloured windowpanes rattled. Dandolo twitched.

'Brother *Smit*. But your counsel is not required. Your aid is of course most welcome. And since I am Governor of this city, you are now under my command. To the bastion of Costanza with you now.' He spoke to them as he would to schoolboys. 'Off, off with you! We have other matters to attend to.'

Outside the palace, Giustiniani turned on Smith in a fury.

'We are here for one reason and one reason only. To offer counsel and advice to that fool Dandolo. It is our only value here.'

'And advice I offered!'

'Not immediately, and clumsy as a bull at a cardinal's dinner, you blubbering vainglorious idiot!'

Smith was open mouthed, but Stanley too looked angered with him.

'I had it all planned,' said Giustiniani. 'After a day or two of, frankly, gross flattery and servility, we might just have begun to offer Dandolo the most tentative and subtle advice about how to rescue his wretched Nicosia from its doom. But you blunder in and offend him instantly. He will never listen to us now. We are wasted here.' He walked on ahead, bristling.

'We can still fight,' said Smith stubbornly.

'Yes, seven of us,' snapped Stanley. 'No, six, the Moor is gone. To fight this besieging army of tens of thousands. Who the devil are you, Achilles himself come back from Hades, or just John Smith? Now into his fifth decade, well paunched, out of breath, scarred like an old bear, but with only half as much wit in his skull!'

'Brother, I—'

'Out of my sight. You are a burden to me. To us all. You have made our entire journey, all our struggle, and our coming deaths, entirely without purpose.'

Sorrowfully John Smith turned away.

The elderly sergeant-at-arms wheezed up the stone steps to the west wall, where the bombardment was lightest. A long-serving soldier, never of the first rank, but faithful as an old hound, doing his service to the last in this city of the plain, surrounded by hills and guns and under sentence of death.

Around the walls, things were indeed, as Smith said, a bloody shambles. Men lay dead and dying, unattended. Walls were left unbulked, broken battlements unrepaired. A woman lay on her side, an apron to her mouth, choking. One of the disturbing, unreal sights you saw in the midst of battle.

Stanley knelt beside her and gave her a sip of water. Then he signalled to Mazzinghi, who helped her back down the steps. She never stopped trembling on his arm, seeming crazed in her wits. What had she been doing up on the walls anyway?

'A whore,' muttered the old sergeant. 'They do it for a crust of bread now. And the soldiers still swive like beasts, not knowing if tomorrow they might be dead.'

'What of the dying here, man?' demanded Stanley. 'Are there no medics?'

The sergeant shrugged. 'The priests and the monks were serving as such but most have been killed, as has the Bishop of Paphos, with a breastplate on his chest and a sword in his hand. And all medicines are long gone.'

A stray musket ball kicked off the top of a nearby battlement, stone chips flying. They ducked lower.

It was hopeless. There was no La Valette in command here, only a few hundred Venetian and Spanish infantry, and worst of all, an uncertain cause to fight for.

'We're too late, aren't we?' said Nicholas quietly.

'If I was Lala Mustafa,' said Stanley, 'I'd have sent my men in already.'

Giustiniani snapped, 'Stamp on such thoughts, Brother! We are here to fight and win, to make Nicosia another Malta. Or at least to hold out until a Venetian relief force might be sent. Just another month or two. Look at the walls! It is still possible!'

The sergeant-at-arms creaked upright again and gave a salute. They glanced round.

There was a lean, dark-eyed man behind them with an intelligent light in his eye.

'Captain,' said the sergeant.

The newcomer nodded. 'And you are the relief party?'

'Such as we are,' said Giustiniani. 'We have known a siege or two. You command this bastion?'

'I do. My name is Captain Paolo dal Guasto, Venetian infantry.

The Greek levies are not to be trusted, and all our best command-ers are dead. Our fighting Bishop of Paphos, Bollani, Thomas Visconti, Colonel Palazzo. The best always go first. The mediocre,' he grimaced satirically, 'stagger on a little longer.'

'Show us the worst-hit bastion.' They walked on round. 'And tell us all you know of how things stand.'

And so Paolo dal Guasto told them. Of how Nicosia had had a defending force of several thousand to begin with, defending three miles of walls. But there were only a thousand arquebuses between them. Governor Dandolo had said they could trust to fixed defences rather than manpower or sortie.

'Which you never can,' said Stanley.

Dal Guasto did not comment. He said there were now barely three or four hundred fighting men left. Morale was so low, some had fled across the lines to join the Turks. The end must come soon. 'Meanwhile,' he said to Stanley, 'that soldier lying there. He died well. Now I think his breastplate may fit you, sir.'

Stanley did the grim work of waving off the flies and stripping the dead man and Mazzinghi laced on his backplate. It was a fair fit. The rest began to look about them likewise.

'The moat is dry,' said Giustiniani. 'Lala Mustafa diverted the river upstream?'

'No need,' said Dal Guasto. 'The moat was dry when the Turks came in spring. Governor Dandolo had not thought to fill it. He said our bastions were mountains.'

'And why was the invasion not resisted from the start? On the coast? It is always easier to keep men from landing when they are in the water.'

Dal Guasto's words were studiedly neutral, giving nothing away. 'It is not for me to explain. Governor Dandolo is our supreme commander.' But his tone betrayed his quiet contempt. 'The Turks landed unopposed at Lemessos Bay. Lemessos surrendered without a fight, like Kyrenia.'

Now they stood and looked across the half-ruined bastion of Costanza. Some mountain. Half the stonework was already in the dry moat below. It seemed as if there was nothing substantial between them and the entire Ottoman army. Why didn't they just march in?

'One village,' said Dal Guasto, 'Lefkara by name, actually rose in support of the Turks, sick of Venetian rule and heavy taxation. Besides, the Turks have cunningly offered all our Greek serfs their freedom if they join with them. Governor Dandolo ordered his militia to ride out and massacre all the inhabitants of Lefkara in punishment. Fortunately I myself was not under order.'

'You jest.'

'I have no sense of humour,' said Dal Guasto.

Nicholas studied him sidelong. The narrow face, deep lined with tiredness. The high brow. No, Dal Guasto had a sense of humour. But Dandolo did not make him laugh.

'Enough,' said Giustiniani. 'Is there any wine?'

'Some dregs,' said Dal Guasto. 'You may not want a second cup after you've tasted it.'

They arranged themselves in a small chamber off Dal Guasto's barracks in the heart of the city, laid out their blankets, inspected their weapons, their motley collection of armour. The sun was in the far west now, the Turkish bombardment dying off again. Perhaps they would attack tonight and finish it?

'Perhaps,' said Stanley. 'Then at least we will die peacefully in our sleep.'

They ate from wooden trenchers with the soldiers, a grim stew of lentils and unnameable bones, perhaps mule, perhaps dog.

'This,' said Hodge, 'has to be the worst supper I've ever tasted in my travels. And that's saying something.'

'Don't worry,' said Stanley. 'It'll get worse. It always does.'

And then there was a figure in the doorway. It was Smith.

'Brothers, I have offended,' he said abruptly.

Giustiniani stood and bid him welcome.

Smith said, not moving, 'I have ever been an ill judge of men, and the fault was all mine today. Forgive me.'

Smith was not a man who found it easy to admit fault, least of all before an assembled company. It was an act of true humility.

Giustiniani's heart was full. 'Of course you are pardoned, Brother. I spoke with a bitter tongue. You only did according to your nature. Come and eat.'

'Thank you, I have eaten.' He bowed and went out.

After a moment, Stanley rose and went after him. Out on the walls, in the gold light of the setting sun, they would stand side by side, in utter silence, their old friendship healed. Brothers like no other.

Nicholas and Hodge came to join them.

'Need some fresh air?' said Stanley.

Nicholas nodded, looking a little green. 'That supper.'

After a while Smith said, 'You know, I have always struggled with the vow of obedience?'

'I know it,' said Stanley wearily.

Smith unslung his knapsack, knelt and unstrapped it. Then he stood and triumphantly shook out a faded banner. It was the scarlet standard of the Knights of St John, emblazoned with the white cross of Malta, which he had brought from De Andrada's galley.

The one that Giustiniani had ordered him to leave behind. The one he had pretended to bury.

'And what was it you called me?' said Stanley. 'A crafty devilish schemer?'

Smith gave a rare grin, a light in his black eyes that was positively boyish. He held his arms aloft and the banner hung down listlessly in the still evening air.

'You'll have to confess this to Giustiniani too.'

'I will,' said Smith. 'Maybe tomorrow.'

And then a fortuitous gust blew along the walls, slight but just enough for the banner to open up and show itself. Along the wall, a couple of Venetian pikemen smiled.

'We heard there was a party of knights among us!' they called. 'Now that banner gives good cheer!'

'Venice has not always looked with favour on the knights,' Smith called back, obstreperous as usual.

They were walking over, keeping an eye always on the Ottoman lines beyond in the gathering dusk. No torches, no linstocks. Pray it might be a quiet night.

'Whatever our Fathers of the Republic may think,' said one pikeman, 'it does me good anyway. Here. Use this staff.'

In a minute they had the standard strung up high, the staff in an iron flag-loop behind a morion, and the light wind opened it up. A small thing, tiny compared to the great satin banners of the Ottomans, faded and frail compared to the magnificent sceptres with long white horsehair tassels, raised high on silver poles, standing amid the vast encampment of the besiegers. Yet the white eight-pointed cross on its scarlet background, a symbol feared and respected across the Mediterranean world, blazed out against the golden walls of Nicosia like a rose in bloom.

Nicholas looked out over the Turkish trenches, no more than two hundred yards off. And then he clearly saw a Janizary start up and stare, shielding his eyes against the sinking sun, regarding the dreaded red standard with steadfast eye. He nudged Stanley and they all watched. A few moments later, the Janizary leapt from the rear of the trench, seized a white horse by its bridle, vaulted on to its back and was away to give the unwelcome news to the Pasha.

Smith whooped and guffawed. He nearly capered.

'Before heaven,' said the Venetian pikeman, grinning broadly, 'did you see that? Did you see the Turk run? Just the sight of it. Before heaven it does me good. Luigi, you saw that?'

His comrade was grinning too. 'Couldn't mistake it.'

'How it'll rattle 'em!' bellowed Smith, his voice unnecessarily loud considering they were right next to him. 'The sight of the old red standard will be about as welcome to them as an outbreak of galloping pox!'

Indeed, word was already spreading fast through the Turkish camp: the almost unbelievable news that, despite Nicosia being ringed around with Ottoman besiegers, it seemed Knights of St John, those devils and djinns, were now among the defenders. How many, no one knew. Some said it was a feint, a bluff, a mere piece of cloth. Others doubted. And among older soldiers, the terrible shadow of Malta rose in their minds.

Those Knights Hospitaller, those Knights of St John ...

They were the soldiers of Shaitan.

They were the mad dogs of Christendom.

6

Smith unslung his Persian jezail. Since its soaking in the sea, he had spent hours cleaning and polishing it, and once in Nicosia he had stripped it completely, oiled every part and reassembled it as lovingly as a Geneva clockmaker.

Now it was time to put it to the test. While cleaning the barrel one last time, wadding it with guncotton and powder and ball and tamping it well, he said to Nicholas, 'Boy, is it my ageing eyes or do I see a Habsburg banner out there? On the highest hill there, the hill of St Marina, I think.'

Nicholas had already seen that banner: the two-headed eagle of the Habsburgs before one of the largest tents on the plain, with clear ground all around. 'Is that the tent of Lala Mustafa?'

'I presume so. And that's a captured banner, to taunt us. Well, let's see.'

The air was clear, the wind was light. But the tent of the Pasha might have been half a mile off.

'Waste of a ball, Brother,' said Stanley.

Smith ignored him, crouched silently behind the battlements, the long smooth barrel of the musket resting on the stonework. He took his time, sighted, measured his breathing, tightened his finger on the trigger. Moments passed.

The tension was unbearable.

Then he said, 'Maybe, instead ...'

And he swivelled the barrel just a couple of inches to the right, sighted swiftly once more, breathed out and fired.

It still must have been two or three hundred yards off, an

astonishing shot. But a moment after the musket fired, a tall Janizary half out of a trench turned sharply, clutching his upper arm. Then he turned back and howled at the walls of Nicosia: cries, Stanley said, of considerable irritation.

'Keep 'em on their toes,' said Smith. 'We're not beaten yet.'

In the night, Nicholas and Hodge walked the half-ruined streets of Nicosia, hungry and weary yet unable to sleep. People begged at every corner, nobody was asleep. The night air still hot, wind rustling the palm trees, everything a dream.

'These mighty Venetian walls that seem so solid,' said Nicholas, waving the nearly empty flask of vile wine, 'cities of men, kings and their thrones, everything ... It was all built to fall. All but the dream of God.'

There were old women in black, praying by candlelight in a small but beautiful church, a black-bearded priest intoning the ancient liturgy of Byzantium. The church of the Virgin of Chrysaliniotissa, its walls covered with icons, the air heady with incense. They lurched in half drunk, and the old women glared. They peered into the mystery of the inner sanctum behind the screen, the priest muttering, 'Franks and barbarians,' moving over to throw them out. But there was nothing in there but a table and a bottle of oil. God doesn't wait in some inner room for you. The mystery is not to be seen with such pragmatic eyes.

They finished the wine sitting by a fountain, heads warm and cloudy, stars winking through the acacia tree overhead. So peaceful, in this city about to fall in slaughter to the Turks.

'We might be in the Orient,' said Hodge softly.

'We are nearly,' said Nicholas. 'Much closer to Jerusalem than London. Not so far from Damascus, even Baghdad. Listen hard and you can hear the muezzin cry from Rhodes, from Beirut. Soon there'll be mosques in Nicosia.'

'You really think it?'

'Of course. We are finished here, before we even started.'

'I'm not going back on the galleys in Turkish chains.'

'Nor me. God knows how.'

Maybe they would die soon. Nicholas drained the bottle.

Hodge shivered, not from cold. 'The farther I get from England, the more I love her. But you like it here.'

'We are exiles, old friend. I have not kept you from England. Prisons and galleys and slavery and damned war have kept us.'

'Aye,' said Hodge. 'We must lay our heads on what pillows we find.'

'But you never give up hope of England, eh, Hodge?'

'Never.'

'One day we will go back.'

Hodge regarded him. 'You would rather wander and drift in and out of danger than come home to it all. The daily round.'

Nicholas said no more, but Hodge knew him well. He had come to love danger, and she would destroy him before long. But it was the daily round he feared.

They weaved down a dark street that had some promising lanterns on hooks over open doorways. There was a young girl on the step. She looked at them boldly and stroked her bare leg as they passed.

They went into a small chamber with an old woman eating pistachio nuts, the floor around her stool strewn with shells, and a plump girl who looked Greek or maybe Bulgarian. The girl on the step was young and fair skinned.

'What coin have you?' mumbled the old woman, her mouth full of nuts and no teeth.

'We'll all be dead in the morning,' said Nicholas, as the fair-skinned girl took his hand and pulled him towards an inner room.

The old woman scowled and held out her hand. He gave her a ducat.

She peered down at it and then stared at him. 'A Venetian ducat! Who do you think she is, Helen of Troy?'

Nicholas just shrugged and said again, 'We'll all be dead in the morning.'

Once in the inner chamber, drawing the curtains behind them, the girl said, 'Will the city really fall to the Turks so soon?'

'Aye. What will you do then?'

'Be taken captive, no doubt.'

'Does it not worry you?'

She shrugged off her dress and sat naked on his knee. 'Whores are survivors. And I've lived through worse. Now stop talking and kiss me.'

They got back to their quarters in the early hours, stumbling over the prostrate forms of their comrades. Stanley stirred and looked at them as they collapsed on to their blankets.

'Happy now?' he said.

'Not particularly,' said Nicholas. 'But I'll sleep better. You?'

'Perfectly well, thank you.'

After a while Nicholas said, 'I don't know how you do it. The celibacy.'

'It's because it's so difficult that it's worth doing. Like anything else. I like the melancholy of celibacy. The spartan melancholy of saying no. No night with a whore is worth the pride of that.'

'You haven't met my whore here,' mumbled Nicholas, already asleep.

Stanley lay back and grinned, despite himself. Whoremonger Ingoldsby. He'd learn.

Nicholas awoke from a sweaty nightmare of falling towers, infants smashing to the ground. He lay panting, and then Stanley kicked him.

'Up, up, tosspot and whoremonger. It's a filthy conscience gives you bad dreams.'

'Go to hell.'

'Here. Some bread. The mould adds flavour.'

There was a mighty hubbub outside.

Smith came back to say that Governor Dandolo himself was riding out their way. 'On the finest white charger left in the city uneaten, and a very heavy bodyguard too. I wonder why. Can he not be popular?'

They hurried out, buckling on swords, Nicholas and Hodge still swallowing down mouldy bread and stale water. They found Captain Paolo dal Guasto locked in argument with a stout, impassive fellow in a tall helmet.

'The Jews?' Dal Guasto was saying angrily. 'Why the devil are we to round up the Jews?'

192

The fellow shrugged. 'Order from the Governor's palace. All Jews in the city to be driven to the Famagusta Gate.'

A crowd came surging round the far end of the street, some wailing.

'There you are,' said the fellow. 'There's your first batch.'

And behind them came a finely dressed gentleman on a white horse fringed with scarlet trappings, and a mounted bodyguard of eight men around him, all with long lances at the ready.

Giustiniani snapped. He hurried up the street, pushing his way through the crowd of Jewish men, women and children, clutching the few pitiful possessions they could carry, and stood four-square before a disdainful-looking Dandolo. Smith, Stanley and Mazzinghi followed close behind, and Nicholas and Hodge hovered near by. On adjacent steps, unnoticed by any, Paolo dal Guasto ordered four of his men to load up their crossbows.

'Any moment now the Turkish bombardment is going to start up anew!' roared Giustiniani, so loudly that Dandolo's horse shied and backed up, colliding with the one behind. 'Or maybe the Janizaries will just come marching in direct. And we are busy herding the Jews like sheep. What in hell is *going on?*'

Dandolo was white faced and furious. 'I understood that I was Governor of this city, not you, sir knight. Now out of our way. Guards! Ready the sally port!'

Suddenly Dandolo and his eight bodyguards found themselves facing not one but four tough-looking Knights Hospitaller, hands on their swords, and those two tatterdemalion English volunteers lurking near by too. Among the Jews, some of the men were beginning to mutter and refuse to be driven any farther. Damn it all.

Dandolo tightened his reins and held still. Composed. Lordly.

'In Caesar's *Gallic Wars*,' he declared, 'we have read that at a certain dangerous siege, he drove the townspeople out between him and the besieging enemy.'

Giustiniani was lost for words. Dandolo was no Julius Caesar, and his account was garbled anyway. Did he mean the siege of Alesia?

Dandolo pressed on. 'There are more than a thousand unchristened Jews still living in this city, eating our food, drinking good clean water. And so we have decided that they shall be driven out before our walls, as a form of protection. That will fox that brute Lala Mustafa!'

'Sire, that is barbarous!' cried Giustiniani. 'And pointless besides. A man like Lala Mustafa will have no hesitation in mowing them down with grapeshot, and using the corpses for sandbags.'

'Then upon his conscience be it. It is a necessary policy and we have made our decision. Open the sally port! Drive them forth!'

Guards drew back the final crossbars and the low entrance gate to the long dark tunnel of the sally port creaked open. Like all sally ports, just wide enough to admit a man at a time.

'If you drive them out, we go with them,' said Giustiniani.

Dandolo smiled. 'Go with the *Jews*?'

'Just so.'

'Well,' murmured the Governor. It was not a prospect that displeased him. All troublemakers together ... 'Off you go, then.'

The knights were speechless, even hesitant. Their estimation of Dandolo, which they had thought could sink no lower, had just sunk lower.

But there was a blur on the steps leading up to the walls. It was Nicholas. He had run to retrieve the Standard of Malta.

'What's up?' said a pikeman, looking puzzled.

'We're going,' he gasped. 'Dandolo's throwing us out.'

Word flew like a hawk. Even as the first Jewish elders were being poked and prodded into the tunnel, Paolo dal Guasto appeared before Dandolo.

'Sire, if the knights are driven out of the city too, I cannot be sure of the loyalty of my company of men.'

Dandolo's expression set frosty again. 'Do I understand you correctly, Captain? You are threatening mutiny?'

'Not threatening, sire. Predicting.'

Dandolo's mouth worked furiously, his lips writhed.

On the stone steps to the right, there were four of Dal Guasto's men, uncouth common soldiers, and their crossbows were already loaded. Then one of them – Dandolo's heart missed a beat – one of them actually raised his crossbow, slow and silent, and aimed it directly at him.

For several moments, Dandolo could not speak. Then he said quietly, 'Close the gate. Let them be.'

The soldier slowly lowered his crossbow. The Jews shuffled backwards out of the tunnel, to the amusement of onlookers.

Dandolo pulled his horse around and trotted swiftly back to the palace.

Nicholas dropped the standard and grinned.

At that very moment, with cruel irony, a huge marble cannonball came in on a neighbouring bastion, an exact hit, shattering into a hail of hot shards as marble was meant to. Two soldiers huddled just below the parapet were hit, one screaming and writhing.

It was the Turks saying good morning.

And then all along the Turkish line, the cannons opened up. The ground trembled, the noise was deafening, enough to make a man shake at the knees, to sink down in a corner and cover his head, ears ringing. Two hundred black mouths belching black smoke and fire, two hundred balls of iron and stone and marble hurtling through the air to rain down with ferocious destructive power upon the nearly broken city. Women and children wailed. A few skin-and-bone mules tore free from their tethers.

'The very rats in the sewers will be pissing themselves!' roared Smith.

'This is the main attack,' said Stanley. 'After this, the Janizaries will be coming in.'

'God damn the Christian kings!' cried Giustiniani. 'Boils and plague on 'em! Where is Don John now, where is the fleet of the Holy League? Why is Cyprus abandoned like this?'

But there was no more time for words. They ran to the bastion where the two soldiers lay stricken, others gathering round.

In the street below there was already mass panic. Someone said the Turks were already through the Famagusta Gate, others denied it. Fighting broke out.

Stanley knelt by one of the wounded soldiers. 'Can you walk, man?' But it was foolish to ask. 'Hodge, lad, take him behind the knees there.'

The other soldier pulled himself upright and leaned heavily on Nicholas, bleeding so heavily his own shirt was drenched. He glanced down. The fellow was wounded in the stomach, almost black blood leaking from his midriff.

195

'Hold up, friend,' he said. 'These are Knights of St John. Famous medics.'

The soldier stared at him for a moment, unfocused, and then coughed a single, violent cough. A hot blob of blood struck Nicholas on the shoulder and then the man slumped. He was dead.

He laid him down.

'The nearest hospital, for God's sake!' Stanley was shouting. Another soldier shrugged. Field hospitals had not even been set up.

'The city is lost!' someone cried from the street below. 'The day is come, the heathen are upon us! Fly for your lives!'

7

The people were fleeing into the heart of the city, taking to roofs or cellars like maddened animals. An old man, stark naked, crawled into a barrel and started to giggle. But Nicholas had seen such sights before. The madness of war. Now it was time to steel yourself. Nothing was normal. He wound up his shirt front tightly and wrung out the dead man's blood. It trickled to the dusty ground, still warm.

'Below!' cried Smith, sword in hand. 'To me!'

All was chaos, but at least the rumours about the Famagusta Gate were false. As cannonballs hurtled in overhead, the ground shaking with huge thumps, and walls and buildings behind them collapsing with a slow, distant rumble, they formed up before the great eastern gate of the city. Paolo dal Guasto was already there with his company, pikes at the ready.

But the gate, at least, had been heavily bulked, on Dal Guasto's initiative. On the outward face the stonework was all shock-absorbing slopes and angles, and the huge oak gates themselves were covered with overlapping plate metal. Behind that, most simple but most effective of all, was the bulking. A mix of bales of straw, barrels full of sand, stone blocks and sacks of earth, as deep as a barn full of hay. Unlike impressive stone walls, such soft bulking actually absorbed the hammer-blows of cannonballs rather than resisted them. No cannonball on earth could go through it.

Smith grunted approval. 'The Turk will have to start building defences for himself, right up against the walls, before he can begin

197

lifting and carrying away all this. Like a peasant carting bales of hay from the meadow.'

Stanley joined them. There was blood on his sleeves, and another dead soldier back in the street behind. He had died without even a taste of opium. There was none in the city.

Giustiniani said, 'It's mining that brings down cities.'

There was a lull in the bombardment again while the Turkish guns cooled. They crept up on to the walls once more. Stanley peered out, and told the younger three to do likewise.

'What are we looking for?' asked Mazzinghi, whispering un-necessarily.

Stanley grinned. 'You're looking for where there's nothing.'

Smith started almost immediately. 'There, damn it. Just off to the left.'

They all looked. There was one section of the wicker breastwork and earth rampart where a gun barrel poked out, but no gun team was working to cool it with buckets of warm water. Cold water could crack the barrel, even a piece of bronze weighing more than a pair of oxen. It was as if this gun hadn't been fired. As if it was merely for cover.

And then Nicholas saw a man with a spade.

Smith was already unslinging his jezail.

'Take us to the countermining tunnels,' said Stanley. 'Fast.'

Dal Guasto wore a look of shame on his face.

Stanley said, 'Don't tell me . . .'

Dal Guasto said, 'The Governor thought we had not the manpower to countermine. He said our walls were impregnable anyway.'

Smith lowered his jezail in sheer despair. This siege was almost over. And the end would not be good.

They had come too late. Always too few, always too late.

'Truly,' murmured Smith, shaking his head, 'truly my Lord Niccolo Dandolo, you are a dunce and a dog's arsehole.'

They threaded their way back into the city, the four knights in a silent daze. Past the haggard gaze of the last few groups of soldiers, past the heaps of the slain, past the emaciated faces of the towns-people. The general stench of decay and exhaustion told their story.

'Nicosia is lost. We must plan for Famagusta.'

'Aye,' said Smith, 'we know when Lala Mustafa will be in now.'

'When?' said Mazzinghi.

'Just as soon as the mines have been blown and the last stones have fallen back to earth.'

'I am sorry,' said Giustiniani, bowing his grizzled old head. 'My brothers, my brave souls, we have come on a suicide mission. Just in time to see Nicosia fall. And if we ourselves are only taken captive in chains, we'll be lucky.'

'If we become separated,' said Stanley, 'we should head towards the Governor's palace. The last act will be there.'

'There are three courses open to us, I think,' said Giustiniani. 'We can lie down and play dead, and hope to escape. A fairy-tale escape, in truth. The Turks will just throw us alive on to a pyre. We can fight to the death, heroic to the end, achieving nothing for the world. Or we surrender and live to fight another day.'

'Never,' said Smith.

'Fighting to the death is wasted,' countered Giustiniani. 'We are needed at Famagusta – if we can get there, after this, somehow.'

'It is over for us,' said Smith, buckling his plate tighter.

And then the mines went up.

Nicholas had never seen or heard anything like it, nor ever would again. The final assault on Birgu at Malta had been nothing compared to this: destruction so total and unopposed.

In a matter of seconds, so perfectly organized was the Ottoman assault, all three of the city's great gates, Famagusta, Paphos and Kyrenia, were sent sky high. It was as if an earthquake had been cross-bred with a volcano.

The arch where they sheltered trembled with the explosions. Nicholas looked up to see the very keystone above his head shaken and half dislodged. But Stanley yelled, 'Stay where you are! Cover your heads! Do not step out from the arch!'

All the massive bulking behind the gates, that barn-deep mass of material which no cannonball on earth could have ploughed through, was hurled clean into the air. For the expert Armenian and Mameluke sappers had tunnelled precisely underneath it, barely a foot below, the thin ground above their heads held up by little more than pit props. Then they had rammed the tunnels tight with as many as two hundred barrels of highest-quality gunpowder, lit the long matchcord soaked in pitch ... and run.

Bales of hay and sacks of straw too heavy for a man to lift were sent spiralling into the air as if in slow motion, coming back to land some time later, thumping down on to rooftops or in distant squares. Some bales simply detonated, the air filled with dried grass and grass halms, and the sweet scent of summer hay meadows, along with the black, bitter tang of gunpowder. A drum of marble from some ancient column was tossed up and then crashed down on to a pretty little fountain in a street behind. A barrel rolling as fast as a horse could gallop smashed into a fellow trying to run away.

And then there came a great roar of thousands of men, rushing all three gates simultaneously, spears and scimitars ready for close-quarter work. Men who had waited for weeks under the blazing sun, bored, restless, sometimes falling sick, for the fall of this stubborn city which had so foolishly refused surrender. Now it was time for just punishment.

'Not Janizaries!' came one last desperate cry from a wall. 'Bektaşis!'

Irregulars, dervishes, fanatics. God-crazed connoisseurs of opium, rape and slaughter.

Only moments later, as the six of them raced down a narrow alley, heading for the Governor's palace and the last stand, there was another gigantic explosion. A deafening eruption of timber and stone. It must have been a powder store. Why hadn't the powder been brought up to the walls for use? But now either some last desperate defender still in his wits had put a flame to it to destroy it, and deprive the Turks of the use of it, or it had been detonated by some stray pot-bomb or spark.

They would never know. The alley collapsed around them, silently, for they were already deafened, and they were lost to each other in a sandstorm of limestone dust.

*

Later Nicholas tried to find his way to the palace again, alone, ears ringing, swordless, wanting only to be reunited with his comrades so he should not die alone. Amid the dust clouds and chaos he wandered like a wraith, amid the terrible randomness of the city's sacking. As if he were marked like Cain, it seemed no man, not even a Mussulman, dared to raise his hand against him. He reeled rather than walked, his own blood now around his neck, and a strange shaking weakness in his left arm that he did not investigate further.

He saw a little girl of no more than six or seven, stone dead but still standing as if stuck to the wall. He thought of his sisters, and pulled her from the wall and laid her down and cursed that he had no covering to give her, looking over her heartful and speechless. He didn't even stir when another cannonball, fired pointlessly now the city was taken, smacked into a wall only feet away and covered him afresh with dust.

In a nightmare without sound, he saw people wandering about as slowly as himself, but purposeless. He saw a Turk come up behind a woman walking along with her head down, thoughtfully, and run her through. Once she was down, the Turk knelt and started to rummage under her skirts.

Wait, wait, he said to himself, dust gritty between his teeth. Make it to the palace. Find them. Fight another day.

He saw terraces and balconies pointlessly raked by point-blank gunfire, and from the Tripoli bastion, Turks fired down canisters of shot into the crowded, wailing square. He saw them cut off an old woman's head and toss it in her serving maid's lap, and other images that engraved themselves indelibly in his mind and memory, and would waken him from nightmares, sweat soaked and panting, for many years to come.

Everywhere there was treachery and despair, bickering over loot, petty vengeance. A defeat was always soul destroying, but especially one so cowardly and chaotic as this. And yet even amid the carnage and chaos, he saw a mule peacefully tearing little weeds from a wall, and a cat licking her kittens in a cellar doorway.

His hearing came back, accompanied by ringing. He armed himself like a peasant with a long-handled goad he found inside a stable doorway, slipped down a back alley and through a house, then made it over flat rooftops until he was close to the palace. There was a group of Turks singing down below in a courtyard, as if it was all over, but from within the palace came the sound of gunfire. Twice he was challenged as he clambered along, and once a crossbow bolt clattered over the roof near by. He waved his makeshift spear in the air and called *Allahu akbar!* and pulled down his shirt to show his own blood. None of it made any sense, but they left him in peace.

He went as far as he could go along the rooftops, dropped down into a yard with a tethered goat, went through a stone barn and a back window thick with pigeon droppings. He wedged the goad under his back-belt, climbed up a wooden post and over a loosely tiled roof, sending them skimming to the ground below, climbed in another window, and dropped down on to cool flagstones. He was in a larder. There was even a stone basin in the corner, and a ewer.

He drank the ewer almost empty, poured the rest over his head, rubbed his face with his sleeve. His head felt clearer. He remembered a stag hunt back in Shropshire, when he was still but fourteen and had never killed a man. The stag reach the river's edge, exhausted, trembling in every limb, almost finished, as the hounds bounded towards it, spittled tongues lolling. The stag drank about a gallon of water and was revived as if by magic. It forded the river and then bolted away up the steep hill faster than any hound could run.

He breathed in the cool damp air of the larder, then headed towards the gunfire.

He ran down a corridor thick with black gunpowder smoke and up a fine carved wooden staircase. He vaulted over a dead man with his throat slit. Somewhere in this palace, the last battle was being fought, and he knew his comrades were there.

The mood was coming upon him again now: ferocious and sublime. The mood he lived for. He knew that some power watched over him, that he would not die, not today. That he could do anything.

He grimaced as he ran, other men's blood still on him, thinking that this was what the Bektaşi felt.

*

Musket fire raked over his head and splintered a fine wood-panelled wall behind him. A ball may have whispered past his cheek. Then he jabbed a musketeer's throat with the goad and pulled him down. He seized the musket like a club and struck a second fellow sidelong, but it was a poor blow. He had to draw the musket back and use it again in an instant, not easy with so heavy a weapon, as the fellow brought down his barrel in a long jabbing motion towards his stomach. He just managed to parry the blow and knock it aside while rolling, came up and kicked the fellow behind his knees. Then he was on him and had smashed his head two-handed into the floor so he didn't move again. He dropped the musket and took his sword. It was an inferior weapon but better than an empty hand.

He dropped into a small room and knelt against the wainscot, gasping. They were fighting room to room, and he was behind the Ottoman lines.

He went climbing. In a narrow, shadowy corner of the palace he ascended a steep spiral staircase until it reached a high-vaulted attic room, leaned out of a narrow window, turned on his back and looked up. Possible. Then he was out and drawing himself up, slowly, slowly. Weight on your legs, arms will tire. Climb it like a ladder. Feet sideways on, sometimes perching on nubbins of stone no bigger than crab apples, fingers clutching cracks in the stones. But enough, holding himself tight to the wall. Forty feet up from the ground. A startled white dove took off and almost killed him.

He pulled himself over a ledge and moved along between two steep-pitched rooftops. He knew he was near when a wooden shutter erupted in a deadly hail of splinters just feet ahead of him. He dropped down, crawled beneath it and then bobbed up as fast as he could and glanced within. With the accelerated senses that danger brings, he saw a dark arquebus barrel already turning on him, the matchcord smoking. He ducked down again as the gun fired a ball through his hair, and yelled out, 'St Michael and St George!'

A mighty hand, black with powder smoke and burns, grabbed him by the edge of his jerkin and hauled him inside.

Smith.

'What kept you?' he growled.

'I thought you were dead,' said Hodge.

'How did you all find each other?' said Nicholas.

'We never lost each other. Only you.'

They were in a lofty vaulted chamber with a huge stone fireplace, bearing the lion crest of Venice above the lintel. But now was not the time to appreciate architectural features. Besides, the chamber was still drifting with black smoke.

One end was massively barricaded with a dark oak table on its side. Stanley crouched behind it. He stood swiftly, fired straight through the wooden panelling, reloading furiously. The muzzle smoked.

There were about twenty men in all here. Four or five were dead or dying.

Why had he come?

Then the doors at the other end of the chamber were flung open, and there stood none other than Governor Niccolo Dandolo himself. He had donned his finest crimson robe for the occasion, and wore neither sword nor armour.

Their guns fell silent. Beyond the barricaded door, the Turks were still shouting.

'Gentlemen,' said Dandolo, imperturbably serene. 'We have done all we can. It is time to give ourselves into Ottoman hands, with dignity intact.'

Not five feet from him, a young Venetian pikeman was spluttering his last breath, a musket ball in his lungs.

There was a sudden movement, and Captain Paolo dal Guasto was at Dandolo's side. His expression was dark and contorted as he drew back his sword.

'Dal Guasto, no!' cried Giustiniani.

Dandolo turned, oblivious of danger to the last. But then one of his bodyguards standing behind him raised his pike high in the air and brought the heavy iron head slamming down upon Dal Guasto's bare skull. He fell like a poleaxed heifer.

Stanley ran to the fallen captain. He who had held the bastion of San Luca to the very last minute, even after half of it was destroyed by the mines. Dal Guasto was taut and shaking, his eyes rolling. Stanley knew he was done for.

The pikeman was impassive. What point was there in anything

now? It was all too typical. But let the last wretched scene be played out.

'Draw back that table,' said Dandolo. 'We shall present ourselves.'

They hauled back the heavy oak table and then hurried to the opposite end of the chamber, fifteen desperate, panting men. Dandolo stood alone before the holed and splintered double doors and drew them open.

Beyond, it was carnage. The Turks were dragging away the dead bodies of their comrades to make space for further attacks. Somewhere below, a team was actually trying to bring a field gun up the stairs. They had fought half the length of the palace, room by room, a savage and bitter fight in a city already fallen. But rumours flew that there were Knights of St John in the palace, guarding Dandolo to the end.

That would explain it.

Finally the smoke cleared, and there was a Janizary commander with his hand raised, his men twitching but obedient.

Dandolo gave a curt bow. 'At your service.'

The commander grinned an unsettling grin and strode into the room. His scimitar was gripped tight in his right hand.

'We have our orders for your capture already, from Lala Mustafa,' he said. 'I shall have pleasure in following them to the letter.'

Dandolo frowned. Understanding nothing to the last. The commander took a two-handed grip on his scimitar and swept it cleanly through the air at shoulder height.

The head fell to the floor with a hollow thunk, brains leaking. The surprised trunk in its crimson robe toppled sideways a few moments later.

The commander signalled to his men and they swarmed in. One picked up the severed head and dropped it into a sack. Two more took the headless trunk by its arms and legs and went over to the window. They swung it back and forth a couple of times and then slung it out.

The mortal remains of Governor Niccolo Dandolo tumbled through the air, crimson robe billowing, and came to land with an ugly thump. A great cry went up from the soldiers outside. It was over.

The Janizary commander eyed the huddle of men in the far

doorway. A mere dozen or so, but their expressions were grim rather than placatory or pleading, and they still gripped their weapons. They had fought hard. He indicated the floor with the point of his scimitar. Behind him, a dozen arquebuses were trained on them.

Then one of their number, a bull-like figure with burning eyes and black beard speckled with grey, produced something from behind his back.

Something with a smoking matchcord.

Smith tossed it in the air.

8

They ran from the chaos behind them like boy sprinters, with no plan but to keep running. There was still a chance they might hide themselves somewhere, in the maze of alleyways and courtyards of the ruined city, or some dank cellar.

Arquebuses cracked out behind them, only two or three rooms back.

They clattered down stone steps and into a small courtyard, where Stanley and Smith whirled their swords and cut down two astonished guards on the gate. A hue and cry went up and a hundred men came after them.

Bektaşis.

Somehow they found a moment's respite in a quiet street, beneath an archway. But they would be found soon.

They sank down wearily and Mazzinghi took a slug of water from his flask. A last drink.

'On your feet, my brother Luigi Mazzinghi,' said Giustiniani, his voice very gentle amid the approaching yells and curses. He took the young knight's arm, for it was trembling as he held his sword. 'On your feet, my courageous English gentlemen. Before heaven, I know you have been brave fellows, and I would as willingly die beside you as any Knight Hospitaller.'

There were tears in the old man's eyes. They had all heard the cry of the Bektaşis, surging towards them like the sound of hell unloosed. *Allahu akbar! Death to the unbelievers!*

And, more soul destroying, they heard an old woman calling out

207

in Greek from an upper window, 'There they are! There are the Franks!'

There would be no call to surrender now. This was a sack, with no quarter given: chaotic and bloody yet carefully calculated by Lala Mustafa, most ruthless of military commanders, so that Famagusta should hear of its atrocities and promptly surrender without a fight.

Smith raised his sword high. 'Acre! Jerusalem! Malta!'

Round the end of the street came a horde half hidden in a cloud of roiling dust. They glimpsed topknots and henna tattoos, white teeth, flashing steel. There was a dervish racing towards them with a scimitar in one hand and a severed head in the other. Most fought naked, already daubed with blood. Some were sexually excited. Their eyes were bloodshot and maddened, rolling in their heads. The Bektaşis were so holy and beloved of Allah, they even allowed themselves to drink alcohol. Nothing impure could harm ones already so purified by fire and blood and the love of God.

Much of the Ottoman army, especially the Janizary regiments, had nothing but contempt for these savages, and others said they were no part of the religion of the Prophet, but of Shaitan. Nevertheless, as Lala Mustafa well knew, they had their uses. Savagery and terror, principally.

Nicholas laid his hand on Hodge's shoulder one last time.

Hodge raised his sword too. 'For England,' he said softly. 'For what it's bloody well worth.'

Giustiniani pulled them back into the archway, where at least they could not be outflanked, and might pile up the bodies before them.

The Bektaşis were not thirty yards away. They had seen their armour, their swords shining, and were howling, running.

Smith glanced back into the small courtyard behind them, open to the sky, surrounded by low buildings. At the back of the courtyard was a high wall. With a door in the far corner.

He glanced out of the archway again. They were coming. One came ahead of all the others. He flailed his arms at them. Stanley struck him down.

Smith sprinted back across the courtyard and tried the door. Bolted, unyielding as a rock. The wall was twelve feet high. Stanley had one pot-bomb left hanging from his belt, just one, but it was too precious.

Giustiniani read him immediately and drew the others back to form a small triangle, standing five abreast across the corner. They formed a tight line that could not be outflanked, bristling with blades. God send the Bektaşis had no guns or they would simply shoot them down. But they always preferred scimitars. More blood.

Now the howling dervishes swarmed through the archway towards them, a flesh-coloured tide.

Stanley reached out and grabbed a donkey-barrow that stood against the wall, and with one giant heave, turned it on its side. A singe small obstacle, but it might help.

Behind them, Smith was hurling himself at the bolted door.

It wouldn't budge.

The crowd of fifty or more came towards them, chanting, jabbing spears in the air. Many more surged on down the narrow street. Somewhere a woman screamed.

Stanley reached for the single pot-bomb on his belt.

'A moment more,' murmured Giustiniani. He held a smoking matchcord close to the pot-bomb's short fuse. Even his veteran hands were shaking. Sweat stung his eyes.

The Bektaşis were doing a kind of dance of death.

Oh, to have one small field gun full of grapeshot. But it would be hand to hand and ten to one.

Smith hurled himself at the door again. Still it did not budge.

One Bektaşi rushed at them, ecstatic, smiling, swinging his spear almost uselessly. Mazzinghi clouted it aside, took a single brisk step forward, skewered him through the throat with a thrust of his sword, planted his foot in the fellow's chest and pushed him off it, and took one step back into line as the fellow was still falling to the ground.

The horde howled, dancing, their spears weaving in the air before them. Six feet in front of them. A single charge and they were done.

And more were climbing up on the roofs of the buildings around the courtyard, coming almost behind them to hurl down tiles and stones.

Smith drove himself at the door.

'Now!' said Giustiniani.

The matchcord touched the fuse, it fizzed into life, and Stanley lobbed it high over the horde before them.

'Down!'

They ducked low, squatting, faces lowered, hands over their heads. The pot-bomb exploded in the air. They stood again, instantly reforming.

The heart of the horde had been flattened by the blast of nails, glass and potsherds like a field of wheat under a hailstorm.

'Forward!' cried Giustiniani, and as one they stepped up to the front rank of still-bewildered dervishes. Nicholas bent one knee and drove his sword forward long and hard. He caught his man in the thigh and he went down groaning, surprised. He could not finish him off before two more came forward and they all stepped back into line within the enclosed space of the walls.

Then they were under full attack.

Nicholas had not fought like this since Malta, and yet for the first few moments that seemed to last so long, it was horribly easy. These were no trained soldiers but fanatics, ardent to die and go to paradise. They came on to the sacrifice willingly. Yet after only a minute or two of duck, thrust and skewer, the five were blood-slathered to the shoulder, and all but Stanley, perhaps, were beginning to tire in the sword-arm. It was exhaustion that would kill them, exhaustion alone, swamped by sheer numbers.

Then Mazzinghi was cut, a long spear thrust more calculated than most, which laid his temple open to the bone and blinded him in one eye with his own blood, so that he could no longer judge distance and scale.

'Get that door open, Smith!' roared Giustiniani, hacking down another spearman. 'Hit it again!'

Hodge took a savage blow to his left arm from a studded cudgel, and sank to one knee with the pain. Nicholas whirled his sword over him and caught the assailant a shallow slashing cut across the side of his neck. The Bektaşi stepped back, not mortally wounded, and another came on in his place.

Beyond the howling, there were sounds of a city being raped. But for them, for now, the whole vast battlefield of the central Cyprus plain, the fall of this great walled city of ten thousand, had shrunk to this single courtyard, and an old wooden door with a bolt that wouldn't budge.

Then Mazzinghi cracked.

He shot his bloody sword home in its scabbard, vaulted forward on to the side of the donkey-barrow, and then leapt up with a spring that only a young man in terror could perform. It was just enough for him to reach the top of the courtyard wall, holding on by his fingertips. He swung left and right, legs flailing. A spear clattered into the wall not a hand's breadth away from him, and then he swung far enough to hitch his right foot up on top of the wall. He rolled over, dropped down the other side and was gone.

The cowardice made them redouble their ruthless sword-work. At least they'd not die like that yellow Florentine.

Smith abandoned the door and drew his sword and pressed forward into the line.

'Remember Acre!' he bellowed.

It was in the final flurry of slashes and thrusts, all of them half blinded now by dust and sweat, arms barely able to raise their blades, that they heard the sound of a bolt being shot, and knew from the way the sound opened up that the door behind them was ajar. And there stood Mazzinghi.

They seized the moment of chaos and opportunity, Nicholas kicking one last fellow hard on the kneecap, and then they were back through the doorway.

Smith put his less battered shoulder to the door and slammed it shut again. A dervish had his arm through the door. It must have been half severed by the door slamming shut with all of Smith's weight behind it. Smith wrenched the door open one last time, as if exasperated, punched the fellow full in the face, and slammed it shut a second time, shooting the heavy bolt.

It would buy them all of a few seconds. Other Bektaşis were already coming over the wall above them.

'Run!'

They tore round the corner into a wider street, and there was a column of two hundred fresh Janizaries ahead of them, eight abreast, long wheel-lock muskets held across their chests.

They might have been a different army.

Behind them they could hear the soft thunder of two or three hundred bare brown feet. Silent now. Intent.

The Janizary captain shouted an order, and the front rank raised their muskets, setting the butts not against their chests but nestled hard into their shoulders in the modern style.

The Bektaşis came on behind them.

They were done for.

Yet even in this last moment, Giustiniani had to speak.

'Fra Luigi,' he gasped, 'forgive me, I doubted you. I thought you had fled us.'

Mazzinghi actually managed a last grin as he raised an empty, bloody hand, facing the execution of the Janizary muskets. 'Forget it, Brother. Pardon all.'

The captain shouted again, and dropped his straightened arm imperiously.

'He means us!' shouted Stanley, suddenly understanding. 'Drop!'

They hit the ground just as a disciplined volley cracked out from the Janizary front rank. It was aimed to sheer just over the heads of the onrushing Bektaşis, who even in their opiate delirium and bloodlust came to a jumbled halt, scimitars trailing, staring.

'Hold yourselves back!' roared the Janizary captain. 'These six are in our custody now!'

The six lay still in the dust while the two factions stood opposing one another. Then the captain called out once more, clear and commanding, and used the name 'Lala Mustafa'.

The Bektaşis muttered dark curses and eyed each other. Then they slunk away and were gone.

The six lay still. Out of the frying pan, into the fires of hell. They had been found out. They had been taken prisoner as knights. And instead of quick slaughter at the hands of the Bektaşis, a far worse fate now awaited them. Led captive to Lala Mustafa himself, and death by slow and exemplary torture.

9

A voice said, 'Yes, it is them. The Venetian embassy.'

'You are certain?' said the Janizary captain gruffly. 'They look like very martial and sword-ready ambassadors.'

'They went armed,' said the other. 'There was necessity. But this is them. They should not be harmed but taken in safety. They came into the city with orders for Dandolo to make peace.'

Nicholas looked up, face begrimed. Blood everywhere, and his neck throbbing. His arm tingled likewise.

Beside the Janizary captain, serving as his translator in this ravaged polyglot city, stood a thin-faced, clever-looking Moor.

Abdul of Tripoli.

'On your feet,' said the captain.

As they hauled themselves up and wiped the sweat from their faces, Abdul gave them a surreptitious wink and murmured in English, 'An eye for an eye.'

They remained expressionless.

The captain looked at him sharply. 'What tongue was that?'

'Italian,' said Abdul in Turkish. 'But Venetian dialect. An old proverb.'

The captain grunted.

By the beard of the Prophet, thought Abdul to himself, a liar and cheat has to think fast.

'Your weapons,' said a Janizary sergeant.

Smith shook his head.

Giustiniani said, 'Brother John, I order you to surrender your weapon. It may be returned to us after.'

Smith threw his beloved jezail at the sergeant, who caught it smartly. He raised it and admired the perfect barrel, then slung it over his shoulder and smiled. They were chained and marched back through the city towards the Famagusta Gate and the Ottoman camp beyond.

Up a ladder, a drunken Greek dragged down the flag of St Mark and hoisted the Turkish standard.

'You see why we lost,' murmured Stanley.

They saw an old woman being beheaded where she knelt in the dust. Old women, beyond work or childbirth, were always regarded as particularly useless booty of war. Then they threw her with other bodies on to a pyre.

Smith, even weaponless and in chains, seemed to bristle visibly with fury.

'Wait,' murmured Stanley softly to him, 'wait. Hold it all in. Our time will come. Now is the time to be strongest of all. To watch all this and do nothing. That takes strength.'

Giustiniani nodded grimly to him too. It was a humiliation almost beyond endurance, yet by a strange fate, they might yet survive the charnel-house of fallen Nicosia.

There was a fire burning in a side street, and they glimpsed a group of Janizaries, wearing expressions of grim disgust, beheading two naked, kneeling Bektaşis. Near by they saw a boy of no more than twelve years of age hanging crucified from a wooden gate.

That Lala Mustafa should still regard this hideous sacking of a city as a personal triumph and a great victory told them all they needed to know about the enemy commander.

They halted to watch. Their guards raised their muskets to belabour them onwards, but they stood as stubborn as mules.

A big bearded Janizary waved at the murdered and crucified boy. 'Get him down!' And then he rained curses on the dead Bektaşis at his feet, and finished by spitting on them.

The Janizary captain glared at his captives, as if angry with them for even witnessing this shame upon the armies of the Sultan.

'The sack of a city is always a foul thing,' he growled, 'and only the lowest can take pleasure in it. But those dogs of Bektaşis are nothing but a disgrace to us all.'

Giustiniani said sharply, 'You cannot unloose such men on a fallen city and not expect carnage. But carnage has a habit of returning on those who commit it.'

The captain said, 'Walk on,' and they were jerked forward in their chains.

They were left in a large framed tent surrounded by guards.

'What happens to us now?'

The captain, still angry and mistrustful of them, grimaced and departed without a word. A little later a black slave brought them a little bread and water.

All night the fires of Nicosia burned, and their hearts burned within them for shame and sorrow.

'The shame of the survivor,' murmured Stanley.

On the second day, a small, slender Turk stepped into their tent, flanked by two burly bodyguards who looked like wrestlers, bare to the waist, shaven headed but for nodding topknots. They were too dark skinned for Bulgars. Perhaps Kazakhs or even Tajiks.

The Turk wore a fine silk robe, unspotted by battle. He had darting eyes and a moustache as thin as a blade of grass, and standing in their tent he wrinkled his nose. They lay and sweated, still exhausted, defeated. Their own bloody shirts and boots lay on the ground around them.

'You fought hard, I see,' he said. 'For peaceful ambassadors.' His voice was very crisp and he spoke fast.

Ottoman intelligence. There was no mistaking it.

Time to sharpen their thoughts. The feel of the rack was in their joints and bones.

Giustiniani got to his feet and bowed, pulling his filthy shirt on over his powerful frame. The others shuffled upright and did likewise.

Giustiniani said, 'We were cornered in the palace and attacked, even as we tried to urge Governor Dandolo to make peace. Yet we came as ambassadors, not soldiers. My name is Federico da Mosta, at your service.'

The Turk's eyes narrowed. 'Ertugul Bey. Most humbly your servant.'

Stanley said, in the fluent Turkish that might be expected of a Venetian ambassador, 'Be assured, My Lord, that it was bitterly frustrating for us to be so ignored and overruled by the gallant and fearless Governor Dandolo, who so longed to taste the glory of war.'

As Stanley spoke, Nicholas saw his fists clenched so tight behind his back he thought his knuckles might pop.

Ertugul Bey said, 'Well, though I have no doubt at all that you are ambassadors, you are officially captive for the moment, and indeed a part of that fifth of all captive booty set aside for the Sultan himself.'

'So now we belong to Selim,' muttered Smith. 'There's a funny twist.'

Giustiniani caught his eye warningly. And Ertugul Bey in turn caught his warning. He said, 'Now that Nicosia has fallen to us, we hear that the Venetian relief fleet has already turned and sailed for home. Without a shot being fired!' He smiled. 'Your masters must have decided that Famagusta, too, is a lost cause.'

He eyed each of them in turn. Not a flicker.

'If you would release us,' said Giustiniani, cold to the heart at this appalling news but hiding it with absolute mastery, 'we would willingly ride on to Famagusta in embassy once more, and persuade them to sue for peace.'

'I'm sure you would,' said Ertugul Bey. 'But there are a few more matters to be gone through with you first. There was a Malta standard seen on the walls. And a rumour went round that there were Knights of St John fighting in the palace. An idle rumour, of course.'

'Of course,' said Giustiniani.

Their inquisitor turned on Mazzinghi like a polecat. 'Grand Commander de la Valette was a tall man, was he not?'

'I, I never met him,' stammered Mazzinghi, 'but I believe so.'

'Taller than Commander Piero del Monte?' Ertugul Bey snapped, still staring at Mazzinghi, 'would you say, Da Mosta?'

Pietro Giustiniani didn't miss a beat. 'I couldn't say, My Lord. I have not met him, but Del Monte is accounted a fine commander.'

Ertugul Bey whipped round and smiled at him again. A smile more disconcerting than any scowl.

Then he eyed Hodge. Light brown hair, blue eyes, rosy sunburned cheeks. 'God save the Queen!' he said in heavily accented English.

They stood in frozen agony, but Hodge merely frowned and shrugged.

Ertugul Bey patted him on the shoulder. 'Rumours said the knights in Nicosia were English, or perhaps had English among them. Very far from home, no?'

'And very implausible,' said Stanley. 'The Protestant English and the Catholic knights are no friends.'

'No. Yet the world is very complicated and confused these days, is it not?'

Stanley nodded. 'That it is.'

'With spies, traitors and partisans everywhere?'

'Alas, all too true. One longs for plain dealing.'

Ertugul turned on his heel. 'But delightful though it is to talk with you, I am needed elsewhere now. Meanwhile you will be cared for with all our customary Ottoman courtesy. We will talk in much more detail later, yes?' He glanced back. 'Perhaps I will talk to you each individually? That will be interesting. But meanwhile you will not mind me saying that your odour is strong, as men who have fled from battle. You will have water to wash, better food, drink. We bid you farewell.'

As Ertugul left the tent, they all breathed out.

Large basins of water were brought before the tent, scented with thyme and rosemary. They filed out and washed their hands and faces, their necks, their feet. Even that much felt like luxury.

'Wash that cut on your neck well,' said Stanley to Nicholas. 'Rosemary is good for preventing infection.'

Nicholas had almost forgotten the cut he had received, but remembered it when it stung. It was not a deep cut. Smith had a powder burn or two, and Hodge's left arm was painfully bruised and swollen from the blow of the cudgel. Smith himself rebandaged Mazzinghi's head where the Bektaşi's spear-point had cut across his temples. Yet they had survived the fall of Nicosia comparatively unscathed. Enough to fight another day.

A few minutes later, a basket of sweet, fresh-baked white bread rolls was brought to them, some new cheese, and four bottles of fine red wine. No water.

'Have a single mouthful of wine,' said Giustiniani quietly to Nicholas, looking longingly at it, 'and it may cost you your life. You need all your wits about you. Everyone.'

So they ate bread and cheese and thirsted more than ever.

'The torture's already begun,' muttered Smith.

10

Towards nightfall, Giustiniani drew the tent door closed.

'And now we shall sing a psalm,' he said. 'Psalm Twenty-three seems appropriate. *Yea though I walk through the Valley of Death* ... Sing lustily, and,' he dropped his voice and eyed Nicholas and Hodge, 'for God's sake remember to sing in Italian. Or else just hum.'

Hodge looked puzzled. 'Must we? My throat's as dry as sand.'

Stanley grinned. 'You really must.'

So they began to sing loudly. The guards outside turned to stare at the tent sourly, but did not intervene. *Christians.* And then Nicholas and Hodge understood. Under cover of the psalm, the knights took it in turns to whisper.

Outside, the boy already positioned there by Ertugul Bey, his ear to the canvas at the back of the tent, could hear nothing but this Christian caterwauling.

Stanley whispered, 'Interrogation from this Ertugul is going to be as hard as anything we have yet faced.' He resumed singing.

Smith said, weary and low, 'In a duel of wits with a weasel like that, I tell you now, I at least will soon be defeated. I know how to judge a man in a sentence or two. And there is a man of such cruel cleverness, he'll pull us apart in moments.'

Giustiniani nodded. 'And once he knows we are knights, we will be committed to questioning under severest torture.'

Nicholas felt icy needles on his back. On Malta he had heard the screams of the Chevalier Adrien de la Rivière as he was tortured by the Turks. He had heard the sound of skin being ripped from flesh, and would never forget it.

'And the irony is,' said Stanley, 'we have nothing to tell. When will the Holy League attack? Where? What is its strength? Is King Philip of Spain with it? Who is commanding?' He shook his head. 'We know nothing. Perhaps there is nothing to know. So the torture may last a while.'

'The only path left to us,' said Giustiniani, 'now we have escaped Nicosia, is to escape again. Ertugul will be back tomorrow morning.'

'From what I know of Ottoman intelligence,' said Smith, 'and indeed, our own practices in the Order, he will be back some two or three hours past midnight. When a man's defences are weakest, his wits most sluggish.'

'Keep singing!' said Giustiniani as the others fell silent for a moment.

'As soon as night falls,' whispered Stanley, 'we must try and break out.'

'How?' said Smith. 'There are half a dozen guards outside, and they will be watching us like hawks. They know that if they allow us to escape, they will all be killed.'

Their heads hurt. Escape was quite impossible. It had privately occurred to all three of the older knights that the only path left to them might yet be to kill each other.

Darkness fell and they sat in mental agony, unable to move, unable to sleep, ashamed even to look each other in the eye. Ertugul might return at any moment. They had not even weapons to kill each other or fight a suicidal last stand, here in this tent. At least Smith thought he might get his hands around that weasel's throat long enough to kill him. But what was that worth anyway? Despair crept into their bones like cold.

They picked at their nails, fidgeted, heads hung low. Outside they could hear the change of guards pacing, armed, fresh and very alert.

Then there was a stir outside the tent, the flap was pulled back and a chest was dragged inside by the black slave boy. A voice beyond said, 'Some clean robes for these unwashed Christians. Stand aside, boy.'

Nicholas looked up.

Into the tent stepped Abdul of Tripoli. He carried an oud, a Berber instrument something like a lute.

He sat down cross-legged on top of the chest and began to sing in a plangent wail, plucking the strings in accompaniment.

'Twist my ear,' muttered Nicholas. 'I'm dreaming.'

Hodge twisted his ear. He wasn't dreaming. But it was so mad a situation he almost wished he was.

After some Berber verses in praise of a beautiful she-camel – 'Surely there is no woman as faithful and loyal as she, my ship of the desert' – Abdul switched into a strangely accented Italian, and sang, 'I am allowed into your tent by special permission of Ertugul Bey. I told him I knew you were Knights of St John, and could prove it.'

Smith was on his feet in a moment, mighty fist clenched.

Nicholas's head spun. What was going on?

'Be seated, pray,' warbled Abdul. 'How else was I to gain access to you, you bearded fathead?'

Giustiniani gestured, and Smith sat down, very slowly, eyes blazing.

'In this chest beneath my fundament you will find robes.'

Smith mimed: A sword, a gun?

Abdul raised an eyebrow. 'Don't be stupid. You think a man like Ertugul would let that past? Ssh, and listen to my sweet song. In the chest are fine silk robes. Of dark hue. There are extra cloths that might be wrapped around the hooves of horses to silence them in the night. There are horses in a large corral on the eastern side of the camp. Last time I looked they were unguarded, Lala Mustafa so little fears a counter-attack across the plain from Famagusta.'

Giustiniani pointed in the direction of the guards walking outside.

Abdul sang, 'I knew you would be wise enough not to drink this dangerous gift of wine. Now, here is another gift.' He raised his elbow and from his armpit fell a small bottle.

'Tincture of opium in alcohol. Add it to the wine, quickly.'

They unstoppered the bottles and did as he said. Stanley began to smile. It was just dawning on the six prisoners that they might yet escape, thanks to this extraordinary, devious, brilliant Moor.

'Now there is enough drug in each bottle,' sang Abdul, 'to

make an elephant dream it is Emperor of China.' He sprang to his feet and strummed the oud in staccato little chords and sang very rapidly now. 'I shall offer the wine to the guards as I go. You should pray to your God on his little wooden cross that the guards take the risk of a swig. Then I am going straight back to Ertugul to tell him you are Knights of St John. His tent is fifteen minutes' leisurely stroll away. I will take five minutes to tell him, with much characteristic Moorish circumlocution and flattering slipperiness of tongue. The kind that so sickens you pure-hearted Christians. He may be back just ten minutes after that, with his favourite box of pincers and tongs.' He stopped singing and bowed low.

'Gentlemen.'

Giustiniani mimed a last, puzzled Why?

'Out of the great love I bear you, my brothers,' said Abdul softly, with a reproachful look. Then he beamed. 'But if we meet up again in Famagusta, as is my plan – Famagusta, reputed wealthiest city in the world – then perhaps you will bestow on me some reward? Your Order is rich, and so is Venice. My own weight in gold should suffice.'

Then the tent flap whipped open and shut and he vanished.

There were quiet voices outside. Tones of casual offer and decline. A shared joke. Hesitation.

Inside the tent they could hardly breathe. Stanley was scratching letters on a flat stone.

And then there was the sound of a bottle being unstoppered. Abdul himself took a fake swig, hoping that the mere touch of that drugged wine to his lips was not enough to put him in a swoon.

Smith and Stanley were on their feet already, throwing open the chest and passing out silk robes. All of black or midnight blue. And extra squares of silk and cotton too. That Moor was as cunning as a thousand foxes.

Then Smith began counting to four hundred.

'Make it six hundred,' said Stanley. He pulled on his boots and flexed his powerful hands, rubbed his arms and stretched his broad shoulders.

*

On Giustiniani's orders, Smith and Stanley alone came out of the tent, fast and silent as panthers. There were muffled grunts and groans, a single drowsy shout of surprise, and the sound of bodies slumping to the ground. Then the other four slipped out to join them.

Six guards lay dead or unconscious on the ground, heads twisted at strange angles.

Smith looked swiftly around.

'That was close,' muttered Stanley. 'None of them were entirely asleep even then. Just slow witted.'

'I'm getting too old for this,' said Smith.

Stanley reached down and tucked the flat stone he had been writing on into the jerkin of one of the guards still breathing.

'Come,' said Giustiniani, already heading off into the darkness among the farther tents.

Mazzinghi bent to pick up one of the guards' spears.

'Leave it,' said Giustiniani. 'Move.'

'What was that stone you wrote on?' asked Smith.

Stanley said, 'If you wake, flee. Save yourselves.'

Smith grimaced. 'In a foul war, that was not a bad deed.'

They walked confidently through the camp in their dark robes, looping round south and then east.

'Heads up, not too hurried,' said Giustiniani. 'Walk as if you were born and bred in this camp. Walk as if you own the very ground beneath you.'

He and Stanley conversed in Turkish, audibly, Stanley's shaggy flaxen hair and beard quite evident in the half-moonlight.

Most of the Turkish army were asleep, wine-parched mouths agape, though some were awake, admiring their loot or dicing. The six greeted all they met with calm authority. A guard dog lunged and barked at Smith, its chain jangling. He took time to hold the back of his hand out to its nose, pet it. The dog wagged its tail.

Sweat ran down Nicholas's back in rivulets.

No one had challenged them yet.

But it was a long walk.

*

They reached the huge, wooden-fenced horse corral just as a shout went up from the heart of the camp. Then a loud bugle call.

Too late to use those cloths to silence the horses' hooves.

They vaulted into the corral and seized their horses by the manes, calmed them, drew them to the side, using the fence itself to mount them. No saddle, stirrups, bridle – nothing.

'Hold on tight!' said Stanley.

Smith kicked his horse into the centre of the corral, where the horses clustered, watching them, uncertain. Then he leaned forward and began to growl at them, a low lupine growl, baring his teeth. His own horse shied and others skittered backwards, one or two rearing half-heartedly. He lashed out and caught one a blow on the muzzle. They nickered and began to panic, rolling their eyes, ears back, and then starting to move in a great circle. Dust arose silvery in the moonlight.

There came a shout, a crossbow bolt thocked into the wooden rail of the corral, followed by an angrier shout.

Giustiniani and Stanley leaned from their mounts and drew the gates open and the six galloped forward. The panicked herd came after them.

'There'll be other horses!' cried Mazzinghi.

'Of course!' said Giustiniani. 'With stirrup and bridle too. So move!'

The panicked herd covered the plain to the east of the camp with hoofprints and kicked up an immense cloud of dust from the hard summer earth. But soon they began to fall back, and the six were out on their own. Then behind them they could hear another, more determined drumming of hooves. Ottoman lancers, Sipahis, armed and in full pursuit.

11

Nicholas leaned down low behind his horse's stretching neck, hair and mane blown back in the hot night. His thighs gripped the horse's belly, his hands on its withers, kicking furiously all the way. And no idea what quality of horse this was, but unlikely to be a match for the beautiful Arab horses of the Sipahis.

Dust and stars, sweat and terrible thirst. He twisted and looked back. A dust cloud coming on, a dust cloud with white Arab stallions emerging ghostly from it, white horses riding on waves of dust. Even as he felt the cold dread of a lance in his side, there was the unspeakable beauty of it all. The starlit world, the night, the thunderous galloping, the terror and the coursing of his blood.

They burst into a sparse pinewood and veered back and forth through the trees, whiplashed and torn by low branches, horses stumbling, dangerously close to being lamed. The horses' hoof-falls muffled on the needles, the sullen drumbeat of the Sipahis' horses behind them, as many as fifty men.

'Oh, for a sword, for one damn blade!' cried Smith.

But all they had was the silk robes they wore.

'It is having no armour or weapons that may yet save us,' called Giustiniani. 'At least we travel light!'

'Then more speed!' roared Smith, heeling his horse's flanks without mercy. 'I'm as light as a giddy girl!'

They came out of the wood again and across a dry burnt plain, then a stubble field burned black. Greek peasants had destroyed all they had, even their own fields of wheat, before the oncoming Turks. They would rather starve than feed the enemy, now they had heard of the agony of Nicosia, the treachery and the despair, and most of all the sacking of the churches, the desecration of the holy icons. Gradually the atrocities of the invader were doing what such atrocities always do: they were hardening the people against them.

At last the drumbeat of pursuing hooves seemed to fall back. They dared to look round – the dust cloud was far behind.

Yet still they rode on, the moon overhead, a few thin clouds racing.

After some more miles, Mazzinghi let out a great whoop.

'Brother,' said Giustiniani sharply. 'Less noise now.'

Then he relaxed his own horse into a trot and they all did likewise. He looked around at them and his eyes gleamed. Despite the bloodshed, despite the loss of the city, this was a moment of unreal exhilaration. They still lived, to fight another day.

Beyond a rise they came to a halt. The flanks of Nicholas's horse were foaming and going like furnace bellows, and then it put out a hind leg and leaned at an unnatural angle.

'Off!' cried Hodge, and, seizing Nicholas, he dragged him sideways as the horse toppled away and fell on its side. Nicholas clambered to his feet where he sprawled in the dust, swiped his face and moved round to examine the poor beast.

The stricken animal's breathing was shallow; blood coursed from its nostrils and its wide white eyes saw nothing. The breathing suddenly stopped, the flow of blood came to a halt.

'Dismount all,' said Giustiniani.

Even if the Sipahis still came on now, they had no dogs with them to follow the fugitives' traces. They were surely safe.

They led the other five horses into an orchard of lemon trees. The air was sweet.

Nicholas looked back at the dead horse. Innocence died easy.

They found a deserted village and enough stale water in a stone trough to slake their horses' thirst. But no more mounts, not even a mule or donkey. Nicholas would have to ride with Hodge. It was only another two or three leagues to the walls of Famagusta. They should make it by dawn or soon after.

They rested for half an hour and then walked on. They found a goat, tethered and unmilked, and drank her milk, a few mouthfuls each. Then they turned her loose. A little farther on there was a well, and Stanley pronounced it not poisoned. Nevertheless they drank slowly and carefully.

Behind them all was darkness still, and fallen Nicosia still burned. After three days of looting, no doubt the churches would be washed clean of Christian blood. The cathedral would be turned into a mosque and sanctified by prayer, the uncouth flagstones covered in fine carpets for the bare feet of the faithful. A Christian church was like a stable, and the Christians tramped in still wearing their dusty and grimy boots, even before their God.

In the east the sky was greying.

'I think I can almost see the towers and spires of Famagusta,' murmured Stanley. 'Hear the waves breaking at the foot of her mighty walls.'

'Is she really so beautiful a city as they say?' asked Hodge.

'A fairy-tale city built on sand, tawny as a lion ... I think she is the most beautiful city I ever saw after Jerusalem.'

They shivered. Even the name sounded like poetry.

City of the vanished Lusignan Kings.

Lost city of the sand.

Fabled Famagusta ...

The outlying country around Famagusta was burned black, with barely a tree standing nor one stone upon another.

'I'm impressed,' said Smith. 'What was his name again?'

'Bragadino. Governor Bragadino. You remember we met his two sons in Sicily?'

Smith nodded, and Nicholas remembered them too. A pair of green-eyed panthers, softly spoken, watchful and lethal. He wished they were with their father now.

The sun was just up and the day brightening fast. They wanted to be within the walls soon.

There was a pool in a hollow, but it smelt foul. Already poisoned, like every well in the district. Nevertheless Mazzinghi knelt down beside it.

'Drink that, you'll never see the fair ladies of Famagusta,' said Stanley.

Mazzinghi said, 'Just checking my bandage.'

Smith frowned. 'Let me see the wound.'

Mazzinghi sprang to his feet again. 'The wound is fine. I just want my bloody bandage to look its best when we ride into the city.'

Smith's eyes bulged.

Mazzinghi turned side-on to give the battered older knight a view of his damnably handsome young features, offset by the broad white bandage around his wide forehead. 'I think, of all the accessories a soldier can sport to win the ladies, a fresh bloody bandage about the forehead is the best,' he said. 'Somehow a bandage about the foot or the thigh is just not so effective. It doesn't set off one's noble visage nearly so well.'

Smith said, 'Though as a Knight of St John, the thought of fair ladies never crosses your mind.'

'Of course not,' said Mazzinghi with a grin. 'Heaven forbid.'

There was one hut suspiciously untouched, and inside a table with a ripe goat's cheese on a wooden trencher. Nicholas eyed it longingly.

'I wouldn't,' said Stanley.

'What if we cook it?'

He shook his head. 'That won't destroy the poison.'

Smith kicked the table hard, the cheese shot to the floor and he stomped it into the earth. 'That wouldn't have fooled the Turks for a moment,' he said. 'But they'd have fed it to a prisoner, to test it, and he'd have died.'

It was Hodge who first said he could see towers and spires through the heat haze. They rode on a little, and then it was unmistakable. A fairy tale of a city indeed, something out of an ancient chapbook or prayerbook, Gothic lances of stonework rising into the shimmering burning air. A mighty wall all around it, and the tang of the sea on the air.

Nicholas twisted behind Hodge and reached into his small knapsack and drew out a familiar square of old cloth. He shook it out in front of Smith, red rag to a bull.

The Standard of Malta.

'You ...' Smith scowled. 'You took it down from the walls? You carried it through captivity? Why on earth did you not hand it to me, then? If they had found it on you, boy, they would have put you to the torture in an instant.'

Nicholas pushed the cloth into Smith's hands. 'I forgot I had it,' he said vaguely.

'You *forgot*? You lie.'

The boy turned away and he and Hodge heeled the horse and it clopped forward again, tired head nodding.

Smith and Stanley and Giustiniani sat their horses a moment and looked after them. The rising sun haloed the two riders in bronze sunlight, their thin grubby figures almost silhouetted. Each of them but twenty-two years of age, and to veteran knights like these, mere boys still. And yet what a pair. The faithful, long-suffering Hodge, shrewd survivor; and Nicholas himself, wanderer, exile, vagabond, robbed of his rightful inheritance, world-weary but still full of young desire for the world.

'If I didn't know him for a worthless tosspot and whoremonger,' murmured Stanley, 'I'd say Master Ingoldsby had kept a hold on that standard deliberately. So that if it was found by our captors, he would have been punished for it and not you.'

Smith rubbed his beard. 'As tosspots and whoremongers go, perhaps he isn't the worst.'

Then Giustiniani pointed towards a scurry of dust over the plain, and said, 'We have company.'

'Another good sign,' said Stanley. 'Dandolo never did outriders.'

'Draw up!' cried Smith. 'No weapons!' And he shook out the Standard of Malta and held it high.

Stanley had a vision of how it might appear to a passing bird. Their tiny group, so small upon the vast burnt plain, six men on five horses, surrounded by a troop of disciplined cavalry, lances lowered, forming a tight circle.

The cavalry captain sat his jouncing horse and demanded, 'Who goes here?'

'God with you,' said Giustiniani. 'Knights of St John and gentlemen volunteers. All six of us.' He smiled, nodding towards Famagusta. 'We are come to save your poor city.'

The captain said, 'We know Nicosia is finished. How far off is the Turk? Our scouts have reported nothing.'

'Another day or two,' said Giustiniani. 'We have ridden hard all night. And we are not pulling cannon.'

'Follow me. Fast trot!'

12

As they neared the city Nicholas saw how magnificently built it was, three landward walls and a fourth seaward, the waves indeed lapping at its base as Stanley had said. Walls second only to those of Jerusalem or Consantinople, so it was said. But the walls of Nicosia, too, had been impressive. What gave him most heart, after the wretched past few weeks, was the sense of crisp order and efficiency. It had him sitting up straighter on his nodding horse, weary and famished as he was.

A postern gate was opened and they rode in and dismounted. They led their horses through a maze of hot dusty streets, gloomy arched passageways and steeply-roofed towers. Everything was an orderly bustle, soldiers everywhere, men and women with barrows, a little boy and girl, brother and sister, carrying a single cannon-ball between them in a sling of cloth. Two burly bearded priests, perspiring heavily in their black robes, silver crosses on their chests, carrying rocks on their shoulders to the walls.

The sense of steely determination was palpable. Their hearts swelled within them. A city of men and women and children pre-pared to stand and fight against a huge invading army. Nicholas had half forgotten the pity and the pathos of it. Malta all over again. And then, far more than Malta, Famagusta was a city of such ghostly, breathtaking beauty. A city of three hundred and sixty-five churches, it was said, one for every day of the year, and each more lovely than the last. Neat Orthodox chapels with rounded walls and golden domes, lancet windows and Gothic arches in the French style, St George of the Latins, St George of the Greeks, churches

of the Armenians, Nestorians, Syrian Jacobites, Copts, Franciscans
... and everywhere, priests in black and friars in brown, working
among the people, sweating and dusty as any.

'Like Outremer before the fall ...' murmured Stanley.

All of it surrounded by two miles of formidable walls fifty feet high,
twenty feet thick and now massively bulked by the ceaseless labours
of the citizens. Five main gates, fifteen bastions, a deep dry ditch. The
great Lion of Venice, carved in stone, high over the sea gate, glaring
out unblinking over the burning Mediterranean. The citadel and the
Great Hall of the Lusignans, the palace of the Governor ornamented
with granite columns taken from nearby ancient Salamis, palm trees
rustling in the breeze, and gorgeous flags and standards high on the
battlements. The streets a swarming entrepôt of Levantine exiles,
Phoenician merchants from Beirut and Tyre, Jews, Syrians, Greeks,
Italians, Alexandrians. Crusader chapels, fountains and courtyards,
back alleys with cool, shadowy taverns exuding the aroma of
sweet Cyprus wine. And in the heart of the city, the magnificent
St Nicholas cathedral, modelled on the cathedral of Rheims itself.
Like a Gothic fantasy stranded on the shores of a desert island ...

It was like being back in the times of Saladin and Richard Coeur-
de-lion. Jerusalem the Golden was near now, where Christ himself
had walked. Just across that sparkling sea.

'Farthing for your thoughts,' said Stanley, but Nicholas just
smiled.

He was thinking, Here would be a fair place to fight and die, if
I must.

'I'll tell you my thoughts,' said Smith.

Stanley sighed. 'If you must. But I'm not paying for them.'

'I'm thinking, Famagusta is the toughest nut in the eastern
Mediterranean. She will stand for months. And if Don John and
the Holy League attacked the Ottoman fleet at sea, once siege is
engaged here, we could destroy the power of the Turk utterly.'

'Hope and pray, Fra John,' said Stanley. 'Hope and pray.'

Grooms took their shabby, tired horses, and they were led into
a courtyard of the Governor's palace. No waiting this time. The
moment the Governor heard there were fugitives from Nicosia, he
came out to them.

A tall man of some sixty years of age, scion of one of Venice's noblest families. Black doublet and hose, long white hair elegantly combed back over the ears, a grave expression, and searching eyes. Green eyes, like his sons.

'God save you. You come with news of Nicosia?'

'All bad news,' said Giustiniani. 'The city is fallen with great loss of life, great brutality. We escaped only by the grace of God and trickery. Now the siege army of Lala Mustafa is marching this way. He will expect your instant surrender, like Kyrenia and Lemessos.'

Governor Bragadino grimaced. 'Numbers? Our scouts estimated some fifty thousand.'

'More. Seventy thousand, and with the usual complement of guns. But it was the mines that finished Nicosia.'

'As usual. And a relief fleet from Venice was seen near Crete, but has now turned back. You heard this too?'

'Aye. We heard it.'

Bragadino's eyes glittered, impossible to read. 'Come. You look half starved. Eat and drink.'

Giustiniani introduced them all as they walked inside.

'Knights of St John are always welcome at a siege,' said Bragadino. 'Although I see you have not a weapon nor a scrap of armour among you. And Commander Piero del Monte might have sent more of a relief force than four.'

'With respect, sire, we hardly made it across Cyprus as it was. And Piero del Monte is holding the knights in readiness for the Holy League, and the final confrontation. He believes it will be a sea battle. A clash of two galley fleets, such as the world has never seen.'

Bragadino nodded thoughtfully. 'Well, you are welcome now, especially after Malta. And as for the two travelling Englishmen ...'

'They too fought at Malta.'

Bragadino eyed Nicholas and Hodge with a new curiosity. 'Did they indeed? Hm.'

He ordered platefuls of food for them all, jugs of cool water fresh drawn from the well, sweet Cyprus wine. 'After this, you can sleep.'

Nicholas felt tired even as he ate.

'After this, we would be glad of a tour of the walls,' said Smith.

*

Bragadino called for a map, and showed them what his latest intelligence told him.

'Famagusta will stand as long as it can. But look. It is an island in a Mohammedan sea. The Ottomans are already far to the west. On the Adriatic they hold the coastal forts of Dulcigno, Antivari and Budva. You know that Kara Hodja, the Black Priest, even briefly blockaded the basin of St Mark itself? A disgrace.

'That most cunning Grand Vizier, Mehmet Sokollu, orders raids on Crete, to keep Venice distracted there, but still afraid to commit to total war. Spain is similarly distracted by the internal revolt of the Moriscos, again manipulated from Constantinople, we are sure. All of Christendom is in turmoil, the Ottomans outfox us at every turn, both on the battlefield and in intelligence and diplomacy. They sow discord, keeping us at each other's throats. They may be arming the Protestants in the Netherlands. And with Cyprus taken, we have heard one rumour that they plan the most breathtaking attack of all. On Rome.'

They stared. '*Rome?*' said Nicholas softly.

Bragadino said, 'Centuries ago, the ninth century after Christ, Muslim hordes also took Rome. They held the Pope himself to ransom. Why should they not do so again? Imagine what would happen. All of Protestant Europe would rejoice at the fall of the Great Babel of Rome, would it not? Rush to congratulate the Turks? Or would England, say,' he fixed Nicholas, 'finally realise that Europe must stand together, or it is lost?'

Nicholas stammered, lost for words.

'Meanwhile, we hold them here in Cyprus.'

'This last corner of Cyprus, you mean,' said Stanley.

'Just so. And we pray that the Holy League realises the extent of the peril, and comes together at last.'

A messenger whispered in the Governor's ear. He nodded curtly, looked around at his new guests unseeing, and then whispered a reply. The messenger departed, with Bragadino following close on his heels.

He reappeared a minute later. 'Another tasty dish has just arrived,' he said drily.

Giustiniani mopped his mouth with a napkin. 'Sire?'

'A head on a plate. Can you guess whose?'

Stanley said, 'God save us all, the fool has followed us here. Or the least-thinking part of him anyway.'

'We saw him beheaded before our own eyes,' said Smith. 'It was a very clean cut. I take it you mean the topmost part of Governor Dandolo?'

'The same,' said Bragadino. 'With a note demanding our immediate surrender. He comes with as much style as he ever mustered, his head on a silver platter. A look of surprise set cold on his face.'

'Garnished with pigeon livers and white lilies?' said Mazzinghi.

Bragadino gave a very quick, faint smile, and then said, 'In truth, it was the folly of Venice to appoint him Governor on this front line, right under the nose of the Turk.'

'We are told the Governor of Famagusta has more belly.'

Again the faint smile.

Giustiniani asked, 'How will you reply, sire?'

'Will? Nay, the time is short and I have replied already. The reply is plain. *With your own blood you will capture this city.*'

There was a moment of silence. Nicholas's heart thumped. There was to be no relief and no surrender. He had always known, but now it was certain. Such a reply was a blast of the bugle.

It was coming. And soon.

He took another gulp of wine. Then another. Heaviness and dread and that dangerous excitement in the blood.

Sir John Smith, Knight Grand Cross and lover of battle, meanwhile, leaned back in his chair, stretched luxuriously and grinned through his thick black beard. 'Lala Mustafa Pasha will not like that.'

'No,' said Bragadino. 'He will not like it one bit. But life does not always go according to plan, even for the greatest.'

Stanley grinned too. This was a man to lead them.

Bragadino stood, popped a morsel of bread in his mouth, and said, 'Come and see the walls. Before you fall asleep.'

They toured the broad tops of the walls, marvelling at their massive breadth and strength, and the busy efficiency of work going on.

Bragadino indicated the moat below. 'Plentifully spiked with small mines, tripwires, grenades buried just beneath the sand. More primitive are the planks studded with poison nails, and the baskets of vipers we have in store.'

'Vipers?' said Hodge. 'What d'you want with vipers, sir?'

Bragadino looked rueful. 'Something for the boys to do. I sent them all out to catch vipers, and gave them a copper per head. When it comes to the attack, we tip them out on the Turks' heads. What say you, master Englishman?'

'I say, vipers aren't great distinguishers between Mohammedan and Christian, and tend to bite any man that passes. And I should know,' he added feelingly.

Bragadino smiled. 'You may be right. We shall see.'

'I see dust,' said Nicholas softly.

All turned. Smith knelt and laid his hand on the stones. Was it imagination, or could he feel a deep rumble, as from the underworld itself? He stood again. But Ingoldsby was right, eyes like a hawk. The horizon was losing the definition of the hard Mediterranean light. A gigantic dust cloud was arising.

'Here they come,' said Mazzinghi.

13

They found billets and, with the Ottoman army only a few hours off, managed to snatch a few hours of uneasy sleep. They awoke again as it was growing dark.

'Like a ruddy bat,' said Hodge. 'My eyes will wither in me skull.'

Nicholas was staring at the whitewashed wall opposite. Now washed red in the setting sun. He felt sure one of them would die here.

They wandered through the streets, and a woman called down from a balcony. 'Evening, my gallants!'

Nicholas glanced up. A woman old enough to be his mother, dark hair piled high, low-cut dress displaying ample bosom. He bowed politely to her and she laughed, a rich, throaty laugh.

They found their way to the armoury and Smith and Stanley were there already. They chose basic arquebuses and powder pouches and balls, and found breastplates and backplates and the small morion-style helmets which they liked best. Little more than steel caps, doing nothing to protect the face or neck, only the skull, but they left the vision free and weighed little. Ideal for those who moved fast.

Smith started to object, saying a flying splinter could take a jawbone off, but Stanley said, 'They're right. Their strength is their speed, remember.'

Stanley and Smith went heavy armoured, with a pair of poignards at their waists, mighty swords hanging from their left sides, a pair of pistols each.

'But oh for my old jezail,' murmured Smith. 'I could take out Lala Mustafa from the walls with just one shot.'

'That would change things,' agreed Stanley. 'It would mean the Ottomans *mustafa* new commander.'

'Please,' said Smith. 'Not now.'

He hung as many as a dozen grenades from his belt.

'Don't stand too near me,' said Stanley. 'You'll go up like a powder store.'

Smith's teeth showed white. He was burning to begin.

Nicholas swished his own light sword. He knew how Smith felt. It was the only way to manage the tension and not run mad. The only way without women.

They stood on the walls and watched the vast Ottoman camp establish itself by torchlight. A magnificent sight, hundreds of camels and mules, companies of slaves, great squares of tents and broad avenues, just like at Nicosia.

'They look like an army fresh from home still,' muttered Smith.

And it was true. Many of them had barely fought yet, merely sacked, and were as keen as any for the battle to begin.

'Bragadino said we have four thousand men,' said Stanley. 'Venetian and some Spanish. You sure that's seventy thousand out there?'

'Thereabouts,' said Smith. 'Why, do you want more to get your teeth into?'

Gangs of slaves began earthing up ramps for the cannon, and they saw one huge shadowy shape in the darkness, a gleaming bronze barrel like some monster from the ocean deep. Its team of twenty-four powerful draught oxen strained under the lash to drag it forward over the flat dusty earth.

'The first bombardment will start tomorrow,' said Smith. 'Not full assault, just ranging shots, testing shots.'

'Still,' said Hodge, 'best not try to stop the balls with your belly, eh?'

Stanley grinned. 'That's the spirit, Master Hodge. That's the spirit.'

*

But the next night brought someone else into the siege. A legendary name. They were not alone.

Famagusta harbour was closed off by a giant chain, hanging from two stone windlasses the size of castle keeps. It rendered the harbour and the few galleys within both safe and useless. The Turkish fleet bobbed at anchor beyond it on the mild summer sea.

But at night a single galley came in among them as the sky clouded over and the stars were lost. It moved without a single torch or lantern, a black shadow on the dark sea.

Then its guns roared out at near-point-blank range into the hulls of the sleeping Turkish ships, and three of them were sunk within minutes.

The black galley came to the mole beside the great chain, where all but two of its passengers and crew crawled on to the harbour wall under the pikes of the guards. The last two aboard scuppered her immediately outside the chain and swam for it. The galley sank in the shallow water, forming yet another obstacle in the path of any enemy trying to break into the harbour.

A messenger came to Bragadino, dining late with the knights.

'An arrival by sea, sire!'

'By sea?'

All looked up. There in the doorway stood a man of some sixty-five years of age, perhaps seventy. It was hard to tell, for he still gave off the strength and energy of a much younger man. A long fine nose, straggly beard and deep-set eyes circled with dark rings.

The Chevalier Romegas, Knight Commander of St John. The most feared sea-wolf in the Mediterranean.

They embraced heartily.

'Before God it does me good to see you here!' said Giustiniani after Romegas had told his tale. 'And leaving three Turkish galleys sunk in your wake! The Chevalier Romegas does not become any milder with the years.'

The old sailor's eyes gleamed. 'I'll become milder when the Sword of Islam is beaten into a pruning hook.'

They drank to that.

'I bring you all of six marines to fight,' he said, 'no galley, no supplies. But still more than Venice or any other power sends you, eh?'

'Bitter truth.'

'I also bring you fifty Muslim pilgrims, on the haj, whom we took captive coming here. They have been well treated. You may find them useful bargaining chips.'

Bragadino absorbed this surprising news. 'What of the Holy League?'

Romegas's dark-ringed eyes looked pained. His heart was sorrowful for this courageous governor.

Bragadino read him instantly. 'None?'

Romegas shook his head. 'In consistory they continue to argue. Don John presses very hard, but the Genoese are against any joint operation with the Venetians. The French are as elusive as ever, Philip urges caution—'

'Their world is coming to an end!' cried Smith. 'Now is no time for caution! Why, I'd take Genoa and Venice by the scruff of their haughty necks and dash their heads together till they clanged like bells. *Do they not understand what danger they are in? Do they not realise?*'

There was a sombre silence.

Then Bragadino squared his shoulders. 'It is as before. No help will come. We are alone.'

'We should get more sleep while we can,' said Hodge.

'Sleep now?' said Nicholas. 'That's a joke.'

The Ottoman miners would already be cutting into the ground with picks and shovels, behind their wooden and wickerwork screens. Among the tents, Janizaries would be sharpening their scimitars, combing and waxing their fine black moustaches, praying their last prayers to Mecca.

'Well, I'm sleeping,' said Hodge, and he vanished back to their billet. Nicholas followed a while later.

He came down an alleyway and there in a doorway was the woman he had glimpsed on the balcony. She must have been not far off forty, yet she was a handsome woman, tall for a Greek, her dark hair piled up and offset with a red ribbon. The black dress and lace mantilla of a widow in mourning went ill with her voluptuous figure and the wicked light in her bold dark eyes.

'Ah, it's my fair-haired gallant,' she said when she saw him. 'Give company to a poor widow, far from home?'

'Me too,' he said. 'Farther than you. I am from England.'

She looked him up and down as if inspecting a ham in a butcher's shop, almost smacking her lips. 'A young Englishman? I am from Venice.'

'That explains it,' he said drily.

'Explains what, Baby-face?'

'The Greek women are more … guarded. Whereas your Venetian women are well known to be more *generous* in every way.'

She scowled, hands on her hips. 'Impertinent baby-faced whelp.'

He sighed. 'How much?'

It was terrible how the imminent prospect of death caused such lust.

'I was going to offer you a favour for nothing,' she said, 'seeing as the battle starts tomorrow and you'll be stretched out dead by nightfall, while we women with more wit will live happily for many another day. Men, though, they go over the cliff like lemmings and call it heroism.'

He considered. Then he bowed and said, 'Madam, please pardon my impertinent words.' Half her age he might be, but she was alluring and life was short. Besides, he had never found the mock battle between men and women so hard to engage in. Indeed, the enemy, whether wives, widows or maids, had often enough taken him by the hand and drawn him into their bedchambers without even an assault on his part. He thought of the jailer's daughter in Djerba. That had been risky indeed.

He smiled and took her hand now, the fingers brightly beringed, gazed into her eyes and murmured, 'I was confused for a moment there by your unspeakable and heavenly beauty.'

She pulled her hand free, tossed her head, and said, 'You lie like a Roman cardinal.' Then she put her arms around his waist and pulled him to her.

Ah, the little feints, the charges and retreats …

He could smell the perfume in her hair.

'We poor widows,' she said, 'the downtrodden and oppressed,

241

who are we to be proud? We need protection. Come inside, then, English soldier boy, though it feels wrong, you being about the age of my own son.'

They stepped inside the doorway and he kissed her full and generous mouth.

Didn't they say a woman her age was most warm and passionate? 'Like a fine wine,' he murmured.

'You,' she said. 'Never trust a man so smooth with words.' And she nudged the door shut with her bare foot.

He had leapt from the bed and was standing naked in the chamber before he realised why.

In his last few seconds of sleep, he had heard the distant roar of a great gun, and then the thump of an iron ball against stone.

It was dawn. It had begun.

She sighed and stretched, hair tousled across the pillow. 'Come back to bed.'

If he didn't get his breeches on immediately, it would be too tempting.

'Didn't you hear that?' he snapped.

She opened her eyes. 'What?'

'The Turkish guns. It's started.'

14

He hurried through the streets to their billet, and was directed to the landward bastion of the west wall. Below the bastion was a maze of tunnels, chambers, powder stores and, most important of all, gun rooms, where the dark muzzles of slim culverins and field guns nosed out through narrow niches, ready to give enfilading fire across the entire breadth of Famagusta's walls. Any attacking enemy would be mown down like summer grass.

He raced up the steps, head low. At the top, lying behind the sloping ramp where the defenders sheltered, he found Smith, Stanley and Hodge.

Hodge eyed him. 'You look drained. Refreshing night's sleep?'

'Just jealousy.'

'Where's your helmet, you ass?' growled Smith.

In his hurry he had left it at the widow's.

Running back with the helmet he heard a voice call from behind.

'Master Nicholas of England!'

It couldn't be. He spun round.

It was. Abdul of Tripoli.

'If I didn't know better, I'd think you were stalking me. How the devil did you get into the city?'

'The fortunes of war,' said Abdul, typically vague. 'Look.' And he produced a long, slender object wrapped in oiled white linen. 'Where is your friend Smit?'

'Follow me. That's not ... is it?'

*

It was. Abdul knelt before Smith and unwrapped the bundle. There lay his beloved Persian jezail.

Smith snatched it up, eyes shining like a boy's on his birthday. He leaned on the wall and sighted down the barrel. It was perfect.

Behind him, Abdul coughed. 'I am glad you like my musket, sire.'

Smith snapped back, '*Your* musket?'

'Indeed. Many dangers I endured to keep it to myself. Now I will sell it to you.'

'Sell it to me?' Smith looked as if he was about to reach out and wring Abdul's neck where he knelt.

'He's right, Smith,' said Stanley mildly. 'It was yours. Now it is his. You must pay the man.'

Eyes now shining with a darker, more dangerous light, Smith said, 'How much?'

Abdul named his price.

'Curses and leprosy on you, Moor, I don't have that kind of money.'

'Yet you know it is worth twice that amount.'

The damnable thing was, the Moor was right.

'I will take a promissory oath from you, for the full amount to be paid within the month.'

'We'll be dead in a month.'

'You, perhaps. Not me. Then I will just take back the jezail from your cold hands. Like a pawnbroker. Otherwise, that is my price. Plus ten per cent.'

'You sure you have no Jewish blood?'

Abdul just smiled.

'And why the devil is a Moor selling guns to a Christian?'

'Christians sell guns to Moors often enough,' said Abdul sharply. 'I have seen English arms merchants with my own eyes in Casablanca and Marrakesh. In return they take back good quantities of saltpetre, that key ingredient in the single most delicious recipe ever cooked up by the hand of man: ten parts saltpetre, two parts charcoal, a measure and a half of sulphur. Grind to a fine powder, and there you have it. Boom!'

Smith scowled furiously.

'Yes,' said Abdul, enjoying himself very much now, 'you

Christians may have plenty of sulphur and charcoal, but the very finest saltpetre is in Morocco, Syria, Egypt and Iraq. The lands of Islam! It is all ours, and yet Christendom cannot run without it! Truly we are blessed by Allah.'

'Devil.'

'I watch,' said Abdul. 'Others see but I observe. I wait, and I take my chance when it comes. I intend to die a very rich man.'

'What's the point of that?' said Nicholas. 'You can't take it with you.'

Abdul smiled and tapped the side of his long thin nose. 'I shall find a way. I shall negotiate with Azrael, the Angel of Death himself.'

'He bloody well will too,' said Hodge.

'Observe now,' said Abdul, 'while we have been talking. The guns have been pulled back. I think Lala Mustafa is going to have a parade.'

'A *parade*?'

He nodded. 'To dishearten you. I overheard them discussing it, not forty-eight hours ago.'

And he was right.

The guns were rested after their brief opening barrage of ranging shots, and instead the great plain between the Ottoman encampment and the city walls began to fill with division after division of the Ottoman army on full dress parade.

'Is this a siege or isn't it?' grumbled Smith.

'Mental warfare,' said Stanley. 'Good tactics.'

At a safe distance of half a mile away was spread out what seemed like all the manpower of the Ottoman empire: Constantinople, Antioch, Damascus, Alexandria ... Those ancient, teeming cities of the East were inexhaustible.

A rumour was spreading along the city walls that the Mohammedan army numbered a quarter of a million. Another rumour said that Lala Mustafa had promised to make a pyramid of severed heads. Panic was spreading, the Turks were already winning.

'We need to do something,' said Smith.

Upon the plain, long trumpets blared, cannons fired blanks,

pipes wailed and cymbals clashed. The great squares of Janizaries in their white silk robes and plumes of heron and ostrich feathers turned and wheeled in perfect order, to the audible shouts of their captains. There were holy men in green turbans carrying banners inscribed with the names of Allah in gold embroidery, horses champing and lavishly caparisoned, great goatskin drums beating out a slow stately march. The numbers of their besiegers were beyond telling.

And out in front of the vast parade rode a man in a midnight-blue robe on a white stallion, a drawn scimitar in his hand.

Lala Mustafa.

Stanley pointed along the wall. 'Bragadino's having words with the gunnery team there, look.'

'Guess what he's planning.'

They went over, passing by a young Venetian arquebusier who was watching this intimidating display with eyes flared wide like those of a frightened horse. He was shaking so much, the barrel of his arquebus rattled on the top of the wall.

Stanley laid his big, heavy hand on the fellow's arm and he shook a little less. 'Watch this display of ours, son,' he said. 'It'll put new mettle in you.'

A gunner was just ramming home a fist-sized iron ball when they came alongside.

'Gentlemen,' said Bragadino with a quick bow. 'A reply was called for. Now,' he said to the gunnery team. 'Hit them.'

'That'll have to be a mighty good shot,' said the gunnery sergeant.

'Then make it a mighty good shot,' snapped Bragadino.

Nicholas caught Stanley's eye and they both smiled. Who did that remind them of? Grand Master Jean de la Valette, victor of Malta. To the very letter.

They quickly rolled the gun carriage forward into position, the muzzle at the niche. A gunner held the smoking linstock to the powder hole at the cannon's breech.

'Permission to fire too, sire?' said Smith.

'Knights of St John rarely take orders from any but their own,' said Bragadino drily.

Then Smith was a blur of movement, astonishingly deft and precise. He slid the rod free from the long musket, cleaned the barrel, loaded it with paper cartridge and musket ball, and took position with eye along the barrel and finger on the trigger, all by the time the cannon near by roared out.

The gunnery sergeant had calculated both detonation and elevation finely. The iron ball arced high into the air, perfectly visible to both defenders and besiegers, watching in irritation the moment they heard the cannon. And then it began its descent towards the close-packed front ranks of the Sipahi cavalry.

It would just make it.

There was an unseemly sidestepping and barging of horses, wild shouting, a cavalry commander galloping down the lines in fury, before the iron ball smacked into the earth where moments before it would have killed both man and horse.

Out in front of his army, the figure in a midnight-blue robe on a white stallion pulled angrily around and glared at the walls of accursed Famagusta. And then, in violent *lèse-majesté*, a single musket shot rang out from the walls. Evidently a musket of incredible power and accuracy, for the expertly aimed ball kicked up dust not ten feet from his horse's hooves. The horse reared; the rider remained in his saddle – but he dropped his scimitar.

He settled his horse. A moment's ominous silence.

Smith rapidly reloaded.

'Why bother?' said Stanley. 'You missed.'

Smith said, 'You'd not have hit within a hundred yards of him.'

Even at this distance, Nicholas thought he could see the expression on Lala Mustafa's face. As black as a burnt stubble field.

Then a slave ran out and retrieved the fallen scimitar and handed it back to the Pasha, head bowed.

Lala Mustafa looked down at the slave as if contemplating beheading him where he stood. Then he raised the scimitar high and bellowed out an order, voice like a lion's roar.

'In the name of God,' said Stanley softly.

'What?' said Nicholas, palms sweating, scalp prickling 'What is it?'

'It'll be bloody murder. He's sending in the Bektaşis already.'

They came racing across the dusty plain to paradise. Thousands of them, with not a square foot of armour between them. Naked but for turbans and loincloths, otherwise just bare skin and fanatic hearts. They clutched spears and daggers, and some had slashed themselves already in their zeal, blood coursing down their arms and legs, while others had battered their own foreheads with stones for the love of Allah.

What was Lala Mustafa thinking?

'If he treats his own men like this,' murmured Stanley, 'think what he does to his enemies.'

'All reserves to the walls!' bellowed Bragadino. 'Every second company to the west wall, volley fire on company command! Sergeant, ready the gunners below, linstocks at the ready. Grapeshot and chain-shot, close-quarter firing and no respite. If Mustafa wants to see what we've got, then let him see.'

'That's just what Lala Mustafa wants,' said Stanley.

'And the corpses of his Bektaşis will start to fill up the moat as well, and sicken us with the smell. That's what they are to him: sandbags that lay themselves down where needed.'

Stanley closed his eyes. Though they were savages and fanatics of the worst sort, yet he had an image of every screaming killer there as a boy once, smiled upon by his mother.

He started to ram the barrel of his arquebus.

Nicholas held his arquebus and trembled. Was it six years ago that he last faced such a horde? It felt long ago. He trembled like any novice, holding gun and rod, feeding it in. If Hodge had not been here, stolidly working away, if Stanley and Smith had not flanked him, he might have broken and run. But it was like a wild game of village football, he reminded himself. Like a long horse ride. You eased into it, the blood heated. In an hour or two the shakes would be gone and he'd be killing as well as any other.

The Bektaşis came to the lip of the moat and Smith fired.

'Now!' he urged the company captains. 'On the level!'

He was right. Once they were in the moat below it would be harder to shoot from directly above. The captains raised their arms, dropped them, and there was the deafening roll of hundreds of arquebuses in volley.

Nicholas pulled his own short arquebus back hard into his shoulder, sighted roughly, though there was little need, and pulled the trigger. The hard bark of the gun, the fierce recoil, the drift of smoke to the eyes. Impossible tell to where or even whether it had hit. But surely it had hit someone.

The moat filled with more and more attackers, hundreds jumping and slithering down the twenty-foot drop into the dry moat. Some twisted ankles, or worse, painless with opium. Some fell along with dead men, toppling into the moat with their hands clutched to chests or bellies.

And then the mines and grenades started to go off. It was atrocious, a spectacle of horror.

Nicholas saw men shredded into pieces even as they ran, saw a fountain of blood and limbs where another was blown high in the air. Others fell down clutching their feet in agony as they found the poisoned nails hammered into planks. They tried to stand and pull away, but were trampled down again by their screaming fellows.

Nicholas fired again at those opposite, waiting to drop into the moat. Impossible not to hit at this distance, with that close-packed mass of brown flesh.

He looked over the packed ranks of Bektaşis, and thought he saw through the dust and heat haze and drifting smoke the figure of a man on a white horse, cold as a statue.

'God damn you,' he murmured, reloading again. Yes, the shakes were already subsiding. 'Truly, God damn you and all your kind to hell. May the devil drink your blood as you have drunk men's.'

The Bektaşis had come on in such a wild rush that few even brought scaling ladders, and the few that did fumbled and struggled at the foot of the walls. They had come to die as much as to kill.

Nicholas leaned over, ready to seize one that thumped against the wall below and throw it back, but some infantrymen were ready with more efficient long grappling poles. Then Smith roared, 'Down!'

They ducked back, for he had see the fizzing breech of a culverin in one of the side towers, and a moment later a hail of grapeshot sliced across the flank of the wall and blasted the men off the ladder. Then they reached down with the grappling poles and shoved the ladder clear.

More mines were going off in the moat all the time, more concealed grenades and pot-bombs and booby traps in pits. The bastions roared their enfilading fire and, from the walls above, soldiers tossed down more grenades, sacks of quicklime, incendiaries of that evil mix called Greek fire in glass jars. Made from a mix of rock-oil, turpentine and anything sugary – date wine, fig syrup, even honey – it burst into flames and clung to men's flesh even as it burned. Men rolled in the moat in hoops of their own flames, howling like the damned, as others fought to get away. Sweet Cyprus honey was turned into a device of slaughter, and any comradeship was destroyed by mutual terror.

The assault of the Bektaşis, so early in the siege and with so little damage done to the walls, was as Stanley predicted. Bloody murder.

Then the Bektaşis suddenly broken and fled. They had had enough. Paradise could wait.

The smoke slowly cleared and the defenders peered out. The moat was a vision of hell, a ditch of perhaps a thousand stretched and writhing bodies, men and parts of men.

The defenders had sustained a single casualty. One novice had burned his hand firing up a pot-bomb.

'There'll be more to come,' said Bragadino grimly. 'Like the ranging shots of the cannon this morning, this was only a test, was it not? Now the moat is already half filled with the slain. And almost all our traps and grenades down there have been detonated.'

Then he held his sword aloft and cried, 'A famous victory, my brothers!' and a great and heartening cheer went round the walls.

Sometimes the best thing a commander could do was put new spirit in his men by lying.

15

The Ottoman guns were being brought forward again.

This time it would not be a test. This time Lala Mustafa and his very finest gunnery masters would be aiming at the bases of the walls, towers, gates and bastions.

'Keep your heads down,' said Smith. 'And wad your ears up or you'll be deaf by sundown.'

The entire length of the west wall of Famagusta was under sustained assault from hurtling iron and stone. Nicholas had forgotten what it felt like to be under bombardment from two or three hundred cannon simultaneously. That is, his mind had not forgotten, but his body was shocked anew. His eardrums fluttered, his bones juddered, the air itself shook. The sound beat against him in blows and bludgeons.

And from within the city arose slow wails. The sickening thump of cannonball hitting walls and courtyards, fountains, chapels, churches, fine merchant houses and humble timber shacks. Infants screamed in their cradles, little girls buried their heads in their mothers' skirts, still unable to shut out the terrible unceasing thunderstorm of the guns.

'Return fire!' cried Bragadino. 'Hit their guns! Take them out one by one!'

But the Ottomans had such vastly superior manpower and resources, their slave gangs had already built for every gun a miniature earthen fortress. Still they must try.

'Every day we hold out,' said Stanley, 'brings the Holy League one league nearer.'

Please God it was true.

Boys came round with pails and scoops of water, and they drank greedily. Others, called powder monkeys, came round with fresh powder and whatever smaller missiles they could carry. The gunners themselves brought up the bigger cannonballs. They returned fire as best they could. Smith kept trying with his jezail to take out a single gunner, even a gunnery master.

A church bell struck twelve noon.

And then three hundred black mouths of the enemy guns roared again and they all took cover.

'Coming in!'

Most hit home with cruel accuracy, thumping into the base of the walls, sending up huge clouds of stone and mortar dust. The whole wall juddered.

A breathless messenger came running, saluting even as he ran, and gasped, 'Big crack opened up beneath the Martinengo bastion, sire.'

'Bag it up, man!' cried Bragadino angrily. 'We're all out of mortar!'

A few balls went high and struck the sloping bastion tops, losing much of their power as they kicked up high above them, clearly visible.

'One in the air!

Then everyone would watch and stumble out of the way as it came hurtling back down, on to tops or battlements, or falling within the city upon some house or tavern or shop roof, or thumping heavily into a sandy street or alley.

Boys came running out to see if they could pick it up.

'Watch out!' called Nicholas. 'It'll burn you!'

One boy squatted and touched the ball, half buried in the sand, with a wisp of dried grass. It smoked. He stared up at Nicholas wide eyed.

Sometimes a fired cannonball was hot and sometimes merely warm, without obvious reason. Later the boys would retrieve the balls in coarse slings and carry them back up to the walls to be used in return. Soldiers would scratch messages on them with their knives.

'Eat this, Mehmet.'

'Up your Mohammedan arse.'

'This one's for the Prophet.'

Then again, some of those coming in from the Ottoman guns had the Lion of Venice stamped on them. Taken from Nicosia, and garlanded with similar greetings.

Stanley knelt and peered, and then said, 'These fellows can't even spell *turd*. Disgraceful.'

'Coming in!'

And from the Martinengo bastion came a terrible sound. A multiple strike from three or four huge cannon, the ones they called basilisks – and another sound beneath it.

A deep, groaning judder: the sound of a wall giving way. The air filled with a cloud of ochre dust, far greater than any yet, blinding them all. And through the cloud of dust, from the Ottoman lines, a huge cheer.

Bragadino cried, 'Smith, Stanley, take your men! I'll send Baglione's own company too, one of the best. Hold them back at the bastion, report to me what damage.'

They ran.

Across the plain, two huge columns of Janizaries were already racing towards the stricken bastion.

Even as they ran, another monstrous volley of cannon fire juddered through the air. A big gun needed resting and cooling for as much as half an hour after firing. Lala Mustafa must have such vast numbers of artillery pieces that he could fire rolling volley after volley, resting them in turn. There would be no respite, all day and all night. The Ottoman Empire was determined that Cyprus should not prove another Malta. And so far, everything was going as planned.

There were Venetian infantrymen streaming away from the Martinengo bastion, some covered in white plaster dust like ghosts.

'Back to your positions!' Smith bellowed at them. 'Where are you going?'

One barged past him. 'Who the fuck are you?'

A giant fist struck him down senseless.

'That'll really help,' said Stanley.

The others clustered uncertainly, staring at this burly, terrifying-looking Knight of St John with his blazing black eyes.

Then the company commander, Astorre Baglione, came at the trot with his hundred-strong hand-picked company, the finest reserve troops in Famagusta. He barked orders even as he trotted, puffing with the effort for he was short and stoutly built.

'Fall in, you sons of bitches! Martinengo's not done yet! And it'll be a whole lot worse for you if the Turk breaks in! Now move your lazy arses!'

Buoyed up by the fresh troops, the soldiers from the Martinengo bastion turned and lumbered back the way they had come.

The fellow at Smith's feet stirred and groaned.

'Lie there,' said Smith. 'Sun yourself a while.'

Then there was a cruel whirring sound in the air, and they all ducked down, heads low, in the shadow of a wall.

But not a powder-boy, a leather satchel of black gunpowder over his shoulder, staring open mouthed into the blue air. No more than six or seven.

'Get down!' screamed Nicholas, and made to run to him.

Then the missile struck. It was marble, specifically intended to shatter on impact, and send shards of sharp white stone flying in all directions. It struck the top of a wall, exploded, and the boy went down.

Nicholas raced to him and pulled him over on his back. His smooth young face was stuck with lean white splinters, and he was screaming.

Then Stanley was kneeling beside him too. 'You go on!' he shouted to the others. 'We'll join you!'

He raised the boy's head from the dust, fingers in his hair. There were more splinters in his skull, but he didn't find what he dreaded. A split in the skull, or a shard as long as a man's finger, embedded straight down.

The boy screamed and screamed; it was no good telling one so young not to. He had a right to scream. With astonishing

254

concentration and gentleness, kneeling there in the dusty street with cannonballs flying and falling beyond them in the heart of the city, and the sound of many people running, shouting, a ruinous pandemonium, Stanley's powerful fingers moved with the delicacy of a lacemaker's. He plucked the shards from the boy's cheeks, forehead, one from his neck, one from just above his lip, and several from his skull beneath his child-fine hair. Numerous little trails of blood ran down the boy's face, trickling into the corners of his mouth, and Stanley wiped them away with his neckerchief.

At last he was satisfied and stood and raised the boy up in his arms.

'I'll take him,' said Nicholas. 'You go and fight.'

Stanley considered briefly, then nodded and passed him the sobbing child. 'Not over your shoulder. Keep his head up or he'll only bleed the more. Find the Franciscan friars if you can. Though they'll be busy.'

'Will I die? Will I die?' wailed the little boy as Nicholas hurried as best he could through the streets, almost blinded with the dust, ducking into doorways every time he heard another whine, another thump.

'You won't die,' said Nicholas. 'I won't let you.'

'It hurts! Why does it hurt so much?'

One of those questions no man could answer. He hurried on, arms already aching with the sobbing burden.

He came into a small square – a dead mule, a shattered bell tower, a hubbub of people. Then through the dust clouds he saw a familiar shape in a black dress. She saw him and came towards him.

'You're limping,' he said.

'It's nothing,' she said swiftly. 'Just my age.'

He glanced down. Beneath her dress he could see that one of her bare feet was bloody and bandaged.

'Let me take him. You are needed on the walls.'

He passed her the boy, and she kissed away the bloody trickles on his forehead. 'There, my lamb, my pet. Tell me your name.'

His sobbing diminished a little at this warm maternal touch, the rich smell of her dark hair. He stuttered, 'Andreas.'

'Come then, Andreas, we will find your mama and make you better.'

'My mama fell down in the street this morning.'

She exchanged an agonised look with Nicholas.

'Men in black robes took her away,' the boy said, starting to sob again.

Sweet Jesus.

'Maybe the Dominicans,' said Nicholas, 'they've been caring for the wounded too.'

'I'll try.' She was already going.

'What is *your* name?' he called after her.

'Evangelina.'

And she was gone.

He ran back to the Martinengo bastion. The sound of grim tumult and steel on steel came to his ears.

He prayed as he ran. For the little boy, for his mother. For the widow Evangelina.

For the whole damn city.

The little boy's pain, and the running, sweat coursing down his forehead from under the tight-fitting morion, and the unreal sights of a city being pulverised yet still refusing to surrender – the chaos and cruelty of it all, too great to be reduced to words – all of it filled him with the familiar old battle fury that seemed to slow everything down around him. As he ran into the mêlée, he saw ahead of him that the great south-west Martinengo bastion was already half in ruins. A gaping wound opened straight out on to the plain where the south wall had stood, and yet above, a huge, half-broken arch still hung overhead, apparently supported by thin air, threatening to crash down upon them at any moment and bury them in a hundred tons of Cyprus sandstone.

All of them. Venetians and Spaniards and Ottomans alike.

For the Janizaries were upon them.

The wall had collapsed into a massive ramp of rubble and broken stonework, steep sided and some thirty feet high, and two groups of men were bitterly contesting this piece of worthless ruin. The ramp was hemmed in between those walls still standing, forming a front no more than fifty yards wide. Yet beyond, many more Janizaries pressed forward, rank upon rank. If they could only break in here, form a bridgehead of this one bastion and throw open the gates – the city could be overrun by thousands of enemy troops in minutes.

And they were nearly in already.

Nicholas clawed his way up the rubble ramp with drawn sword just as an Ottoman order rang out and all the Janizaries fell back and crouched.

'Down!' yelled Baglione, but many of the inexperienced pikemen were too late. Over the heads of their crouching front rank, the rear rank of Janizary musketeers fired a perfectly timed volley from less than twenty yards away.

Two of their own were hit by musket balls that spun erratically from the barrel – it was a dangerous tactic – but the rest of the volley raked into the stumbling line of defenders, taking down as many as twenty or thirty still standing. One fell backwards on top of Nicholas. He dragged himself out from underneath the dead weight, sheathed his sword and snatched up the man's pike.

'Attack!' roared a familiar voice. It was Smith.

Maximum aggression, surprise, ferocity at every moment. Especially the least expected moment. That was the secret of the knights' fearsome reputation.

Now desperate, exposed, a key bastion already half blown away, defenders outnumbered ten or twenty to one, and their attackers without question the finest infantrymen in all of Christendom or Asia, Smith was leading his comrades in a sudden assault, scrambling down the ramp and into the startled enemy ranks.

Below them, the crouching Janizary front rank were just getting to their feet once more and reordering the line, when several fire-breathing and heavily armoured men crashed into them: Smith and Stanley, Mazzinghi and Giustiniani, drawing with them the bolder of Baglione's own pikemen. Mazzinghi was momentarily reduced to using nothing but a bare wooden pikestaff for a weapon, his sword having just snapped off at the hilt in an enemy shield. But he managed to avoid a panicked blow from a kneeling Janizary, knock him senseless and then fight on with the fellow's own scimitar. Smith himself swung a glaive, a grim, short-handled pike, having abandoned his sword as far too delicate for this bludgeoning close-quarter butchery. He opened a man's belly, cut away another's hand and half severed the head of a third in three swift slashes.

Nicholas ran up to join them, slipped and stumbled on something. Glanced down. A hand, diagonally severed at the wrist. The sole of his boot smeared with its blood. He pressed forward, swerved and kicked down a sword-thrust with his boot, kicked his assailant again in the face, and then killed him with a clean thrust to the heart.

The Janizaries fell back, rolled, tripped, stumbled into their own second rank, and were impaled by blade upon blade. It was a classic case of their superior numbers, in a confined space, telling against them. Behind them, their own line of musketeers was panicking, trying to reload.

Smith saw a bugler raise his bugle to his lips, rushed him, slapped the bugle aside and knocked the fellow senseless with a titanic blow of his gauntleted fist.

'It's called cutting the lines of communication!' he called to Stanley near by, stomping the bugle flat in the dust.

Lala Mustafa sat his white horse.

'What is delaying them? Why are they not in yet?'

'Some sort of counter-attack, esteemed Pasha.'

'Counter-attack,' snorted Lala Mustafa, flicking a fly away with his crop. 'Send in another regiment.'

A scimitar swept inches in front of Nicholas's stomach. He sucked in, raised his arms, for all the world like a Spanish matador, and then drove the point of his sword in a thrust straight enough to please a French fencing master. He impaled the fellow's left shoulder, pulled swiftly back. The fellow, burly with a hennaed beard, came at him again, not even feeling for the wound. Then a crossbow sang and the bolt went into his stomach below his belt, and he doubled up and knelt. Nicholas finished him with a second straight thrust.

He glanced back.

Crossbowmen were swarming up the broken walls of the bastion behind like Barbary apes, some with their bows clutched under their arms as they climbed. They crouched where they could, trying not to slip and fall, and loosed off steel bolts into the oncoming Janizaries as fast as possible. Even so awkwardly positioned, cranking back the powerful crossbow arm while struggling for balance, they could achieve a much faster rate of fire than any musketeer could manage.

Baglione's order. Good thinking.

Baglione himself, meanwhile, had taken thirty hand-picked men and come out of a small sally port on the west wall to savage the flank of the Janizary attack before they even knew what hit them.

'Imagine you are cavalry!' he shouted. 'Hit them and run back! Do not get caught up!'

They followed orders with perfect discipline, emerging from the sally port at a sprint, racing round to attack the startled Janizary flank, loosing arquebuses, pistols and crossbows into them, killing or downing as many as twenty of the enemy in an instant, and then sprinting back again through the sally port and heaving it shut, barred and bulked before the Janizary captain even knew what had happened.

The assault was weakening.

Smith and Stanley pressed on, hacking and swiping, closely followed by the rest of Baglione's elite company, and more Venetian pikemen. They emerged on to the open plain before the front line of Janizary musketeers, still reloading, eyes flaring wide.

The damned Christians! It was a counter-attack, a sortie. In broad daylight! And so hugely outnumbered. But the Janizaries had shamefully lost their battle order for a moment. They were unprepared.

An instant later they were reduced to using their unloaded muskets as clubs to fend off a furious frontal assault of flailing swords and pikes. Out on the Janizary right a pack of crossbowmen in studded black leather jerkins had run at the crouch, knelt and were firing into their other flank. Devils and djinns, where were the Sipahis when you needed them?

Here they came. Red plumes and lances, glinting helmets, the thunder of galloping hooves in the dust, thirsting for the shame to be avenged.

They were expected.

'Fall back!' cried Baglione. 'At the double. Crossbowmen, one more volley at their horses and then the sally port!'

Then they were clawing their way back over the rubble ramp and falling down within the shadow of the broken bastion, utterly exhausted. Behind them they heard the stricken whinnies of horses as crossbow bolts thumped into rumps and flanks, and red-plumed Sipahis tumbled and rolled with their wounded mounts.

Fifty fresh men stepped between the defenders up the ramp, arquebuses already smouldering. Another fine order of Baglione's. They shouldered arms and waited, the matchcords sending a thin drift of smoke into their eyes. And then the Janizaries were reforming and coming back, a thousand strong, with two entire companies of light archers to give extra fire. The arquebuses roared out.

Some damage. Some sop to morale. But never enough.

The defenders had also lost men, with far fewer to lose. They were cut and bruised and weary, eyes blinded with sweat, sword-arms shaking and burning. And there were no reserves to take their place.

Against the length of the west wall, and especially Martinengo's twin bastion on the north-west corner, the monstrous Ottoman guns kept up a constant battering.

Something clanged on Nicholas's helmet. A musket ball? What did it feel like to be shot in the head? A slow, oozy blurring? But no, it was just a small fragment of stone falling from above. He looked up. That huge half-broken arch overhead, suspended by nothing but habit.

'Here, boy!' Baglione was beside him, plucking a grenade from his belt. 'You're still young enough to climb trees. Get up there. And for God's sake remember to shout a signal when you fire it up!'

Nicholas stared at him bewildered, clutching the pottery grenade to his chest, the roar of the Janizaries coming ever closer. They were no more than two hundred yards off now, coming at the trot.

Down among the wounded, a man screamed a high, crazed scream and then was suddenly silenced.

His head spun.

'There, boy, there!' shouted Baglione, thumping him hard on

the back. 'Climb! Lodge it there, look, where the plaster is streaming from that crack!'

Then he understood.

Baglione thrust a squat wheel-lock pistol into his belt.

He took a deep breath and closed off his senses to the world
around him and forgot any fear. All men must die. Perhaps it will
be now. But Christ, let me die and not be maimed. Then he froze
out even that thought. There was just him and this arching wall.

He kicked off his boots and climbed barefoot. He caught a
stream of plaster and rubbed it in his hands for more grip. He
moved slowly and steadily upwards, never looking down. But from
below he heard the first ring of steel on steel as it began again. Shut
it out. Nothing but him and the wall.

Now he came to a jutting pillar top and for a moment had to
reach up and hang suspended by his fingers alone. Something
smacked into the wall beside him, a puff of dust. Musket ball or
crossbow bolt? Ignore it. He swung a foot up and pulled himself
over the lip of the cornice. There was no decent handhold here, the
arch above was smooth stone, but there was a vertical crevice where
he could jam his hand and then cramp it into a fist. It would have
to be enough.

His foot slipped, he cramped his fist harder and his arm was
wrenched so painfully he cried out. He scrabbled with his bare
right foot and found a tiny hold with his curled toes. His foot
began to burn and ache immediately as it took almost all his body
weight. Then he pulled the grenade from his belt and forced it into
the crack. Plaster coursed down. Beyond him stretched the huge
arch that had formed the vault of the bastion. Impossible that it
still hung there in empty space. But it seemed miraculously sturdy
still. This mere pot-bomb would do nothing. Yet he must try.

He pulled the squat pistol from his belt and reached after the
lodged grenade. His other arm burned as if aflame with Greek fire
to the bone. The matchcord was well soaked in volatile oil. All he
needed was a spark and the fuse would start to fizz. A fuse less than
an inch long. Only a few seconds of burn time.

He pulled the trigger and the little wheel spun. Nothing. He
fired again. His arm trembled, hot to the core; his foot was about
to go and he would fall. He wondered if he should let himself

261

surrender to it. He would land in a mess of men and steel blades. O Christ let me not be maimed.

He could not fire the pistol again, he hadn't the strength. He was going. This one, he prayed. He demanded of God. *This one.*

The wheel whirred and sparks flew off in a bright little roundel like a tiny Catherine wheel. The oil-sodden fuse began to smoulder and then smoked. Very fast indeed.

He dropped the pistol down his shirt front. Pulled himself painfully upright with both arms and shouted down below, 'She's going!'

No one heard.

The fuse was half burned already. Not just smouldering but burning, a spitting white flare.

'*She's going!*'

Then Stanley's broad, ruddy face looking up, an arm signal, and suddenly the defenders dropped back. The Janizaries roared and pushed forward.

He must climb down. But he could not. He was trapped.

Deaf, blind, crippled, buried alive.

His foot slipped and he hung by his hands alone. He would die here. He could not move any further. His heart burned, his tongue stuck to his mouth, every muscle, every tendon, burned with a red fire.

He buried his head between his arms, scrabbled with his feet. Nothing. Not a hold. He could smell the burning matchcord, the oily smoke mocked him. His fingers were slipping from the stone ledge. He tried to cover his ears with his upper arms even as he hung there.

And then the grenade went off.

16

Like any great building, like a great beast brought down by a
hunter's spear, the arch seemed to fall slowly, hesitantly. It broke
away from the wall where the grenade had blown and gave a half-
turn in the air as it came down, blocks the size of boulders. And
then the Janizary front line was crushed and buried, and the rest
fell back aghast.

His eyelids fluttered.

Stanley was below, his arms outstretched. 'Fall, boy! Let go!'

Something was dripping from his right leg. Coursing down. His
foot had gone.

He closed his fluttering eyelids and fell.

'To the hospital with him!'

The lower slopes of the ramp were covered with the slain, Christian
and Muslim commingled. Cloven helmets, broken spears, dead
men, white silk robes wet and stained red. An arquebus that had
exploded on firing, its muzzle a shredded steel flower.

'Back off the ramp!' cried Baglione, perspiring, pale. 'Sandbags
coming up. Time to get building.'

Bragadino meanwhile ordered every spare gun and arquebus
on to the walls beside Martinengo to give covering fire while they
worked. The more Janizaries Lala Mustafa sent in at this point, the
more would be killed.

'We need to fill this bastion up and pack it tight,' said Baglione.
He looked uncharacteristically anxious.

'Aye,' said Stanley. 'They're coming round.'

It was true. Well out of range, the Turks were bringing a whole column of guns on their carriages round to the south. Within hours they would be freshly earthed up and ready to fire. Just as night fell.

'We can take it,' said Baglione. 'You know from Malta – you are of the Order of St John, are you not?'

'Knight Grand Cross Edward Stanley.'

Baglione nodded. 'Happy you are here. You know from Malta, nothing stops a cannonball like a few yards of earth.'

But Smith was glaring around, up, down, eyeing every man that walked wearily past him with ferocious suspicion.

Stanley murmured, 'Less obvious, please, Brother.'

Smith kept his voice lowered, with great effort. 'I am thinking, there is no way a few volleys of cannon, not even those two-hundred-pounder basilisks of the Turks, could have brought down these walls so easily.'

Stanley's expression was grim. 'But they could not have mined this far either. Not so soon.'

'Yet there were mines under this tower.' Smith's expression was as dark as a storm at sea. 'We have traitors among us.'

Baglione gasped. Stanley looked at him; the man was paler than ever, his arms clutched tight over his belly. Then he realised. It was not fear. It was agony. Baglione was hit.

'Sir, you must retire.'

'I cannot. No one else ...'

Then he fell against him. Blood leaked from beneath his breast-plate.

Stanley held him with his strong right arm. 'Stretcher!'

'Remember it was just on noon that the Turkish guns opened up!' said Smith as he and Stanley ran. 'When our own church bells rang. It was co-ordinated. Someone lit a fuse underground, and the whole thing blew.'

Shouted messages were passing along the wide wall above.

'Tell us the news!' shouted Smith.

A pikeman looked down. 'Fort Andruzzi bastion! The Turks are bringing guns round north as well!'

'Tell the Governor to find us there! Urgent!'

They ran faster.

Malta was a rock, but Famagusta was built on sand. It took little to tunnel beneath.

They came to the north-west corner of the city and a familiar figure emerged from a small house near by. Abdul of Tripoli.

Smith seized him by the collar of his robe. 'Talk, Moor. This is where you are living?'

Abdul put his finger to his lips and said very quietly, glancing back over his shoulder, 'There are buckets inside.'

'What?'

'More buckets than you would expect in an ordinary household. And a pile of earth in the fireplace, which seems curious, does—'

Smith tossed Abdul aside like a discarded cloak and hurtled inside. Stanley steadied him and kept his hand heavy on his shoulder.

'You still think I betray you, Christian? After all we have been through.'

'I advise you to be silent a while.'

The Moor stood placidly with his hands folded before him.

'Show me your hands.'

Abdul did so.

Not a spot of earth on them, fingernails as clean as a queen's.

'What were you doing in this house?'

'I thought you told me to be silent.'

Stanley gave him a gentle shake, which made Abdul's head loll like a puppet's. 'I am kinder than my Brother John,' he said, 'but not that kind.'

'Very well, very well. I keep my ear to the ground. I observe. I trade in fine garments, in jewels, in muskets, but most precious of all, information. The moment that south-west bastion went down, I started looking about me. It just took you a little longer to work it out.' He shrugged. 'Had I been Governor Bragadino, I would have ordered every house within fifty yards of the walls to be razed to the ground before the siege even started.'

Stanley felt his jaw tighten. The Moor was right, damn him.

In a city as mixed and polyglot as Famagusta, there were always traitors.

*

Smith hauled two men out howling, apparently by the hair, and dropped them like sacks in the dust. From their bruised and bloody faces, it looked as if he had banged their heads together like bowling balls quite a bit already.

'One Bohemian, one of the Kingdom of Serbia, I think. Look at their fingernails.'

Stanley trod on their hands. 'How much are they paying you?'

One howled. The other jabbered.

'In Italian, or some cultivated tongue at least.'

One said, 'Our freedom only! No gold, no silver, just our lives at the end of it.'

'Fools as well as traitors,' said Smith. 'You really think Lala Mustafa would trouble to find you and save you if this city falls?'

The man sobbed. Smith drew his sword and touched the edge to his neck.

Bragadino came cantering down the street on horseback with two lancers.

'Is there any more to learn? You two vermin, are there any more saboteurs among us?'

The man wept and shook his head. 'I do not know.'

'Understand this,' said Bragadino. 'You are to die before nightfall. Think carefully and tell me all you know. Soon you will be before the Throne of Judgement.'

He controlled his sobbing and said softly, 'There are no others I know of, I swear it.'

'You mined the Martinengo bastion? Just the two of you?'

'Impossible,' said Smith.

'We stored powder in the crypt of the church of St John Chrysostomos. It was not so far to dig, and there was an ancient culvert too. It was not the best mining, but with the cannon fire as well it was enough.'

'You have been the death of many good Christians,' said Bragadino. 'You should fear what is to come.'

'I fear it,' the man said, trembling. 'Sweet Jesus, I do fear it.'

'They have no more to tell,' said Bragadino. 'Imminent death often makes a man truthful.'

Smith and Stanley nodded their agreement.

266

Bragadino relieved the knights themselves of the squalid task, and ordered his men to dismount and draw their swords.

The traitors' heads were struck off in the street before a watching crowd, and their bodies thrown over the walls.

Bragadino looked grave. 'It was my error,' he said, 'a gross error.'

'May we ask why the houses were not razed before?'

'To appease the damned merchants. They demanded not a building should be touched. Now they are overruled.'

Every house, every stable, every donkey shack within fifty yards of the walls was pulled down and razed that night, the material carried to the walls for precious bulking. Some of it was used to refill the tunnel they found under the traitors' house, a foul damp burrow badly propped and leaking sand. A poor thing, but stretching underneath the walls of Fort Andruzzi, in concert with a heavy barrage from beyond, it might have played a crucial part.

Even a fine acacia tree was cut down, along with two merchant houses with splendid courtyards and upper galleries, an ancient Byzantine chapel, first hurriedly deconsecrated by a priest. He carried away the icons by torchlight, his face wet with tears.

Groups of merchants in fine robes and gowns looked on, muttering among themselves.

Nicholas awoke with a Franciscan friar bending over his leg and bathing it.

'My foot has gone,' he mumbled. 'Blown away. I am lamed for life.'

The friar looked up. He was slightly hunchbacked, with a snub nose, and amazingly bushy grey eyebrows which curved up at the ends, making him look like a comical demon.

'Both feet still present,' he said, 'though one a little cut about and worse for wear. Brain soused in opium, though. I'd sleep if I were you.'

It was dark when a visitor came. Stanley himself.

'I brought you an orange.'

Nicholas turned his head on the pillow. 'Opium.'

'You've had enough to fly to the moon and back.'

The knight squeezed the fruit to a pulp in his bare fist and the juice poured into a silver goblet.

'Show-off,' murmured Nicholas.

Stanley grinned. His hands were black with powder and burns, and his knuckles grazed and bleeding.

'I don't mind the gunpowder so much,' said Nicholas, 'but I'd rather not taste your blood.'

'It'll be good for you. The blood of English earls runs in these veins.'

He held up the boy's head and put the goblet to his lips. The juice was sharp and sweet and delicious.

He lay back. 'More.'

'I'll bring more.'

If I can find more, he thought. The city was already feeling its isolation, cut off from the surrounding countryside and no ships coming or going in the harbour. And the Ottoman guns had already destroyed two grain stores.

'What happened at the bastion?' asked Nicholas.

Stanley set down the goblet. 'Your heroic little endeavour did some good. The arch came down, a few enemy were killed, just when we were hard pressed. Baglione was hurt in the fighting, though.'

'Badly?'

A second's hesitation. 'He will mend, I'm sure. The Turks pulled back disheartened. Though I know you are strong enough to want the truth, and not heroical bombast. What really saved us, while we hacked and bludgeoned away there, was the work of Bragadino in the city. The moment the Janizaries gave us respite, we looked around and there were – I do not exaggerate – a thousand, two thousand, of the townsfolk in perfect columns, bearing sandbags, earth sacks, pushing barrows. They filed in one by one and filed out again, obedient as nuns. Bragadino supervising. Each one left and then came back and rejoined the queue with another sack. Cushions full of stones and sawdust. Pillowcases stuffed with straw. Anything.

'The people worked the rest of the day, in rotation. Perhaps one in every ten citizens was there, helping bulk up the broken Martinengo bastion. The work will go on all night, and by dawn that shattered wall will not matter so much any more. For Martinengo will just be a great, squat, solid block of ... *stuff*. We can't use it any more, alas. But neither can the Turk take it. And it was this – the citizens and peasants and humble sacks of sand – that have really saved us for now.'

Nicholas said, 'I am glad of it. Hanging there from my fingertips, I felt no hero. I felt like a Bedlam fool.'

Stanley grinned. 'I'll get you some more oranges.'

Outside, he paused for a while. Yes, he had told Ingoldsby the truth. It was an insult not to. But not the whole truth.

Not the dismal rumour that more and more of the town's citizens, especially the wealthier and more influential of them, were talking about negotiated surrender.

The sturdy peasants and plain townsfolk would have none of it. They lived with death every day, and hated the Turk more than anything. But the wealthy merchants, many of them Venetian or Levantine, said they had no quarrel with the Sultan Selim. What matter who governed, as long as they could continue their trade in peace? And they wept to see their fine city houses and courtyards reduced to rubble and dust. Their wives harangued them further.

'Surely,' they said, 'some *accommodation* can be made?'

Oh for a city full of Malta peasants, thought Stanley. They were a people made of rock.

There was one other strange turn that day. An Ottoman ball had gone into the house where the fifty Muslim pilgrims of the haj were sheltering, and it killed two of them. Some time later, the leader of the group came to Bragadino, and pleaded to be released.

'Released? In the middle of a siege? Released where, man?'

Then he told their story. They were Muslim converts, from Wallachia. Only two generations ago, their families had still been Christian. But they were so oppressed and impoverished by the relentless taxes and punishments of their Muslim overlords that eventually, 'God forgive us, we abjured the Cross and bowed to Mecca. As so many have done before us.' And before the Governor's astonished eyes, he crossed himself.

Bragadino decided to trust them. In a few days' time, he promised them, under cover of darkness, they would file silently aboard a galley in the harbour under the command of Romegas himself, slip past the Turkish patrols, and sail into the west.

Night time. Torchlight and cooking fires, dogs barking, muted talk. Eating and drinking, grimy faces, bowls and goblets slurped and guzzled. Water still plentiful, drunk by the quart.

No news from the lookouts on the walls, no sign of activity around the Turkish guns.

Suffering Christ, they might even get some sleep.

Two soldiers rigged up a pipe and pumped from a cistern, a cool gout of water at head height. Exhausted and filthy soldiers stripped and stood naked beneath it.

Women passing by screamed and giggled, half hid their faces with their headscarves and turned the other way. But not before having a swift look.

One well-built handsome Spaniard, muscular chest coursing cold water, scooped back his thick black hair, shook his beard and grinned at the women and called out, 'I am glad we give you something to smile about, fair ladies, in these straitened times!'

They passed on with heads lowered, giggling like schoolgirls. More than one of them would dream of him tonight.

Priests of the Greek Church, Armenians, Dominicans and Franciscans, friars and nuns, said nothing to condemn such bawdiness, or the scenes they saw in taverns, stables, back alleys. *In extremis*, men and women would take what comfort they could.

They forgot their doctrinal differences and worked on through the long hot night.

They tended the wounded, drugged the dying, and buried the dead.

17

At dawn, word came that Astorre Baglione, Famagusta's single finest military commander, had died in the night of his wounds. His last words were, 'No surrender!'

Moments later, a huge bombardment opened up on the north-west corner of the city, against the sloping walls of Fort Andruzzi.

Dust went up. Flakes fell.

Nothing else.

Towards noon they stopped firing and the guns were rested.

Smith smiled grimly. 'Think on it well, Lala Mustafa, you dog. It won't always go your way.'

Bragadino looked grey. The responsibility was almost too much, even for so strong a man. His refusal to surrender had already sent a thousand soldiers to their deaths, perhaps another five hundred civilians. Ten thousand more, old men, women, children, depended upon him. And now he had lost Baglione.

'He was my best commander. I have the military experience of any gentleman, but Astorre Baglione was my stay and staff. I will need your advice now.'

'That's why we're here,' said Giustiniani. 'With our memories of Malta.'

There was another long, exhausting assault all afternoon until night-fall by countless regiments of Janizaries, infantry and dismounted Sipahis fighting as infantry as well. At one point Bragadino esti-mated there were as many as ten thousand men coming against them. They brought up protective barriers, huge bundles of brushwood which they rolled into the fast-filling ditch, scaling ladders, ropes and grappling hooks.

'If the moat is completely filled,' said Giustiniani, 'or strongly bridged, they could bring up siege towers.'

But they had enough on their hands as it was. Turks swarmed up the walls; many were cut down by enfilading fire from the towers, but they quickly learned that the Martinengo bastion itself was now unable to offer return fire. They scaled the walls nearest to it, and scores of men came up over the battlements. Only rapid reply by Bragadino saved the day, with two whole companies of pikemen already stationed there on the wide walls, able to encircle them and then cut them down.

There were no more sorties from the defenders. They were fighting to the point of exhaustion and beyond just to hold the walls.

At dusk the Turks pulled back.

Bragadino ordered a count.

Half an hour later came the sombre tally.

Of the four thousand men he had had under his command a week ago, over two thousand were now dead or severely wounded, beyond fighting. He had around 1,800 fighting men left, and few of them were unscathed.

Hard to estimate the Turkish losses. Four, five thousand at least.

'But that still leaves us facing an army of sixty or seventy thousand,' he said. 'Pietro Giustiniani, what would you judge?'

'As I have always judged,' said Giustiniani. 'We can still hold out a while. We can inflict great losses on the Turks, to the bitter end, forcing them to accept a victory at high cost. But we cannot win. We can only pray for relief.'

'Yet no relief is coming. What then?'

'Just possibly we could hold out until the onset of winter. Then they would have to abandon the siege anyway.'

'Winter? It is still August. You truly think we could hold them back another three or four months? Another one hundred and twenty days' assault like today?'

Giustiniani sighed and did not reply. Both men knew they could not.

Nor was it only the day.

Lala Mustafa knew all about the power of sheer exhaustion to win battles and sieges. He sent his engineers and sappers forward at night, and they filled the moats with more bundles of brushwood and timber, drenched in heavy oil. They lit them just before dawn. With the wind on their side.

'Plague on them,' said Smith. 'On it all.'

A warm, soft wind came from the west, the gentlest zephyr. Their worst possible enemy now.

The oil-drenched brushwood burned green and slow, giving off thick black coils of smoke, a roiling tarry curtain that rose as high as the walls of Famagusta and then drifted gently, blindingly, into the smarting eyes of the defenders.

Worse still, they began to smell the aroma of burning human flesh. The hundreds of corpses down in the moat were roasting, human fat seeping forth and feeding the oily flames.

Lala Mustafa, master of tactics, then threw everything into the mix.

Cannons roared against the south wall, and huge two-hundred-pound cannonballs began to curve in over the battlements and pulverise the city yet further. The streets gradually filled with dust as well as lung-searing smoke, people lost their bearings along with all hope, and the sound of the guns booming yet again was almost enough to drive them out of their senses.

Lala Mustafa piled on dread upon dread. Safe behind the vast veil of smoke, he had Sipahi drummers parade below the battered west wall on their biggest horses, and the trembling people heard, in between the booms of the guns, the harmless yet more nerve-racking boom of great goatskin kettledrums played to an ominous, relentless rhythm.

Hodge and Nicholas huddled below the ramp on the west wall with the four knights. Nicholas's leg was still bandaged where it had been deeply cut as he detonated the pot-bomb beneath the arch. But he was young and in the last few days he had healed fast. All had kerchiefs around their mouths, eyes tight shut. Fists around the hilts of their weapons, but nothing to fight except this blinding smoke and growing terror.

'Come at us again, damn you,' murmured Stanley. 'We are ready for you. Smoke will not take a city.'

Smith began coughing violently.

Stanley said sharply, 'Do not encourage them, Brother.'

Smith, red eyes streaming, looked ready to strike him. 'There must be something we can do!' he spluttered at last.

'Blow the smoke back in their faces? Cut it to pieces with our swords?'

'Can we not try to blow up our own moat?' wondered Nicholas. 'Just with grenades, dislodge the tinder, scatter it ...' He tailed off.

Stanley shook his head, hesitated, then told him. 'We do not have enough grenades or powder left.'

The smoke thinned for a moment and Mazzinghi saw something. 'They've brought up a wooden catapult in the old style, and another ... four, five in all.' He dropped down again. 'I pray they don't start catapulting in putrefied bodies. I hate that.'

'You've never experienced it,' said Smith.

'No, I've read about it. The Turks did it at Constantinople.'

'It's not as bad as you think,' said Stanley.

'No?'

'No. It's worse.'

'You are a great consolation.'

'Here's a real consolation. A besieging army is far more likely to get sick than people in a fortified city, with fresh wells, water cisterns, latrines ...'

'But they are all being smashed to pieces even as we speak.'

Stanley had no reply. The young knight was right.

A massive stone cannonball came in from the south, whining unseen through the clouds of smoke so that no one could even cry out a warning, One in the air! It smashed home not fifty yards from them, still unseen. The west wall juddered to its foundations, and Mazzinghi threw himself flat. Then he sat upright again, looking ashamed, shaking.

For all his bravado, he was frightened. The bravado was an act. That only made his bravery all the greater.

They heard the muffled release of a catapult beam and then the mighty thump against the padded crossbar.

'Report!' cried out Giustiniani. 'Anyone?'

Now a distant screaming was added to the din of cannonade and kettledrum, and strident Janizary trumpets not far off through the smoke.

They could not abandon the walls, the attack might recommence at any moment. Smith said they'd send the Bektaşis again. 'Coming dancing barefoot and burnt across the flaming moat, inhaling the smoke like incense. As happy as drunken stoats.'

Then a messenger was running along the walls, head and face heavily wrapped in wet cloths, his lungs seared.

'What are the catapults for, man?'

He knelt, wheezing, eyes streaming.

Another catapult thumped. Then another. Through the smoke and din, they saw flashes of light, and in the city below, Nicholas thought he saw the bright lick of flame.

'Incendiaries!' gasped the messenger. 'Some sort of sack, filled with metal fragments, perhaps salt of magnesia, and tar and Greek fire and the bleeding Jesus knows what—'

'Mind your blasphemous tongue,' said Smith.

The messenger wheezed at him, wiped his eyes, then stood and ran on at a crouch.

Their facecloths were drying out and no sign of the water boy.

'I'll go,' said Nicholas.

'I too,' said Hodge.

Two more catapults thumped, sounding as if they were right up to the edge of the moat and still unseen through that pitch-dark pall. Down the steps and into the narrow street, the smoke was thinner and they saw buildings aflame. The nearest well was shattered, filled with stone, and near it lay a dead boy still holding a pail. Nicholas took the pail from his stiff fingers and he and Hodge ran. They found a marble fountain in a ruined courtyard, sweetly decorated with nymphs and dolphins, laid the pail on its side and half filled it, ran back.

There was a wooden warehouse aflame, a roaring inferno, too hot to approach. Another near by, already burning down to a smouldering ruin, a stench like burnt sheep.

'Listen, Nick,' said Hodge, gasping. 'You take the water. It is more than I can stand to be up there, doin' nothing. I am for the

Franciscans in the hospital, where I can do some good. I know a little medicine, and if nothing else I can mop up the blood.'

Nicholas clapped him on the shoulder. 'We will meet later.'

Clawing his way back up the half-shattered steps one-handed, pail in the other, lungs poisoned, leg still hurting, he felt the city hot behind him. The incendiaries were taking hold.

They dunked their facecloths in the water, retied them, drank the rest.

'This smoke must clear!' said Smith, almost shouting.

'Be thankful,' said Stanley. 'The chronicles also say the Turks at Constantinople used flame throwers mounted on siege towers, trumpets the size of cannon belching out flames fifty feet long and as hot as hell itself.'

'Fool,' said Smith. 'Now you've said it, you'll probably bring it. And you'll be the first one to burn up like ...'

He started to cough again violently.

Giustiniani got to his feet, keeping low. 'Time to get below,' he ordered. 'We're dying up here, and we need to report to Bragadino.'

They found him in the hall of the palace. His left hand was wounded and bandaged. Three men were speaking to him at once. He looked exhausted beyond death.

A plump, hysterical merchant held his arms wide and cried, 'The entire warehouse! Filled with priceless carpets of Tabriz and Kurdistan! I am ruined!'

'Aye,' snapped Bragadino, 'and at the Franciscan hospital is a child of two covered with burns from crown to toe, whom I confess it pains me to think of even more than your precious carpets, Signor Spinelli.'

The merchant stamped his slippered foot, until Smith moved him bodily out of the way.

Bragadino looked at them with relief. 'Gentlemen.'

Signor Spinelli looked at them with disgust, his nose wrinkled.

Bragadino said, 'We have heard news that Lala Mustafa's own son has been killed. Do you think this can be true?'

They were speechless for a moment. This complicated things.

'It is possible, I suppose,' said Stanley. 'A long-range shot ...'

Bragadino turned back on the merchant. 'But now we cannot surrender, do you understand? If we make terms, they will not be honoured. It is now a personal matter. Lala Mustafa will lie, we will open the gates, and he will kill us all.'

Twice, rumours ran through the frantic city that the Turks had broken in, twice they had to be quashed. There were further rumours that the wells and cisterns had been poisoned. Bragadino went out and drank from them himself to show it for a lie. But still a sense of barely suppressed panic dominated.

Then one of the biggest grain stores in the city went up in flames.

Everywhere, rich merchants and bankers talked of surrender, looking at their fine houses, their glittering wardrobes, the classical statues from Salamis in their courtyards.

'Think of the women and children,' they said.

They slept that last night on the walls, huddled in blankets for comfort, not for warmth. The smoke had at last died down. Their lungs burned, they coughed frequently.

'I think it will come tomorrow,' whispered Smith, passing Stanley the last of the bottle.

'Aye,' said Stanley. He saw Nicholas's eyes shine. 'You awake, boy?'

Nicholas sat upright and held out his hand for the bottle. A church bell struck three. After he had drunk he said, 'Will it be like Nicosia?'

'Perhaps worse,' said Smith. 'Lala Mustafa has lost many more men here than at Nicosia, as well as his son. So if he wants revenge ...'

There was a long, brooding silence. Then Nicholas said, 'Still, if we are to die here tomorrow – I am glad of it, though I wish Hodge were with me too.' His throat was full. 'I know I had more to do—'

'We all had more to do, old friend,' said Stanley. 'Life is always an unfinished story.'

Nicholas nodded. 'But I am glad enough to die here as anywhere. I am happy you found me, took me to Malta, and all that followed. Even the pains and the griefs. What it has all been about, I do not know. But you always say it is not ours to understand much, as mortal men. Ours to do and die.'

277

'So I do.'

Smith looked over the walls. Beyond the last shreds of drifting smoke there were many lights out on the dark plain.

'I think they will come just before dawn,' he said. 'Maybe two hours from now.'

He was right.

The sky was grey, the sun not yet above the horizon, and it seemed the whole Ottoman army came at once.

Columns surged towards the walls at the fast trot, five thousand skilled musketeers spread out and keeping up a steady rate of fire at the defenders pinned on the walls. As many more archers, Armenians and Syrians, did likewise. Smith's jezail cracked out and a musketeer spun and fell. Another took his place. Thirty seconds later it cracked out again. Another died.

They began to come over the blackened, foul-smelling moat on wide pontoons, carrying scaling ladders and ropes. They were concentrated particularly on the towers, to try to capture them and silence the murderous enfilading fire of grapeshot and chain-shot.

And then a mine went up.

Not the troublesome mine of the saboteurs, weakening a wall already under attack, but a mine laid over the past two weeks by teams of Ottoman engineers working all day and all night, with the labour of hundreds of roped slaves. And it went off where they least expected it. The south wall.

An entire thirty-yard section of the wall seemed to lift into the air and then settle back into place, albeit leaning forward more than before. An agonised wait, and then the whole thirty yards leaned out further ... further ... ripped from its own foundations, and toppled forward into the moat.

A column of two thousand Janizaries was a minute away.

'To the tower!' cried Smith.

They ran past a hospital with walking wounded spilling out on to the street, worse wounded under awnings, shielded from the hot sun as they lay dying. Flies were everywhere, fever and a universal stench of death.

'Remember Malta!' they cried.

They scrambled up the spiral stairs of the tower and found two gunners lying dead beside a small culverin. The Janizaries were crossing the fallen wall.

'Pull the gun round!' cried Smith. 'Bring me that grapeshot!'

They cleaned the gun out and rammed it with powder and Nicholas brought a fistful of grapeshot, tripping over one of the dead gunners.

'Cover!'

The breech hole fizzed, the gun bellowed, and the grapeshot tore into the entering Janizaries.

'Pull her back, reload! Find me more powder!'

Down below, a Janizary officer had already got his men under cover within the walls and sent a party to take the tower.

They heard footfalls on the stairs. Stanley drew his sword.

'More powder, damn it!' cried Smith.

'Patience,' said Stanley. 'Occupied at present.' He gripped the stair column in his left hand and held his sword low. A Janizary's tall white hat appeared and then ducked back. A moment later a grenade landed between Stanley's feet.

'Fire!'

The gun roared and tore into more of the enemy picking their way in. The forward company of Janizaries inside was feeling trapped. Where was the follow-up? And down the street came a company of grim-faced Spanish pikemen.

Stanley fumbled for the grenade. A pistol fired and the ball ricocheted off the wall and clanged off his breastplate. A spear jabbed at him, he swiped it aside and thrust forward. A fellow rolled back down the stairs. He reached for the grenade. The fuse stuttered and went out.

He stared at it, cursed and tossed it down anyway.

A split second later he felt the full blast of the explosion as hot air in his face, knocking him backwards. He sat up and felt his face, his ears. Nothing missing.

'What are you *doing*?' roared Smith. 'The gun's cracked, get downstairs!'

They came out into a ferocious mêlée of pikemen and Janizaries. If the whole enemy column had pushed forward they would have carried everything before them, but for some reason the column commander held them back and the forward company, isolated and bewildered, was cut to pieces.

There was a respite. The defenders stood and sagged, leaning on pike butts and spears.

It was hopeless. The wall before them could never be rebuilt in time. The Janizaries could be back in at any moment.

'Sire, the guns are overheating,' reported a gunnery sergeant to Bragadino. 'We must cease fire a while.'

'Then bring down the guns from the Andruzzi bastion.'

'Only two still working there, sire. The rest are out of action. Also they are low on powder and no more is being brought up.'

'We haven't the manpower to hold them otherwise!' cried Bragadino.

The gunnery sergeant hesitated, and then said quietly, 'No, sir. We haven't.'

Bragadino turned his head and regarded him. No plump merchant this, but a tired-looking, hard-bitten, clear-eyed professional soldier. He carried two wounds on him already, bloody-bandaged knee and thigh. His face and hands were caked black with powder smoke, his eyes reddened, his lips chapped dry and cracked by the heat.

'Envoy from the enemy camp, sire,' said a breathless messenger. 'Do we wish to seek terms?'

Bragadino hung his head.

Then he raised it again and cried, 'Would to God I had died here!'

It seemed an ominous cry.

Smith, Stanley and Nicholas, nearly ready to fall to their knees in the street and weep for defeated exhaustion, raised their swords one last time with trembling arms and shot them home in their sheaths.

'I want to find Hodge,' said Nicholas.

They went back through the streets towards the Franciscan hospital. Women were weeping, and in the middle of the street there was a powder monkey curled up and still, a young boy, the black shining powder leaking from his leather satchel.

Nicholas cried, 'No!' and fell to his knees beside him and rolled him over.

His face was pocked with scabs and young scars.

It was little Andreas.

Nicholas raised him up in his arms and wept.

Smith and Stanley stood close either side of him, as if guarding him from greater grief.

18

By nightfall the terms of surrender had been agreed. Bragadino decided that he had no choice, and they must take the risk that Lala Mustafa would keep his word, despite the death of his son.

'The same self-delusion, the same appeasement,' said Smith – though he did not blame Bragadino himself. 'The Crescent has won again, advanced a little further across the world. We have done nothing to stop it, and it has all been in vain.'

Nicholas thought of the ordinary infantrymen, heroes all, and of stout Baglione, and of the little powder monkey, Andreas, buried in a nameless mass grave with a hundred others in the hurried twilight.

It could not all be in vain.

Worse than the despair of defeat was the terrible tension that held the city from sleep all night long. Would the sack come?

At one point they heard a huge roar from across the plain, and thought that the Bektaşis were coming. Grown men and women whimpered and knelt, the most irreligious now prayed in the street, crossing themselves feverishly; some lost control altogether, and children looked on wide eyed as the adults around them went mad.

But still the sack did not come. The roar they heard was merely some celebration.

Instead the city was ringed around with a disciplined row of guard tents. The great chain was lifted and the harbour filled with Ottoman galleys. A red crescent flag flew from the towers of St Nicholas Cathedral.

Whether the last grain stores had been sabotaged from within, they never knew. The poorest had been eating asses and cats the last few days. Wine stores were so low, most drank water with vinegar.

'And some say the whole operation to take Cyprus was because of wine,' said Stanley. 'There's an irony.'

'How so?' said Nicholas.

'Because Cyprus wine is famous, and Sultan Selim is a great lover of it. So, some say, that wise confidant and adviser of his, Joseph Nassi, encouraged the conquest of the island even more forcefully than the Grand Vizier, Mehmet Sokollu.'

'Joseph Nassi? Who is he?'

'A rich Jew,' said Smith. 'Maybe the richest in all the world. Close friend of the Ottoman court. You may even glimpse him soon.' He spat into the fire. 'He is to be the King of Cyprus.'

There was a figure standing at the edge of the firelight. Nicholas saw the long, thin face, lit by the orange glow. He beckoned him over. The man shook his head, so Nicholas went over to him.

'If you do not mind,' said Abdul softly, 'I shall not join you. I do not think your knightly friends trust me stilll. I will go into the mountains, I travel faster alone. I have had enough of sieges for now. I have repaid my debt to you handsomely. I believe I saved your lives once, perhaps twice. May you prove lucky under,' he coughed, 'the new Ottoman rule. I have in my possession certain valuables,' he patted the canvas bag over his shoulder, 'which will stand me in good stead. Two months ago they were Nicosia's. A month ago they were Sultan Selim's, strictly speaking. Today they are Abdul of Tripoli's. In another two or three weeks, if all goes well, they will be with a banker friend of mine in Aleppo. What a merry-go-round it is!'

'Then?'

'Then, I long to go on the haj to Mecca.'

Nicholas stared at him. 'Are you sincere? I did not think you a pious Muslim.'

'Not pious,' said Abdul with his enigmatic smile, 'nor entirely orthodox, no. But ... mysteries are many in the world that is. And I would like to see Mecca one time before I die.'

Nicholas nodded. 'Well,' he said at last, shaking his hand, 'Allah go with you.'

'And God with you,' said Abdul. Then he gave a strangulated little laugh. 'Ah, if only men of all creeds and nations could live together in such sweet peace and harmony as we,' he laid his hand on his heart and fluttered his eyelashes like a dancing girl, 'then how soon we would all die of boredom!'

And he turned and made for the darkness.

Life was strange. You could not account for it. You could only do what you thought right. A Moor could prove a friend, for a time, and in battle you found yourself killing a man without even judging him.

Abdul turned back one last time. 'By the way, Master Nicholas of England, did you and your knights never think it strange that our paths should keep crossing? First we met in the prison of Pedro Deza, back in Cadiz, and at Nicosia, and then I appear again in Famagusta. Like your shadow.'

Nicholas looked puzzled. It seemed far fetched, certainly. He shrugged. 'The Mediterranean is a small world, I am beginning to think.'

'Think on that way!' said Abdul. 'Do not think suspicious thoughts, such as that I was always in the pay of the Great Sultan, and paid to track you across the sea. And to find out about you and your close comrades, those two wandering Knights of St John who seemed to know so much.'

'You …' He was momentarily lost for words, head spinning. Then he said carefully, 'If that were the case, what would you do now?'

'Why, I would make for Aleppo via Constantinople and the Court of the Great Sultan, my beloved master. I always take roundabout routes, they can't track you so well that way. I would report on all your travels, rich in detail and colour, and conclude with your heroic death at the siege of Famagusta. And then I would collect my handsome reward and go on my way. Whistling a little tune, perhaps.'

Nicholas shook his head wearily. 'But I do not believe you have ever betrayed us.'

'You can tell it from a man's eyes,' said Abdul, 'his mouth, his

284

expression, his hands. A hundred things. Liars are not so hard to identify, after all.'

'Truly you are a man in a thousand.'

'Do not insult me! Abdul of Tripoli is a man in a million, nay, entirely unique!' Then he said more gently, 'God watch over you anyway, Master Nicholas of England.'

'And you, Abdul of Tripoli.'

Then he was gone.

Nicholas turned back and almost bumped into a figure just round the corner.

Smith.

'You move quietly for a fellow of such bulk,' he said.

Smith nodded after the departed Moor. 'I tell you something even more amusing than the Moor there spying on us all this way, or pretending to. We knew it all along.'

This game of spy and counter-spy. It could drive a man mad.

'Why did you let him?'

'Perhaps,' said Smith, 'the Moor told us more than you realise.'

The next day the half-ruined city was taken over by an impressively orderly occupation, far different to Nicosia. Huge gangs of slaves worked to clear away the damage, and the defeated saw with a strange dismay that much of Famagusta, especially around the harbour, was barely touched. It would be rebuilt as magnificent as ever by winter, a prized new jewel in the Ottoman crown.

Sultan Selim had acquired a very fine harbour and city, along with the third-biggest island in the Mediterranean.

Bragadino and his immediate counsellors were invited to dine at the palace: until yesterday, Bragadino's palace. He was now billeted with the others, on a hard horsehair pallet in a grubby airless room, while Joseph Nassi, the rich Jew, was already in occupation.

'It is a trick,' said Smith.

'I do not think so,' said Bragadino. 'Joseph Nassi is a man quite independent of Lala Mustafa, who shows no sign of wanting even to enter the city of the Infidel.'

'Let us go,' said Giustiniani wearily, 'and see what this triumphal Jew has to say to us.'

Nicholas found Hodge in the hospital, washing his arms clean.

He shook his head. 'Not I. The fighting's done but we're as busy as ever here. You go to dine.'

Nicholas said hesitantly, 'You are not angry?'

'No. I'm just learnin' fast, that's all.'

Slaves had already scrubbed and cleaned the entire building, new tapestries were hung and carpets were laid, another column from Salamis was sent for by ox wagon to replace one that had been shattered by an unfortunate Ottoman cannonball. A galley came into the harbour with fresh furnishings, linens, silks, magnificent gilded lamps and lanterns. And Joseph Nassi's beautiful wife, Dona Gracia, daughter of a fabulously wealthy Portuguese Jewish banking family.

The party of Christians were invited early to bathe themselves, and fresh robes were laid out for them on velvet-upholstered divans.

Nicholas chose a blue silk robe, belted with a gold sash, feeling sick. In the Franciscan hospital, men, women and children still lay dying of fever and gangrene. Hodge was up to his elbows in blood and filth.

Smith looked blackly rebellious, almost refusing to bathe.

'Just co-operate,' said Giustiniani. 'That is an order, Fra John. We are Venetian counsellors. We are hear to listen and observe. Joseph Nassi is a man of high civilization, confidant of the Sultan, yet also personal friends with Prince William of Orange and the Emperor Maximilian, connections with the Duchy of Burgundy. He is even said to have masterminded the election of the King of Poland. Now suppress your mulish will for once. The time for fighting is over.'

It was not a grand hall, however, but a much smaller chamber where dinner was laid. A table, white linen, silver candlesticks, ivory-handled knives. Dishes of fruit, jugs of wine. Discreet servants, and still more discreet though well-armed guards at the door.

They were led to be seated. Just the five of them. There was no sign of the new King of Cyprus.

All so quiet and elegant. Their ears still ringing intermittently from the cannon fire of just two days ago. Beneath these fine silk robes, many a cut and burn.

'I don't like this,' said Smith. He eyed the knife in front of him.

'Mind your manners,' said Stanley quietly. 'No stabbing the host now.'

Then the doors were opened and in came a man and a woman. Nicholas, at least, felt more at ease, and took a quick, deep gulp of wine as he stood. You were less likely to be slaughtered at the table, he felt, if there was a lady present.

Joseph Nassi smiled at them, hands held wide. 'Gentlemen, please, be seated.'

He sat at the head, his wife at the other end, Nicholas and Stanley either side of her. She was dark, hair threaded with silver, although no more than thirty-five, and immensely beautiful. Nassi himself was of medium height, wore a plain back robe, had dark curly hair and bushy eyebrows. He bristled with energy. Nicholas had been expecting something much smoother, plumper, more pompous; less disarmingly likeable.

The host clapped his hands and the servants bustled. He raised his goblet.

'Gentlemen, and my beloved wife, the incomparable Dona Gracia: I give you Peace!'

They all drank. Smith concentrated hard on swallowing.

Then Nassi said something quite incomprehensible, adding afterwards, 'As the old Venetian proverb has it.'

They smiled and nodded. Bragadino looked puzzled.

Fish was brought.

'Caught this morning,' said Nassi. 'In the coastal waters of my new kingdom.' His tone was light and dancing, teasing and testing, and he eyed them all one by one as he spoke, assessing them like an inquisitor. 'An offensive idea to you, I am sure—'

Bragadino shrugged. 'The verdict of Providence.'

Nassi smiled. 'Then again, since Cyprus is now under my rule, from the moment Famagusta surrendered, there has been no further sacking. You may have noticed.'

So you could keep it all for yourself, thought Smith.

Nassi read his thoughts as if reading a book.

Stanley recalled that cunning Turkish interrogator at Nicosia,

Ertugul Bey. Joseph Nassi could outwit an army of Ertugul Beys.

Nicholas nodded and his goblet was refilled by a silent servant. He glanced sidelong at Dona Gracia. There was a slight flush on her cheek, and her mouth was beautifully shaped. She really was very lovely. For a moment she reminded him of a more elevated, more graceful version of the Widow Evangelina.

'So,' said Joseph Nassi, 'you will no doubt form a judgement of me. You are very well informed, you n … You Venetians.'

Was he about to say knights? Did Nicholas just imagine it? He felt a cold thrill.

Did Nassi even want them to know he knew?

He played at life like it was a game of chess.

'I was sorry to hear about the flood at Venice in this recent summer storm.'

Stanley tried not to tense, and spoke in his most perfect Venetian Italian. 'Indeed, sire. Most regrettable.'

'Was there much water damage?'

'I believe some.'

Joseph Nassi smiled. 'There was none. I know you four, you are Knights of St John.'

Forks and goblets stopped halfway to their mouths. Then Smith quickly laid down his fork and reached for the knife. Stanley slammed his hand down upon the back of Smith's so that the goblets jumped. Dona Gracia gave a soft scream.

Joseph Nassi said with a sharp note of command, 'Gentlemen, *please*.' He turned in his chair and had quiet words with the steward. A moment later the doors were opened and the armed guards departed.

Smith relaxed slightly.

In came a musician.

'Play outside, in the hall,' ordered Nassi. 'We do not wish to hear you, but we wish no one to hear us either.'

The musician, thin and pale as a weed starved of sunshine, bowed very low and sorrowfully, his lute held at arm's length, and then retired. A few moments later, he and his three fellow musicians began a plangent madrigal outside the door.

Joseph Nassi smiled around. Smith laid his fork on his plate and his hands on the table. 'Forgive my rashness,' he blurted.

'My husband will have his little jokes,' said Dona Gracia, her voice soft and low. Smith looked at her, and under that thick black beard, Nicholas could have sworn he saw a blush.

It was a strangely intimate dinner, just Nassi and Dona Gracia, the four knights and Nicholas himself. This would be the only time in his life, he thought, when he would have dinner with a king! A Jewish king too, like Solomon and David. Life was a dream.

They were eating with the enemy, whom they would have fought to the death two days ago. Yet the food was delicious – lamb followed the fish – and Nicholas drank more of the fine wine and felt light headed and ludicrously merry, for all the bloodshed of the past weeks, the dead bodies, the stench of the hospitals. He knew what it was. It was sweet, strong Cyprus wine, and the animal joy of the survivor, stronger than any guilt.

A steward refilled his goblet again. He turned to Dona Gracia.

'More wine for you?' He hesitated and then risked, 'Your Majesty?'

She laughed. 'How ridiculous,' she murmured. 'But you know, the terrible thing is, I think I could grow to like it.' She sipped her wine. '*Your Majesty* indeed. You are a charmer, young knight.'

'I'm not a knight,' he said.

'No? Then what?'

'A gentleman adventurer.'

'Indeed?' She arched her beautiful eyebrows and said no more.

'No,' Joseph Nassi was saying, leaning forward on the table, 'there was no summer flood at Venice, and that was not an old Venetian proverb I gave you. In fact it was Aramaic, the language of Jesus. But we hear there *was* nearly a massacre of sorts at Nicosia. There were four Knights of St John, two Italians and two Englishmen if we hear correctly, who stood in the way of the late Governor Dandolo driving my people out of the town. To be mown down by the Turkish guns between the lines.'

They said nothing. He seemed to know everything. Nicholas even wondered, a little blurrily, whether Nassi had contact with Abdul of Tripoli. Who could say?

Nassi said, 'The Knights of St John have not always been so kind to the Jews. Nor were the Templars of old.'

'It is true,' said Giustiniani. 'All men are fallen.'

'Among my people we use the phrase "The Righteous among the Nations" for those Gentiles who risk their lives to save a Jew.'

'You do those four fellows too much honour,' said Smith. 'It was a street skirmish in Nicosia, a small, ugly thing. Little more than schoolyard bullying.'

'Nevertheless,' said Nassi, 'my people are so accustomed to being bullied, it always comes as a pleasant surprise to have a Gentile stand alongside us.' He held out his hands. 'Come, let us not quarrel. The story of the Jews and the Christians is not always a happy one, but there are beacons of light. This deed of yours – this street skirmish, you call it – I call it a righteous deed in the sight of God. Tell me your names.'

Still they hesitated, though all there knew they could judge this extraordinary Jew already. He was both cunning and open hearted, a bewitching mix of lightning intelligence, manipulation, charm and sincerity. Joseph Nassi, who sat at the right hand of Selim the Sot himself.

'Fra Pietro,' said Giustiniani finally.

And then they all gave their first names, until Nicholas, who firmly announced, 'Master Nicholas Ingoldsby of the Country of Shropshire in England, and rightful heir to the estate of my father, Sir John Ingoldsby, knight.'

Smith glared at him, Stanley sighed, Dona Gracia touched her napkin to her mouth to hide her smile, and her husband regarded him with amusement and curiosity.

'Very well,' he said. 'One day you will have your reward, in this world or the next.'

Nicholas made himself slow down on the wine and eat more. It was a delightful dinner, now he felt sure they were not to be stabbed or poisoned.

Joseph Nassi was as entertaining a host as they had ever known. He risked drily disparaging remarks about Lala Mustafa himself – 'sitting in lonely triumph in his tent,' he said, 'having his feet rubbed down.'

And he amused them with a lengthy tale about how he cornered the beeswax market. Dona Garcia leaned towards Nicholas and murmured, 'Do say if my husband is boring you.'

'On the contrary,' he said, 'I have always had an intense fascination with beeswax.'

Her eyes danced. This young Englishman!

'We had two bad summers,' Nassi was explaining, 'and the bees did not fly. I asked about the orchards of Bursa, and the bees weren't flying there either. Truly, a schoolboy could have worked it out. I could have bought up fruit as well, but it does not store so well. And so I, Joseph Nassi, sinister and mercenary Jew as I am, bought up as much beeswax on the open market as I could, at the going rate, cheating nobody. The following year there was inevitably a shortage, the price doubled, tripled, and I made a fair but handsome profit. At which many indignant voices were raised, saying, See the Jew, how he stuffs his pockets!'

He sighed. 'In truth, money does not interest me. I am only interested in what it can buy. Safety for myself, my family, my kin. For the wandering Jews have no abiding city. Only our Bible: our portable Jerusalem. We have no armies, no war galleys, no land of our own. We must live by our wits, as God intended.'

'Since we are being so open with each other,' said Giustiniani, 'tell us, sire. What will come next? Do we need to fear? How can there be peace?'

Nassi spoke carefully. 'Of course I cannot make you privy to Ottoman state secrets. But there are those, will always be those, who wish for an Islamic Caliphate to stretch from eastern horizon to west. I do not think the Sultan Selim himself wishes this. *I* do not wish this.' He smiled faintly. 'What room would that leave for my own people?'

Giustiniani said, 'We hear you have a bold plan to repopulate Palestine with Jews?'

'How well informed you are, for humble travellers!' said Dona Gracia.

'It is true,' said Nassi. 'The Sultan has gifted me the Lordship of Tiberias, including the village of Saged, ancient centre for the study of the Kabbalah. A subject close to my heart. We have rebuilt Tiberias' walls, irrigated, planted mulberry groves to develop a silk industry – though so far, I confess, few Jews have been prepared to quit Christendom, with all its difficulties, for a new life in a hard land. But it may come yet.

'Meanwhile, Christendom herself needs to bring about some final confrontation with the Ottoman Empire, on equal terms.' He popped a grape into his mouth. 'Some accommodation, some *balance*, must be found in the Mediterranean. A balance of power. Then we can all have peace.'

When they left, Joseph Nassi returned their weapons to them, and assured them they would not be harmed within the city.

Dona Gracia held her hand out to be kissed. It was sweetly scented, orange oil perhaps, and as he kissed, Nicholas glanced up and his eyes met hers, dark and dancing.

I am drunk, he thought, as he weaved after his comrades down the street. What a fool.

'You know,' Stanley was saying, 'though he is an operator straight out of Machiavelli's rule-book, and close adviser to Selim, and clearly the brains behind this entire Cyprus operation, which for the Turks, after all, has gone so smoothly – yet I cannot help but like this fellow.'

'For a Jew,' said Smith, 'perhaps he is not all bad.'

'His heart is not in Cyprus,' said Giustiniani, 'but Palestine. Even Jerusalem itself.'

'Also sacred to the Mohammedans,' said Mazzinghi.

'And to *me*,' said Smith.

19

That candlelit dinner was a strange and magical interlude between two horrors. The power of Joseph Nassi to charm, to make peace, could not embrace everyone. Lala Mustafa still had his grievances, and the mummified body of his son in a lead casket.

'Hear me now,' said Bragadino, his voice more grave than they had ever heard it. The tone of a man who has made a decision which is not merely important but fateful. 'We believe that Joseph Nassi is a just man, and will rule Cyprus fairly. But let us not be deceived. Christendom has suffered a terrible loss. Without some desperate act, it will barely realise it. There will still be no Holy League. Next year the Turks will push further west, and further. They will attack small heroic Malta again, and Sicily. There will be no stopping them. And so I am going now as summoned, to the tent of Lala Mustafa, a cruel and vindictive man. And I shall insult him in such a way that he will kill me.'

They were stunned and silent.

'By my sacrifice, Venice will be brought into the war.'

'Sire,' said Stanley, 'if the loss of Cyprus could not rouse Venice, how will your death?'

'I believe it will,' said Bragadino. 'Because of my sons. They will rouse Venice, for they are powerful characters. Though it sounds a little absurd,' he looked down, 'I had a dream last night. I saw my sons breathe out vengeance upon the heathen like the sons of an Old Testament king slain in battle. So I am going now to my death. On my walk there, I shall take pleasure in thinking up the foulest insults I can heap upon a Turkish head. This will provide entertainment and distraction as I go.

'But you must promise me this. You will get back to Venice with the story. I know not how. But you have done special service, Smith and Stanley. I know you have travelled in strange and Orient lands, you are more than ordinary soldiers. You have picked locks, opened dungeon doors, you speak many languages, wear many disguises, know how to handle weapons of which I have never even heard ...'

Stanley tried to protest, 'It is not that easy, My Lord,' but Bragadino raised his hand.

'I know this. You need not deny it. Not now, not to an old man going to his death.'

Stanley felt his eyes blur despite himself. In the fallen world there was still nobility, like fire in the dark.

'So. Promise me only this, you will get to Italy. Tell my story. Rouse the Lion of Venice.' Bragadino rose too, and stood like an old greying lion himself. 'Rouse that mighty Lion! Let her shake out her golden mane and roar! And let the Turk know that at last he has brought ruin upon himself, with his vaunting ambition and his false creed. And his empire will come to dust, like all empires of this world.' His voice softened again. 'Let me not die in vain.'

Then Stanley seized the old man's right hand in his own mighty hands and clasped him as he would his father, and said, 'You shall not. By God, old comrade, you shall not.'

At Vespers on 5th August, Bragadino went to take the keys of the city to Lala Mustafa with all solemnity. He went with a small retinue of unarmed advisers.

Lala Mustafa's was a large, plain white tent with horses tied outside. No ostentation. He made them wait, and then they were admitted before him. They saw a man of small stature, grey moustache, short grey hair brushed back hard off his lined forehead, and cold hard eyes.

'You are welcome,' he said, voice flat. He took the proffered keys. No drinks were brought.

Bragadino gave an insultingly faint bow. 'It has pleased Almighty God to permit you this victory. This *temporary* victory.'

'It is the will of Allah. If you had acknowledged this earlier, many lives could have been spared.'

'Including your son's. If you had not come conquering other people's lands, your son would not have died.'

Stanley thought he saw those cold, hard eyes waver a little. But the mouth was compressed hard.

Bragadino pressed on. 'Cyprus so far must have cost you twenty thousand men—'

'A wild exaggeration.'

'But you will lose many more. How many sons have you left?'

The cold eyes burned. Grief, hatred, and fury that this whipped dog of a governor should dare to humiliate him before his generals.

'Have a care, my friend,' he said.

'I have many,' snapped Bragadino. 'Why are we here? Can we now depart, and leave you to your treasure?'

'Where are the Muslim pilgrims?'

This was an unexpected turn.

'The fifty pilgrims on the haj? We know you took them prisoner.'

He meant the fifty pilgrims captured at sea by the Chevalier Romegas. This was difficult. Bragadino couldn't tell Lala they had converted to Christianity and were ready to sail west. His fury would know no bounds. He would demand they were handed over, and then kill them all as apostates from Islam, in accordance with the law of the Koran.

'They were all killed in the bombardment,' said Bragadino.

'*All?* All fifty, clean killed? Not one even injured?'

'All killed,' he said, 'by a single ball. A most unusual occurrence.'

The cold eyes glittered. 'You mock me, Christian.'

'Indeed not, sire. They were all killed, and then they were drowned at sea, then they were burned to death in a great fire, and then ...' He laid his hand on his heart. 'We ate them.'

Lala Mustafa sprang up roaring and hurled a table over on its side. 'You damned Christian dog, I will have you whipped of your hide!'

There was chaos, shouting, drawn swords, and Bragadino shouting back, even as he was grappled from behind by two huge body-guards, 'Did you not eat your own son, you filthy Mohammedan hog? Curses on you and your family! I fart in your father's beard and wipe my arse with your stinking Koran!'

Lala Mustafa nodded and the bodyguard knocked Bragadino unconscious.

Lala stared down at him. The fellow was mad. But he would pay.

The four knights looked on in grim silence, their own wrists bound with rope, as Bragadino was tied to a horse-post.

'Cut off his ears and nose,' said Lala.

'My Lord, no!' cried Giustiniani, stepping forward.

Lala turned on him. 'One more word from you,' he said, 'and I will cut out his eyes.'

He meant it.

They stood silent.

A man came with a big-bladed knife, pulled Bragadino's ear and sawed it through. The Governor came to and groaned. 'Knife's too blunt,' he muttered.

Another horseman arrived, cloak billowing. It was Joseph Nassi. He might have demanded an end, being lord of the island now, but he knew it was too dangerous for that, Lala Mustafa too far gone. He could read his eyes.

He dropped from his horse. 'My Lord,' he gasped, 'this has no dignity. I beg you, let us show clemency.'

'Clemency!' said Bragadino, neck coursing with blood. 'That dog-fucker couldn't even spell it.'

'My Lord,' said Nassi, 'he is driven mad by something. By grief. I beg you, this is not the way for—'

'He has provoked it,' said Lala, his voice once again without emotion. 'I do not know why. But now he must face the punishment. Let it be an example for the whole island.'

Nassi, rarely for him, raised his voice. 'Sire, I insist, on behalf of the Sultan Selim—'

It was enough. Lala Mustafa had been humiliated already today. Who commanded the army, he or this upstart Jew? He would not be overruled by any Jew, no matter how close to Selim. He nodded to two mounted guards and they obliged Nassi to remount, hands on their sword hilts. They then escorted him back towards the city gate. As he went, Nassi's head hung down.

All the cruelty of the Ottomans came to the fore then, after all the valour. And Smith and Stanley, Giustiniani and Mazzinghi, witnessed it with their own eyes. They let their memories be burned with it.

They cut off Bragadino's ears and nose, and mounted him on an ass. He looked like a mutilated old lion. The soldiery jeered as he rode among them, and wild rumours flew that Lala Mustafa was going to allow a full-scale looting of Famagusta after all. Men rushed to their tents to collect bags and sacking.

Bragadino was driven into the city, and his retinue insulted and then turned loose. And that was where Nicholas and Hodge, along with the rest of the citizens, saw the final horror.

Their noble old Governor was tied to a post before the cathedral of St Nicholas and left for a night to suffer. Meanwhile the Turks began to run riot, and there was no order for them to stop. They bullied people of all ages and estates into gangs to clear away the corpses, and then they began to beat people, ravish the women in alleyways and cellars, and help themselves to any valuables they found. Fights broke out, and more people were briskly put to the sword.

'Remember every detail,' murmured Stanley, his face stricken. 'Be a witness, a chronicle.'

The next day, Friday, the Muslim day of prayer, Bragadino was marched with drums and cheers to the harbourside and tied to a chair. He was hoisted to the top of a galley's mast and then ducked in the sea. Raised up, ducked, raised up, ducked. In salt water. With his open wounds.

The cruelty of it was beyond all reckoning and sense.

Finally, almost delirious with pain, he was dragged back to the Cathedral square, and there a weeping butcher was ordered at spear-point to skin him alive. The butcher refused, saying he would rather die. So they killed him, and found an animal skinner. He too refused, but they found his wife and daughter, and said they would kill them before his eyes if he did not do their bidding. The animal skinner begged for wine, drained a pint jug, and then began the work. Some said afterwards that Bragadino had murmured to him as he was dying that he forgave him. It was not his fault, and he would not be held to account for it before God.

Bragadino cried out, '*Domine, in manus tuas commendo spiritum meum!*'

He died before the animal skinner reached his waist.

He was quartered and each quarter was blown out of a gun on the wall.

His skin was stuffed with straw, dressed in crimson robes and shielded by a red parasol, mounted on a cow and paraded through the streets, crowned with thorns.

Nicholas heard a man in the crowd say to his neighbour, 'Christ forgive us, why did we not resist these savages harder? What madness made us think we would live as well under their rule as the Venetians?'

'This will not go unpunished,' said his neighbour. 'It cannot.'

20

The Cathedral square was cleaned of blood and the cathedral itself reconsecrated as a mosque. Lala Mustafa himself sat on the high altar as if on a throne for the prayers of dedication.

'We sail west after nightfall,' said Giustiniani. 'Romegas will get us there somehow.'

They stowed aboard the small, crowded galley with nearly fifty wide-eyed Christians, lately Muslims. People everywhere were fleeing Cyprus, many for Crete, and the Turks did nothing to stop them. They would bring their own people in from the Turkish mainland soon enough.

They sailed through a hot starlit night on a south-east wind out of Egypt. Nicholas stared down into the black depths, thinking of pyramids and Pharaoh and Joseph. And then he feel asleep on deck, exhausted and defeated, and woke up screaming, seeing the flensed skull of Bragadino, red as raw meat, the skin hanging down around his neck like an obscene ruff, the eyes staring, the ruined lips still moving in prayer.

Stanley laid a heavy hand on him. 'He is free of it all now. Rest, little brother, rest. It will pass.'

Messina, eight days later. A Byzantine council chamber.

All the greatest warriors of Christendom were there. The Chevalier Mathurin Romegas and Gil de Andrada for the Knights of St John, Gian'andrea Doria for Genoa, great-nephew of that famous Andrea Doria who had been the most brilliant naval commander of his age. Don John of Austria for Spain, and doughty Spanish admiral Don

Álvaro de Bazán, Marqués de Santa Cruz. Two brothers from one of Venice's finest families, Antonio and Ambrosio Bragadino, quietly and steadfastly pressing for war against the caution of Genoa and Spain. There was Marco Colonna, commander of the papal galleys, adamant that Pius V still believed in a new crusade.

And a late arrival, striding belligerently into the chamber, salt spray still in his white beard, the ferocious old lion of seventy years or more, commander of the Venetian galleys. Sebastiano Veniero.

'Truly a meeting of Olympians,' murmured Don John of Austria. Half their age, a third of Veniero's age, he may have been, but not a whit abashed. He was still, after all, half royal.

Veniero glared first at Doria, his ancient enemy, and then at this puppy of a bastard prince. His lip curled in contempt. Veniero was never a man to hide his feelings or fake courtesy for anyone. They could call him a sullen and difficult cur, but at least he was an honest cur.

This Don John, this Spanish-Austrian-German mongrel prince, looked nothing like a veteran commander. Ridiculously young, slender, all of twenty-four, clad from top to toe in pale green, gold-trimmed velvet, and high soft boots with ornamental golden spurs. Moustaches and beard immaculately trimmed. He sported the insignia of the Order of the Golden Fleece, and on a table beside him lay a fancy lion-mask helmet. The most arrant fop you'd see this side of the French court.

'Christ's wounds,' growled Veniero, loud enough for all to hear.

The papal nuncio winced.

'Sebastiano Veniero,' said Don John, bowing low. 'You are most welcome.'

He didn't falter for a moment. Others there already knew that beneath the foppery, this prince had a sharp wit and steely determination. It seemed nothing could dismay him.

'So what have we come to?' demanded Veniero. 'We haven't the guns, galleys or manpower to take on the Turk. Why are you still discussing it?'

'Veniero is a great and venerable seaman, no doubt,' said Gian'andrea Doria sarcastically, 'but is ill placed to judge such matters. For alas, he has had no opportunity to fight the Turk face to face, since his own beloved Venice and Constantinople have been living in such close harmony for so long.'

'Unlike Genoa and Spain,' snapped Veniero, 'such famous enemies of the Turk, though they gad about the sea and never quite dare to come to blows. When the Lion of Venice goes to war, believe me,' he thumped the table so that Don John's helmet rattled, '*she goes to war!*'

Don John intervened. His greatest achievement so far, he thought with private bitterness, was to have prevented Venice and Genoa going to war with each other.

'Gentlemen,' he said, 'I still say, now that we have the beginnings of a League, if we do not sail east and defeat the Turk, we are lost. This great force is assembling to do one thing only: destroy the Ottoman fleet, and with it any Ottoman plans of jihad against the West.'

'Hear hear!' cried a deep voice, as the doors flew open. The assembled commanders looked and saw a group of ruffianly travellers straight from the sea.

'Knights of St John from Famagusta, my lords!' said a herald.

There was a great hubbub. Romegas and De Andrada embraced the newcomers, others demanded to know news.

'Grave news,' said Giustiniani simply. 'Famagusta is fallen. Cyprus is lost.'

There fell a dejected silence. Marco Colonna put his head in his hands, Veniero clenched his fists.

Stanley took up the task, speaking quickly, in the heat. 'Next they will fall on Crete, then on Corfu. Kara Hodja already holds Ragusa and Avlona on the Adriatic. Then Venice, then all of Italy. Sooner or later you must take your stand against them. You cannot appease them for ever.'

After a moment, a calm voice said, 'What of our father? Is he in captivity? What is the ransom demanded?'

It was Ambrosio Bragadino.

Then the knights called for chairs, and sat before the two brothers. The rest listened in silence. The very air felt cold.

A few minutes into the account, Don John said quietly, 'Knights, you have looked on horrors, but – brave brothers Bragadino – are

301

you certain you wish to hear all this story in company? If you wish to go away in private ...'

'No!' cried Ambrosio. Then more quietly, 'No. You will all hear this tale of our father. All of you.'

Giustiniani told everything. Not a detail was spared.

Half an hour later the sons of Governor Bragadino were white faced, jaws clenched, but they shed not a tear.

Then Sebastiano Veniero came before them and bowed and said, 'Sons of a noble father, Marc'antonio Bragadino was a dear friend of mine. The galleys of Venice are in my command, and now they are in yours. I wait for your word.'

The brothers' green eyes were cold like emeralds shining under water.

'For my part,' said Don John quietly, 'I shall show myself a bastard to the Turk in more ways than one.'

'Listen to me, all of you,' said Veniero. 'It is true what I said, that all of Christendom united would still be outnumbered by the Turk and his great empire. Nevertheless, there are sixteen thousand Venetian shipwrights working round the clock in the vast docks of Venice. They complete a new galley in only seven hours from ready-cut timbers. The Men of St Mark have fifty ships or more to add to this fleet when last I heard. If Spain is with the League, then so is Venice. I await the final word of the Senate, but I know now what it will be. This insult to our much-loved Bragadino cannot go unavenged. When the Lion of Venice finally stirs herself, knowing the time for peace and commerce is over, then believe me, it is a sight to see, and even Suleiman might give pause. And that is what his fat drunk of a son has to face now.'

Don John could have taken his old hand and kissed it.

The knights had done it. Bragadino's sacrifice had done it.

'Gentlemen,' said Don John, 'are you for me, for Christ and the Holy League?'

'Aye!' said Veniero. 'For Bragadino and for Venice!'

'Aye,' said the papal nuncio, 'you know the papal galleys are with you.'

'I believe my King will now command it,' said Santa Cruz with a little more care. 'Holy Spain sails east.'

'At last,' muttered Veniero.

All felt a fire within them. With Holy Spain came also her vast dominions in the Americas, and those in Italy too: Naples, Sicily, Milan, all subject to Philip of Spain.

'The Knights of St John I need hardly ask,' said Don John. 'They know a little about fighting the Turk.'

Romegas stared, unsmiling. Superb naval commander, thought Don John, but never noted for his sense of humour.

'And Genoa?'

Genoa's thirty or forty galleys were crucial, but even more so, her centuries of experience fighting at sea. Gian'andrea Doria looked from man to man, Veniero last. The old white-maned lion stared him down. He nodded. 'Aye. If Spain is in, then Genoa is also with you. For better or worse.'

At last, it was forged. The Holy League. An alliance of Christian powers that might just be a match for the Ottoman fleet.

Part III

THE RED SEA

1

There was a furious bustle for days after, lading ships with provisions, caulking and tarring, checking cannon, loading powder and shot, bickering, trying to keep the whores off the galleys at night. Two whores were even found, stark naked, aboard the galley of the knights, celibate as they were. Puzzling.

There was endless paperwork and administration, which Don John swiftly delegated to secretaries. He preferred to spend time on the quayside.

'I know nothing whatever of sea battles, ships, sailing, ropes or any of that tarry nastiness,' he said gaily. 'I couldn't float a cork in a bathtub. Which is why my saintly half-brother Philip has made me Supreme Commander of the Fleet. It makes sense, does it not? The blood of the Emperor Charles flows in my veins, along with the blood of a German trollop, my beloved mother, and I am therefore but a bastard and misshapen homunculus of the great Emperor. But this is enough for me to be Supreme Commander, is it not? No need for any vulgar knowledge of how to command ships at sea, or wage a battle?'

Veniero's habitual scowl deepened, his sunburned face riven with new creases. This one was clever and dangerous and talked half-gibberish. Was he mocking himself, or Veniero, or Philip of Spain? He would arch a fine eyebrow and mock God himself, this one. Veniero didn't know what to make of him. You never knew what he was going to say or do next.

And still there was fighting in the streets of Naples and Messina between the squabbling factions. There was a widespread rumour that King Philip had secretly commanded Santa Cruz to hold back the Spanish fleet and let the rest take the brunt of it. A rumour impossible to disprove.

Don John received several urgent missives from Madrid which he read swiftly and then tore to shreds and dropped in the harbour.

'What news, sire?' his old tutor, Don Luis de Requesens, would anxiously ask.

Don John looked blank. 'Dear me, I've forgotten already.'

There was a threatened mutiny at La Spezia over pay. Don John rode down in person, arriving with the words, 'I do beg your pardon, I was detained tupping my *fille de chambre*.' He smoothed out his waxed moustache. 'What is the problem here?'

He quelled the mutiny with personal assurances and promises, earning a grudging respect from the hard-bitten, low-paid veterans.

As he was leaving he dropped his sword. A mariner retrieved it and said pointedly, 'Fine piece of work. The handle alone is worth more than a year of my pay.'

Don John smiled. 'Well said, sir. Take it. It is yours.'

The mariner gawped.

'On one condition. You sail hard against those damned dog Turks and use that blade to part at least a dozen of 'em in two.'

The mariner scowled and grinned at the same time.

For a velvet fop he wasn't such a bad bugger.

Nicholas and Hodge were accosted on the quayside one evening by a fellow they vaguely recognized. Lean and pale and sickly looking, with an effortful moustache that looked like a drooping bootlace, he seized them by an arm each and said, 'You are the English gentlemen volunteers? You fought at both Malta and Cyprus?'

They acknowledged it warily.

'Ah,' sighed the fellow, 'would that I had been there, in the midst of all that glory and heroical death!'

'You're right about the death, anyhow,' said Hodge.

'You seem familiar,' said Nicholas. 'Did we meet at Messina before?'

He bowed low. 'My name is Don Miguel de Cervantes Saavedra, from Alcalá de Henares, in Old Castile. My father is the universally renowned Rodrigo de Cervantes, knight at arms and sometime apothecary-surgeon, in reduced circumstances. Through him I claim descent—'

'I remember now,' said Nicholas.

'—from the ancient kings of Castile, from Alfonso and Pedro, as well as Eleanor of Navarre, and ultimately from the Visigothic kings themselves, Rodrigo being the name of—'

'Aye, truly, engaging stuff. And you are a poet, are you not?'

The fellow gave another small bow. 'I follow the muse Calliope where'er she leads me. It is my dream to write a great epic of this noble war between Christian and Turk, to rival that of Homer. A vaunting ambition, perhaps. Yet is it not true that this great conflict takes place over the same lands and seas as that of the Achaeans and Trojans, the eternal battle between East and West, in which Achilles—'

'I don't know as I'd turn out a heroic epic, from what I've seen of it all,' said Hodge.

'Would you not? Yet you were there, in the very midst?'

'So I was. And if wrote an epic about it, which is fair to middlin' unlikely, I admit, I'd make it full of wrong starts and false turns, dreams and daftness. More like a comedy, only with a lot of knocked-about heads and fallin' off horses. If you could of seen us landing on Cyprus that first time, and skedaddlin' down a cliff to get away as soon as we were landed, you'd know what I mean. And if you could see that damn fool Niccolo Dandolo, who thought he was such a fine commander of men, you'd know too. War's full of it. Piss and wind, just as much as your heroism and martial glory, if you want my version of it.'

Miguel de Cervantes stared at Hodge. Nicholas smiled to himself. The Spanish poet seemed momentarily lost for words.

'And on that note we bid you farewell,' he said. 'May luck go with you in the days to come.'

Joseph Nassi was walking in the gardens of the Topkapi Palace in Constantinople, talking with a clerk from the mint, when Selim summoned him to audience.

'Bragadino's sons,' he stammered without introduction, 'we have heard from agents in Venice that they are accounted two of the finest naval commanders in Christendom. This Holy League is coming for us, isn't it?'

Nassi had prepared for this moment with luxurious frequency. 'Admittedly, the severity of Lala Mustafa at Famagusta is in danger of uniting our Christian enemy against us, in a way that nothing else could have done.'

'Y-you,' stammered Selim, looking hunted, 'you think he was *too* severe in his punishment of this wretched Bragadino? You think he made a terrible mistake, that this mighty armada now sailing against us is all his fault?'

Nassi gracefully laid his hand on his heart, giving a little bow. 'My Lord and Master, Shadow of God upon earth, I would not dream of suggesting such a thing. That would suggest that Lala Pasha was nothing but a vainglorious and overambitious fool, who has triggered an attack on our Empire greater than any before, by sheer stupidity and viciousness.'

He suppressed a smile. How easy it was to put a thought in the Sultan's head, so vividly worded, while denying it! The Greek rhetoricians called this trick *paralipsis*, and a most delightful one it was too.

He continued, 'The Pasha is, of course, Your Majesty's greatest general. Yet in his torture and execution of this Bragadino ... Well, as I say, it was a severe punishment, and not perhaps without some risk ...'

To be an enemy while seeming a friend. To destroy while seeming to defend. Such were the low arts of palace politics. Nassi excelled in them, exulting in his own abilities, even as he felt some mingled disgust. All this was only to serve a far higher purpose, God be thanked. Or his own cleverness would sicken him.

Selim brooded uncomfortably, eyes darting.

Yes, Nassi felt sorry for this fat little man, the weak, unhappy son of Suleiman the Magnificent. It was always a curse to have a great father. Absalom, Absalom ... And it was a terrible fate that he had become ruler of so mighty an empire. A burden more than his puny, sloping shoulders could bear, which was why he took to gluttony, and dulled his fears with wine. He always slept badly, rising up out of bed, jabbering with nightmares, bringing his Nubian guards running, spears at the ready.

'They are trying to kill me!' he would scream, writhing in his bed. Always the same nightmares. 'I am drowning! Save me!'

Or he awoke thinking he was trapped underwater, or most often of all, that the palace itself had collapsed in an earthquake and buried him alive. He was in darkness, alone, beneath tons of rubble, unable to breathe ... It needed no Persian soothsayer to interpret his dreams.

Like all such men – burdened, anxious, weak, and knowing that they are despised as weak by all around them – Selim was given to wild, ill-considered outbursts of belligerence. Suddenly he sat upright, as befits the Lord of the Lords of this World, and snapped, 'We must engage this Holy League. They must be destroyed!'

'Majesty, is that wise? Our galleys have been at sea all summer, theirs are fresh, their guns—'

'My generals will do as I say!' screamed Selim, puce with sudden ferocity, rising up out of his seat, spittle flying. 'They will obey me, or I shall have them and all their kin dismembered at the Edirne Gate!'

Nassi bowed. 'A noble threat, Your Majesty.'

So the two massive fleets must come face to face, bow to bow, and battle be joined, he thought. They would annihilate each other, and peace would follow.

Selim sank back in his seat, exhausted, eyes rolling.

'Destroy them utterly,' he said. 'They must not come near.' His gaze darted back and forth over the patterned carpets, but all he saw in his mind's eye were triumphal Christian galleys rowing into the Golden Horn.

'That is my final command. Engage and destroy them, *now*.'

'How can we lose?' murmured Nassi. 'With Allah on our side?'

Don John sent word that he wanted the survivors from Famagusta aboard his flagship, *La Real*. They could tell him inspiring stories as they sailed. And so it was that Stanley and Smith, Giustiniani and Mazzinghi, Nicholas and Hodge were again given space aboard that resplendent scarlet-painted galley. Romegas and De Andrada would fight from the knights' own galley, the *St John of Jerusalem*.

Mazzinghi grumbled, 'What action will we see aboard a flagship? None.'

'I wouldn't be so sure,' said Stanley. 'From what I know of our commander, we could be right in the heart of it.'

'I s'pose it means we'll get better food, at least,' said Hodge.

Smith took his place upon the fighting deck immediately, sword drawn, as if the great battle was about to begin in a minute or two.

'We have suffered much defeat lately,' he rumbled, 'a whole damnable summer of it. And Sir John Smith, Knight Grand Cross,' he thumped his sword on the deck, *does not like defeat!*'

'Mind your sword there, Brother.'

He shot it back in its sheath and glared balefully round, black eyes burning. 'But this summer will have a better ending. I demand it.'

A messenger came to Don John.

'How many?' he asked crisply.

'Some fifty sailing down from Venice to join us at Brindisi. And here already, over a hundred, sire.'

'I did not ask for an estimate,' Don John snapped, sibilants hissing, 'I asked for a number. Come back with a precise number within ten minutes or I throw you in the sea.'

The messenger was back in six minutes. 'One hundred and eight galleys and supply ships in all, sir.'

Don John nodded. 'Apart from mariners, we will have some eight thousand soldiers aboard, all told. What say you, brother knights? Is that enough?'

'It is never enough,' said Smith. 'But it will serve.'

In the harbour there was one particularly striking galley, low and lean and predatory, draped all in black.

'The Bragadino brothers,' said Stanley. 'Truly, something even in my blood chills to think of them.'

At night, a strange boat slipped into the main harbour under cover of darkness. A spy party sent by Kara Hodja, surprised to enter Messina so easily, unchallenged.

'Deliberate,' drawled Don John the next morning. 'They will have counted the ships in the main harbour and come to about sixty. We spied on them spying on us. They entirely missed the other forty or so galleys in the inner harbour, and have not reckoned on the Venetian party either. An enemy's false sense of superiority can be very useful.'

The oar slaves appeared in a shuffling column on the quayside. They had been kept busy mending sails with needle and cord, loading pebble ballast, even polishing cannonballs. Now they were stripped naked and searched. One was found with a hidden needle. An inch-thick rope-end was wetted in seawater and he was condemned to fifty blows. Don John stopped them after ten.

'I need him for rowing my ship,' he said.

'But discipline, sire—' said the boatswain.

'Enough,' he snapped.

Their heads were shaved and they were driven up the ridged gangplank.

'Give me your blasphemers, your sodomites, your forgers and drunks,' murmured Don John, 'and I shall set you free.'

They were chained to the benches below by one leg. The benches were roofed over with planks to make for easier movement above. They would row in sunless gloom, blind as moles, though once they began to sweat they would be glad to be sunless. In the heat of battle they would hear the din and bellow of the guns above them, the deafening explosions, the ship lurching, and shake in terror that any moment an iron cannonball might erupt through the hull and smash them into pieces where they sat. It was all a matter of luck who survived.

'Tell me, boatswain, who we have here.'

The boatswain indicated each grimy, despairing face in turn.

'Bernardino here: took three wives. The devil knows how, to look at his poxy face. Sentence, five years at the oar.

'This scumbag, Ercole di Benedetto, cheesemaker: sodomy. He can row till he rots.

'This is Lorenzo di Niccolucci: heretic.'

'The Book of Revelations says—' began Di Niccolucci, before a mariner struck him a blow on the shoulder with an ugly-looking maul.

'This gallant fellow, Senso de Giusto: rape and deflowering of a thirteen-year-old girl. Two years at the oar.

'This one, Ahmed, a Turk—'

'Syrian,' corrected Ahmed.

'Shut it, shitskin. Next to him, Salem, moor of Tunis, half lame. Next to him, Il Cazzogrosso, missing his two front teeth, and blind. But he can still row.'

Il Cazzogrosso grinned miserably.

'They're all under sentence of *beneplacito*.'

'Meaning?'

'Meaning until whoever is well pleased to set them free.'

'A rather vague and sinister sentence.'

The boatswain grunted with satisfaction. 'That's the idea. You want more, My Lord? There's every vice under the sun down here.'

'I get the picture,' said Don John. Then he raised his voice. 'Listen to me, you scum of the earth. Most of you will die at the oar if you do not die in this coming battle. And it will be a terrible battle, we are still hugely outnumbered by the enemy. The sea will foam with blood. Most of it will be yours. You are as good as dead already. But – I give you one thin lifeline. When our galleys hit theirs, and heads start rolling, the boatswain here will unlock your chains. Every man that rows for us or fights for us and lives to tell the tale will be set free. Even the sodomites and heretics.'

The oar slaves stared. Nothing seemed real to them for now but their misery and the huge, heavy oar before them.

'Good,' said Don John. 'I'm glad that cheered you so well.'

It was late afternoon when the boatswain blew his silver whistle. Gradually a wave of whistles sounded across the harbour.

The mighty fifty-foot oars creaked in their leather collars, between four and six men chained to each haft, and slowly, slowly, *La Real*'s gleaming prow eased forward through the sluggish harbour waters and towards the open sea.

Nicholas and Hodge looked at each other with excitement and dread. They were going. No turning back now.

On the harbour mole stood Don Luis de Requesens.

'Be nothing rash!' he called in a quavering voice. 'Remember the wise caution of princes!'

'Caution,' Don John called back, waving a white-gloved hand, 'is the daughter of lechery and the wet nurse of impertinence!'

Don Luis muttered and crossed himself. Beside him stood the

papal nuncio in his crimson robes, arms raised in blessing upon the departing fleet.

'We need it,' murmured Stanley. 'After Preveza, Djerba ... We've lost every major battle at sea with the Turk these past fifty years.'

'That's because I wasn't there,' said Smith.

Stanley roared with laughter and clapped him on the shoulder. Nicholas wasn't so sure Smith was joking.

2

At Brindisi they were joined by the fifty Venetian galleys, as promised. Cannon salutes rang out, and huge cheers echoed across the sea.

As the great flotilla went east, they communicated with each other constantly by signals, and in person in smaller, faster boats. On the third evening, Sebastiano Veniero came over to *La Real*.

Don John questioned him closely.

'Aye,' said Veniero, 'the longer a ship has been at sea, the more its hull is fouled with weed and barnacles, the timbers half eaten with shipworms. And the crew sick and hungry, the pitch and caulking going, the slaves working ever harder daily to pump the bilges clear, and the sea leaking in faster all the same ...'

'And the Turks have been at sea all summer, as we know. Many at Cyprus?'

'Most of 'em, aye.'

'And our galleys are all clean of hull?'

'That is true.'

'Then we go faster than them? And are more manoeuvrable?'

'In theory. But if the Turks head for home, the autumn winds are with them—'

'They must not! We must meet them now and finish this.'

Veniero rubbed his beard. 'I hope for it too. But ... By October the storms in the Mediterranean are terrible, especially the eastern Mediterranean, the Aegean. The winds—'

'Then now is our chance.'

'In truth, it is not the season for fighting sea battles, sire.'

'Because it is not considered the season,' said Don John, slow and solemn, '... it is the season.'

'If only the Holy League could have sailed earlier, and saved Famagusta,' said Giustiniani with a sigh.

'My fellow knights,' said Don John, 'my brothers. Let me at last confide in you. I too delayed the League, by multiple evasions and lies.'

They stared at him, astonished. 'You, My Lord?'

The young prince spread a map on the cabin table and spoke crisply, every inch the most seasoned military commander. 'Famagusta would have divided our forces. I wanted the Turk in one place: one great armada. Let Famagusta fall, let the Turks garrison it with some two thousand men, let the rest rejoin the fleet to meet us. Then let us fall on them and destroy them altogether. A knockout blow.'

Stanley said dully, 'You never intended to come to the relief of Famagusta after all?'

'We had to bring Venice into the war. The Vengeance of Venice.' Don John looked at him and his eyes had less of the dancing light, more of an older man's sorrow. 'Brother Eduardo,' he said softly, 'war is never separate from politics. If you know what agonies such delay cost me – what thoughts were mine, as I danced in a golden mask at that *ballo in maschera* in Genoa, knowing that even as I laughed and danced, brave men fought and died for a Cyprus that was already lost ...' He tailed off.

Stanley looked away. 'I would not have to make such decisions as yours for all the world.'

'The privilege of princes,' murmured Don John.

Even now they went painfully slowly.

It was those six great lumbering supply ships, the galliasses, that the Venetians had brought down from the basin of St Mark where they had lain up mothballed for months, even years. High sided, wide beamed, round at stem and stern, they took a tow from three oared galleys each to shift at all.

On their broad flat decks, each had a curious round tower with black portholes.

317

'New-fangled rubbish,' muttered Smith impatiently. 'Do we really need so many supplies with us? Can we not use Corfu, Crete?'

Don John ordered a jug of wine and gave them each a cup. 'Let me tell you about our six galliasses,' he said.

When they were still fighting at Nicosia, Don John visited the Venetian dockyards. He tracked down that genius of a shipwright, Master Franco Bressano, who had the heavily bowed legs of a horseman, beetling grey eyebrows and a permanent scowl.

They talked about ships and guns.

Don John said, 'If we wanted more guns aboard—'

'You can't,' said Bressano. 'There's a pay-off. On *La Real*, you have five forward guns, with a centre-line culverin, no?'

Don John raised an eyebrow. 'You are well informed, Master Bressano.'

'There's nothing about ships I don't know. I know how many barnacles there are on your hull.'

'How many?'

'Same as every other ship on God's ocean. Too bloody many, that's how many.'

Don John smiled. A pleasant if rough-hewn wit.

'But there's always a pay-off,' said Bressano. 'Guns weigh heavy. And every extra pound of bronze and iron has to be rowed by men. Men have to be fed and watered – so more food and water have to be carried. The ship gets bigger and bigger, moves slower and slower ... Follow? The Turks go lightly gunned so they can stay mobile and fast, and I'm not sure they're wrong. There's a limit to how many guns any galley can carry and still move herself, and your *Real* is about at that limit now.'

'What if,' said Don John slowly and carefully, 'forgive a prince as ignorant of ships as of shrimp fishing, for the Lord be praised, I have spent little of my pampered life hammering nails, and ... *sawing*, and that sort of thing – '

Franco Bressano eyed him dourly. He was a funny one, this bastard royal.

'But what if you loaded up multiple guns on to a ship that *didn't have to move*?'

Bressano scowled. 'Then you'd have a godalmighty big hulk of a

318

ship laden with ordnance, half sunk in your own harbour. Where's the bloody point in that?'

'The biggest ships afloat are Venice's own merchant galleys, are they not? The *galia grosse*, the galliasses.'

'Aye. Fat lumbering beasts that move at a snail's pace, but carry their grain or cloth or whatever cargo there eventually. What use are they to you?'

'How many in the basin now?'

'In dry dock, half a dozen or so.'

'Take them,' said Don John. 'Strip them down, remove all the ballast—'

'They'll tip over.'

'Remove all the ballast – and replace it with guns.'

'Guns sit too high on their decks. They're merchantmen, not men-o'-war.'

'Then put them on the lower decks, make portholes through the walls, what do you call them …?'

'Bulwarks.'

'Bulwarks. Fit the guns down among the rowing benches, even number of guns on each side.'

'A heavy sea will swamp 'em, a storm sink 'em.'

'They don't have to endure for years, not even for a summer. Just three weeks, until we meet the Turk. Then they may sink. Before that, they do not have my permission.'

Bressano made a noise like a bull hawking phlegm.

'All this done in secrecy, of course. As much as possible. Imagine a galliass stripped of everything, shorn of all fittings, cabins, quarters, stores – no other cargo except guns, cannonball, powder and gun teams, and maybe a squadron of heavily armoured marines to repel boarders.'

'Hardly needed,' said Bressano. 'The sides of a merchant galley are too high for any Turks to come aboard. Like scaling a cliff face.'

'Well, a few marines, just in case. Then how many guns could you put aboard?'

Bressano rubbed his stubbled cheek. 'To equal a full cargo of grain, say … Well, I suppose you could have as many as forty or fifty thirty-pound culverin … '

'Is that all?'

'Thirty pounds is the weight of the shot, not the gun. You know that, don't you?'

'Is it?'

'Aye. Take it from me.'

'Of course. Well, go on.'

'Maybe thirty-pounders, even some forty-pounders. Some swivel versos for grapeshot and chain-shot, plus five more guns at the bow.'

'She'd be quite a ship, wouldn't she?'

'She'd be a floating fucking gun tower is what she'd be,' growled Bressano. '"Scusing my language. But she wouldn't *go* anywhere.'

'Instead of a flat deck at the front, what do you call it?'

'The bow.'

'The bow, that's it, build there a stout oak round tower housing another six or eight guns, covering every point of the compass.'

'She'd tend to fire way over any nearby galleys. And demolish her own gunwales when she fired.'

'Then clear everything in her line of fire. I mean stripped bare. As you say, nothing but a gun platform. Put a sail on her—'

'Then you're entirely dependent on the wind.'

'And if the wind was right, how many rowers—?'

'But the rowing deck is full of guns.'

'Rowers between the guns. The bare minimum.'

'They'd barely move her. Especially in a live sea.'

Don John bit his lip. Patience was required. Bressano was a shipwright of genius, the greatest in Christendom, some said. But by God he was an awkward dog. Must be related to Veniero way back somewhere.

'Imagine this great – as you put it in your colourful dockyard vernacular – this great *floating fucking gun tower* – then being *towed* – by, say, three lightweight, ungunned, stripped-bare galleys, no more than galliots, say fifty oars in each – one towing her at the bow, the others either side. Would she move?'

'A hundred and fifty oars? Pff.' Bressano stared into nothing, picturing it. 'Yes, she'd move. At the pace of a drunk snail. But she'd move.'

'And if the wind was at her back?'

'Then she'd move at the pace of a sober snail.'

'But she'd move. So, given time, you could get her into position?'

'Given time, given money, given enough guns – and enough gunners, you'd need no fewer than two hundred trained gunners on every one of 'em—'

'And then imagine what would happen if one of these *floating fucking gun towers* – I confess, this refulgent phrase of yours is growing on me apace – imagine what would happen if this galliass so armed, towed into position and turned side on so that her flanks gave fire, as well as those in her bristling round tower on deck – all roaring at the same time from her starboard side ... She could always face into the oncoming sea and keep steady, and *have numbers of guns facing the enemy, whichever direction they came from.* Imagine a flotilla of, I don't know, as many as twenty light galliots and oared galleys rowing against each galliass, but none returning much fire, or none to speak of – arrows from their marine archers, yes, but nothing to trouble the gunners behind their oak bulwarks – imagine the very finest gunnery teams working like demons on the gun deck, faces black with powder, loading, reloading, urinating on the smoking barrels as I believe they do, with all the finesse of French courtiers urinating in the corners of the Elysée Palace – then what would happen? Come, Bressano, picture it! What do you see?'

'I see – if, if, if, as you say, and it's one fat If, God alone knows how it would all come together like you say – but if, if, if – then I reckon ... I reckon your galliasses would blow those incoming galliots into fucking matchwood.'

Don John stood and smiled. 'Signor Francesco Bressano, give me your hand.'

They shook. When they parted, Bressano found a gold ducat in his palm.

'It'll cost you more than that to fit out half a dozen galliasses.'

'That,' said Don John, 'is my next task. Start wrighting, Master Bressano. As of now!'

Then it was money matters, tedious meetings, persuasions, negotiations, the writing of florid and oleaginous letters. One by one the galliasses were commandeered from their plump, suspicious merchant owners, remuneration paid or promised. In the docks there was hammering twenty-four hours a day, riveting, strengthening, doubtful looks from the quayside, some mocking laughter. But Franco Bressano was now fully committed to the immense project with scowling passion, and roared back at them that people had laughed at Noah once like that. 'And look what happened to them. The fuckers *drowned*!'

If the cost of refitting the galliasses was huge, the cost of that many guns was eye-watering. But the money came in. Venice opened her immense treasuries, which the Serene Republic had been filling for five long centuries, and slowly but surely, the six colossally gunned beasts of the sea were armed.

Don John set down his cup of wine. 'So there you are, gentlemen. That is why those galliasses go so slowly. But they will be worth it.'

Stanley breathed out slowly. 'I pray it is so.'

The prince said, 'In my youth, I was always one for gambles and wagers. But I have grown out of that now.'

Stanley smiled, a slightly pained smile. Nothing could be farther from the truth. Don John of Austria was gambling everything – the whole fate of Christendom – on a single throw of the dice.

3

It was a clean, blue September morning when they passed the
Malta Channel. Beloved Malta. Nicholas inhaled the sea air. This
coming battle would be different, from Malta, from Nicosia and
Famagusta. It would see all of Christendom united under a blue
Mediterranean sky, and no women or children caught up in the
scenes of carnage. Two forces, a clean fight, and all on a single
day. And a Christian commander with a ludicrous dress sense but
undoubted force and charisma.

But a wind was getting up.

A cold end-of-summer wind, herald of winter. The Bora, blowing down the Adriatic from the north, from the Balkan mountains
and the Carpathians.

The sea began to rise and run, the galleys to roll. The rowers
flailed their oars above the waves. From *La Real* they watched
anxiously as the six great galliasses behind lumbered and lurched in
the white-combed swell, their towing galliots struggling desperately
to keep control, their sails and ropes straining and groaning under
the savage strain. They had visions of those great vessels, Don
John's wild gamble, going down and taking three galliots apiece
with them.

'Difficult sailing conditions,' murmured Giustiniani.

'We want difficult sailing conditions,' snapped Don John.

'Sire?'

'Because we are better sailors than the Turks. The Genoese, the
Aragonese, the Venetians have been sailing these waters since long
before the Turk. What is difficult for them, this blustering chill

Bora, will be quite manageable to the old sea dogs of Genoa, who have been to the Indies and back. The Aegean in October is no gentle sea. She blows up many a foul storm. We should hope for more.'

The prince needed to do everything in his power to keep his force together. Matters were not helped when Veniero hanged some mutineer Spanish soldiers on his ships. The Spanish and Venetian fleets actually primed their guns and faced each other for some hours, before Don John managed to calm them. He urged them to save their anger for the Turk.

At Corfu they took on fresh water, and heard of churches desecrated recently by Kara Hodja, around the coasts of the island. Don John and his commanders visited them. They found broken crucifixes, frescoes of saints stabbed and defaced or used for pistol practice, the sickening stench of profanation by ordure.

'Tell all your men,' said Don John. 'Spread the word throughout the fleet. Not only how they tortured and killed noble Bragadino, but also this. How they have mocked and abused Christ's handmaiden, the Church. Nothing unites men like a common enemy. Stir them to vengeance.'

A message came to Don John from another ship in his immediate squadron.

'Sire, there is a woman on board.'

'How lovely,' murmured the prince. 'What age is she? Is she dark eyed?'

The man looked shocked. The commander was missing the point. A woman aboard ship was as bad luck as a cat.

Still the prince seemed unconcerned. 'Is she a whore?'

'No, sire, it seems not. She is a,' he almost spat the word, 'a *dancer* by profession. Maria la Bailadora, disguised as a boy, going to war with her lover.'

Don John smiled. 'Like an old romance. The question is, can she fire an arquebus?'

'Can she ...' The man swallowed. 'Certainly not, sire.'

'Then teach her, man, teach her. She may dance as well as Salome, it won't save her now.'

They sailed south from Corfu, keeping within the Corfu channel. They passed by the fortified base of Parga on the coast, another recent capture by the Ottoman Empire. It was 4th October.

As they approached the wide Gulf of Patras, every man's heart was in his mouth. The sea was grey and uneasy, winter was approaching. And all of them felt they were closer by the hour to the lair of the Turk. Around every headland and island, every spit of that broken coastline, they expected to encounter a numberless armada, bent on destroying them. Many there dreamed of turning and retreating to the safety of their old ports in the west. But Don John reminded them continually that there could be no retreat. The Turk would always come after them.

Gil de Andrada went out scouting in a fast unarmed galley, and vanished into the winter gloom. It was dirty weather, squally and buffeting. On the night of the 6th, they hove to and dropped anchor in the narrow channel between Cephalonia and Ithaca. It should have offered some shelter, yet men and oar slaves alike still vomited with the roll.

Don John went tirelessly from galley to galley in a longboat, his fine clothes drenched with salt spray. With brilliant eloquence, he reminded Veniero and the Venetians of their many losses, of Rhodes and Cyprus, not to mention the bloody insult of Famagusta. He told the ardent Spanish that when they met their turbaned enemy, they should give the unbelievers no chance to sneer, Where is your Jewish Saviour now?

'Show them our right cause with your swords,' he cried, 'and win yourselves everlasting fame!'

In the heart of the night, sailing dangerously over seas black as pitch, Gil de Andrada returned. His face in the lantern light was as grim as the face of a storm-dark sea.

'Speak, man,' snapped Don John. 'Do you expect us to sob like girls at your news?'

Gil de Andrada drew breath and said, 'They are certainly not fleeing back to safe port, but are readying to meet us. Selim has clearly given order for battle. The whole Gulf of Corinth is full of them. An armada from horizon to horizon. Two hundred sail in the foreground, but more beyond. And they will move to pick up more fighting men from the garrison at Galata.'

'Excellent,' said Don John, 'excellent.'

'There are Algerine ships among them as well. I know the rigging. Corsairs of the Barbary Coast, and Kara Hodja's too, of course, which explains their vast numbers. We face all the power of both Africa and Asia combined. Kara Hodja will take their left wing, if I know him.'

'Then he will face Doria and Genoa on our right,' said Don John.

Doria said quietly, 'The city of Genoa against the whole coast of Africa. And I have faced Kara Hodja before. He knows how to fight, an enemy of great skill.'

'And the Turks have the harbour of Lepanto to fall back on,' said Gil de Andrada, 'we have none.'

'All the more reason why we must destroy them utterly and win,' said Don John.

He retired to his cabin with his valet to arm, and soon reappeared in a golden suit of armour with silver clasps, which blazed out even in the night. A relic of the True Cross hung about his neck, and he wore a sheepskin cape of the Order of the Golden Fleece of Castile.

He found his commanders downcast and perturbed, full of foreboding. Gil de Andrada was not a man to mince his words or gild a harsh truth.

The Ottoman force they faced, he reckoned, both in ships and fighting men, outnumbered them by two to one.

Veniero looked grim, Doria's eyes darted about with anxiety. The knights kept a silent composure, but they were men long since sworn to die in battle, not to live long. What of the mariners and the foot soldiers? And what of the brothers Bragadino, so silent in their black grief? They were full of thoughts of vengeance but they might lack steadiness if they did not mind dying, so long as they took many Turks with them. The outcome of the battle, the fate of Christendom, mattered little to them. Let doom come, so long as many thousands of Turks were sacrificed with it, in expiation of their father's atrocious death.

'So,' said Don John, 'we are certainly outnumbered. They crowd together so, we cannot fail to hit them.'

'That is true,' said Veniero. 'Look on the bright side.'

Don John ignored his glum sarcasm. 'This battle will be about gunpowder and gun power, and ours is far superior. Numbers are nothing. If you saw a sea battle between one ship versus a hundred, who would win?'

'The hundred,' said the old Venetian sea dog.

'Wrong. You have not asked for enough information. If the one was a great galliass, and the hundred were mere fishing skiffs ...'

'Those Ottoman galleys are no fishing skiffs.'

'But many of them are barely more gunned. They still fight as soldiers on floating platforms, dispatching a few cannonball but really wanting to close and board us with scimitar and pike. But they will not even get near before our great guns roar.'

'I pray God it is true.'

'Make it so, my gallant captains, make it so!' His tone was not scolding but inspiring, full of the belief that they could and would win, that they were truly gallant captains. It was infectious.

'If your gunners follow orders, if they work hard and do not rest, we will win. I have every confidence. Are they not the finest gunners in the world?'

'They are very well drilled.'

'Then numbers are irrelevant! The Turks are sitting ducks. If the wind is against them, so much the better.'

'It is for them now, it blows from the north-east, more behind them than us.'

'It will change by noon, and then it will begin. And then they will see our fighting spirit, our martial fire! Courage, gentlemen! It is courage that wins battles, in the end, and I also think cheerfulness a weapon of no little power. All else aside, cheerfulness certainly vexes the enemy mightily. And are we not Christian men, proud Italians, fiery Spaniards? Santa Cruz, does not the blood of El Cid run hot in your veins? Generations of great crusades, of high chivalry? Doria, I know today you will do honour to the memory of Andrea Doria. Do your family not claim descent from Scipio Africanus himself? Rome ruled the world once, and perhaps it will again ...'

327

Gian'andrea Doria swelled at the compliment.

'And God knows, dear sons of Marc'antonio Bragadino, you have reason enough to be here.' Don John waved his hand. 'The Turks are nothing – those turbaned upstarts! They are just bitter because of their frightful food, their harsh braying music and their lamentably hairy women. They know ours are so much prettier.'

Laughter.

'Now go forth and teach them a lesson: Europe is not theirs for the taking! Let them know that Christendom does not bow before them and never will. They can never defeat us. We are greater men than they. Let them learn the taste of defeat. Destroy their dreams of conquest. Win yourselves glory, glory that will redound across the nations, and for centuries hence! And when they hear the news, they will ring every church bell in Christendom at our feats of arms. Crowds will cheer your name, men will curse themselves they were not here at your sides, beautiful maidens will swoon at the very mention of Bragadino and Veniero, Doria and Santa Cruz!'

The commanders smiled despite themselves. Don John painted a picture.

'No beautiful maidens for me, alas,' said De Andrada.

'Fear not, my dear monkish brother,' said Don John. 'In a great act of personal self-sacrifice, I shall take up your complement of girlish admirers myself.'

They laughed again, even Veniero smiling in his tangled white beard and shaking his head.

'And as for me, I shall lead from the front!'

'Are you certain, sire?' said Santa Cruz. 'It will be a firestorm once the guns open up.'

'Of course I am certain! I might even have a stool drawn up for me to stand on, to get a better view of our glorious victory!'

He would too, the mad prince. No point reasoning with him. He was as stubborn as a mule, and possibly as brave as a lion. His spirit was irresistible.

Suddenly Veniero shoved his chair back so hard it fell to the floor, stood and roared, 'By God, I think you are right!' He slapped the startled Doria on the back as if they were brothers. 'Sire, bastard you may be, and barely a third of my years, and I dislike the colour of your armour mightily, but I think you are the man to lead us after all! Let us go out together and give 'em hell!'

And as one, the formerly forlorn commanders stood and cheered their prince, and themselves, amid a flurry of backslaps and bear-hugs, and then went back to their longboats and their ships, still burning with rivalry, but rivalry now turned outwards, not upon each other but upon the Turk.

The energy of Don John, the sheer self-belief, burned in their veins like raw grape spirit, and now it spread throughout the fleet as each commander called his own captains to him, each squadron and each ship heard that, though they were outnumbered, they had more guns and better gunners, and Don John of Austria, their royal leader, had every confidence in a famous victory.

Above all, they were impressed to hear that their dauntless, dashing captain-general would be in the heart of the battle, upon the fighting stand of his flagship, *La Real*, in his blazing golden armour, beneath the gorgeous yellow standard of Holy Spain – perched on a stool, so he could witness the glorious victory! Caps were snatched off and thrown in the air, and a mighty rippling cheer spread over the dark waters of the Gulf of Patras.

The Turks had intelligence of the enemy too, and soon the harbour of Lepanto and the Gulf of Corinth were filled with the rattle of mighty anchor chains. Trumpets blared, kettledrums boomed. Marine Janizaries whetted their scimitars, Barbary corsairs their daggers. Gold earrings flashed, teeth gleamed white in the darkness. At last it had come to battle.

4

Don John talked last tactics with his knights.

'The Turks still use many archers,' said Stanley, 'and a good archer can shoot twenty or thirty arrows in the time an arquebusier fires once.'

'To even it out,' said Smith, 'every shot must count. For the arquebusier, the report and the impact should be almost identical, i.e. point-blank range. A great commander I knew used to say you should only fire your arquebus so close to the enemy that their blood spurts in your face.'

'An unpleasant image, but instructive,' said Don John. 'I will send word out. For our line, I propose to range our ships like Barbarossa at Preveza. Spread wide enough not to tangle, but not so wide as to allow a Turkish ship through our line. Oh, and,' turning to a messenger, 'send the order to all galleys to shear off their rams.'

'Off, my lord? But—'

'Do galleys ram each other any more these days?'

'They come close, they clash, they—'

'But they do not ram? Not as a key tactic? So I am told.'

'No, but—'

'Then have them sawn off. They are useless decoration.'

In the grey dawn light he had them move forward as slowly as possible out of the narrow channel into the open Gulf of Patras, towards the little island of Oxia. His hundred and fifty ships were divided into three great squadrons of roughly equal numbers.

They would form into line with Don John of Austria himself in command of the centre aboard *La Real*, with some of the biggest and heaviest Spanish galleys and those of the Papacy, Veniero and the Venetians in close support. On the right would be Doria, commanding Genoese, Milanese and Sicilians, and beyond him was the open sea. On the left, the Bragadino brothers aboard their black-painted ship, commanding the main Venetian contingent with some Spanish galleys and a strong force of Spanish infantrymen aboard. Immediately to their left began the rocks and the shoreline of Scropha Point and the Greek mainland. How they negotiated their enclosed position would be crucial.

In reserve position behind Don John's centre squadron drew up the veteran Spanish commander Don Álvaro de Bazán, Marqués de Santa Cruz, ready to feed men and ships into any breaks or weakness in the line, and with him was a single, fast galley flying the much-feared Cross of Malta, and captained by one Chevalier Mathurin Romegas.

Out in front of the Christian line, six huge galliasses were towed forward to wait silent and impassive for the fray.

For so many ships to come to order after passing through the narrow channel of Oxia in file was a fantastically difficult and complex manoeuvre. But Don John was served by the finest naval commanders in Christendom, and it was vital they succeed. The moment a Turkish force got among them or behind them – a favoured trick of Kara Hodja's – they were lost. But the wind and the sea had begun to calm as the sun rose, which was some help.

The near-silent glide of a forest of masts over the blue waters. The faintest creak of oars in the leather-collared rowlocks, the occasional shiver of the rigging. The wind gentler by the hour, as Don John had promised. The banner of the Holy League softly waving overhead, blue damask embroidered with an image of the King of Kings, Judge of All, and a golden chain linking four escutcheons: the lion shield of Venice, the red-and-silver-striped arms of the Papacy, the heraldic castles and lions of Spain, and Don John's own arms. The warm autumn day, the gentle sea, the proud banners and the gorgeous colours – Nicholas stared around, dazed with the beauty of it, though his guts were tight with fear. How could war be so foul and yet so glorious?

Then he coped with his fear, Hodge and he both in silence, as they had always coped. By keeping busy. They buckled on each other's breastplates and fitted their helmets, and then along with the mariners and the soldiers aboard, they laid out grappling irons, and greased pikestaffs so that boarders couldn't grasp them and haul themselves up. In the rear of the ship, as far from the guns as possible, the ship's surgeon laid out his bandages, his handsaw, his leather flask of alcohol. All glass would shatter.

Friars sprinkled holy water on ships' prows, and gave absolution for sins. Priests prayed fervently to San Marco and San Stefano, San Giovanni, Santiago. The Christian archers, islanders from Sardinia and the Balearics acknowledged the finest among them, tensioned their bows and filed their arrowheads. Mariners smeared the planks with oil to slip up any boarders, and brought up barrels of sawdust, to strew on the decks as the battle progressed and soak up the blood.

Visibility improved, and the lookouts stared over the blue sea from the tops.

'Can we see them?'

'Aye,' one called down evenly. 'We can see them. Estimate eight miles off and closing on us steady.'

It was 7.30 in the morning.

'Hold the line.'

Don John gave the order for the oar slaves to be unchained. Down below, Bernardino the bigamist, Ercole di Benedetto the sodomite and the blind Il Cazzogrosso rubbed their red raw ankles in disbelief.

'They range out like the horns of a bull!' called down a lookout. 'And no reserve!'

'No reserve? Are you certain?'

'Quite certain, sire.'

'They will try a breakthrough in our line,' said Giustiniani, 'feeding fresh troops in where needed with small, fast fustas and galliots.'

'How very confident of them. Overconfident, perhaps. Good for us.' Don John mused. 'From overhead, their line would look to a passing bird like a huge crescent. While ours, a straight line, with Santa Cruz behind, and our galliasses out front – like a huge cross, perhaps?' He smiled. 'Everything men think real is a symbol. Only the symbols are real.'

It felt real enough for now, thought Nicholas, knuckles white on the rail.

The two vast fleets approached each other, five miles apart, then three, then two. They slowed and waited, the oar slaves skulling back and forth, holding formation.

It was a battle-front some four or five miles wide. So many hundreds of ships, so many tens of thousands of men. There had been no clash of galleys like this since the days of the ancient world. Since Augustus fought Mark Antony for the Empire of Rome, in these very same waters. Then as now, the whole of history would turn on a single day.

Nicholas leaned from the rail, teeth clenched to stop them chattering. The enemy seemed numberless. And it was only a fraction of the fleet that he could see. Was the Holy League really supposed to destroy it, send it all to the bottom, make Christendom safe again for a generation? It was a madman's dream.

And this was the powerful Ottoman fleet that had defeated the Christians in sixteen sea battles in succession now. He narrowed his eyes against the sun and made out poop decks adorned with silken awnings, exotic oriental hues of indigo, gold and green, and huge stern lanterns topped with silver crescents, glittering and swaying gently in the sun. Across the calm waters he could hear the sound of trumpets, drums and cymbals, the reedy piping of zornas. There the Turks and the Egyptians, the Arabs and Moors, would be listening to a last recital of the Koran, kneeling and kissing the decks beneath their green banners embroidered with the ten thousand names of Allah. As ready as any to die for their God.

'The beauty of it,' whispered Miguel de Cervantes. 'Oh, the beauty of it.'

On the red-hulled flagship of the Ottoman commander, the *Sultana*, Ali Muezzinzade and his captains were full of high confidence, both wind and sun at their back. Yet as they surveyed the line ahead of them, they felt a slight puzzlement.

Why had the Christians been so careless as to let those great lumbering supply ships of theirs drift out in front of their line?

Idiots. Their commander, this base-born boy of twenty-four years, Don John, was evidently even more of a fool than they had heard.

Yet deep down, Muezzinzade felt some foreboding he could not explain.

'Give them a blank shot!' he ordered. 'By way of invitation.'

The *Sultana*'s centre-line gun gave a crack, a giant's handclap, and black smoke drifted over the sea.

'Return fire!' cried Don John. 'Live firing!'

'At this range, sire? It must be ... twelve hundred yards.'

'Crank up the barrel or whatever you do. Hit something. 'Tis not far off, and God knows there's enough targets to choose from. Hit them, that's an order!'

Utmost aggression with supreme confidence. It had always been the way of the knights. And Don John himself was, among other things, a Knight of St John.

On the deck of *La Real*, every man's gaze was upon her centre-line gun, now raised at an angle of forty degrees or more, and that first cannonball. Every other ship round about watched for the response. It was ridiculous – yet on that first ball, they felt, depended the mood of the Holy League itself, and the fate of this battle. And on this battle depended the fate of Christendom.

So may it please God, prayed the roughest mariners, chapped and salt-dried lips moving in prayer. Blessed Virgin, let it do its work, and let every ship in the fleet behold it clear.

Never such concentration.

The master gunner stooped and sighted one last time, felt the gentle tip and tilt of the deck under his bare feet, judged the precise timing of the burn. He glanced out at the masts of the enemy fleet, and then put the matchcord to the touch-hole, stood back and blocked his ears. The powder fizzed and spat sparks from the touch-hole, the muzzle lowered and then rose again in the swell, and there was a thunderous detonation and a whine. A perfect trajectory, the powder generous but not so much as to damage the barrel, the ball arcing high as a rainbow.

The destructive force of an iron ball was reckoned as its weight multiplied by its speed of travel. Like those terrible rocks from heaven that astronomers called meteors, falling so fast through the sky that they burned up, or made giant craters in the earth. This ball came down faster than any swift or falcon in its dive.

Chroniclers afterwards were often disbelieved, but in a wild stroke of luck, that first ball fired from the Christian flagship hit the flagship of the Turks at its stern lantern. The *Sultana* seemed to shiver and roll, followed a moment later by the sound of the impact travelling over the water to *La Real*. They saw the wooden gunwales of her stern explode in a halo of splinters and could even hear screaming. It was a devastating hit.

The effect on morale was tremendous.

Amid the cheering, Don John's high, carrying voice was heard. 'God is with us! Attack, all speed ahead!'

Ali Pasha, the muezzin's son, face bright with anger, had evidently given the same order. The great kettledrums boomed out from the slave decks of three or four hundred galleys, and the two mighty fleets surged towards each other over the mild blue sea.

5

Gunners readied their guns, palms sweating, arms shaking so badly they wondered how they'd ever manage to fire them. In only a minute or two, these wooden walls around them would be erupting in their faces. Some among them would never hear anything again, not the song of the birds nor the voices of their own wives and children. Strangely, dread steeled them. They'd better goddam win, if that was the price they'd pay.

Arquebusiers crouched with their wheel-locks or more primitive matchlocks, murmuring their rosaries and prayers to the saints. They thought of their women. Hearts raced, blood pulsed, expressions tensed white, ready for the approaching cannonade.

A seabird wheeled overhead and gave a cry.

And in the prow of *La Real*, their crazed commander, Don John of Austria, was seen in full suit of armour, dancing a galliard to the music of pipes and a viol. It was high noon, the zenith of the day's golden glory, before the slaughter to come and the bloody fall of the sun.

On the Turkish left, Kara Hodja narrowed his sun-wizened eyes and thought he understood what those great, silent galliasses must mean. He gave the order for his huge force of some ninety galleys and galliots to pull to larboard, well wide of them and out into open sea.

'Their left wing moving out, sire!' called a lookout.

'Flanking movement,' said Giustiniani.

'Make sure Doria moves out to meet them!' called Don John.

Meanwhile a low, well-oared fusta was moving off from Kara Hodja's squadron fast, with an urgent message for Muezzinzade's central squadron. It was Stanley who spotted it and advised Don John to give the order to hit it.

'That speck? Why?'

'A hunch,' said Stanley. 'I think Kara Hodja has suspicions of our galliasses.'

'Damn it, yes, you're right!' exclaimed Smith. 'The Turks will hold back if they get wind of the plan.'

Don John gave the order, and sent the same to the galleys to left and right. The *Merman*, the *Fortune*, the *Santa Ana*, the *Wheel* and the *Serpent*.

'Hit that fusta travelling from the Turkish left to the centre! Blow it out of the water!'

The sea erupted in white geysers around it; the low boat was soon swamped, yet still it struggled on. Then it was low-raked again, savagely splintered, dancing wildly in troubled sea. It took more than twenty cannon shots to finish it. It rose and came down again no more than a shattered skeleton of its former self, and quickly went under with all hands.

On the *Sultana*, this skirmish was briefly noticed then dismissed. The Christians were practising ranging fire.

Kara Hodja raged. He made a move to send a second fusta, a third. But already the Turkish centre was now approaching the silent galliasses. It was too late.

Francesco Duodo commanded the centre galliass, with Jacopo Guoro to his left.

The mighty Turkish centre split apart to move around them. They were obstacles, nuisances, but no more. A feeble ploy by the Christians to break up their line, but only for a few moments.

The Turkish line was now almost parallel with the galliasses.

Aboard the galleys of the Holy League, forty thousand men held their breath.

Duodo raised his arm.

All along their high sides, portholes fell open and black muzzles appeared.

Kara Hodja stared through his telescope, and his mouth fell

open. Twenty, no, thirty guns a side. No wonder they could hardly be moved.

By the beard of the Prophet.

On the deck of the Turkish galleys passing nearest to these silent supply ships, men's eyes flared wide. There was a gasp, a wail.

Duodo's arm dropped, and matchcords were lowered to the touch-holes.

Each galliass fired a volley from its open side so massive that the entire ship rolled sidelong with the recoil. But this had all been reckoned for by master shipbuilder Franco Bressano back in Venice. The guns were safely roped on their carriages, allowed to run back on their wheels and the huge ships well able to roll with the blast.

The effect of the volleys left and right into the Turkish line, effectively an explosion of enfilading fire, was devastating. The galley nearest to Duodo's ship was momentarily rolled clean out of the water, coming back down in pieces. The one beyond was blown into two halves when its powder stores were ignited. Other balls ripped onwards down the line, and five or six more galleys beyond were badly damaged.

'Return fire!' screamed the nearest Turkish captains. 'Sink those monsters!'

Even as they moved to reply, their oar slaves pulled desperately to move beyond the dreaded ships. Duodo and Guoro then ordered a second volley, for only every alternate gun was fired each time, with an interval for cleaning and cooling. The two galliasses turned a few degrees into the passing fleet, the guns lowered as far as possible. Any height and they might begin hitting their own wings behind.

'Fire!' cried Duodo, and again the guns roared.

Hulls splintered open, sails tore from shattered masts, seawater poured in. Chained oar slaves panicked and began to turn their stricken vessels around wildly in the centre of the line, oblivious to the savage beatings from the mariners, and soon became entangled with the neighbouring galleys.

Still untouched by a single shot, the two central galliasses began to wheel slowly though a complete half-circle, their minimal complement of oarsmen just enough to effect the manoeuvre. Then they could give fire from their other sides with guns still cool and ready.

In desperation a small, fast galliot full of corsairs came rowing at those evil ships, determined to scramble up the wooden walls somehow and cut the throat of every man aboard. Then the small band of marine arquebusiers stationed aboard came to the fore. They fired from the gun portholes into the close-packed galliot and soon every man aboard was either killed or wounded. The galliot floundered and came to a halt, the least scathed throwing themselves into the sea. The rest died where they sat.

The gun teams worked like demons, the two Venetian captains bellowing insult and encouragement at them in one breath. And the Turks saw to their dismay what would come next. Another ruinous broadside. Yet they must continue moving forward.

Ahead of them, the Christian line was fast approaching. One lookout cried that there was a man in a suit of armour dancing on the prow deck of the flagship. The captain ordered him down to be beaten. Evidently sunstruck, or hallucinating with fear, the fool.

Don John removed his helmet, slicked back his hair, and regarded the approaching line.

'A fifth of them hit, I'd say,' muttered Smith.

'An excellent start.'

They ploughed through the water.

Smith knelt now and lined up his jezail.

Stanley gripped his sword.

La Real was heading straight for the *Sultana*. What else did they expect from Don John? Commander would clash directly with commander, and on the fate of that single encounter, much depended.

'Give fire!' cried Don John. 'Let battle commence!' And he waved his jewel-hilted Spanish rapier above his head.

The guns opened up all along the line as they raced towards each other.

The Turkish galleys came on with lateen sails raked back, guns blazing.

'I thought we reckoned they were light gunned!' bellowed Smith. He loosed a round from his jezail. 'What would heavy gunned feel like?'

'Keep firing, Brother!' cried Stanley. 'One day you might just hit something!'

'Hodge,' said Nicholas. 'We will fight together, as always. Yes?'

'As always. At least till I sicken of the blood and go to aid the surgeon below. If he is still living.'

Nicholas nodded. 'As you will. And if you see me mortally injured, beyond help ...'

'Aye. And you will do the same for me.'

'I will. I swear it.'

The guns of *La Real* bellowed out again, and Nicholas could have sworn one of them struck the *Sultana* a second time, but it was hard to judge damage. Still the Ottoman flagship came on fast, oars churning the water, kettledrums thumping like the heartbeat of some great sea monster.

Then *La Real* shuddered. She was hit.

It was the wretched oar slaves in the bow who were killed or maimed. Their oars dragged loose in the sea and began to ruin the rhythm.

'Get those men off the benches!' cried the boatswain. 'Pull those oars in! Give me the damage!'

The bow walls were holed but not shattered, and little sea came in. But five or six men had been dismembered or killed. The mariners moved to bundle them overboard.

'To the surgeon with them, damn ye!' bellowed the boatswain. 'Captain's orders!'

The mariners cursed, every curse under the sun. Risking their lives to save the dirty skins of bloody unbelievers. One of the slaves screamed, his sundered arm on the bench beside him, as a mariner pulled him up by his remaining good arm and heaved him over his shoulder.

'Shut your wailing or I'll split your belly, you son of a 'Gyptian whore.'

They lugged or hauled the maimed Mohammedan slaves back to be treated. Before going for'ard again ready to fight and kill more Mohammedans.

'It's a merry round dance, is it not!' rasped one mariner to another.

'Servants in a madhouse is all we are!' roared the second.

La Real gave another lurch beneath their bare feet, and then the arrows started thocking into the deck around them.

The lines were barely a hundred yards apart.

'Arquebusiers, hold! Any man fires, I'll suck his eyes out!' cried their sergeant.

La Real managed one last, ferocious blast of her five prow guns in close unison, the sheared-off ram enabling them to fire low and hit the oncoming galleys almost at the waterline, doing great damage. Yet the Turks seemed to be using guns more than expected, and galley after Christian galley was hit and began to sink. Nicholas actually felt the heat in his face as a galley a good hundred yards off, targeted and then struck by a brutally concerted bombardment from three Ottomans, simply blew up as it rowed forward, breaking into two in midair. Timbers and limbs came down in a mingled debris, oil and gore and intestines.

Then one hundred galleys or more drove into each other. A rolling, brutal clubbing sound of timber upon timber, wooden drums thumped by giants, a forest of masts dashed together by the angry hand of God.

The two flagships smashed into each other with single-minded fury, trembling and juddering. Arrows hissed in the air, a mariner fell crying with a bolt in his shoulder. Turkish archers swarmed high above in the rigging, but hopelessly exposed against the blue October sky. *La Real*'s arquebusiers returned disciplined fire at close range, and archers fell from the rigging like leaves from a shaken tree.

Amid the chaos, Don John's pet marmoset, from the Americas, scampered up and down the main mast, plucking out arrow shafts and snapping them between his teeth, then throwing them into the sea with a chatter.

Then Muezzinzade showed his veteran skill. He gave a rapid signal, and with astonishing deftness, two more galleys, one on either side, closed in on *La Real* and isolated her. She was suddenly an island surrounded by three Ottoman ships, each thickly clustered with fighting men, corsairs and Janizaries.

'Signal for reinforcements!' yelled Don John. 'Someone to break through!'

But Muezzinzade, still with greatly superior numbers, had already given the order for any galley going to the aid of *La Real* to be intercepted and engaged immediately, at any cost.

He was determined to avenge the damage done by those accursed galliasses, and capture the Christian flagship as soon as possible.

A great roar went up from all three ships surrounding them. Hardened mariners trembled.

'Ready yourselves, all aboard!' bellowed Smith. 'Here they come!'

The Turks had it their way. It had already come to hand-to-hand fighting on deck. Their preference every time.

Ropes whistled, grapples clanged. Plank bridges crashed down.

From three different sides the enemy swarmed across, swords gleaming, eyes bright with the joy of battle.

The gallant *Merman* struggled to come alongside and attack the Turkish galleys from beyond. In the rigging, a woman with long dark hair plastered across her cheeks yelled out wild curses, shrieking at the enemy like some crazed banshee. It was Maria la Bailadora, a squat pistol in her hand. But the next moment, two more Ottoman galleys came along either side of her and the *Merman* was overrun. Maria la Bailadora fired into the midst of them but she could not reload, and a corsair swarmed up the rigging, dagger at the ready. She screamed and flailed at him, and he managed only to cut her arm rather than her throat.

His comrades screamed up from below, 'Skewer the bitch!'

It was eerie to see a woman aboard any fighting ship, and bad luck for all. She must be a witch.

The corsair grinned and slashed at the rigging around this wild woman. She lunged at him, unarmed, ready to tear his eyes out. But her arm was weakened by the wound, the rigging ripped, and she lost her hold. He gave her a final kick in the chest and she fell to the deck below, in the thick of the enemy.

'La Bailadora!' cried a Spanish soldier. 'Break through!'

Then there was a ferocious onslaught, swords clashing, pistols and muskets fired into faces at point-blank range. Even half-pikes seemed too long and unwieldy in that bloody close-quarter mêlée.

The Turks were finally driven back and there lay La Bailadora, cut with a thousand sword cuts.

The last of the enemy fled from the ship, some throwing themselves overboard. The *Merman* turned about, ready again to come to the aid of *La Real*, breathing vengeance. But in the chaos of the fighting, one of the Turks or corsairs had found his way to the powder store in the bows and lit a fuse. Even as she turned, the powder went up and the bow of the ship, where most of the fighting men crowded, went up in fifty-foot flames, a beacon of fire carrying nothing but bad news.

On the right, Andrea Doria and Kara Hodja were playing a desperate game of manoeuvres. The renegade Dominican priest was moving wide and south into open sea, aiming both to avoid the guns of the galliasses, and to outflank the Christian line altogether. Then he could reform, turn and drive into them from the south, prow guns blazing.

But Andrea Doria had the blood of generations of Genoese sea dogs in his veins. He moved out and matched Kara Hodja's squadron stroke for stroke, though the corsair ships outnumbered his own two to one. It was a damnable frustration for Doria, still barely a gun fired, while to his left the battle was raging. But he knew it was the most important thing he could do: hold off Kara Hodja, and engage only when safe to do so.

On the Christian left, it was desperate. Here, the Turks under the command of Sulik Pasha had driven forward with the fiercest speed and greatest weight of numbers, determined to break through fast.

Among the Christian ships they saw one painted midnight black, as black as a raven in mourning.

'What ship is that, do we know?' demanded Sulik Pasha.

'That is the ship commanded by the sons of Bragadino of Famagusta,' said a lieutenant.

Sulik Pasha regarded the sinister black ship in silence. Then he simply raised his arm and ordered the whole line forward at battle speed.

Minutes later, all hell was unleashed.

The Christians were outnumbered on every blazing,

blood-slathered deck, yet they fought like demons, and not one single Turkish galley could break through the line.

The decks of the *Raven* were awash with blood, the stern cabins were aflame, and yet even amid the sheets of flame and the coils of black smoke, men hurled fire pots and grenades, and arquebuses banged out of dense clouds where surely no man could see.

Ambrosio Bragadino reeled backwards as a soldier fell into him, head half blown away. He pushed the corpse aside.

'Guns overheating, sire!' called the master gunner.

'Keep firing on them!' Bragadino bellowed back. 'Fire till they crack!'

And so the relentless rhythm went on: guns primed, priming iron driven down the touch-hole to clear it, shake of powder from the horn, gunner's mate near by with the slow-match in the fork of his linstock, sputter and sparkle, and then boom, the gun reeling back on its carriage, and woe betide any novice standing behind.

Turks crowded up a ladder hooked over the prow of the *Raven*, yelling for the Prophet, but then they were burned away like leaves in a forest fire. Bragadino had set up a brazen trump for such an assault, and now it roared like a furnace as huge gouts and sheets of superheated flame blazed from its trumpet mouth, a blaze of fire cleansing the sides of the galley as enemy troops poured over. It burned deep into the wooden walls of his own galley too, but he seemed not to care. Let the *Raven* go down, if she took a thousand Turks with her.

His brother fought ferociously at the stern as more Turkish soldiers swarmed aboard. He was bleeding copiously from a neck wound, face white with blood loss, but quite oblivious.

Some soldiers donned rope-soled shoes so as not to slip in the blood.

'Sand here!' cried a voice. 'More sawdust and sand, for God's sake!'

The afternoon was now as dark as dusk with cannon fire and powder smoke. Like an untimely nightfall, thick with ashen clouds and streaked with burning meteors, red-hot lava. Nuggets of Greek fire burning even underwater, dancing tongues of flame devouring sails and rigging above. An infernal scene.

'Fall back, sir!' cried a Spanish captain. 'You'll be hit!'

'Better hit than not heard!' returned Bragadino. 'Press on 'em, men!'

Any signalling between ships was all but impossible, few there could either hear or see beyond their own little world of ship-bound slaughter. Yet through the dense smoke, even as he fought with a sword chipped along its edge like a woodman's saw, Antonio Bragadino glimpsed the rocky shore of Scropha Point, barely a hundred yards off to larboard. He shouted desperately to his brother. And Ambrosio, knowing the power of the unexpected, sent word as best he could to all captains and rowers to press north towards the shore.

'We'll be ripped open, sire!' cried the captain.

'So too the Turk,' said Bragadino.

The chaos on the left was now indescribable, yet it was chaos in part deliberately created by the brothers Bragadino.

'The devil love chaos,' muttered one boatswain, peering into the smoke, trying to see any rocks around them, before taking an arquebus ball straight through his forehead.

And then Ambrosio Bragadino at the prow saw a Turkish standard ahead, arising out of the smoke like a castle turret out of an early morning mist, and he knew that below, in that dense smoke, was the command ship of Sulik Pasha.

'Straight ahead!' he cried, even thumping his foot on the boards as if the oar slaves below would hear him.

The *Raven* drove blindly into the smoke, and moments later struck Sulik's galley astern and carried its rudder clean off. In the choking smoke, every man there was half blinded as well as gasping for clean air, red of eye like rabid dogs. Yet Bragadino still urged them forward into another fight, vaulting across on to the Ottoman galley. Hanging from the stern, he flailed his battered blade at the great silver lantern there and dashed it into the sea. He would slaughter everything he found on that ship. Commander, mariners, soldiers and slaves.

Fighting almost alone at times, cut with a dozen wounds, Bragadino found in a lower cabin four fine hunting falcons and a single shivering greyhound, Sulik's personal menagerie.

He slaughtered them all.

Sulik Pasha was captured, bound and made to kneel on the ruined deck of the *Raven*. Somewhere behind in the smoke, Turkish galleys were foundering on the rocks of the Greek shore. So too were Christian galleys. It was madness.

Sulik Pasha began to ask what ransom the Christians might demand for him.

Ambrosio Bragadino kicked him in the mouth. 'You know whose ship you are now aboard?'

Sulik spat blood, shook his head to clear it, determined to show no fear. 'I know it. Your father was Bragadino, Governor of Famagusta.'

'Well then.' Bragadino raised his sword.

'It was no doing of mine. You should understand, you should—'

The words were choked off as Bragadino's sword drove down into the back of his neck and out of his throat.

'Sire!' came a cry. 'Turkish galleys have broken through! They are behind our lines!'

Lighter in the water and shallow draughted as they were, four or five Turkish galleys had slipped through between the Christian line and Scropha Point.

'Kill them!' cried Ambrosio Bragadino. 'Kill them all!'

6

As soon as the Turkish galleys were behind the Christian line they turned again and bore into the hard-pressed centre, guns ready loaded, gunners exultant. Suddenly the galleys under the command of Don John of Austria, already outnumbered by an enemy that attacked them fore, found themselves fired upon from behind as well. The most unnerving experience for any fighting men, on land or at sea.

'They have come through! We are surrounded!'

On the battered galley of Sebastiano Veniero, twice holed in her hull but still afloat and mobile, one Spanish pikeman, a lad of no more than eighteen, snatched off his helmet and began to unbuckle his breastplate, ready to throw himself over the side and swim for the Greek shore. This battle was as good as lost.

In a trice, the point of Veniero's sword was at his throat. The lad felt its startling pressure just under his Adam's apple. The old Venetian sea dog glowered at him from beneath snowy-white eyebrows.

'Armour stays on, lad. You stay fighting. Or I will kill you where you stand.'

Grapeshot from a nearby fusta raked over the deck, men ducked, pellets clanged and ricocheted off steel helmets and brass fittings. But Veniero did not move. The whole volcanic force of his will was bent on this one trembling soldier, and this example before his men. The lad rebuckled his breastplate with clumsy fingers, set his helmet back on his head, and took up his pike.

Veniero turned and gave fresh orders to his captain. 'Make for

347

the centre, at all speed! Master gunner, clear our way! *La Real* needs us!'

In the reserve squadron, the Marqués de Santa Cruz kept an eagle eye on the progress of the battle at all points. He was aware of the Turkish breakthrough below Scropha Point even before the Bragadino brothers heard of it, and immediately sent six of his strongest galleys to face them. They raced across the rear of their own lines at exhausting ramming speed, the wretched oar slaves lashed by the boatswain and his hated wetted rope-end, yet soon past feeling any pain other than their own arms and hearts and lungs, burning fit to burst. Such a speed could not be maintained for more than three or four hundred yards. Yet they closed on the rogue Turkish galleys over five hundred yards, six hundred ... A slave collapsed over the oar, blood pouring from his nose and mouth. Mariners unshackled him and pulled him free, dropped him in the bilge, face up out of kindness. Others groaned and pulled onwards.

They hit the five Turkish galleys from behind, firing at close quarters and very low to ensure they hit only the enemy and not their own. Despite the exhaustion and sickness of the slaves, the marines and pikemen aboard were fresh for the fight, and amid the chaos, Santa Cruz's six galleys made short work of the Turkish five, sinking all but one of them, raking the other clean of soldiers and gunners at close range and then firing her. They pulled back slowly enough for the Spanish pikemen to lean over the sides and skewer enemy soldiers and sailors where they swam, bewildered and bleeding, through the smoking wreckage of their own galleys.

The Bragadino brothers closed up hard against the rocky shore, even as one, two of their own galleys were grounded on submerged rocks. The Turks too suffered grounding, their galleys suddenly groaning and tilting, the sound of twisted and tormented timbers ripped asunder adding to the general din.

It was only aboard one single Ottoman galley that it happened, yet it was the catalyst for what came next: a galley called the *Star of Antioch* happened to have a complement of oar slaves made up entirely of Christian captives rather than Muslim criminals. Their boatswain was particularly cruel, even by usual galley standards, and had laughingly sodomized one of their number only two days before the battle, when he discovered he was a novice monk.

'And so white of skin!' he roared as he worked, to the cheers of his mariners.

One of the oar slaves, a blacksmith by trade, had managed to break free of his chains. Now in the deafening press of battle, the *Star of Antioch* closely engaged with a Christian galley and every mariner and fighting man up on deck, the blacksmith hurriedly broke off the shackles of his fellow slaves with a boathook, biceps bulging, veins like pulsating cords. Moments later, led by this redoubtable blacksmith armed with his boathook, the slaves swarmed up from the benches on to the fighting deck. The mariners and soldiers, already holding off an attempted boarding by Spanish pikemen, were aghast to find themselves attacked from behind by a filthy, howling horde of their own slaves, half starved, skeletal thin, infested with lice and covered in sores, yet suddenly given a terrifying new strength by that strongest of instincts in the human heart: revenge.

There was wild butchery for a few moments, and then the greater part of the Turkish soldiery threw down their weapons and hurled themselves into the sea. Some of the slaves were so maddened by bloodlust that they instantly leapt after them, to stab them or drown them in the foaming, reddening water.

A neighbouring Turkish galley heard the desperate cries, saw their comrades abandoning ship and swimming for the Greek shore – Turkish territory, after all, and safety – and in a mass panic that can so easily take hold among exhausted and frightened men, did likewise.

'Abandon ship!'

The cry spread like a contagion in crowded streets, and soon the Turks were abandoning their galleys all along the line.

The guns on all sides were firing less now, some having cracked, some simply too hot to work, and the scene became clearer to the commanding Bragadino brothers.

'To the longboats, all swordsmen, all pikemen!' they ordered. 'Press after them hard! Let not one escape!'

They went after them crying 'For Famagusta!' They rowed over them and drowned them, they trapped them in the shallows or on the very shoreline, trampled over them and butchered them where they lay.

'There is not enough sea,' said one pikeman, 'to wash this much blood away.'

But in the centre, the crux of the battle, it was going much worse for the Holy League.

Every man capable of wielding a sword or a pike held the line around *La Real.* Don John had given orders for the oar slaves to quit their benches and find arms of any kind, and they fought with the crew and soldiers in gallant comradeship. But with three enemy galleys surrounding her, it was desperate.

Yet again, Nicholas knew what it was like to be under siege from vastly superior forces.

The roar of cannon, the crashing and sundering of ships, oars snapping like whip-cracks, the hiss and thock of arrows, the ships' sides bristling like a porcupine. Cries and shouts, grenades and splashes, bombs and fire pots, and everywhere the gritty black billowing smoke. You could drown in another man's blood, and men's eyes showed as no more than bloodshot balls in a mask of soot.

A Spanish arquebusier crawled up on to the roof of the stern cabin to try to give fire over the heads of his comrades, but was immediately struck down by flights of arrows from the Turkish rigging. *La Real's* mast was cracked and fallen. From the stores were dragged up makeshift wooden pavisades, covered in fat and oil, and used to build up the sides of the ship.

Something detonated below. They could not even be sure in the chaos whether they were hit, whether it was a powder keg going up, or what. Perhaps *La Real* was sinking under their feet even as they fought to the death for her.

Nicholas felt another arrow sheer off the side of his breastplate, glanced down to check it hadn't gone into his arm. Safe. A match-cord on the *Sultana* fizzed white and Smith bellowed,

'Ball coming in!'

Men ducked, the arquebus banged. A man screamed. A Turkish scream. The arquebusier himself. The gun had exploded, the muzzle flayed out like a flower. He was blinded for life.

Down below, Hodge worked alongside the surgeon. Then a savage burst of chain-shot from one of the Turkish galleys ripped straight through the window that should have been boarded up earlier, a window of finest stained glass, depicting the Virgin and Child. Rainbows of glass filled the air. Hodge ducked instinctively and was unhurt. But the surgeon clutched his raked belly and collapsed across the legs of the dying man before him. Hodge seized him by the shoulders and pulled him up again. The surgeon gave a last cry to heaven, a glimpse of the stars, sick of the blood-dark timbers, falling, falling ... He thrust the hacksaw into Hodge's chest and his head fell forward.

'I cannot,' cried Hodge, 'I cannot!'

He laid the surgeon down, snatched up a wooden crate and wedged it in the shattered cabin window as best he could.

The whole ship lurched. Timbers groaned and split. The dying man on the table groaned in the semi-darkness. Sweat beaded his marble-white face.

'Take it off, for God's sake,' he pleaded softly, waving towards the red pulp that had been his foot.

Hodge gripped the hacksaw. Oh for alcohol. But there was no more alcohol.

There were only a last few grenades. Stanley hauled himself as high up the mast as he could and hurled one at the very last moment into the air. It exploded too high, though the defenders aboard the second galley, the *Trebizond*, ducked down, and shrapnel clanged off a few helmets and shoulderplates.

'Make it count, Brother!' cried Smith.

Stanley grimaced, teeth and lips black with powder where he had torn open so many paper-and-ball cartridges. He ripped off his neckcloth, wrapped up his last grenade, lit it, and hurled the whole bundle like a sling direct at the stern cabin of the *Trebizond*. The grenade detonated just as it struck the wooden sides and blew out a plank quite cleanly. Moments later a Janizary officer reeled out, clutching his bloody head.

A corsair leapt across the narrow divide between *La Real* and the *Sultana* and clung to the pavisade like a monkey, dagger between his teeth. Nicholas leaned out to cut him away but he dropped back with lightning agility. Nicholas hung over the side, one arm gripping the ropes of the pavisade, and slashed again. Again the skinny corsair dodged him. Then he plucked the dagger from his teeth, held it by the point and threw it hard and fast. It flew past Nicholas's ear and hit someone behind. A cry. Stanley.

Nicholas didn't even look back. He did what the corsair least expected. He let go his hold on the pavisade and dropped straight down upon him, hurling them both into the channel of water below. An instant later, two arrows thocked into the pavisade where he had just hung.

The water was narrow and choppy, the sides of the ships perilously close together. Any moment a lurch would knock them together again and Nicholas and his enemy would be crushed. Nicholas heaved himself up on the flailing corsair's shoulders and pushed him down, expelling air from his own lungs as he did so by sheer will, against every instinct. They went under.

At any moment he expected to feel a stab in his side. Corsairs rarely carried just the one blade. But nothing. He held the corsair's shaven head between his hands, trying to ram it against his knee. A cannonball came fizzing through the water near by and sank away into the darkness. His eyes wept, his lungs burned. The corsair bit his hand. He gouged and fought, and felt his thumbs sink unspeakably into the corsair's tightened eye-sockets. The corsair thrashed and went limp.

Nicholas rubbed his thumbs clean in revulsion, swam for what he hoped was the stern of *La Real*. A rope splashed in the water near by; he clutched it with both hands, his bitten hand seeping blood where the villain had bitten him. A strong grasp pulled him up like a drowned puppy. He swiped the water from his salt-reddened eyes as he lay there gasping on deck behind the barricade. An arquebus ball slammed into the timber near by. He stared blearily.

'Stanley, you still have a knife in your shoulder.'

The knight pulled it free and stowed it under his belt for later use.

'Are you not wounded?'

Stanley slipped his hand under his breastplate and his fingers came out unbloodied. He patted his bulging torso. 'Not all muscle, lad. Wadding too. All horsehair and bombast, I am. Now you need to bandage that hand, and get some brandy on it.'

Then the whole boat rocked and boomed, the *Sultana* alongside rocking even more violently, as Sebastiano Veniero's heavyweight galley charged into her far side like a mad bull. A whole line of well-drilled arquebusiers stood swiftly and delivered a volley at point-blank range across the decks of the *Sultana*, laying low at least a dozen men.

Cheers went up, Don John swirled his rapier overhead and cried, 'Veniero to our aid! Press on!', and with that near-miraculous renewal of morale that comes to any group of fighting men, no matter how beleaguered and weary, when reinforcements arrive, the soldiers aboard *La Real* surged over the pavisades and threw themselves at the *Sultana*.

Nicholas glimpsed Veniero himself, the old sea dog, the old sea lion of Venice, standing at his fighting post, a bloody bandage round his thigh, one arm crooked round the mast, the other holding a stout crossbow it would have taken most men two hands to use. He raised it and fired from the hip, and a Janizary on the *Sultana* went down in a tumble of white silk.

'Sire, you need to get below and have that leg freshly bound!' cried a young musketeer.

'Time enough when the Turks lie six fathoms down! Find me more bolts, damn you!'

A second later, a huge explosion sent the *Trebizond* rolling away on her side, and half her men slithering towards the far rails. Then she settled down at a steeper and steeper angle. She was sinking fast.

Someone had made it to her lower decks and sabotaged her with a well-placed keg of powder ... There was no sign of Smith.

'Make sure they don't grapple us as they sink and take us down!' cried Stanley. 'Cut all ropes!'

There followed vicious hand-to-hand fighting on all sides, as refugees from the sinking *Trebizond* tried to press aboard *La Real* in final desperation, and those aboard the *Sultana*, under assault from two sides themselves now, were steadily pressed back along their decks, flailing and tripping over their own wounded and dead.

At last, crowding back to the stern cabin, they threw up make-shift, unlikely-looking barriers.

Smith reappeared and stared blearily through the smoke, a wheel-lock pistol in each hand. One of his eyes was badly cut about. 'Mattresses!' he bellowed. 'Goose-down mattresses! What do the devils think this is, the Sultan's seraglio?'

Yet they would make bizarrely effective barriers to their capturing the stern cabin and Ali Pasha within.

And they needed to move fast, seize this momentary advantage. Nicholas yelled out and pointed. Across the water, not a quarter of a mile off, three or four fast galliots were ploughing towards their stricken flagship, densely manned with a fresh hundred or more best Janizaries.

'Hit those galliots, prow gunners!' cried Don John. 'Don't let them get close! And Smith, Stanley, get men on the roof! Tear the timbers off with your bare hands!'

Then a familiar voice bellowed out from beyond, 'Get your heads down there!'

Veniero. And without a second warning, he put a matchstock to an ancient petrier he had mounted on his starboard side: a stone thrower.

An instant later the barrier of mattresses exploded in a storm of feathers, blood and bone. Smith and Stanley and Nicholas, with many a grim-faced Venetian pikeman, fought their way forward in an eerie snowfall of white goose-down, falling gently to the deck and turned red beneath their slithering boots.

7

On the right, Andrea Doria did everything he could to shadow Kara Hodja and prevent him from some ruse that would tip the battle his way. Kara Hodja's flagship even signalled that they were preparing to move off and save themselves, but Doria did not believe it for a moment, and held close to him.

Yet Doria and Genoa had barely half as many galleys as the enemy, and as they moved further out to sea, shadowing the African squadrons, the brilliant renegade commander switched direction in a trice. Some eighty galleys came about with sails tight, smooth as a skein of geese, and moved fast into the gap that had now opened up between the Christian centre and Doria's ships.

There was something else. Behind the Christian centre, flanking the reserve squadron of Santa Cruz, Kara Hodja had glimpsed a certain standard which made his blood burn.

The accursed white cross on red. The Standard of the Knights of Malta.

Doria pursued manfully and fired on the enemy even as they closed on Santa Cruz's reserve, and the single galley of the knights under the Chevalier Romegas. Yet as the massive squadron bore down upon them, Doria saw something that made his heart miss a beat, then swell with mournful pride. He saw the single galley of the Knights, out on the right of the whole reserve, turn steadily and face prow-on the oncoming force of eighty ships. There was no sense or reason in it, but it was magnificent.

*

Within minutes, the *St John of Jerusalem* was surrounded, battered and half overwhelmed, knights lying dead across the deck or hanging over the rails. Yet still a last few fought furiously at the prow and the stern, even as their own awnings and sails blazed fiery above them.

Below, Pietro Giustiniani lay dying, his left arm almost hacked off. But it was his own Mohammedan slave who had carried him below, and then wadded up the door with clothes and blankets.

'Over the side with you,' murmured the dying knight. 'Go.'

The Mohammedan slave wept, and shook his head, and stayed.

'Kill them all!' cried Kara Hodja, frustrated even at this delay. 'Finish them off!'

For in the time it had taken to destroy the knights – he had expected his squadron simply to mow that single ship down in an instant, but typically the Knights had already held out for twenty minutes now, and *were still fighting* – Kara Hodja had seen the reserve galleys of Santa Cruz turn about and draw up in a well-ordered line, ready to give fierce fire the moment Kara Hodja's galleys came within range.

'Yet again,' muttered the renegade black priest sourly, 'those gallant Knights have bought precious time for others by their sacrifice.' He spat at his feet.

Moments later there came a massive first volley of cannon from the reserve fleet of the Christians, now moving towards them fast. And the smaller force of Andrea Doria was also approaching steadily from the south.

Kara Hodja ground his teeth.

But at last he decided, as many times before, to retreat and save his own skin. They had captured the Standard of Malta, and most of the Knights lay dead. The ship would soon burn itself to a cinder and sink.

His squadron pulled back, not a ship lost – though more than a hundred men had died trying to take the *St John of Jerusalem*. Kara Hodja retreated well out of range, almost out of sight, and then waited like a vulture for the verdict on the battle.

*

There was no final moment, no trumpet call of retreat or triumph. Skirmishes continued over the wide sea late into the afternoon and even as dusk fell. All along the shoreline of the Gulf of Patras, Turks, Arabs and Moors lay in the salt shallows, panting, flailing: fugitives from the galleys of the Ottoman right, so mercilessly savaged by the galleys of the brothers Bragadino. Spanish and Venetian infantrymen marched among them, kicking up saltwater spray, thrusting long sword blades through chests and backs.

Across the gulf, men floated on spars and timbers, men lay face up in the water. Shattered galleys flamed and belched black smoke. Occasionally there were desperate cries for help.

The flagship of Savoy drifted silent and haunted, not a man on board left alive.

The Naples galley, the *Christ over the World*, blew itself up in the late afternoon, taking with it the four Turkish galleys still locked in exhausted battle with it.

In places, the victors were too bewildered, deafened and weary to know they had won.

Amid the ruinous debris of the left flank, two galleys still faced each other, a Christian and Turkish, after hours of skirmishing. Two exhausted beasts, backs broken, masts tumbled and splintered, knocking gently into each other in the evening swell, soft twilight coming up out of the east over drifts of powder smoke, distant cries.

Paolo di Mazzarino, a soldier of Sicily, sat clutching the stump of his right arm across his chest, too weak from loss of blood to move. He croaked for water. His arm was gone above the elbow, bone showing. But he felt calm. The rest of him had survived. Two legs and an arm. Maybe he shouldn't complain. There was more of him left than many men there. Below him on the benches, most of the oar slaves lay dead in their chains. But he might live on yet, if this wound didn't kill him in the next week or two. He might yet live to see his village and his vineyard and his girl again. He could please her as well with one hand as with two. He smiled faintly, lips cracked, and whispered again for water.

The galley was slowly sinking. Longboats moved across the water among the wrecks in the setting sun, picking up survivors. And on the other galley, also sinking, just twenty yards away, flying the crescent of Islam, Turks lay in a similar state, limbless, bandaged, blinded, beyond exhaustion, strangely calm. Some were now up their waists in the gently rising water. Warm Mediterranean water, mild October. It stung their wounds but it was gentle.

The enemy soldiers regarded each other in silence. The guns were all overheated, the barrels cracked or warped, swords chipped and broken, powder gone.

Suddenly a voice rang out from the Turks. 'How can we fight each other now, eh?'

With their powder-blackened faces, their turbans gone, used for bandages, their standards and pennants ripped or burned, they all looked uncannily alike, thought Paolo. Then he spotted the fellow who had shouted. Half naked, bare headed, grimed and bloody, cropped hair, big moustaches: a hairy barrel-chested Turk if ever he saw one.

Nearby there floated a casque of oranges and lemons, split open, the fruit floating free and bobbing in the water. Paolo raised his eyes to heaven, reached out and seized an orange, bit into the peel and squeezed the juice from the flesh into his mouth. The taste of Sicily, the taste of heaven.

A little revived, he took another orange and hefted it, felt the weight, and then threw it across at the Turks. It hit the bulwark and dropped.

The big Turk grinned. 'You throw like a girl!' he called.

'I am sorry for that, my infidel friend! I am used to throwing with my right hand, but alas you shot it off and it is now down in the deeps, fattening the fish. That was the best my left hand could do.'

A nearby Spaniard, still in one piece, gave a gruff laugh. 'Here, send one over here.'

Paolo threw one over. The Spaniard caught it and lobbed it high in the sky at the Turks, like a grenade.

'Here,' said the Turk, 'lend me one.'

Paolo tossed another to him underhand. The Turk caught it, weighed it up, narrowed his eyes and then hurled it suddenly at the Spaniard.

It skimmed over the deck close to him and then harmlessly away.

'Hey!' cried the Spaniard angrily. And then all three, and a dozen more, saw the absurdity of his anger, and there was helpless laughter on all sides.

'Be careful, we might hurt each other!' cried Paolo. He and the Spaniard gathered more oranges and lemons from the crate and hurled them over. The Turks began to catch them and throw them back.

Another Christian waded into the deeps where the water rose dark over the deck, pushed aside a corpse floating there face down, and retrieved another armful. Precious ammunition.

'A hit, a fine hit, enough to take my arm off!' cried the Turk.

Others cried out 'Allahu akbar!' as they threw. The Christians laughed with them. They were like boys throwing snowballs. Men splashed in the water, oranges and lemons flew brightly through the air, some bearing bloody handprints. Amid the floating corpses and the sinking galleys, the mirk of drifting powder smoke, it was like a mad scene from some painting of doomsday.

And then from the bowels of the Turkish galley there came a deep rumble and heave, and it began to go down faster, bubbles erupting from below. The childish game ended and they were back in the real world, grown men again, and dying.

The fight of the oranges and lemons ceased and silence descended once more, along with an obscure shame.

The Christian galley was sinking fast too now, and no sign of a longboat. It was far to shore, a mile or more, and few men aboard, none of the wounded, still had the strength to swim. All were dying slowly as if in a dream.

In the far distance, very far away, it seemed, occasional guns still fired pointlessly on other galleys, men shouted and screamed. But here between these two dying galleys, there was utter silence and stillness.

Facing each other, eyes fixed on each other, each man saw men like himself, fathers and sons. They could see the very earrings in their ears, the wrinkles about their eyes, teeth missing or carious like their own. The water swirled more strongly around their legs, over their knees, sluicing and slurping, rapid whirlpools in hatchways and out of portholes, The man sprawled against the mast went below the water without another word, head bowed. Paolo winced with the sting of his arm, thinking how ridiculous, to wince at a little pain when he was nearly dead. How comical, almost.

One Turk still held an orange, but at last he simply let it drop. The mild waters rose over them and the galleys surrendered with a bubbling sigh, buckled and sank, dragging them all quietly down. Not another word was ever spoken, they went in a kind of solemn and reverent silence. As if in this last instant of their lives, some revelation had been granted, and for all of them there, Christian and Muslim and unbeliever, the revelation was the same.

The galleys gurgled and tipped and raced to the bottom and the men went with them. Some tangled together in the deep, indistinguishable now, arms outstretched towards each other as if they were dancing, or as if they were brothers greeting each other after long years apart. Drawn silently full thirty fathoms down, down to settle upon the soft white sand, among the waving weeds.

8

Nicholas trembled in every muscle and nerve end with fatigue. There was Stanley beside him, cleaning his sword, head hung low. There was Smith, bloody bandage around his neck, and another about his forehead, half over one eye.

'You are not blinded?' said Stanley.

'Time will tell.'

Nicholas stumbled down the narrow steps, black with blood, and there was Hodge, red to the elbows. The odour of blood in that confined space was sickening.

'Is it a victory, would you say, Nick?' said Hodge.

'I would not call it that.' He shook his head. 'No, I would not call it that.'

'Nor I.' Hodge reached for a cloth and wiped down his arms. The man on the low table in front of him was dead. He covered his face with the bloody cloth, so he could sleep now. 'But the Turks will surely not return again after this.' They looked at each other and then, both shaking, they embraced.

Ali Pasha Muezzinzade was led out on to the deck of the captured *Sultana* and, on the order of Don John, allowed his final words.

He spoke with fine dignity. 'I die as I have lived, obedient to Allah and in the service of my Sultan. A fighting man before fighting men. Give me an honourable death.'

Then he was cleanly beheaded, and both his head and the banner of the Holy League run up the mast of the Ottoman flagship.

Though desultory fighting still went on over the wide sea, little

361

islands of warfare in a growing calm, the news spread fast. The *Sultana* was captured, the Pasha was dead. Allah had spoken, and the day was lost.

Don John allowed Ali Pasha's head to be displayed for only ten minutes, and then it was lowered again, wrapped in a clean white cloth and cast into the sea. A sea so chocked with timbers and spars and corpses, masts and oars and bobbing casques, there was barely space for it to sink.

They rowed slowly over to the burning hull of the *St John of Jerusalem* in a captured Turkish longboat.

The timbers flaked black under their feet, the sweet smell of smouldering wood filling their nostrils as they came aboard.

In a cabin below, breathing his last, lay Pietro Giustiniani. Five arrowheads buried in him deep.

'Care for my slave Ali,' he whispered.

'We will,' said Stanley. 'What of Romegas?'

'He fought to the last,' said Giustiniani. 'And then he went over the side, two Turks in his grasp.' He gasped and stretched in pain, and Stanley laid a giant hand on his arm.

Then he said, 'Do not weep, Brother. I die happy.'

'We know it,' said Stanley. 'I only weep to say farewell.'

'The day is won, is it not?'

'Aye. The day is won.'

Giustiniani's breathing became a deep rattle in his throat, his face sank into the immobility of the dead, and then he breathed no more.

Out on deck, they found the body of Ali, Giustiniani's faithful slave, his throat cut by Kara Hodja's men. They wrapped him in a strip of sail and lowered him gently over the side.

Nicholas gently touched a body half burned, legs charred almost away, but head and face miraculously preserved, a handsome face, a fine scar over the forehead. A faint smile on his lips, he thought.

'Luigi Mazzinghi,' he whispered. 'A year younger than I.'

'A gallant death,' said Smith. 'A knight's deepest wish. He would not have wanted to be old and grey and toothless, and turn ladies' heads no more.'

'No,' said Nicholas, smiling through his tears. 'No, he would not.'

'They will be taken back to Malta,' said Stanley. 'Giustiniani and Mazzinghi, unique as heroes of both Cyprus and Lepanto. They will be buried in Valletta with the highest honours of the Order.'

It was a sea of fire, burning on into nightfall. The mariners cleared away the bodies and swabbed the decks. The extent of the destruction became clear as they passed down the shattered line, rowing carefully among the burnt-out hulls and half-sunk galleys.

Truly the death of Bragadino had been avenged, and the Vengeance of Venice had wrought an unimaginable destruction.

A single blank shot was fired from *La Real*, and the Christian galleys saw that she had hoisted the storm signal. And it looked likely. A sharp wind had whipped up suddenly across the Gulf, white horses were dancing.

They picked up the last survivors they could find, and then made for shelter at Porta Patala.

'And move fast!' cried the captains. 'The storm comes on apace!'

Darkness had fallen long before they rounded Cape Scropha, clouds thickened and the stars were extinguished. Half-shattered lanterns swung violently from their posts, and the north-east wind whistled in the rigging as they finally struggled into harbour,

In the darkness, rolling at anchor, the soldiers diced and drank and roared their filthy songs as the rain hammered down on the battened-down canvas awnings or on their bare glistening heads.

Meanwhile those remaining Turkish galleys that could still move themselves were doomed to struggle back in the teeth of the wind for Lepanto harbour in a heavy and rising swell. Galleys so gilded and magnificent when this day had dawned, now ravaged and humbled before the majesty of nature, tossed about by the almighty storm wind that blew down from the cold mountains. They prayed to Allah the merciful, little creatures clinging to their little wooden toys, as the thunder rolled overhead like the horses of heaven.

Don John of Austria leaned back and closed his eyes. He dreamt he was playing *Moros y Cristianos* again in the dusty streets of Leganés, as he had when a little boy.

'Well, sire,' said a voice. He opened his eyes. It was the big Knight Hospitaller, Eduardo Stanley. 'You did it.'

'Aye.' He closed his eyes again. 'Aye, I suppose I did.'

The rain came down harder than ever, cold but clean, and washed the blood away. Men went out on deck, shivering but exhilarated, and raised their faces to the black wind-torn sky. The wind roared and bellowed all along the Greek coast. They held their arms wide, some danced on the deck. Out to sea, the wind lashed the waves wildly, scattering and sinking the last remnants of the ruined Ottoman fleet.

At dawn, Don John held a review.

There had been so many deaths. Both the Bragadino brothers had died of their innumerable wounds in the night, received in the desperate fighting along the shore. A lineage was extinct. Pietro Giustiniani of the knights was dead, and that gallant young knight so full of dreams of martial glory and fair ladies, Mazzinghi the Florentine. The great Chevalier Romegas was also dead.

Sebastiano Veniero was badly wounded, though he hid it, and Don John himself had been stabbed in the thigh. He said it would mend. And that mad, rake-thin poet of the Spanish ships, that Miguel de Cervantes, had been hit in the chest twice by bullets and his left hand was also maimed. He was intensely proud of his wounds.

'Wounds are like stars in the sky, to guide others along the great highway to honour!' he cried. Even now, he seemed determined to believe that he lived in an age of high chivalry rather than brute gun power. 'Besides, I can still write my great epic with my other hand.'

'What sort of epic?' they asked him. 'Of this great battle?'

He looked thoughtful. 'I shall have to think about it,' he said.

On the Turkish side, both Sulik Pasha and Muezzinzade had been captured and executed aboard ship. Kara Hodja had made good his escape. Deserters and captives gave Don John a fuller picture of the Turkish losses, and he looked grave as befits a military commander after battle.

'Gentlemen,' he said. 'Our losses were not small. Both our left and centre were badly mauled. But the squadrons of Andrea Doria on the right, and Santa Cruz's reserve, escaped better, though both played a brave and vital role.

'Furthermore, it seems the opening salvos from our Venetian galliasses did more damage than we thought. Perhaps a quarter of the Turkish fleet was damaged right at the start. In all, we estimate some fifteen thousand Christian dead, and at least thirty thousand Turk. Perhaps as many as forty thousand, with significant additional losses in the storm, which was hard against them, by the grace of God. Of our one hundred and fifty galleys, we lost some fifty. Of the Turks' three hundred galleys, as best we can judge, they lost at least one hundred and fifty. Perhaps two hundred.'

There was relief but no cheering. You could not cheer the death of fifteen thousand Christians, nor that of some fifty thousand men. In a single day. Had there ever been such a rate of slaughter in the history of the world?

Don John finished a glass of wine that evening, set it down and then said, 'I think this great battle of the galleys may be the last in this ancient red sea for a long time. Already, I begin to wonder if it was not a greater battle than even we realised. We have so decimated the Turk that Islam's age-old dream of conquering Europe is surely finished. I say Christendom will turn its back now on the ancient Levant. We must look out instead across the wide Atlantic. The future is sailing west.'

All pondered and said nothing. But they all felt they had indeed witnessed something terrible, yet something of destiny.

Then Don John smiled to see them all so exhausted and solemn, and said, 'My dagger wound shows how close I was in the fight, does it not, Sir Eduardo Stanley?'

'Indeed it does, sire.'

'Close enough to smell a Turk's breath, I was. Worse than an onion-eating whore. And a mercy it was not four inches higher, or my amorous exploits would have been severely curtailed.'

'You will be the hero of all Europe,' Stanley assured him.

'A passing worship,' said Don John drily. 'And a dangerous position. My brother Philip will be *so* delighted. And those hailing me today will be demanding my head on a plate tomorrow. That is how it is with men. Hosanna one day, crucify the next. Why this change, men themselves hardly know.'

He stretched back his hands, his fingers. They still ached from where he had gripped his sword hilt, hour after desperate hour. Then he clenched his teeth as the wound in his thigh suddenly made itself known again, but he made not a sound. His courtly code forbade it, and he quickly regained his expression of calm composure, even as his eyes were still watering.

'A hero for a day, then, and still no crown.'

'The cowl does not make a monk, nor the crown a king,' said Smith.

'I would have made a great king, and proved most royal, would I not? See how I commanded and inspired! A great lord of men, wise and well beloved. I would have chosen a queen of both beauty and virtue – a rare combination in women, I admit – had fine sons, ruled a happy and peaceful kingdom. But my father Charles tupped a German whore and there I was, a squawling base-born brat, and that is all my story. My single life upon this earth. I will never sit on a throne.'

The ironic lilt was gone from his voice.

'Yet for a day, 7th October, 1571, I ruled over my watery kingdom well, and guided my men wisely. Was I not king for a day?'

'You were, my lord,' said Stanley. 'You were.'

9

It was said that even before the battered but victorious fleet arrived back at Messina, Pope Pius V knew. He was with his treasurer when he stopped and said, quoting the Gospel, 'There was a man sent by God, whose name was John.'

'Father?'

He stood, his face radiant. 'Come, this is no time for books of accounts. Let us go and give thanks in the Basilica of the Apostles!'

And he named the 7th of October as the Feast of Our Lady of Victories.

The fleet sailed into Messina on 21st October, having battled contrary winds for days. Then the news spread through Italy, across to Sardinia and Spain, over the Alps and through all of Europe as fast as a horse can gallop.

Sicily celebrated until Christmas and beyond.

Don John entered Rome in a triumphal procession such as had not been seen since the days of the Caesars. Captured, gun-shot banners of the Ottomans were displayed on the northern hills of the city.

He went on to Venice, and the city erupted in carnival as only Venice knows how. Business came to a halt, whores gave their services for free, debtors were loosed from prison. Ottoman standards were displayed on the Rialto, and all the Turkish merchants then in Venice hid quietly in their cellars. Only an express order from his Holiness in Rome prevented the Venetians from executing all their prisoners of war as part of the festivities.

All of Spain went wild, and fighting bulls were given turbans in the corrida. Ali Pasha's green banner hung in the palace in Madrid. King Philip declared a national day of prayerful thanksgiving.

In Paris, the young Charles IX, or rather that kingdom's true ruler, his mother, Catherine de' Medici, allowed a grudging Te Deum to be sung.

They even celebrated in the streets of London, in Germany and in Lutheran Sweden.

With the common Ottoman threat now removed, all the tensions and rivalries within the Holy League quickly resurfaced, and not long after Lepanto it was dissolved. With it vanished Pope Pius's dream of a new crusade to recapture the ancient lands where Christianity was born. Not in his lifetime, but one day, Christian pilgrims would go there again, and church bells ring out once more over Jerusalem.

In Constantinople, the disaster was named the Battle of the Dispersed Fleet, and Ali Pasha Muezzinzade was blamed for it – quite safely, as he was already dead.

The Ottoman ambassador came to Rome and Venice, and announced a cessation of all hostilities between the Empire of Selim and the Christian powers. The grim truth was that, for all its immense resources, the empire of the Ottomans was exhausted by the substantial toll taken on its armies at Famagusta, followed closely by the virtual obliteration of its Grand Fleet.

As a small consolation for the defeated, the standard of the Knights of St John, captured by Kara Hodja, was hung in the mosque of Hagia Sophia.

Nicholas and Hodge lodged in Messina for the winter. It was warm and lazy and they had enough loot.

'I wonder about Malta,' said Hodge. 'As our final resting place. Though it is no green England, God knows, yet I did love that island. We would be welcome there as natives, almost, and I know you love it too. For more than one reason.'

'I do,' said Nicholas quietly.

They drank too much. They chased girls. They did little.

Then one day in December, Smith and Stanley came over from Malta and found them.

'We have a message for you.'

'Go on.'

'From one very highly placed.'

'Who?'

Stanley grinned. 'I cannot say.'

'Your cloak and dagger act. Truly—'

'That wine will kill you.'

Nicholas gave a sullen smile. 'I expect it will.'

'A message comes to us at Valletta, suggesting that if the young Englishmen who fought at Malta, at Cyprus and Lepanto, gentlemen volunteers and good Catholics, returned to England, to London, and presented themselves to the Queen there, they may find a warmer welcome than they think.'

'You have a message from the English court?'

'No, not from the English court,' said Smith. 'You're not *that* celebrated.'

'So, what, a couple of sunburned Catholics just walk into Whitehall Palace and bid her good morrow?'

Stanley nodded. 'Maybe.'

'And then – let me see – we are led away from the Palace and taken to the Tower, and hung from the beam and beaten until we abjure Rome and the saints and say we are good Protestants now, like the rest?'

'Catholics are not hunted down and killed like rats, you know,' said Smith with a touch of irritation. 'Elizabeth prefers to ... ignore them. And she likes a handsome young hero. Especially if he doesn't stink of Sicilian wine.'

Nicholas belched. But Hodge's eyes were shining.

Nicholas said, 'We have seen so much war and so much religion. Sometimes I think there is too much religion in the world, and that is why men war with each other. Catholic and Protestant, Mohammedan and Christian. And further east, Turk against Persian, Mohammedan and Hindu, and heaven knows what other wars in other uncharted worlds. But my father always said, there is just enough religion in the world to make men hate each other, but not enough to make them love each other.'

'Your father was a knight and a wise man,' said Stanley.

A day later, sober and shaven, Nicholas and Hodge tracked down Smith and Stanley in a room of the Governor's palace.

'Where will you go after this?' demanded Nicholas. 'No more Turk to fight? Smith, you will go quite mad with peace.'

Smith grinned, after a fashion. 'We have a yearning to visit the lovely city of Constantinople,' he said.

Nicholas and Hodge could not but laugh. 'Is it your first visit there?'

'I . . . I don't recall exactly. But the yearning is strong in me – for a number of reasons.'

'Dangerous, though.'

'Naturally, or else I would go crazed in my wits with boredom.'

'We will meet again one day.'

'You are going to England?'

They nodded. Suddenly they could not speak. Then they wept openly as they embraced each other, the two young adventurers feeling they were losing their fathers all over again, the two knights feeling they were losing their sons.

'Courage, masters Hodge and Ingoldsby,' said Stanley briskly, parting from them. 'Brother Smith, dry your eyes, I do declare.'

Smith made a noise like a wounded bear.

'Let us not weep like women. We have known strange days, such scenes, such battles – and by some miracle, we all live, when so many brave men have died around us. A tale for your children and grandchildren at the fireside, is it not?'

'And perhaps we will have another jaunt to England again soon,' said Smith. 'We are much loved there, I know.'

'And may you come back to Malta one day,' said Stanley. 'Only three weeks' sailing, with God's grace.'

'Perhaps we will,' said Nicholas. 'Perhaps.'

They could find no boat in December to take them from Sicily to Spain, not in winter seas, so they travelled up to Naples, and went overland in three months around the coasts of Italy, France and Spain. They met with many adventures, a few tavern brawls, and some generous-hearted girls.

It was March when they came down to Barcelona, and there found a ship that would take them round to Cadiz.

'Cadiz,' said Nicholas. 'I know a tavern there we like.'

'You again,' she said.

'You remember us? It was nearly a year ago.'

'I could not forget, though how I have tried to rid my memory of your ugly faces. I even brought you food in prison when you were jailed by Pedro Deza. Englishmen, are you not?'

'That we are,' said Nicholas. 'You have heard of the great sea battle against the Turk off Greece? We fought in it. We were its greatest heroes.'

'Of course, and also at the Siege of Malta. I remember. You are the greatest liar I have ever had in this tavern. And I have had a few.'

'Bring us wine, fair maiden. Though I am already half drunk with your beauty.'

'You will only get more drunk and tell still more outrageous lies.'

'We will show our scars from the battle. Lepanto, it will be known as.'

She sighed, hands on her hips. 'Show me your new scars, then, gained in some dirty knife fight in the backstreets of Malaga.'

They showed her. She looked unimpressed, tossed her black hair, and went to serve other customers.

Towards the end of the evening, Nicholas told her, 'We are going back to England now.'

Hodge was snoring gently, head on the table.

'Good,' she said.

'Come with me,' he said. 'Marry me.'

She laughed, a harsh, magnificent laugh. 'You know nothing of me, fool and liar.'

'You are a young widow, your name is Maria de l'Adoracion, your man died fighting in the revolt of the Moriscos in the mountains, and you have a son of four or five.'

She looked surprised, a faint smile. 'You remember that?'

'Of course. As well as your loveliness. Now you need another man.'

371

'Indeed I do not! Or if I did, it would be a decent man, not a drunken fool who is always in trouble.'

'Marry me. I need a good Catholic wife and there are few now in England.'

'England! I might as well go and live at the pole with the perpetual snow and the white bears.'

'It is a little colder in England than Andalusia,' he admitted. 'And they do not like or trust Spaniards. It is a Protestant country, life is hard for Catholics and getting harder.'

'It sounds very desirable. I cannot think why I have not married a drunken English fool before.'

'Also the food is foul, there is very little wine, it is expensive, and oranges too. It can rain on any day of the year. It used to be warmer, some say, two or three hundred years ago, but now it is very cold in the winter. Animals freeze to death standing in the fields, sheep on the wolds are frozen to the ground, and the rivers turn to ice, even the London Thames. Ice so thick they roast oxen on them at the fairs. In midwinter there is barely eight hours of daylight.'

'Tell me the disadvantages now.'

'Hm. You'd have to be my wife. I am a penniless and unpropertied vagabond and soldier who has not seen his homeland for six years. On my return I may be arrested and tortured at any moment.'

'So nothing new there. You are how old now?'

'Twenty-two.'

She tossed her head. 'I am but twenty. You look far older.'

'The Mediterranean sun has played havoc with my fair English complexion, once so fine and lily white. And all my scars ...'

'Scars on a man are not all bad. So long as he fought on the side of God, and with honour. But your face and arms are burned so badly by the sun you will be a wrinkled old man in another five years. You are badged with powder burns like a German mercenary, you are an Englishman and so the enemy of Spain, you are penniless—'

'Though rightful heir to great estates in the County of Shropshire.'

Hodge abruptly woke up. 'I wouldn't say *great* estates ...'

'Thank you, Hodge.'

'More lies,' said Maria de l'Adoracion. 'You look like any other feckless vagabond, wandering this Mediterranean Sea between two worlds, picking off the scraps from this endless war of Christendom and the Turks. And now you presume to take me home as your wife, to your Protestant island of which I know nothing, nor any word of the barbarous language except "goddam". The usual curse of your pious and God-fearing sailors when in my tavern. What a cultivated and intelligent people you English must be!'

'Goddam,' murmured Hodge, gazing up at her, 'isn't she magnificent?'

Then she said, 'In truth, though I do not love the Moors, who killed my man in the mountains – yet it was your intervening, so foolishly but bravely, when those poor Moors were being driven out of Cadiz – and ending up in jail for your pains – it was that which first made me think you were not all bad.'

Nicholas waited.

She said, in a softer voice, her hard tavern mask dropped away, 'Get you to England, Englishmen. Perhaps you will find kind English brides there, who will tame your hearts.'

10

They sailed on a merchantman two days later, and came to London in the bleak days of January. They shivered like aspen leaves in the chilling east wind.

'I had forgotten …' stammered Hodge, nose blue.

They bought woollen cloaks. People stared at them in the streets, one man barged them and called them Gypsies. They tossed back their cloaks and showed their swords and were left alone.

They lodged in Cheapside and requested audience at the Palace.

Stanley had not lied to them, about some mysterious higher influence.

Three days later, they were to attend Her Majesty at Greenwich.

'*Her Majesty*,' whispered Hodge. 'After all I've seen, this is still the most …' He could find no more words.

In an outer chamber they were first addressed by an elegantly bearded chamberlain in a black fur robe. Told to kneel before her, not to look directly at her. Only to answer questions, to ask none.

'And it is known that you are Catholics still, and loyal to Rome. You will, of course, leave off your swords.'

They unbuckled, Nicholas saying, 'Yet I am loyal to my Queen also, and would die to defend her.'

The chamberlain smiled a thin smile. 'She will judge your loyalty for herself. She is a very fine judge of men indeed.'

Hodge could not have looked directly at her if he had tried. He would have been blinded. Her dress was white satin, there were many pearls in her hair, she was as a white of countenance as an angel, though her hair was flame red. A woman still only in her thirties, yet it was wrong to think of her as a mere woman. A *queen*, radiant, from another world.

They knelt and waited for a long time. At last she spoke, her voice feminine yet commanding.

'There is a trusted confidant of ours, a wealthy merchant in Constantinople, who has done us some service in the past. He has no great liking for the Catholic princes of Europe, and in that at least we have a common interest. Now he sends us a letter. A request, in return for the many good deeds he has done us in the past. He says that you are of a party of four Englishmen – the other two being Knights of St John, and Englishmen disavowed.' Her voice was crisp with contempt. 'He says the four of you did brave service to his people, in the city of Nicosia in Cyprus.'

Joseph Nassi. It was Joseph Nassi behind it all.

'Speak,' she said.

'Your Majesty,' stammered Nicholas, head still bowed, 'we did a small thing, to protect some citizens, albeit Jews, from cruel treatment. Families who were to be driven out in front of the Turkish guns. We protested, and the decision was revoked. Not a sword was drawn, nor a drop of blood spilled.'

'Bloodshed is no sure sign of bravery. If you stand firm, peace will often come rather than war. Stand.'

They stood, knees aching.

Her blue eyes were hard upon them.

'Your words are to our liking,' she said. 'Claiming only small courage for yourself, and therefore more credible. You would hardly credit the extravagant tales we hear from our more ... *heroical* sea captains.'

The chamberlain and others tittered.

Nicholas could not help a slight smile. She saw it and smiled frostily too.

'Now, to this request. It is requested that we admit you once more into our kingdom, as free men, to go untroubled.'

There was a pause. A very long pause. Nicholas's heart sank. She could not admit to this. Some other reward would suffice instead, before they were sent on their way once more, into exile.

She seemed to hold her breath, and then breathed out a little. 'We grant this request.'

They were home. In England. With no need to wander more.

Beside him, Hodge began sobbing.

'Come, Master Hodge,' said the Queen. 'It is Hodge, is it not? More manly. You have seen worse things than this in your travels, I am sure.'

'Worse, yes, Majesty,' sobbed Hodge. 'But none better. To be back in England.'

Few things moved the Queen so deeply as an Englishman's simple love of England.

'There's an honest Englishman,' she said. 'Even if he is burned black as the devil's own heart.'

'Please, Your Majesty, it'll soon wash off in the English rain.'

'I don't doubt it,' she said. 'Hodge, it is such as you that shall make our England the glory of the world. And as for you, Nicholas Ingoldsby – Sir Nicholas Ingoldsby, I should say – your late father, Sir John, was by all accounts a good gentleman, though not one for the Court.'

'No, Majesty. He liked the country.'

'Hm. You too?'

'I too. The Court is not my world. The old hills of Shropshire ...'

'After all your adventures?'

'Yes, Majesty.'

She pursed her pale lips. 'Nevertheless, your father entertained Catholic knights in secret at his Shropshire home. During arrest he resisted and died of natural causes. Yes?'

Nicholas swallowed. 'Yes, Your Majesty.'

'His estates passed into the hands of the local magistrates, and their value to our exchequer. We see nothing remiss in this. But now further enquiries suggest that the Justice of the Peace, one Gervase Crake, has provoked widespread dissatisfaction. There are reports of cruel treatment, and worse, peculation against the Crown. Action will be taken against him in due course. But I should say that if meanwhile Sir Nicholas Ingoldsby himself, though still barely more than a boy, were to go back to his native Shropshire and demand the return of his ancestral lands – by force if necessary – the Crown might at least wink at such proceedings.

'In the future, perhaps this Ingoldsby might make a very service-able Justice himself, and servant of the Queen. But for that he would have to abandon his Popish religion and swear loyalty to the Church of England.'

Nicholas said nothing. What could he say?

Her Majesty understood very well what agonies of conscience could make a man say nothing. She herself had spent much of her life in careful silence, not choosing, and would no doubt spend years more that way. Silence was a friend who would never betray.

'You will write of all your travels,' she said. 'I have never travel-led outside England, not even to Wales, nor desire to. You have wandered far and wide. You will write up your adventures, what you have seen. You will tell all. We want to know the customs of Shrove Tuesday in Cadiz, the weather in Naples, the winds in the Messina Strait. The fortifications of Malta and Cyprus ...'

Nicholas bowed. He had never contemplated setting down his experiences in writing, but now it was a royal command, he had no choice in the matter.

'You will have half a dozen men-at-arms to recover your prop-erty.'

'With gracious respect, Majesty, that is not needed. I have a man-at-arms worth a dozen.' He nodded at Hodge.

'He is an Achilles, this Hodge?' she said with irony.

'He is,' said Nicholas without irony.

'I cracked a few unbelieving skulls, Your Majesty, it's true,' volunteered Hodge, against all court etiquette. The chamberlain winced. 'They took some crackin' and all.'

The Queen smiled now. 'Hodge, Hero of Malta, and better yet – Englishman. I decree an annual pension of five pounds for life.'

Hodge gasped.

For many years after in Shropshire, the tale was told. Of how Gervase Crake, the hated but powerful Justice, had been overseeing the whipping of a vagabond girl at the cart's end in a market square one bleak February day. And two grim-faced strangers rode into the square, just as had happened, so folk memory said, some six years before. They were on horseback, and they carried swords, and they looked as if they knew how to use them. They were as

377

sunburned as Spaniards yet they spoke English.

They demanded the weeping girl be set free. Crake opposed them with a sneer. Had he not six ruffians for his guard? More than ruffians. Three of them carried tattoos on their brawny forearms, showing they were mercenaries who had fought with the dreaded free companies, in the German wars of religion.

A fight broke out, and in a matter of minutes four of the ruffians lay dead. The two others fled, sore wounded, and were never seen again in the county. The two strangers bore a few knocks and bruises too, but fewer than Gervase Crake. He was then stripped and whipped and thrown in the dog pound until some later use could be found for him. As a chimney sweep, perhaps, or tavern turnspit.

One of the strangers was the long-lost son of old Sir John Ingoldsby, come to claim his inheritance. The old hall that Crake himself had been living in! So of course it was all shipshape and handsomely cared for. Then the son of old Ingoldsby found his sisters in another gentleman's house, two of them now in service as maids. A third had died in his absence. Their reunion was such a thing to see, they said, it would make a stone weep.

And afterwards, a serving-man said he had glimpsed the long-lost son of old Sir John Ingoldsby go into the barn there at the hall, near sunset it was, and find the things of his boyhood still hanging on the walls. A child's leather saddle, the one he'd learned to ride on. A hoop and a stick. A toy sword made for him by the gardener, long since lain in the churchyard. And the son had fallen to his knees and wept, till his man Hodge came and helped him into the house.

But others said it was wrong of the serving-man to spy and worse of him to tattle. For surely that young Ingoldsby had travelled wide and seen many things, more than most of them in the village would ever see in their lives. And doubtless his heart was full of all the beauties and the sorrows of the world.

EPILOGUE

The Battle of Lepanto was hailed by Cervantes himself as the greatest event in the history of the world. Certainly it seemed to win a general peace, though with occasional skirmishes, and establish the bounds between the Christian world and the Muslim for generations.

Yet there followed some strange occurrences.

Only six months later, in a small back room in a house in Algiers, Kara Hodja was gunned down by two mysterious, hulking masked men carrying four pistols apiece. The assassins were never caught.

The captured banner of the knights in Hagia Sophia vanished from under the very noses of the Turks, and reappeared in the Chapel of St John in Valletta, Malta, only a few weeks later.

Most astounding of all, the stuffed skin of the gallant Marc'antonio Bragadino, still cruelly displayed in the Topkapi Palace, also disappeared. Such a feat seemed almost impossible, and the Ottoman court wrote long letters demanding to know who was responsible.

No Christian prince or prelate could advise on it.

But in 1572, the last mortal remains of Marc'antonio Bragadino were buried with full honours in the magnificent Basilica of San Giovanni e Paolo, in Venice, where they remain to this day.

Pope Pius died in 1572.

Don John enjoyed his hour of fame and had many more beautiful mistresses, including Diana di Falangola, Zenobia Saratosia and Ana de Toledo. There were plans for him to marry Mary, Queen of Scots, or even an invasion to make him King of Ireland. They came to nothing.

His brother Philip sent him to Flanders to fight the unwinnable war there against the Protestant rebels. He died of typhoid in 1578, only seven years after his great victory of Lepanto, aged just thirty-one. In his last year he wrote, 'I spend my time building castles in the air but in the end, my castles and I alike blow away in the wind.'

His brother Philip lived on until 1598, racked with gout and suffocated by asthma.

Sebastiano Veniero recovered from his severe wounds, and in 1577 was given the ultimate accolade of being made Doge of Venice. It is said that in his very last years he mellowed a little. He now rests in the Basilica of San Giovanni e Paolo, along with Bragadino.

Andrea Doria lived on until 1606. He was suspected by some of cowardice at Lepanto for not having engaged more closely. But those who had been there knew the truth.

Don Álvaro de Bazán, Marqués de Santa Cruz, died in February 1588. His death was fortuitous for the English, for this brilliant commander had been leading the Spanish Armada. He was replaced by the markedly less capable Duke of Medina Sidonia. Had Santa Cruz remained in command, English history might have been very different.

Miguel de Cervantes continued for a time to seek chivalrous adventure. He was captured by Muslim corsairs in 1575 and spent five years as a slave in Algiers. Later he spent too much money on a fine suit of armour, went bankrupt and was imprisoned. But by the time of his death in 1616, he had written his immortal *Don Quixote* – the most hilarious yet poignant mockery of chivalric ideals ever written.

Sultan Selim II, 'the Sot', died in 1574. It is said that he was drunk at the time, and slipped over in his bathhouse.

He was succeeded by the peace-loving Murat III, who agonized for eighteen hours before giving the traditional Ottoman order for all his brothers to be strangled by deaf mutes with silken ropes. He spent most of his reign in quiet seclusion in the provincial town of Manisa, where he particularly loved the teachings of a gentle Sufi mystic, who soothingly interpreted the Sultan's nightmares and dreams.

Mehmet Sokollu, Grand Vizier, died in 1579. Many said that his death was arranged by his old enemy, Lala Mustafa Pasha, the butcher of Famagusta.

Joseph Nassi also died in 1579, and all his great wealth was seized by the Sublime Porte for its own use, a seizure also masterminded by Lala Mustafa.

In 1580, Lala Mustafa himself became Grand Vizier, but died after only four months in office.

As recently as 1965, Pope Paul VI returned the captured Ottoman banners of Lepanto to Turkey. In the naval museum in Istanbul can still be seen the standard of Ali Pasha Muezzinzade. Not all banners have been returned. More still hang in the church of Santo Stefano in Pisa.

Of the two Knights of St John, known as Stanley and Smith, nothing was ever certain. But in the harbourside taverns of the Mediterranean, from Cadiz to Aleppo, from Marseilles to Algiers, rumours abounded. Even in the warlike valleys of the Caucasus, it was said, and upon the frozen plains of Muscovy where the Tatar horsemen still threatened, in the burning Syrian desert, upon the emerald coast of Coromandel, and far away into the snow-capped mountains of Central Asia, their names and reputations were not unknown ...

AUTHOR'S NOTE

Originally *Clash of Empires: The Great Siege* was conceived as a stand-alone story. But after finishing, I wanted more of my characters and their adventures, especially Nicholas and Hodge, Smith and Stanley, and it seemed many of my readers felt the same.

Besides, there was another epic moment in history which could very well have involved our heroes: Lepanto. It was actually poetry, not history, which first led me to it, in G. K. Chesterton's thumping good ballad. It's a fine poem to learn off by heart, as schoolboys used to, and makes an excellent companion on a walk.

The other question readers always want answered is, How much is true? And as with *The Great Siege*, I think I can honestly answer: a lot. The biggest liberty I have taken is probably compression of timescale. Nicosia was in fact besieged in the summer of 1570, and Lepanto took place the following year, but I have compressed them into a single summer for greater dramatic tension.

Otherwise, the broad outline of events is pretty accurate. Most of my characters were actual historical figures – even minor players like Aurelio Scetti, the wife-killing lute player, and Maria la Bailadora, the female dancer who fought at Lepanto: a detail so absurdly romantic that if it weren't true I would hesitate to make it up.

Joseph Nassi's plans for a Jewish state in Palestine; the appalling fate of Marc'antonio Bragadino; Don John's pet marmoset, plucking enemy arrows from the mainmast and snapping them triumphantly in half; that last, surreal, exhausted fight of the oranges and

383

lemons; all these things are attested by contemporary chronicles and witnesses.

Among the many books consulted, I am especially indebted to *Empires of the Sea: The Final Battle for the Mediterranean* by Roger Crowley; *Galleons and Galleys* by John F. Guilmartin; *White Gold* by Giles Milton; and *The Renaissance at War* by Thomas Arnold.

For travellers, there is a superb replica of Don John's *La Real* in the Maritime Museum, Barcelona. Cyprus remains as fascinating an island as ever, though sadly divided since the 1974 Turkish invasion. History is still very much alive here. Nicosia is a lively, bustling cosmopolis, whole stretches of its mighty walls still standing, while Famagusta (now in Turkish-occupied territory) is a haunting ghost city of ruined but beautiful Gothic castles, churches and cathedrals. Its massive walls and bastions have survived rather better, however, and remain breathtaking. For armchair travellers, a DVD called *The Stones of Famagusta* is highly recommended.

As for Lepanto – site of that epic sea battle whose destructiveness would not be equalled, as Roger Crowley points out, until the Battle of Loos in 1915 – a UNESCO survey in 1980 found that the sea level has risen by 3.5 feet in the last four centuries, and the coastline altered considerably. There has been very little submarine excavation, but a magnetometer sweep showed up a lot of iron, as well as numerous 'non-ferrous clumps': the remains of galleys, lying at a depth of only 450 feet, and the bones of so many men, both Muslim and Christian, indistinguishable now in the depths of the silent sea.